THE ACCIDENTAL PRESIDENT RETURNS

Volume 3
The Accidental President Trilogy:
A Political Fable for Our Time

By Dixie Swanson

Cover Design by Joe Thomas at Left Brain Digital

ISBN: 098332932X
ISBN-13 9780983329329
Prose Publishing Houston, TX

Library of Congress Control Number: 2011911299
North Charleston, SC

For A.D. and D.H.
The Muse and the Midwife

CHAPTER ONE

REST

January 24
A private island in the Caribbean

Michael bounded up the stairs to their thatched pavilion, hot and stinky from morning fishing with some of the guides. He caught dinner for the two of them and got just enough sun to invigorate him. He might, just might, shave today as a treat for his new bride of a few days.

He noticed Abigail had not moved in hours. Heaven knew she needed the rest. She was still asleep. Her strawberry blonde curls lay in disarray, and her long legs sprawled atop the sheet. She had a small smile on her face. *She even sleeps pretty.*

In the run up to the wedding, she pestered him for details about the honeymoon.

"I need to know what to pack," she'd said.

"You're going to be naked," Michael would reply. "Bring a toothbrush. Or don't. They'll have one. And we're going two places, one week at each location."

Every man in the need-to-know loop stonewalled her: Col. Barnett, the pilot of Air Force One, Albright, the head of the White House Secret Service detail, as well as Michael himself. They adored her and could finally pester her like little boys pulling on her pigtails.

Michael Aston, the actor, director, and one of the Sexiest Men Alive, rented Sir Ronald Bradford's private island in the Caribbean. Bradford Cay could easily hold forty people, but for this week, it held only two guests. Michael checked every detail. Yes, the airstrip would accommodate Air Force One and could refuel it. Yes, the staff was used to heads of state and their security people. Abigail had her Secret Service contingent, and Michael, too, had security people.

He was a low-key kind of guy, not a lot of entourage, but when he married the outgoing President, he wanted to make doubly sure nothing happened to her. After all, she'd escaped assassination once. Michael's publicist deliberately planted a decoy rumor of a destination in the Seychelles, just to send the paparazzi to the other side of the world. It seemed to be working.

"Actually, heads of state are only slightly better behaved than rock stars," Sir Ronald said. "I've stopped renting to most rockers. After all, I use the place, too, you know."

The island came with all the toys any two people could want: sailboats, power yachts, jet skis, parasailing, certified scuba instruction, even golf carts for those too lazy to walk from their pavilion. Bradford Cay even had a "toy" submarine so guests could glide below the Caribbean to see the tropical fish. If Abby wanted to visit another island, there were small planes to take them.

A Michelin three-star chef headed the kitchen. It was a great gig as an off-season vacation from his Paris restaurant. He and his girlfriend had a villa on the property, well away from the guest quarters. He tried out new dishes to take back to Paris, lived in paradise, and got paid for it.

Michael and Abigail's accommodations pleased the senses: the scent of the sea, overlaid with fresh flowers, permeated the air. Their large, thatched pavilion had lazy punkah fans stirring a balmy breeze. Built from native woods, the pavilion looked as if it had grown there. Every annoyance was addressed: drop-down mosquito netting, privacy curtains, even sliding glass and wood doors for privacy, if one wished. The weather was perfect—just enough clouds to make for spectacular sunsets. Extra privacy curtains could be drawn around the bed and bath areas. Michael and Abby could shower outdoors with the fresh green smell of the island and the incredible variety of birdsong on all four sides. Or they could get into a huge indoor, jetted tub in total privacy. Orchids, hibiscus, birds of paradise, and bougainvillea rioted color, and new cut flowers appeared whenever the guests were out of the pavilion. Michael specified different white, fragrant flowers daily for his bride.

The staff never intruded but appeared promptly when summoned. In a twist on the Indian custom for children, all staff members wore an anklet of bells lest a guest be caught unawares while sunbathing nude. The fair-skinned strawberry blonde wasn't even tempted. Ten minutes of this and soon she'd be toast. She was the Queen of Sunscreen.

The infinity pool started under the cover of the pavilion and stretched outside, the Caribbean just beyond it. There was a small, stocked kitchenette and bar in one corner, but through experience, Michael knew neither would appeal to Abigail. She drank almost no alcohol, and her cooking skills were limited to incineration. Luckily, he knew how to run the espresso machine; his face graced billboards for them all over the world.

The chef, being both a haughty Parisian and a food *divo*, didn't like having the Secret Service near his kitchen—much less standing over him while he cooked. He never understood the more he fussed and pouted, the more the agents enjoyed bugging him.

"Private" was a relative term. Forty invisible people existed to meet their every whim below, on, or above the ocean—twenty-four hours a day. Michael, a sports buff, left Abby to rest while he parasailed, snorkeled, and dove with the scuba dive master. Most days, he caught at least a portion of their dinner.

This noon, Abigail stirred and looked up at her husband as he sat on the bed. *Husband is the sweetest word on earth to a woman who thought she'd never marry.*

"Honey, I went out and killed us something to eat," he said with exaggerated pride. "I left it with the chef. I thought it was a bit early to start you on cleaning fish."

"You thought right," she said, rubbing his scruffy face. She didn't have the heart to tell him he looked more like a refugee with a skin disease than the Sexiest Man Alive right now.

"Hey, let's cancel the rest of our lives and live here," he teased. "Go native. I won't shave, and you can grow hairy armpits."

"Mmm, can't wait," she said, rolling her eyes. "Are you planning on shaving anytime soon?"

"No, I thought the Tarzan look would turn you on." He started making chimp noises.

"That's Cheetah the Chimp. I don't do chimps," Abby giggled.

So Michael did a half-hearted holler and beat his chest.

"Think again, Tarzan," she sat up and pecked him on the cheek. "Only one problem. Your face would leave nasty rug burns anyplace it touched. No shave? No shower? No sex."

She stood and stretched. He reveled in the sight of her naked. While he was tan, she had the milky skin of a Botticelli. Put her on half a giant clamshell and she'd look like she belonged in a museum.

She flung a towel over her shoulder and gave him a sultry backward glance.

"Join me in the shower?"

"You don't have to ask twice," he said, taking off his sweaty fishing clothes and leaving them in a pile outside the shower.

They'd been in love for two years before they married, but as she was President, they'd kept things private the first year, and in the second year, they continued to be very circumspect in their behavior. With the Secret Service outside every door, they were pretty tame in bed. Or at least pretty quiet.

Abby still had a protection detail, but security had dropped several notches now that she was out of office. She and Michael showered together in the open air with abandon. The guys were out there; they just weren't watching them. They were watching everything else. Michael, as an A-list movie superstar, had his own security to doubly protect their privacy, especially on their honeymoon.

Time was Abby's biggest luxury. For the last few years, Abigail had showered, dressed, done her hair, and applied camera-ready makeup in less than thirty minutes. She could do it in under fifteen if she didn't have to wash her hair. White tie, black tie, State of the Union, it didn't matter—she was on time, perfectly groomed, with the nuclear launch codes in her bra, and a pleasant smile on her face. She hit her marks, did her homework, and carried out her duties until they became as automatic as the details of her prior career as a pediatric emergency physician.

But not here and not now. She and Michael were honeymooners.

Today, Michael washed Abigail's hair, and then she washed his. They relished the slick of soap and water between them. When finished, Abby begged to shave his face.

"No way. I make my living with this face," he said good-naturedly. "You nick it—it'll cost me money on my next film."

"Hey, I'm a doctor. I've shaved other areas on plenty of people. Remember?" she asked.

"Yes, but those people were sick and desperate. I'm neither."

When they were clean, she wrapped herself in a gauzy robe and watched him shave while she towel dried her curls. Then she combed them out. The island breezes would finish the drying job.

Somehow, they ended up back in bed for the afternoon and then repeated the shower. They called the chef to serve dinner at sunset.

Abigail wore a blue cotton shift just the color of her eyes, and Michael wore some drawstring pants and a white shirt that set off his tan and his big brown eyes. Neither had a care in the world—a miraculous joy for a woman who'd just left the Presidency of the United States. And Michael relaxed because he no longer had to share her with the entire nation, which she had dutifully put first.

The luxury was beyond words.

They watched the sunset from the west side of the pavilion. Michael sipped at a glass of wine. Abby, never much of a drinker, stuck to sparkling water.

The sunset painted the sky in hues too vivid for a painting. To them, the show by Mother Nature was pure joy.

The sun sank quickly so close to the equator. Abby timed it on the watch she always wore. It took just over a minute from the time the sun touched the horizon to the moment it was gone.

After the sunset, they dined by candlelight. The food was fresh and expertly prepared. But what else would one expect? Life didn't get better than this.

After a dessert of a chocolate and orange soufflé, they blew out the candles, grabbed a blanket and flashlight, and walked onto the beach.

They spread the blanket and lay on their backs, looking at the stars. The night sky popped out an infinite number of stars, more than either could have imagined. With the pavilion dark and no moon, the intensity of the stars inspired awe in them both. The ocean lapped softly just yards beyond their blanket.

"Thank you, Michael, for bringing me here," Abby said sincerely. "I've never been anywhere nearly this lovely. And to be able to sleep is an unimaginable luxury."

"You've earned it, Missus," Michael said, using his pet name for her. "Look at all you've been through."

"I suppose so," Abigail replied. "But most people who deserve a rest don't get one nearly this nice."

It had been a busy three years. Abigail had gone from being an emergency room doctor, to tending her dying sister, to serving out the remainder of her sister's U. S. Senate term. She could still recall the click of her high heels on the marble floors of Congress. Then, when Abby was serving as President Pro Tem of the Senate, the President, Vice President, and Speaker of the House all succumbed to accidental death in freak ways. The President, an avid skier, died in an avalanche. The Vice President, a heavy smoker, was out jogging and had a fatal heart attack when the Secret Service told her about the President. The Speaker of the House, known for his horrid table manners, choked to death on a piece of meat when he heard he'd be President.

So Abby became President. She did her duty without hesitation, even firing the Secretary of Defense for insubordination just a few minutes into her term. He suggested she was too young, too naïve for the job. He may have been right, but since the next two people in line couldn't serve (one was foreign born, the other too young), he would be President. She shot him down with icy words, and Marine sentries escorted him out.

Of course, once in the Oval Office, she threw up every morning after the Presidential Daily Briefing, scared witless by accounts of what terrorists had in mind. She cried herself to sleep many a night, feeling pitifully inadequate trying to sleep where men like Jefferson, Lincoln, and Roosevelt put down their cares for the day.

Her learning curve resembled Mt. Everest, but luckily fate sent her Mikey Molloy. An old Washington "hand," he was part mentor and part mischief-maker, first with her in the Senate, then in the White House. His tutelage helped her grow into the Presidency.

Fear stalked her, and her silent mantra was the West Point motto: Duty. Honor. Country. It always calmed her.

Her backbone came from Regina Temple, her childhood guardian and personal North Star. Reege had started out as the family's house-keeper in Houston. Abigail's father, Joe Adams, was a wildcat oilman, so things were boom or bust in the Adams's household. Once when he couldn't pay Regina's wage, she took a share in a well in its stead. They agreed she'd work for six months whether the well hit or not.

It hit.

Big.

Regina was suddenly rich and ready to go to teacher's college in the fall. But then Joe plowed his money into a dry hole and his Cadillac into a broken-down bus on a blind corner. He and his wife were killed instantly. When relatives declined to take on two penniless little girls, Regina stepped up to rear not only the toddler, Abby, but also her teen-age sister, Priscilla. Later, the three took in Regina's newborn nephew, Duke, when his mother ruptured an aneurysm during labor.

While Abby was President, Regina married the curator of the White House, O.T. Wagner, an avuncular sort of gentleman who always smelled of Old Spice. Duke was now an Assistant U.S. Attorney in Washington. Men ten years his senior envied his résumé. He'd married Kim Tran, Abigail's dressmaker, on the White House lawn, and they now had a six-month-old daughter named Priscilla Regina—born on the Fourth of July.

Regina had no use for self-pity, and when Abigail was down, Regina would tell her, "Put on your big girl panties and get to work on the problem."

But if one truly needed comfort, Regina was right there.

Abby got through her term, handling things with a deft hand. She ended the war in Afghanistan when she lured Taliban wives to freedom. Withdrawing with honor was all downhill after the women and children were out of harm's way.

She stopped a drug cartel war on U.S. soil and finally hammered home the message: drugs are a demand business. We are our own worst enemy where drugs are concerned.

When she not only survived an assassination attempt, but also killed her attacker, the country was eating out of her hand. The country would give her anything she wanted.

She wanted to get the special interests to stop buying candidates. The groups could still exist; they just couldn't give the candidates anything of value. They could be advocates for their clients' interests, not purveyors of political prostitution.

She wanted five Constitutional Amendments and got them. The first was Campaign Finance Reform, shutting special interest money out of the electoral process. All money came from voters and went only to people for whom they could vote. The second was The Abolition of Electoral Voting—electing the President and Vice President by popular vote. The third gave the President the Line Item Veto (to cut the pork at least in half). The fourth was a Balanced Budget Amendment, and the fifth limited the President and Vice President to one Six-Year Term, so he or she wouldn't start running for office the day after Inauguration. Both could put all their efforts to the job at hand.

Lying there in the dark, looking up at the stars, she marveled at her life.

"Michael, do you believe in fate?" Abby asked.

"Oh, I don't know, maybe about some things. But I definitely believe in serendipity," he said. "I've been one of the luckiest people in the world, especially to find you."

"Thank you, Michael. If we are blessed with kids, I hope they'll be as happy as we are."

"Well, I'm doing my best to make us a baby," he said. "Don't tell anyone, but I prefer that to fishing."

"Thank you . . . I think," Abigail said, knitting her brows together.

Now she was ready to be a wife and mother, but staring forty in the face, she might not be able to do the mommy thing easily—if at all. Michael had been so funny at Christmas. Just weeks away from their wedding, he'd thrown her birth control pills, Frisbee-style, off the Truman Balcony into a snowy night. She had laughed with delight. Then he'd taken her back to her room to "get her well and properly knocked up."

They'd married in the East Room of the White House the after-noon her Vice President was sworn in as the new President.

President Jerome Lafayette and his wife, Lynne, were probably aglow in the newness of the White House right now, but Abby envied them nothing. She had done her duty, with honor, to her country. It was her turn just to relax. She desperately needed some downtime with her new husband. They'd courted on the fly, seldom spending more than a few days together because of their jobs.

Abigail loved everything about their week on Bradford's Cay. She loved the mini-submarine. It was as if they had an aquarium all around them full of colorful tropical fish. The evening sails were also lovely. Even better, though, was what wasn't there: no phones, no television, and no news. Best of all? No middle-of-the-night calls of world importance.

Abby and Michael were as alone as they would ever be. And each was all the other needed. They read their Kindles, slept odd hours, made love whenever they pleased, and as the week neared its end—Abigail felt a genuine sense of peace.

She could not remember ever feeling this peaceful as an adult. As a child, she had known peace of this magnitude in Regina's lap.

For his part, Michael knew he'd chosen the right woman, and he was damned grateful she'd said yes. At forty-four, he wanted a family and didn't want to be using a walker at his kid's graduation. But wanting a family was something he'd kept to himself. As one of the most recog-nized faces on the planet, he already had a target on his back. If word got out that he wanted children, then he'd have had to put razor wire atop the wall around his Los Angeles area home.

Before he became a movie star, he did okay with girls, but he had to work for them. Once his face was famous, everything changed. Women who were available for sex were like spare pocket change: just there. All the time. Nickels, dimes, quarters, pennies. That was the variety in the world he inhabited. Even before AIDS, he always took precautions. His children would come from his wife, no one else. He could not understand all the men he knew with kids by several women. Children aren't pets. They are yours day in, day out, responsibility number one.

Hollywood had a few rules, and one rule was each star had to have a charity. Michael worked with the UN High Commission on Refugees. At first it shocked him. Then, as he learned more, he was humbled. Some people had dignity in absolute squalor. It made him want more from his charmed life. If these people could behave with dignity, he damned well could, too.

He spent more and more time with his UN work and less time partying. He didn't want the pocket-change women. He wanted a fifty-dollar gold piece: a rare woman, a woman he would have to work to win, marry, and make babies with.

His uncle, Mikey Molloy, was Abigail Adams's mentor. When Abigail asked the elderly Mikey to be her date to a State Dinner, Mikey suggested Michael would be more appropriate, assuming she knew all along he was Michael Aston, the movie star.

She didn't. She didn't even catch his last name, as someone else was calling her out of the room. "The nephew sounds fine," she said, hurrying away. She worried he'd have bad breath and no chin, but she was desperate for an escort.

When that year's "Sexiest Man Alive" arrived to escort her downstairs, she was shocked and incredibly distant to him. Not only was he a movie star, he was also her own private notion of a hunk. She did not trust herself to be anything other than icily formal to him.

He was incredibly smitten with her long, curly, strawberry blonde hair and vivid blue eyes. Here was his gold piece, and she would have nothing to do with him. They danced one dance, badly, and she flatly refused all his entreaties to see her again.

"I honestly do not have time for a personal life, Mr. Aston," she said, her posture imperial, her face in a small smile. And at five-nine, plus heels, she almost looked him in the eye. Her heart was hammering; butterflies were rampaging somewhere way south of her belly button, but she was remarkably composed. Then she turned, and the Secret Service escorted her back upstairs to the Family Quarters and out of his life, seemingly forever.

He had given her his number, but she did not call. He could not wait for her to leave office and/or call him. It took him a month to arrange a second meeting, and it was an ambush arranged by his Uncle Mikey and Thomas Albright, the head of Abby's Secret Service detail. Abigail owned her late sister's penthouse at the Franklin Towers, a five-minute helicopter ride from the White House. Abigail needed some downtime around the first anniversary of Priscilla's death. It was hard to be a bum in the White House, so she went to the penthouse.

Mikey Molloy invited himself for dinner and Scrabble. Mikey arranged with Albright to have Michael show up in his stead.

The Secret Service checked him out in the vestibule. Abigail froze when she opened the door and saw him. She was distant but polite— until she learned she wasn't the only one who had lost a sister to cancer.

"I was ten, she was six. She didn't even get to finish first grade," he said with a catch in his voice. "All she ever got to be was my little sister."

Right then, their labels fell away. They had dinner sent up and played a Scrabble game, which Abigail lost. Badly. She seldom lost at anything, and it irked her. His protestations that he was weaned on Scrabble didn't make her feel better. He came away from the evening with one incredible kiss and her private phone number. She went to bed, alone, convinced their kiss was the best, ever, in this universe. Or in any other universe. For a woman who had trouble remembering her last date, she all but levitated with joy.

After many phone calls and some serious planning, they were able to pursue romance out of the limelight. No one, Abigail included, would put up with an ingénue president publicly in love with a worldwide mega-movie star. That was two years ago. They stayed below the radar for one year, and then announced their engagement. They waited to marry until Abigail was out of office by three whole hours.

"Where are we going next week?" Abigail asked Michael after they made love their last morning on the island.

"I know. I just need some persuasion to tell," Michael said to Abigail whose head was resting on his shoulder.

She persuaded him to his heart's content, and then he fell promptly asleep.

"Hey, Mister, wake up," she said, shaking him. "Where are we going?"

"I forgot. Plane leaves late afternoon." He kissed her and fell back to sleep.

CHAPTER TWO

ITALY

Ravello on the Amalfi Coast of Italy

When one of Sir Ronald's smaller transatlantic jets flew just the two of them and their security people to Naples, Italy, Abigail did miss Air Force One. The Bradford plane had pods that converted to flat beds, but she and Michael could not sleep together as they had on Air Force One.

Abigail would never forget the moment the earth moved at the same time they hit clear air turbulence. Michael put his hand over her mouth, lest her noise summon a cadre of armed men. They ended up laughing under the covers like guilty children.

Still, for a woman who had slept on a ratty futon until a few years ago, the last three years were the stuff of fairy tales. Even though her sister Priscilla wanted to pay for medical school, Abigail wouldn't hear of it. She took out student loans and lived like a struggling student well into her thirties. The only time she went to Neiman-Marcus was to buy Pris her favorite fragrance and to get Regina an Hermès scarf. Abby might eat beans and rice for a month, but Regina deserved the best. Until she became a Senator, the fanciest thing Abby ever bought herself was a leather jacket. Not only was it on sale, but she also had a 20 percent-off coupon. She got it for less than a hundred bucks and still felt guilty.

"Southern Italy in late January is not at its loveliest," Michael said, as Giuseppe drove the big gray Mercedes with one Secret Service agent riding shotgun. "The bougainvillea is taking a rest, but the scenery is still spectacular in Ravello."

Abigail inherited a big chunk of North Texas from Pris, which she had never had time to go see. She'd only seen Michael's house in L.A. once. Everything was new to her in this marriage, including his villa in Italy.

"The home is simply called 'Bel Vedere,'" Michael said. "Beautiful View."

A few minutes after they left the *Autostrada*, the Italian superhighway, they were on the Amalfi Drive, one of the most beautiful coastline roads in the world. The Italians never met a mountain they couldn't hang a road off of, and this was no exception. Its twists and turns were gorgeous, if hair-raising. If the mountain was too daunting, they tunneled through it, often so deep into the rock that just a pinpoint of light far away led the driver back to daylight.

Logically, Abby knew that a security car was in front of them and behind them, but neither could prevent her fear that all three cars would plunge into the sea at any moment.

"Ravello sits high on a promontory overlooking the Tyrrhenian Sea, which is part of the Mediterranean. *Bel Vedere* had been the private home of some nobleman who went broke in the twenties. Gambling, I think. It was briefly a hotel in the thirties, and movie stars flocked to it for their illicit affairs."

"Like ours?" Abby asked, playfully.

"Ours was a courtship, Missus. Neither of us was married, and besides, I was doing my best to get you to marry me," he said seriously. "Do you remember all those black velvet boxes with the pink ribbons? There was nothing illicit about our love affair. We were merely being discreet."

Abigail had to smile.

"Anyway, I was on location near here and saw the place was for sale for a song," Michael said. "So, on a whim, I bought it. I thought I was so smart. I paid pennies for it. Little did I know it had been on the market for years because it would cost zillions to bring it up to code." Michael laughed at his own folly.

"The previous owners had both bad taste and too much money. Some areas had a dead mouse smell. To save money, I'd help the workers myself between films. I can plaster a wall, put in a toilet, even lay tile for a bathroom. Tile is a very big deal around here," he said conspiratorially.

"And I can start an IV in anyone, so we have a good skill set," Abigail said.

"The architect said I had to have all new wiring, all new plumbing, and . . . frankly, I think I would have thrown in the towel except my mom came to help."

"What did she do?" Abigail asked. Abby didn't know Louise well, but she liked her. Like Michael, she was easy going and charming.

"She pronounced the décor 'atrocious' and lived on site, keeping everyone marching forward. She also did the interiors. Has a knack for it. Italians have smaller places now, so antique armoires, beds, and the like are all too big for the newer places. She picked them up for pennies on the dollar. The Italians want everything new, modern, and stainless steel, so she bought magnificent pieces at flea market prices, even the rugs. Of course, everything had to be fumigated, but that's another story."

Abigail was starting to get a little queasy. Perhaps it was the mention of dead mouse smell or fumigation or the twisting-turning Amalfi Drive. She focused outside the car as they went through Positano and Amalfi itself. The stone houses ran up and down the mountains, all higgledy-piggledy, on either side of the winding drive. No one was fat in either town, not with at least a hundred stairs down to the sea and another hundred from the street to the top of the houses.

Then they turned up the mountain toward Ravello. It was a series of switchbacks. Abigail's stomach was lurching. She cracked the window and breathed in the soft winter air with the tang of scrub pine. *I will not throw up in Michael's car.*

Abigail fought down the nausea. Soon they were on top of the mountain and in the middle of a small Italian village, complete with an ancient church. The church square was asphalt and painted for soccer. It was the only place flat enough to play *futbol,* the national obsession. Of course, it was too small for regulation soccer, but it worked for kids to blow off steam.

They drove between a few stores chock full of tantalizing, locally made pottery and stopped at a tall stucco wall with a large wooden door. Giuseppe took a large, old key from the glove box and got out of the car. Abby could hear the snick of the ancient lock opening. Giuseppe opened the door and drove the car through. The tires crunched to a halt on the circular gravel drive at the door of the villa.

The property was pie-shaped with the large, wooden door in the middle of the crust. Old stone walls, some still frosted with stucco and others missing large flakes, enclosed the property and insured privacy. The villa itself sat off to the left as they entered the property, and there was a long, meandering walk to the point of the pie. Hidden in the trees was a house for security staff that Michael had quietly doubled in size during the last year to accommodate the Secret Service Abigail required.

The house's façade was simple. Large symmetrical windows and functional shutters on all three floors punctuated a terracotta-colored stucco façade. Italian cypresses flanked either side of the massive wooden door. Bougainvillea vines twined hither and yon along the façade.

"*Benvenuta a Bel Vedere,*" Michael said, sounding exactly like a native speaker, at least to her untrained ear. Up until then, it hadn't dawned on her she'd have to learn Italian. *I guess Spanish with more hand gestures won't work.*

"What do you want to see first—outside or inside?" Michael asked.

"I want to see a restroom first, and then it's your choice."

He picked her up and carried her inside.

"Put me down, you'll hurt your back," Abigail said, laughing.

"Whew. Thank goodness there weren't any stairs," Michael said, feigning a strain. Then he whispered in her ear, "I might never be able to make love to you again."

Abigail got goose bumps all down that side of her body. She always got goose bumps when he whispered in her ear.

After she washed up, he chose to show her the outside first. The fresh air and *terra firma* blew away the cobwebs of carsickness. The birds were singing, and there was a brisk breeze. Vegetation buffered the sounds of cars on the roads below. The path meandered, so Abigail and Michael could see the views from either side of the promontory. To the west was the winding road up from Amalfi, some thousand feet below, cutting through a patchwork of lemon groves and scrub pine. Abigail could hardly believe they'd driven it without a collision.

"The switchbacks are actually safer at night," Michael said. "You can see the headlights coming. During the day, people honk to tell you they are coming around a corner. It's the scenic route. We can also get here through a mountain pass."

At the point of the pie wedge, there was a patio with a large railing, some statuary, and a covered pavilion.

"This is the *Bel Vedere*, the beautiful view," Michael said, and indeed it was. There was ocean as far as the eye could see. "We are facing south, so the next land you could run into would be Sicily, then Africa."

Abigail was speechless. On the way back to the villa, she noticed they had raised beds for gardens, but in January, the ground was dormant.

"Rafael grows most of our vegetables from here. The meat and fish come up from Amalfi. The pool and tennis courts are behind those trees, as well as housing for security people. The bocce ball court is also over there, but the best games are in the village. The men play for their honor," he said, slapping his chest twice with the flat of his hand. "Take away an Italian's hands, he is half mute."

"And what if I wanted to play?" Abigail said.

"That, my dear, is not possible in the village. Here, of course, you may play. But you are too young and definitely a woman. I owned this place for nearly ten years before I was invited to play one evening in the village. I had the good sense to lose to the oldest man in the village."

"So much for Title IX in Italy," Abigail laughed.

He showed her around the villa, introducing her with great courtesy to everyone they encountered. His manners with his staff were as formal as hers had been with heads of state.

Giuseppe, whom she'd met, was the driver and jack-of-all-trades. He did not live in.

Gloriana and Rafael were in the kitchen when Abigail and Michael entered. Abigail nodded and smiled. *I haven't a clue what they are saying.*

"Gloriana does the cooking, and Rafael is the gardener," Michael said. Then he translated what Gloriana said to the new bride.

"She hopes you will be very happy here and give her lots of babies to take care of."

Abigail smiled, "*Grazie, tante grazie.*"

"You get big points for manners and your accent," Michael said, beaming at Abigail. The ground floor had a huge well in the middle of the entryway.

"The central organizing principle of a *castello* is self-sufficiency, so a water source is essential within the walls. This one is covered over, but it dates from the thirteenth century. How they dug it, I've never figured out. But the Saracens, I think, were marauding around here then."

Louise had made the interiors both serene and welcoming, a hard thing to do with high ceilings and thick walls. Light-colored Oriental rugs covered the terracotta floors, warming the gloom of winter. She'd chosen a palette of honey, melon, and green-grape colors for the plaster walls—a natural extension of the outdoor colors. They set off the dark wood beams across the white ceilings. The thick walls were cool in summer, and a modern heating system made the house toasty in the dead of winter. Winters were mild, as the ocean was a moderating influence. Snow was a rarity.

Michael showed her around the ground floor, then shepherded Abby up to the *piano primo*, the first floor, or as North Americans would say, the second floor. Their bags were in Michael's suite.

"I've always used this corner room as my suite," Michael said, opening a door into a large sitting room, bedroom, and bath. "But you can choose us another if you like. I don't want you to feel like you have to fit into my life. This is our life, and we'll make it together."

"You're very thoughtful, but I haven't seen the rest of the rooms," she said.

"If you don't like the house, we don't even have to keep it," Michael said, looking her square in the eye. "I want you to be happy."

"Michael, this is a fantasy castle to someone who grew up like I did. I'd be an idiot not to like it. I love it. And I love you for sharing it with me," her eyes welled with tears.

He could tick one worry off his list. At least she liked *Bel Vedere*. It was his refuge, and he would hate to give it up.

Each of the rooms on their floor was a suite. The bathrooms were like nothing she'd ever seen at home. They were almost all tile: tile floors, walls, and even some ceilings, often elaborately painted before firing. One bath might be white with minimal blue decoration, another yellow with elaborate designs. In some bathrooms, a shower drain sat in the corner with an elaborate shower above it, but no shower door. Others had circular rods with shower curtains, but most didn't. Each bathroom had a bidet, as well as a toilet, sink, and radiator. There was always a teak bench on which to sit and an assortment of shower shoes, which were mandatory. A wet Italian tile floor might as well be covered with olive oil. Two of the bathrooms had jetted tubs, each big enough for two people. Michael's bathroom had one of them.

On the floor above were rooms with a bath but no sitting rooms. Abigail loved the modern, soft colors with the elegant Italian antiques.

"Let's start out in your suite," Abigail said, bouncing on the bed. "Yep, this should do just fine."

They took their time unpacking, and when it was time for dinner; Abigail found herself oddly food averse. She pretended all was well but just pushed the food around her plate. And after dinner, she conked out.

CHAPTER THREE

THE TESTS

Abigail was jet-lagged and slept late the next morning. When Michael showed up with a big cappuccino and a freshly baked croissant about nine o'clock, one whiff sent her dashing for the bathroom, where she threw up. Not that there was anything to throw up. Her entire body felt like throwing up, but only her stomach could do it.

Michael was concerned. "I want to call the doctor. You could have picked up something in the Caribbean."

"Michael, darling, I see a doctor every morning in the mirror. I'd tell me to wait a while and try salted crackers and ginger ale."

Michael went into the village, noticed a few paparazzi around, and bought the crackers and ginger ale, as well as a dozen things they didn't need, lest Abigail's illness make the front page of some tabloid.

"Well, the vultures have found us," he said as he brought her the ginger ale and crackers. "Only a couple of photogs today. By tomorrow, I expect an entire cellblock of them. We're fine here inside the walls, but I'll have to put extra security on the walls themselves."

He went to his roster of off-duty *carabinieri*, the elite of Italian police, which he kept for occasions such as this. The last time he'd needed them was when he was hosting the wedding of two other stars.

He couldn't imagine what he'd need for his own honeymoon with a past American President.

He also called the mayor and asked if he could get Ravello declared a no-fly zone.

"Michael, I am not sure the flight authorities will agree."

"But my bride is a former President of the United States," Michael said.

"I will see what I can do," the Mayor said. Abigail never knew that her privacy was protected because the Mayor called his old friend, Italy's Prime Minister. The Mayor reminded the Prime Minister that Aston not only paid all his Italian taxes (a rarity in itself), but also paid to have the fifteenth-century bronze doors of the church restored. Anonymously.

When his cell phone rang, Michael was delighted to hear, "Any time your wife is in residence, there will be no flights within five miles of Ravello."

"*Mille grazie, Mille grazie.*"

Abigail was grateful for the ginger ale and crackers but continued to feel queasy. Michael had gone off to consult with his security people to hide them further from the world. Abigail stayed in bed, incredibly fatigued.

The nausea would come and go all day, and the oddest smells would trigger it. Gloriana insisted on bringing her some chicken broth, which sounded like a great idea.

Gloriana's broth arrived, smelling like ammonia to Abby.

Then it dawned on her.

I have morning sickness.

When was my last period? She dug out her smartphone. Just before Christmas. December thirteenth. Michael appeared for a few days around Christmas and threw out her birth control pills. He returned just before the wedding on January twentieth. If she became pregnant at Christmas, that made her seven weeks pregnant. Yes, her breasts were tender, but they'd had a ton of sex in the Caribbean. She stood naked before a full-length mirror. She had a bump. She tried to put on her favorite pair of jeans. They didn't zip. *Oh, holy crap.*

She lay, face up, on the bed and bent her knees. She put her hand on her belly and began to feel around. Yep, there it was, the top of the uterus easily palpable above her pubic bone. At seven weeks, she shouldn't feel it there. It should still be deep in the pelvis.

Time for a test. But how? Michael going into town to buy one would trigger chaos.

Poppy. Poppy could overnight her some in a diplomatic pouch via Rome.

Abigail debated whether to tell Michael what she already knew—she was pregnant. She also debated whether to tell him what she suspected: they were having twins. She knew exactly how big a seven-week uterus should be, and hers was in the twelve-week range.

Abby calculated the time difference and called Poppy. She worked part-time for President Lafayette, while her husband, Logan Chaffee, was his Chief of Staff.

"Pops, Abby here," Abigail said with a big smile in her voice.

"Hey there, married lady. You tired of him yet? Want to pass him down to some of us mere mortals?" Poppy asked. Poppy, her former Chief of Staff and matron of honor, was a redhead with attitude. They'd gotten off to a rocky start but ended with a bond for life.

"Nah, he's great. We're here in Ravello, but you know more about this place than I do, you spent your honeymoon here."

"And I don't think we left the grounds. Gloriana is a fabulous chef, and I'm convinced there's something in the water there—I got pregnant right away."

"Really? And all this time, I thought unprotected sex got people pregnant."

"So what's up that you need me?" Poppy asked good-naturedly.

Abby told her the plan.

"Already?" Poppy was all but crowing.

"I'm pretty sure, but I don't dare send anyone here to get test kits. The paparazzi have already found us."

"They'll be there by noon tomorrow. You'll call me at noon-fifteen with the results. Got it?" Poppy ordered.

After another uneaten dinner, Abby and Michael bundled up and walked out to the *Bel Vedere*. A half-moon splintered into a million pearl shards on the ocean and obliterated all but the brightest stars.

"Michael, my darling, do you remember the night you threw away my birth control pills?"

"Sure, just before Christmas," he said. "Then I took you back to bed to get you well and properly knocked up."

"Well, I'm pretty sure you succeeded."

He could not speak. He wrapped her in his arms, and she felt tears on the top of her head. Then he got out his handkerchief and wiped his eyes.

"When will you know for sure?" he managed to ask between the tears. He looked at her, his eyes full of love and wonder.

"Tomorrow. Poppy is overnighting me some tests in a diplomatic pouch."

Michael must have paced the entire length of the estate a dozen times the next morning awaiting the delivery via the Embassy in Rome. Abigail drank ginger ale to fill up her bladder. Luckily the pouch was there before noon.

They both scurried to their suite and locked the door.

Test number one was positive. So were tests number two and three.

"I think we can stop now," Abigail said, gathering up the clutter to put in the trash. "There's no reason to use the other three in the bag."

Michael deliberated what to do with the trash.

"I can't put it in the trash from the villa, the paparazzi will go through it. I know—I'll wrap it up and mail it to my mom," he said pacing. Then he turned to Abigail, a worried look on his face.

"So what do we do now? Aren't you supposed to be on humongous vitamins? You haven't been drinking, have you? Should I get you special bottled water? I think you ought to put your feet up," Michael paced the floor and prattled on.

Abigail threw up. Again.

He tried to comfort her but found he, too, became nauseated and backed away. He felt awful that he couldn't comfort her.

"It's okay, Mister," Abby said, as she cleaned herself up. "Everyone's like that. Even I had to learn to overcome vicarious nausea in the hospital."

She explained morning sickness is a misnomer.

"It often lasts all day and is a good sign," she said. Michael looked puzzled.

"It means my pregnancy hormone levels are high, and I'll likely go to term," she said.

He smiled and went to hug her. Again, she lurched for the bathroom.

"It also means I'll be doing this for the better part of the next six weeks, at the least," she said. That prospect brought tears to her eyes.

"What is it, Missus?" he said when she finally emerged from the bathroom.

"I was hoping it would take us a few months to get pregnant," she said, still teary-eyed. Then she burst into tears again. "I didn't think we'd be blessed so soon." *Or have twins.*

"I feel awful that you are so sick when we are both so happy," he said, his arms around her. That was code-speak for, "I'm not touching you till the doctor says we can have sex."

"I think I want to see a doctor friend in Houston, if you don't mind," Abigail said, regaining her composure. She wanted to be sure of twins before she told him. Besides, sometimes one just disappears very early on.

"Okay, okay, you get the appointment, and I'll get you there. I'll go start packing."

"I promised Poppy I'd let her know," Abigail said. "Do you mind?"

"Mind? Hell, no," he stopped and struck a muscle-man pose. "I'm so proud of my guys. Tell her they are the Aston Olympic Sperm Team."

Then he headed to get the suitcases and plopped them on the bed.

Poppy was thrilled and promised to tell no one.

"If Regina finds out you knew first, she'll tan my hide," Abigail said.

Regina wanted to be the first to know everything. Any delay came close to lying. And the First Commandment had always been: "Thou Shalt Not Lie to Regina." Whatever you had done was ten times worse if you lied about it.

Abigail called Regina's cell. Undoubtedly, it was buried somewhere in her purse underneath the duct tape, her Bible, knitting, a metal six-foot tape measure, and a disco ball key chain. Abby waited patiently. Regina had the phone set to go to voice mail after the tenth ring because she could hide a small appliance inside that purse.

"Hello, Sweet Pea," Regina's molasses and honey voice was music to her ears. "How is the honeymoon going? I was wondering when I'd hear from you."

"It's great. We spent a week on a private island in the Caribbean, and now we're at Michael's home in Ravello. How are you? How's O.T.?"

"We're right as rain. He's in the next room meeting with the architectural historians about the house we're renovating. It's too cold to go to the site. Thank goodness."

"And Kim and Duke and little Priscilla?" Abby asked.

"Everybody's fine, or I would have called you," Regina said. "So something's going on with you. I imagine you're calling me to tell me you're pregnant."

"Just once, just once in my life, I'd like to tell you something you didn't already know," Abigail feigned anger. "Hasn't happened yet. How did you know?"

"That man wanted babies with you the minute he laid eyes on you. And the grounds keepers brought me your birth control pills they found out on the South Lawn at Christmas."

"Well, I've really got morning sickness, which is good, but I want to see a doctor in Houston. Any chance you and O.T. could meet us there?"

"And get out of D.C. in February? We'll beat you there."

Abby was grateful Giuseppe drove them through the pass and straight to the tarmac at the Naples Airport where a rented G650 awaited them. No winding Amalfi Drive this time.

CHAPTER FOUR

AND THE TWO
SHALL BECOME FOUR

Houston

Clearing customs is pretty easy if you are a former President arriving by private jet. Michael would not allow Abby to be exposed to airline germs, so he'd chartered a plane. It was a lovely, if extravagant, gesture.

In moments they were reunited with Regina and O.T. Regina hugged Abby like she hadn't seen her in a lifetime. *Home would always be wherever Regina was.*

Abby and Regina began chattering away, oblivious to Michael and O.T., who were making sure they had all their bags.

"Oooh, Sweet Pea, you sure are pregnant. I've never seen you green," Regina said fondly, inspecting Abigail to make sure she was still all in one piece. Ever since the assassination attempt, she all but counted Abby's fingers and toes if they'd been apart for any length of time. And the honeymoon was the longest they'd been apart in at least three years.

Regina looked wonderful, as always. Her unlined mahogany skin belied her age, and the gray in her hair didn't detract from her ageless look. She smelled faintly of baby powder, her preferred dusting powder.

"If you two can let go of each other long enough, I'd like my hug please?" O.T. said. He, too, looked happy and healthy, so Abigail relaxed a little. She did worry about them, as they were getting on in years, but she could put one worry aside for now.

"Welcome home, Madam President," the immigration officer said as she and her party left.

"Thanks. I'm always glad to see the Stars and Stripes."

The Secret Service shepherded everyone into vans, one of which held tired agents and luggage. They radioed ahead that Goldilocks and Guy should be at home in thirty minutes.

During the drive into Houston, the conversation hopscotched all over the place.

"You are going to love what the Queen sent you as a wedding present," Regina said. "And since you weren't President when you got it, you get to keep it."

"Michael's house in Ravello is gorgeous," Abby put in.

"How was the bonefishing in the Caribbean?" O.T. asked.

"Great. Abby had one heck of a honeymoon. She slept through the first half and threw up the second half," Michael opined.

"Don't. Don't even say the words, or I'll do it right now."

Michael had never seen the house in which Abby grew up. The ranch-style house smelled like home: clean with a bookish smell. The house was now out of fashion, a teardown really, surrounded by faux chateaux, bastardized villas, and fake Georgian mansions. Its value was in the land.

"No zoning," Abby quipped about the architectural hodgepodge she disliked. "My dad paid cash for the house when it was built in the fifties. There's a picture somewhere of the house with some spindly trees, but now the oaks shade the house all day."

"Wow, it's a lot bigger than the bungalow I grew up in," Michael said.

"Well, the oil patch was boom or bust," Abigail said. "That's how Reege got money to take us in."

Wedding presents overflowed the dining room table.

"Ugh. Thank you notes," Abigail said as she looked at the pile.

"I did them for you, Sweet Pea," Regina said. "As a wedding gift for you. Feast your eyes on this."

Regina held up a large sterling silver pitcher with engraving on its generous bottom, "For Abigail upon her marriage, Elizabeth II R." There was also a handwritten card, "I thought something from Geo. III's era was appropriate for an American President. Elizabeth II R."

"I get the II is for Elizabeth the Second, but what's the 'R' for?" Michael asked, hefting the pitcher that could double as a five-pound hand weight.

"R is for 'Regina' – Latin for "Queen"—just like my darling wife," O.T. answered.

Regina beamed. O.T. laughed.

Miss Penny next door sent a plain Pyrex pie plate and her handwritten recipe for chocolate pecan pie. "I figured you'd get everything else," her note said.

"Too bad I can't cook," Abigail said.

"No, but I have Juanita in L.A. and Gloriana in Ravello," Michael said with a smile.

"Girl, you are so lucky. I've been begging for her recipe for years," Regina said.

Soon it was time for the tour. Regina disappeared for a few moments to copy down Miss Penny's recipe, "before you whisk it away."

"This is my room." Abby showed him into a room stuck in a time warp of her teenage years with boy band posters on one wall and books on the others. "Reege didn't change it when I went to college."

"Oh, my God, you had a mullet?" Michael cringed and held a picture by one corner, as if it were somehow toxic.

"With braces, too," Abby said.

"You should have shown me this before I proposed," he said.

"But Michael, I wanted to marry you," she said.

"And no way are we having sex in this room. I'd feel like a pedophile," he whispered in her ear, and she got goose bumps as always.

"Duke's room is just as bad," Abby said.

His room was full of football and basketball posters. Plus, he had a shelf of trophies and a wall of books. It had a "guy smell" to it, midway between soapy clean and dirty sneakers.

"I threaten to release the mullet picture whenever she acts up," Regina said, coming to find them.

"I am, as a consequence, very well behaved," Abigail said.

"Yes, well, that's up for discussion," Regina said. "Your baby is going to be 'premature' by my calculations. I hope you don't have a nine pounder." Then Regina laughed. Abby had missed the contralto of Regina's laugh.

At least Regina had tastefully updated the rest of the house and long ago made Pris's room into a real guest suite where Michael and Abby would stay.

Dr. Krishna was away at a meeting until February fourteenth, so Abigail and Michael enjoyed their time with Regina and O.T. It would have been fun to take him to some of Houston's fabulous restaurants, but Abigail spent her time either throwing up or trying not to. She couldn't even come to the dinner table; the sight or smell of food was so abhorrent to her. Michael and O.T. ate Regina's cooking with delight, while Abigail read and snacked on crackers and ginger ale.

She could drive without throwing up, so she showed Michael all around Houston. The Secret Service agents enjoyed the tour as well. Abby took the traffic for granted, but the men were shocked at the roar of the ubiquitous eighteen-wheelers.

"I didn't think Houston would be so busy," Michael said. "And the architecture's great downtown. No wonder you're proud of this city."

"Yep. It's a can-do city." She took him on a swing through the Texas Medical Center, a mini-city of thirteen hospitals and two medical schools. "Hermann Hospital was the only thing here in 1947. Now it's the largest medical center in the world."

"I believe it. I've never seen so many huge hospitals in one place in my life," Michael said, craning his neck to see the high-rise hospitals as Abigail cruised through. "And you worked here?"

"Went to med school here, then stayed on for residency and went on to work and also teach," she said somewhat wistfully.

"Do you miss it?"

"I'll always think like a doctor. The process kind of brainwashes you. And I keep up my license. It's a point of pride."

Another day, she drove them around the industrial heart of Houston, Highway 225.

"There are more petrochemical plants and refineries in this area than any other place in the world," Abby said. Michael and the Secret Service men gawked at almost thirty miles of one plant after another.

"And they load and unload here at the Port of Houston," Abigail said, driving up to the Port's main entrance. "Notice there are a zillion rail lines converging here as well."

"But, Abby, I thought Houston was inland," Michael said, slack-jawed.

"It is. The port is sixty miles from the Gulf, but the ships pass through Galveston Bay. We only had to dredge about thirty miles of Buffalo Bayou to get to the bay. And it's either number one or two in foreign or domestic tonnage."

"Buffalo Bayou?" Michael asked. "Weird name."

"Right, there were no buffalo, but it's one of the main drainage ditches…almost rivers…into the Gulf of Mexico. Downtown Houston's only like thirty or forty feet above sea level."

"I'm beginning to see why Texans have big dreams," Michael said.

On Valentine's Day, their appointment with Dr. Krishna fell on a morning he usually reserved for paperwork, then teaching. There would be no other patients. He'd see Abby early and meet the medical students and residents at ten for teaching rounds.

"Michael, before we see Dr. Krishna, I want to prepare you," Abigail said.

"Prepare me for what?"

"If God has a question about a high-risk pregnancy, he calls Krishna. But he's from India, speaks with a very thick accent, and dresses, well, like himself."

"Like himself?"

"Plaid pants with striped shirts, that sort of thing," Abigail said. "But he's super smart and very, very nice. And it was exceptionally nice of him to work us in."

The secretary put them in Krishna's office and the Secret Service Agent in the waiting area. The agent leafed through *Pregnancy Today*. He'd rather take a bullet for a President any day than have to go through what women do to have a baby.

A slight Indian man entered the room, a whirlwind of energy in mismatched clothes under a white lab coat. He wore athletic shoes with orange socks.

"Abby, I am so glad to see you," he said, hugging her tightly. At least Michael thought that was what he said. His accent *was* thick.

"Krishna, I want you to meet my husband, Michael Aston."

His handshake was firm.

"You've got yourself a gem, Michael. Every guy in our residency program was a little in love with Abby."

"Abigail speaks very highly of you," Michael said.

"So tell me, what may I do for you?" Krishna said as he sat down behind his desk, his face now professionally neutral as he snapped open her chart.

"Well, my last period was December thirteenth. I've had three positive pregnancy tests. I'm concerned, because I'm an elderly *primigravida*," Abigail said.

"Ah, yes." Krishna turned to Michael. "That's the term for a first-time pregnant lady over thirty-five," Krishna said. "How long have you been trying to get pregnant?"

"Uh, I got pregnant right after he threw away my pills," she said, pointing at a beaming Michael. "The packet was almost full. I'd had three or four at the most."

"A very, very good sign. Well, let's get you examined and go from there." He showed them into a large examining room. A nurse came in, tried not to faint at the sight of Michael Aston with the former President of the United States, and gave Abigail standard instructions.

"Take off everything, put on a gown, and have a seat on the table," she said. "Mr. Aston, you can perch on the stool there. And I promise to keep my mouth shut, but can I please have your autographs on the way out?" she all but squealed.

"Certainly," he said. "Your discretion means a great deal to my wife and to me."

When Abby was situated, Krishna knocked twice and entered.

"Oh, I told my nurse I'd get her license jerked if she breathed a word of your visit. And I threatened my secretary as well."

"That's very kind of you," Michael said. Everything Abigail had told him about Krishna was true.

Krishna did a full exam on Abby. Michael sat by her, holding her hand, very glad he couldn't see what all was going on below the sheet. How any man could spend his life looking at the business end of a naked woman was beyond him.

"You are a very healthy pregnant lady," he said. He didn't have to tell her the uterus was too big for her dates. He assumed Abby could tell during the exam. She missed very little. He'd let the ultrasound tell the tale.

Michael beamed at this first news. He bent down and kissed her on the forehead. Abby, too, was all smiles.

The nurse rearranged Abby out of the stirrups and draped her so only her bump showed. Soon Krishna had put warmed "belly jelly" on her and took the transducer and rubbed it around Abigail's belly. When he found a fast rhythmic whooshing, he stopped moving the transducer.

"That, Mr. Aston, is your baby's heartbeat," Krishna said. Michael teared up and pulled out his handkerchief, dabbing his eyes.

Krishna and Abby had already seen the two sacs on the monitor, but neither said anything.

"Mr. Aston, would you hold this here, please?" Michael held the transducer in place, listening in wonder to his own baby's heartbeat. He was scared to push too hard. Krishna took a second transducer and located the second heartbeat. It beat at different times than the first.

Michael frowned in puzzlement and then a look of wonder lit up his face.

"Twins?" Michael asked.

"It would seem so," Krishna said.

Michael went pale and sat down, hard, on the stool.

"Put your head between your knees," Abby instructed. "You can't faint on me."

"Abby, get dressed, and I'll see you two in my office," Krishna said and then left the room.

Michael's color returned. He grabbed her and hugged her as soon as she was standing. He was kissing her hair, her face, even her hands.

"You've made me the happiest man in the world times two," he crowed.

Abigail beamed at him, wearing only a smushed paper exam gown with ultrasound goo stains in odd places. Then she cleaned up, dressed, and they went into Dr. Krishna's office, holding hands.

"Do you want a CVS?" Krishna asked, taking in the two of them.

"What is that?" Michael asked.

"It's a test for chromosomal abnormalities," Krishna said simply. "The rate rises with the age of the mother, so we offer it."

"Yes, let's schedule it," Abby answered. "I'll explain it in detail to Michael."

He flipped open his calendar on the computer. "Tuesday, next week?"

Abby knew she, personally, could not handle a child with serious chromosomal abnormalities. She'd seen too much. They seem to suck all the oxygen out of a family, so even the healthy children suffer. She hadn't discussed this concern with Michael but would tonight. He was still on cloud nine.

"Now, Mr. Aston, before you start buying two of everything, I need to tell you that sometimes one fetus simply disappears," Krishna said with equanimity. "We see twins far more frequently at this stage of pregnancy than we do at the four-month ultrasound. It's all part of Mother Nature's mysterious plans.

"And as Abby can tell you, miscarriage is a problem until about the thirteenth week. However, her morning sickness is a good sign. Not at all fun, but a good sign."

He wrote Abby a prescription for ondansetron to help with the nausea as well as prenatal vitamins. Michael and she left the office on two different wavelengths. Abby was in her doctor mode. Michael was simply euphoric.

Later, when they were alone, she shared some of her concerns.

"Michael, I'm going to do CVS, a test for chromosomal anomalies. Older moms have a higher risk."

She explained all the risks and benefits, but he was unfazed.

"My darling, I'm behind you with whatever you want. I'm not the one who is pregnant, thank goodness. You get the final vote," he said with a chuckle.

When they fell asleep, she noticed Michael was spooning her and was resting his hand protectively on her belly.

The CVS was easy, the wait for the results, hard. It was a long two weeks, during which they endlessly discussed the pros and cons of knowing the sex of the fetuses.

When they went in for results, Krishna told them both babies had normal chromosomes. Everything was also fine on the ultrasound that day. When they were back in his office, Krishna asked if they wanted to know the gender of the babies.

"Yes," they replied in unison.

"You have a girl and…" He made them wait while he pretended to look endlessly through the chart. Abby and Michael laughed at his *shtick.*

"You have a girl and a boy. Both perfect." *This is the fun part of my job.*

Then both Abigail and Michael erupted into tears. Krishna's eyes were a little moister than usual, as well.

"Not much longer for the morning sickness; it should be gone by the end of the first trimester. After that, it should be smooth sailing for a couple of months. Then we get into the problem of prematurity in twins. However, Abigail, you're a tall woman, and you have more room for babies. By my calculation, your due date is September twentieth."

Abigail knew the score, and she planned on doing very little between twenty-two weeks and thirty weeks. If she had her way, every woman would sit on a pillow for those eight weeks.

"What about sex?" Abigail asked.

"Sex is fine, just keep it tame," Krishna said.

"Honey, I'm not touching you," Michael said, holding up his hands. "I will not rock the baby boat."

Abigail doubted she'd be able to change his mind anytime soon. Maybe in a month or two. *Besides, who wants to have sex with a woman who might throw up on you?*

"Travel restrictions?" Abigail asked.

"None now. How is the morning sickness?"

"It's there, but my weight is stable."

"Are you taking the anti-nausea medicine?"

"No, but carrying it around makes me feel better," Abby laughed.

Abigail all but tackled Regina with a bear hug when they came back from Krishna's.

"I guess this means good news?" Regina said, hugging Abby tightly.

"The best. One of each, a healthy boy and a healthy girl," Abigail said.

"Sweet Pea, I am so happy for all of us. Just think, O.T. gets married one year and gets three grandchildren in two years. First Duke with little Pris and now you with twins," Regina said proudly.

"And don't forget Poppy and Chaffee's Sweet Baby James. It's all but raining babies," Abigail said.

Abigail couldn't think of a nicer gift for Regina than grandchildren.

She and Michael were on the phone for what seemed like hours that night. Louise cried, saying, "It's about time you made me a grandmother, Michael."

"First shot and I made you two grandbabies," Michael said. Abby was on the other phone and heard him bragging to his mom.

"But Abigail, paybacks are hell, and Michael was an incorrigible little boy. I do apologize," Louise said. "But I shall spoil them rotten and send them home bratty."

"I'll let him handle the brattiness," Abigail said.

Poppy was ecstatic over twins. "So efficient, Abigail. One pregnancy, two babies," she laughed. "James will have 'cousins' about his age."

Duke and Kim were similarly thrilled, "Oh, Aunt Abby, we are so happy Priscilla will have two cousins so close to her age. They can all grow up together."

"Congratulations, Michael," Duke said. "You'll be a great dad, as soon as you get past that first blowout diaper."

"Thank you, I think."

Uncle Mikey Molloy was over the moon. "Finally, a good use of your greatest talents, Michael. You will make a splendid father." Michael couldn't speak; he was so overcome.

"I couldn't agree more, Uncle Mikey," Abigail said.

They were free to travel now, but Abigail knew where she wanted to be.

"I want my babies to be born in Texas. They'll be fifth generation."

"Then Texas is where they'll be born. Do you want me to rent the Alamo and have them born in the shrine of Texas liberty?"

"I don't think they rent it out," Abigail laughed. "It's a long time between March and September."

The thought of being pregnant with twins during the height of a Texas summer was not fun. *Be careful what you wish for.*

CHAPTER FIVE

NEW ARRIVALS

Regina and O.T. left in March and went back to the colonial-era house they were restoring outside of Washington. Regina decreed that one room had to be a "dorm" for the grandchildren, and so, of course, it was to be. O.T. was certainly living his dream, and Regina was pleasantly along for the ride. After a lifetime without a man, Regina had met her match, and it was obvious they adored each other. He'd bait her to get her bickering and then let her have the last word. Abigail and Duke had done the same most of their lives with her. All loved the game.

Michael and Abigail elected to stay in Houston and have the babies on Abby's home turf. He turned down all roles without comment. As a former President, Abigail had funds for an office but didn't feel the need to have one just yet. The only thing she was doing was gestating, and when she finished that, all she'd do was nurse, eat, and, if the babies let her, sleep.

With a few phone calls, they hastily converted one room into a gym, so Michael could stay in shape for the movies. "It's easier to do it every day," he said. Abby found she liked walking on the treadmill at an obstetrically correct pace. Between Michael, Abby, and the Secret Service, it was the busiest room in the house.

Michael imported his Irish secretary, Eileen O'Brien, from L.A. She came in daily to do all the necessary clerical things for both of them, and then she returned to a furnished apartment at five o'clock. She worked out of the office in the back of the house—the one where Abigail's dad had worked—so no one was underfoot.

Marriage hadn't found Eileen, but she was delightful and efficient. Her brogue was charming. She was thirty-ish and on the frumpy side, which was fine with Abigail. Each day she felt more like a whale about to give birth to twin baby whales. If Eileen had been whip-thin, Abigail would have found liking her more difficult.

Eileen decided to do the cooking.

"We've all got to eat, so why am I cooking at my apartment for one, when I could cook here for all of us?" her question was almost musical in her brogue.

Soon Eileen was cooking for them all, the Secret Service included. Once a week they had a movie night, but Michael banned any of his films.

"Too boring for me," he said. "You can watch them on your own time."

"Can you believe what an exciting life we have?" Abby said to Michael and Eileen one evening after dinner.

"When those twins arrive, you'll be glad you were well rested," Eileen said, then left for the night. Of course, there was a mailbox full of invitations for them every day, which Eileen declined. No one wanted Abby-who-grew-up-here; they wanted a Former-President-Married-to-A-Sexiest-Man-Alive-Movie-Star. Time together was precious to them. They'd had so little when they were dating, and once the twins arrived, they'd probably have even less. So they deliberately cocooned while in Houston.

More often than not, they were in the same room. Abby might be reading, Michael channel surfing on mute. They often took an early morning walk and followed it with a shower together. That was as close to intimacy as Michael would get until Abigail was past the first trimester. He marveled at the changes his children were making on her body, and he loved her more for them.

When they announced the pregnancy, they did the publicity thing again. Eileen set everything up, as she was used to doing it for Michael. Andre came and did her makeup.

"Ooh, Madam President, you are glowing. No blush for you or you'll look like a clown. We'll have to really contour the sides of your face so you don't look like a pie plate, but otherwise, you are looking good," Andre said with his usual candor.

Laura Rowe Wicker sent a good pregnancy wardrobe for Houston—lightweight, loose with minimal spandex. It had lots of color, especially cornflower blue to highlight her eyes. Abigail looked like the poster child for pregnant women, even if she did still have an occasional bout of queasiness.

It took nearly a week to accommodate all the press people, but Abigail and Michael had little else to do. They did not want marathon shoots, and Abby loved her midday rest.

Abigail and Michael dissuaded anyone from sending gifts, and instead suggested cash donations to the Infants First Endowment, a charity supporting the Infants First Act.

By then, the morning sickness was mostly gone. Many of the reporters wore fragrances—three weeks ago, Abby would have bolted at a whiff of them.

Yes, she fudged a little on their due date to make it appear she had conceived after marriage. She could fall back on the subject of twins to explain her burgeoning bump.

"This'll be great publicity for the Infants First Endowment," Abby said as she leafed through the *People Magazine* from the grocery store. *I look huge. I look like someone blew me up with a tire pump. How much bigger can I get before I explode?*

They ventured out more. Abigail took Michael to the Museum of Natural Science, and he was enchanted with the Butterfly House.

Hundreds of species flitted about, landing on anyone wearing a bright color. One landed briefly on Abby's bump. Each took it as a good omen. Across the street, The Museum of Fine Arts impressed Michael with its outstanding Impressionist collection.

"Jesse Jones was the mover and shaker of Houston in the early twentieth century. His granddaughter collected all this art and gave it away during her life. She commissioned posters of her paintings and hung them where the originals had been in her house."

People got used to seeing them out and about and pretty much left them alone. Often, if they went to dinner, everyone in the room stood when the couple entered and left. Besides, if anyone got too close, a Secret Service agent would interpose himself, and that was the end of that.

Halfway through the pregnancy, Michael and Abigail chose names. Emma Louise and her brother, Michael Molloy Aston, were not just moving; they began their turf fights at two o'clock in the morning. Abby could swear they were punching and kicking each other. For real fun, they'd use her bladder as a trampoline. Once she nearly fell when one of them stomped on her sciatic nerve. Instinctively, she gently swatted her belly.

"You two stop it in there, you hear me?" she was serious.

Uncle Mikey was thrilled he was going to have a namesake. And judging by the shenanigans going on in her belly, both of the kids would be hell on wheels.

Louise was touched they had chosen to name the girl after Michael's sister, who died of leukemia at age six. She was doubly honored they'd chosen her name as a middle name.

Regina already had one namesake, Duke's little girl, who had just celebrated her first birthday. Priscilla Regina was petite and sweet, like her mother; Abigail feared her own would be lawless brats.

Abby was put to bed at twenty-two weeks because she was threatening labor. It was no wonder, with all the fighting going on in there.

She was terrified of delivering half-baked fetuses. It was her worst-case scenario for this pregnancy. If she shut her eyes, she could hear the hisses, beeps, and dings of the Neonatal ICU, and they terrified her. She remembered the smell of alcohol and the squeak of athletic shoes. Everything about that place creeped her out. It always had.

Abigail was as still as a statue, lying on her left side as directed, and only getting up to go to the bathroom. She needed something to distract her from her terror. This was far worse than anything the Presidency had thrown at her. This was the life, death, or worse yet—the possibility of brain-damaged children. Abby turned to reading like a fiend, including *War and Peace*. She put it on her Kindle for a dollar. It took her five weeks to read it. She loved it, even though it would never get published today. *Too long. Some sleazebag with a reality show can publish a cookbook, but Tolstoy? No way.*

Michael waited on her hand and foot, and he, too, read a lot, usually sitting in the rocker in their room. He did make time to work out when Abby slept.

At thirty weeks, she relaxed. The worst danger for prematurity was passed. Even if the babies were born tomorrow, they had the odds on their side. Krishna let her go back and forth to the kitchen a couple of times a day, usually for ice cream. Eileen kept the freezer stocked with every flavor from the grocery. *Thank God for Blue Bell Ice Cream.* Abby knew the babies were growing at a phenomenal rate. They'd probably each double their weights between thirty and forty weeks. She felt no guilt at chowing down on anything that passed in front of her.

Abigail could go out, but she had little desire to leave the air-conditioned house when it was over a hundred degrees outside. It was even hot indoors. Air conditioning can only do so much, and pregnant women are hotter than your average person. The babies are a degree hotter than the mom, and the placenta acts as a heat exchanger. Abby lived in gauzy nightgowns, with a robe for when the Secret Service was around. She took cool showers at least twice a day and used lots of dusting powder.

Abigail was waddling and shuffling by thirty-two weeks and thought she looked like an overfilled blimp. Everything was big: her face was enormous and her breasts, never small, now deserved their own zip code. Her belly was gigantic, and she resisted the urge to measure her waist, fearing the tape measure wouldn't go all the way around.

She could feel her feet swelling, but she couldn't see them past her bump. She had to put a foot out to the side just to view it.

Even her nose looked big to her in the mirror. *Can my nose get fat in pregnancy?* Sometimes she felt aliens had taken over her body. Other times she was sure they had, like when they did barrel rolls inside of her, and she could only watch her belly writhe with their movement.

To Michael, however, she only became more beautiful. Even during their wee hours brawl, he could somehow calm them, usually with a belly rub and some special cream Eileen bought on her weekly jaunt to the maternity store. Michael got some high-end headphones, but couldn't get them onto Abigail's bump. No Mozart or Sinatra for these two.

Oddly enough, Michael's singing to them along with the belly rubs helped.

"You're going to come in very handy, Mister," she said. "Even if your singing is worse than my dancing."

Jerome Lafayette enjoyed enormous poll numbers. The country was adapting to the "Adams Five," as people had taken to calling the five Constitutional Amendments.

He had immediately gotten the Line Item Veto upon his Inauguration, so "pork" in legislation diminished with the certain knowledge he would ferret it out—and veto it. He was also in for a six-year term, which, as he told Abigail during one of their phone calls, "seems like a bait and switch."

"Does it change the way you think?" Abigail asked.

"Definitely," he said. She could tell he was on speakerphone. And she heard the rhythmic "scratch" of a fountain pen. *He must be signing correspondence while we talk. I used to do that.*

"Reelection doesn't enter my mind. And I take a longer term view," he continued. *Great.*

"What's the downside?" she asked.

"I thought if I didn't like the job, I could leave after 1,460 days. Now I'm stuck for 2,190 days. It's kind of like being in the Army. They upped my enlistment without asking me," he groused with a grin in his voice.

"And the lobbyists?" Abigail asked.

"A lot are just gone. The law firms are laying off the lobby lawyers. The Hill seems like they don't know what to do. They're so used to someone buying every lunch and dinner, they might lose some weight," Lafayette said. "So I'm trying to feed more of them. Maybe we'll work together better."

"And the economy?" Abigail asked.

"It sucks. But it's sucked for a long time. I'm trying to hammer home that we all partied together, so we are all hung over together. At least I have sent legislation to the Hill that I know the lobbyists can't kill."

"Like?" Abigail was happy to think of something other than pregnancy.

"Consumer Credit Reform. No sending people credit cards through the mail without their request. No sending blank checks through the mail. No loan shark credit card rates. It's a sliding scale based on the prime rate. The highest credit scores pay prime plus 3 percent, and it escalates to prime plus 10 percent. The lowest 20 percent of credit scores cannot get credit cards at all. They have to improve their credit before they can get a card without a cosigner."

"I'll bet the people love you," Abby said.

"And the banks hate me," Lafayette said. "And a lot of people who bought too much on credit and declared bankruptcy are ticked they can't run their scam again."

"Sounds reasonable. What about the Balanced Budget Amendment?" Abigail asked.

"We have six years, so this first year, we are trying to get 16 percent closer to a balanced budget. Both parties are working on it."

"How?"

"Don't you read the papers?" Lafayette asked.

"My belly gets in the way."

"Television?"

"I'm supposed to stay calm, I'm on bed rest. I watch streaming videos of fluff movies. If my doctor knew I was talking to you, he'd make me hang up."

"Well, we have a super committee of House and Senate leadership, both parties, the Congressional Budget Office, the White House Office of Management and Budget, plus relevant Cabinet members. They work every Monday, Wednesday, and Friday afternoon—all afternoon—to get a plan within six months for the first three years. It's an enormous job. But, once drafted, it will pass as everyone is fully invested in the project. If they don't, I'll have no choice but to unilaterally cut all spending by 16 percent. No one wants that."

"I'm so glad the country has you and not me," Abigail said, nibbling on a cupcake Eileen brought her.

"You're kind to say so."

"I know you're supposed to hang up on me, but I have to go. I have a bladder the size of a thimble. It's the only small thing about me," Abby said.

Lafayette laughed and hung up.

While Abigail gestated, she shopped online for the babies. She bought enough to see them through two years in yellow, green, and white. She wouldn't have a chance to pop out to Target with twins in tow. She even ordered their car seats online.

Poppy wanted to throw her a baby shower, but Abby couldn't see doing it with everyone flung all over the country. The Secret Service banned any unsolicited gifts from the general public. They were scanned off-site and sent to the March of Dimes to hand out to indigent babies. Eileen sent a printed card of thanks to the donor.

Michael and Abby were happy their plea for donations to the Infants First Endowment had netted nearly two million dollars. It would go to a program for new fathers who had grown up without one. It's harder to be a good dad if you haven't had one.

They didn't go to birthing classes, but a nurse educator came to the house for individual lessons. Abby didn't need them, but Michael was a sponge. He must have read the book on pregnancy at least twice.

"Once for each twin," he quipped.

After the nurse left one evening, Abigail said to him, "You know, don't you, most of the breathing stuff is bogus?"

"Then why do you do it?" Michael asked.

"Distraction from the pain. The mother's cooperation isn't even necessary. When it's time, those babies are coming out."

"And me? Am I irrelevant?" Michael asked, feeling rather small.

"No. You are definitely not irrelevant. You have to teach Mikey how to be a man. You also have to teach Emma how a man should treat her."

Michael kissed her nose.

"And you can't take personally anything I may say when I dilate to seven centimeters," Abigail said.

"Why?"

"At that moment, all women hate their husbands for doing this to them," Abby said. "Then the husband tries some helpful advice, and mom goes ballistic." She'd seen it many a time.

Abigail's water broke in the middle of the night in her thirty-seventh week and the Secret Service drove them to the hospital. A test showed the babies' lungs were mature and Krishna allowed her to deliver. She labored all day on—how appropriate—Labor Day. The epidural helped, but labor is an enormous amount of work, and all she got was a lousy six hundred calories in the IV. Somewhere along the way, the epidural stopped working. She'd gotten the maximum amount of meds but was getting minimal pain relief.

When she hit seven centimeters, an evil woman possessed her body as she screamed several unprintable phrases to the man of her dreams.

"Wow, you weren't kidding, were you?" Michael said.

"And don't you dare give me crap advice. You think you know how to do this? Then do it, Mister. I've had it. I want a C-section, and I want it an hour ago," Abigail yelled. No one on the staff took her seriously. The tirade meant she was progressing rapidly from seven centimeters dilation to nearly ten.

Krishna came in and reassured her all was on target.

"Abby, you know quite well you can deliver these babies vaginally, and it's the best way," Krishna said quietly and calmly. "You're almost there. Ten centimeters, fully effaced. You can start pushing whenever you feel like it."

Abby knew the end was near, and she headed into the hardest part: pushing out the babies. The harder she pushed, the faster it would be over. She clung to Michael with all her strength, bracing her feet against the stirrups and her arms against his strong arms as she pushed.

Within the longest hour of her life, Mikey's head was out. Abigail thought it would be all downhill after the head, but that first shoulder hurt almost as much. Then, before he was fully out, he began to cry. His lower half all but shot out of her. He was a ball of red-faced fury. Abigail could at least rest for a few moments before it started again. The after-birth hurt, but not nearly as badly as delivery.

The second time was easier—but still no picnic. All of her pushing with Mikey had moved both twins into the delivery "chute," and Emma followed five minutes later.

She was a perfect little lady. She looked around and peered deeply into her mother and father's eyes. *I know these people.*

Michael and Abigail were laughing and crying at the same time. Abby, who had looked so imperial as President, was a physical wreck. Wearing a hospital gown, her glasses were covered with smudges; her sweat-drenched hair was scraggly and escaping from the blue poufy surgical cover. Her nether regions hurt like nothing she'd ever imagined. She was the size of a beached whale and totally, completely happy.

The Sexiest Man Alive, who desperately needed a shave, was humbled, crying, and happy at the miracle God had bestowed on him. He also had bruises on his arms from where his wife had grabbed onto him.

Abigail was more beautiful to him at that moment than ever before.

Mikey was six pounds fifteen ounces, and Emma was six pounds fourteen ounces, and both were Apgar 9/10s. In short, they were perfect. One of the nurses snapped pictures of them with Michael's camera. Another put the babies' footprints onto his scrub shirt as a souvenir.

Abby looked in awe at each of her children in the crook of each arm and was fascinated to see them as a mother, not as a doctor.

"Oh, look, Michael," she said holding Emma's narrow long foot, "Italian shoe feet." Michael had trouble seeing Emma's feet through his tears.

"Mikey has shoulders like a linebacker," Abigail said. "No wonder his shoulders hurt so much coming out. He's going to be built just like you, Michael."

The hospital ensured their privacy, and they were allowed to get to know their babies just like any other couple. As for the press, Eileen faxed Michael's statement to his publicist who told the world.

The hospital officially had "no information" on anyone named Aston or Adams. Only their closest friends knew where they were, and they filled the suite to overflowing with flowers.

Regina and O.T. were at the house when they came home. Flowers were also everywhere there, as well as gifts for the babies from family members. The Queen sent antique silver porringers "also from George III's era," for which Abigail wrote a lovely note, including a picture of the babies. Eileen kept up with the regular thank you notes. Gifts from unknown persons were handled as before.

Mikey was the spitting image of his dad, but with light, jade-green eyes. Emma looked like her mother, but had brown eyes from minute one.

Abigail put only one bassinet in their room, as the babies had been "womb-mates" and would sleep best near each other. She made a small chest of drawers into a changing table, and she and Michael took care of the babies while Regina took care of them. Eileen took care of the outside world.

"You have to eat like two pigs, drink like two fish, and live like a princess if you want to breast-feed twins," Regina told her. "And eat ice cream at least twice a day for the first two weeks."

Abigail learned to stay way ahead of the twins. She ate and drank before she fed them, whenever possible, and if one awakened, she woke the other to eat at the same time.

Michael was in charge of the tantrum Mikey insisted on having at two o'clock in the morning, even after he had been fed and changed. He screamed like a banshee, while Abigail swaddled him. Michael held him so Mikey could hear his heartbeat. He'd walk the screaming maniac, jostle him just so, and talk to him. Mikey would eventually settle down, usually within the longest five minutes of Michael's life.

Michael could not believe how much laundry two babies could make. He did at least one load a day, after a lesson from Regina, who wasn't sure anyone so sleep-deprived would get it right anyway.

Emma continued to be very much a lady. She was a gourmet at the breast. Emma would sometimes pat her mother's breast. Mikey was a shark, demanding milk immediately. If enough didn't appear, he'd literally beat on Abigail's breast with his fist.

Mikey couldn't care less if he had a dirty diaper; Emma demanded hers be changed, even if she wasn't completely finished with her business.

The first two weeks were a blur, as Michael and Abigail had no trouble sleeping when the babies slept. Regina told them a successful day was one where each adult got to brush their teeth and take a shower. Many days weren't successful. Some were, but only if judged after five in the afternoon.

For the two-week checkup, they started preparing the day before. Abigail found clean maternity clothes she could wear and laid them out. Michael couldn't remember his last haircut, so he slipped out to a barber the Secret Service guys used. For twenty bucks, it was just as good as the two-hundred-dollar styles he got in L.A.

Abby and Michael could all but see the pediatrician's office, it was so close. Still they were late by twenty minutes. Just getting both babies into the car seats baffled them, and they had to get out the instructions again. Both parents dripped sweat from the late September mugginess, and the babies were crying the whole time.

They apologized profusely for their tardiness to Nurse Amelia.

"No problem. No one has ever been on time for a two-week checkup—ever," she replied as she weighed and measured the babies.

Each baby was over birth weight by a pound.

"I'm very impressed," the pediatrician, Dr. Karen Lawson, a colleague of Abby's, beamed. "Just being at birth weight is, as you know, acceptable for the two-week checkup for a nursing infant. But both twins being a pound over is amazing."

Abigail felt like she'd just won the Grand Champion Mother Cow event at a rodeo.

Regina and O.T. left the next day.

"We've gotten everyone off to a good start, now it's time to bow out," Regina said. "Don't be surprised if Mikey is a holy terror tonight. If all else fails, put him in his carrier on top of the dryer. Then put some towels and a pair of tennis shoes in the dryer."

"Okay, why?" Michael asked.

"It is nirvana to a baby—it sounds like inside the womb."

Abigail cried like one of the twins when Regina left. When Michael asked her why, Abby said, "She raised me and loved me just because I was there, and I needed it."

"There are angels among us," Michael said.

"Now it's just you and me, kid," Abigail said, trying to tame her tears. "Think we can do it?"

"I'm not sure, frankly," Michael replied with a wrinkled brow. "How about you?"

"Well, it's pretty simple. You put food in one end and wipe it off wherever it comes out. It's the repetition that's the killer."

Right on cue, Mikey had his 2:00 a.m. tantrum. It was so bad, Michael had to put him in his seat, put it on top of the dryer, and dry a load of towels and tennis shoes to lull Mikey to sleep. Michael, in his boxers and a T-shirt wet with spit up, fell asleep sitting on the floor, his back to the dryer's door. Abigail found them both in laundry room, sound asleep, when Emma awakened for her 5:00 a.m. feeding. She tiptoed out for the camera, and that picture of Michael would always be her favorite.

With Regina and O.T. gone, the world sort of caved in. Eileen was busy shopping and cooking for everyone, especially Abby who ate an enormous amount of food. Eileen also held the world at bay.

Michael was in charge of the laundry. Regina had taught him how to do it, but he was so tired, he forgot. All he knew was that if he didn't do it daily, the house began to smell funny.

He did at least one load of baby laundry a day and one load of adult laundry a day. He lived in pajama bottoms and T-shirts, and Abby did pretty much the same. Both had all manner of baby effluvia on them, and Abby's shirts also had breast milk on the front. The cups in her nursing bras looked big enough for his whole head, and frankly, the contraptions gave him the willies with the flap down thing. But wash them he did.

So everything got washed on hot for the babies. Once he dried it, he put it in a clean basket, and they fished out what they needed.

He washed all the adult stuff on warm, and then did the same trick with the clean basket. This took up an enormous part of his day. He worked all day long, every day, and the dirty laundry basket was still always full. For a man who consistently made the Best Dressed List, he had no idea how much work was involved in keeping him immaculately groomed. He had staff for that. After a week of baby laundry, he resolved to give everyone a raise.

The babies went through several outfits a day. Abigail gave up on a bath for each baby each day. Every other day was good enough. Bathing a baby is no small feat. Everything must be assembled beforehand. Newborns are not known for being fond of their baths and show their displeasure with gravity-defying contortions—and they are also slippery little devils. Nevertheless, the Aston children were suitably clean.

A cleaning service came daily as Abigail couldn't tolerate dirt around newborns, but they were in and out in under an hour, usually the hour Abby took the babies out under the oak tree in the back for some tummy time. It was still hot in September, but Abigail knew they'd be in L.A. soon and that cheered her.

Abigail sailed through her six-week checkup. She was only five pounds away from her pre-pregnant weight and knew most of that was breast tissue.

"The babies are tapeworms and will get the last five pounds off, though there is no hurry at all," Krishna said. "How long do you plan to breast-feed?"

"I'm shooting for a year. I have an electric breast pump, so I'm storing milk, too."

"Then keep up your prenatal vitamins and don't get much below your normal weight. You can go back, easy, easy, to all your former activities. Sex will feel like the first time ever, so go slow. You can even exercise now."

"May I travel?" Abigail asked.

"Sure, but try not to get the babies out in public much. Too many germs."

Michael and Abigail were walking zombies but wanted to get to California and get settled.

Abigail and Louise had planned the nursery, and Louise had everything ready at her end. It was a cheerful yellow and green room with one crib (to start with) and a bassinette in Abby and Michael's room. The second stayed in its box for now. Her only "extravagance" was two rocking chairs in the twins' room. And two more in the living area.

She and Michael thought long and hard about nannies.

"I want us to raise our own kids," Michael said.

"I agree, but I want someone there if we are going out," Abigail said. "Neither of us is low profile. And we will want to go out sometimes."

"There's my mom, plus my live-in housekeeper and her husband."

"All three of which are a generation older than we are," Abigail countered. "And right now, I'm feeling a generation older. Wait. We did just get a generation older."

They both laughed.

They decided they wanted a system of three or four nannies on call.

"I'd like grad students, as they'll be bright," Abigail said.

"I'll insist on background checks and an ironclad confidentiality agreement," Michael said. They'd pay them all a monthly retainer, and the deal was that when summoned, someone showed up. Most times, they'd give them advance notice, but sometimes they might have to drop what they were doing and come. Michael and Abigail would augment the retainer for time actually worked.

Louise interviewed a number of young men and women and chose a pool for Abigail and Michael to interview. Michael's assistant, Eileen, would close up the Houston house after they'd gone to L.A.

Michael chartered a plane to take the family and Secret Service to L.A. Somewhere over the Grand Canyon, everyone on the plane was ready to bail out without a parachute.

Both babies cried nonstop, whether Abby nursed them or not. Emma squirted diarrhea down her leg and onto the airplane seat.

"At least it's leather," Abigail apologized to no one in particular, as she tried to clean up the mess. Emma wailed, likely because she hated to have a dirty diaper.

Mikey threw up on his father. Twice.

All Abby and Michael could do was look at each other and wonder what happened to their charmed life.

"I'm so glad we love each other. Otherwise, we'd be in deep doo-doo," Michael said.

Mikey, taking the hint, fired a volley of green diarrhea onto his father's pants.

CHAPTER SIX

HOME ON THE RANGE

November
Los Angeles

The babies were angels their first night in L.A., for which Abigail and Michael were profoundly grateful. They deserved something after their nightmare flight.

Their love for their children started at the moment they heard the babies' heartbeats and had grown daily. Michael and Abby fell in love with both babies. It was as intense as the romantic love they had for each other, if not more so. They actually watched them sleep, not for the novelty of it, not for fear one would stop breathing, but for the glorious feeling of seeing perfect, new, little humans who were all theirs. Each loved the snuffly baby noises they made when they slept. And each could not get enough of the smell of a clean baby.

They attended their local Infants First class, which in their school district was pretty ritzy.

Michael admitted he learned a few things at the meeting, like the difference between spit up and projectile vomiting.

"And what is it?" Abigail asked.

"If it hits the wall, it's not spit up," was his take on the lesson.

Both stuck out like sore thumbs, especially since they came with Secret Service protection, but Abigail welcomed the screening for both babies. Each passed with flying colors.

Abby had to call the lady at Neiman's for a post-partum wardrobe. She'd lost all her baby weight, but nothing fit anymore. Her hips had spread, as had her ribs. Her body had indeed been taken over by aliens who, when they moved out, did not bother to put everything back where they found it.

Somehow, with Louise's help, they found their nanny contingent. All had passports and all were shocked and honored to be working for Abigail and Michael.

Angelique, a French grad student in architecture with black cat eyeglasses and a pixie haircut, was quiet and serious but lit up around the babies.

The "manny" was Fred, who was working on his PhD in psychology. He was jovial and could easily keep up with Mikey. As the second of six kids, he knew about childcare.

Third was Ellen, a tall, thin dishwater blonde who was getting a PhD in early childhood education so she could "design educational toys."

Finally, there was Giovanna, the Italian consul's daughter, who miraculously stated, "I have no desire to party. I'd rather play with babies or read a book."

One day, when Juanita, Michael's housekeeper, was speaking Spanish to the babies, Abigail said, "If you only speak to them in Spanish, they'll become bilingual without trying." Juanita had lots more to say to them, as did her husband, Pablo, the gardener.

She made the same request of Angelique who spoke French to them. With Gloriana in Italy and Giovanna here, she hoped her children would be multilingual. She'd read somewhere that kids with normal IQs can learn a huge number of languages if they start early enough. She stressed to all the "language teachers" to spend a lot of time face to face with the children, as that, too, helped with language development, especially in infancy.

"Be sure to babble back to them," Abby said. "Babies love it."

Abigail wanted her family together at Christmas, even though the babies would just be three months old and wouldn't remember anything. Abigail loved having everyone at the White House for Christmas, but no one lived in a house that big. Michael's house had five bedrooms, but couldn't accommodate everyone.

"What about the ranch you own?" Michael asked. "How many will it sleep?"

"I haven't the vaguest," Abigail said. "I'll call Mason in the morning."

Mason Ingram had run Logan Oil and Logan Ranching interests for years. Pris inherited all of it when her former father-in-law died. She in turn left the controlling share of 51 percent to Abigail and divided the rest equally between Regina and Duke. None of the three had ever even been to beautiful downtown Nickel Slot, Texas, not even after they inherited it. All were too busy.

All they knew was that electronic transfer had replaced mailed checks—and the ranch spun off an incredible amount of money. Anytime you own something bigger than Rhode Island, you're going to be rich. The question wasn't how much the ranch was worth; the question was how many bedrooms it had.

"Mason, Abby Adams here. How are you?" Abby asked.

"I'm fine. How are those babies I keep reading about?" His slow drawl sounded welcoming.

"They're fine, but I've learned where gray hair comes from," Abigail said. "I caught Mikey by one leg as he tried to roll off the changing table. And he can't even roll over yet."

"So when are those young'uns coming to the ranch? The ranch house is ready anytime they are."

"Tell me about where you live, first," Abigail said.

"Me? I have my own house here on the ranch, down by a pretty little creek. The ranch house itself is empty. Well, not empty, full of furniture and all, still kept up, still cleaned and so forth, but no one lives in it."

"How many bedrooms?" Abigail asked.

"Golly. The whole house is fifteen thousand square feet or so. I'd have to go count, but I think somewhere around ten bedrooms, maybe eight, maybe twelve."

"I think I will pay you a visit. Would next week be okay?"

"It'd be my pleasure," he said. Abby had met him only once, at her sister's funeral in Houston, but she had liked him instinctively. Pris not only left him in charge of a multi-million dollar operation, but also a nest egg big enough to cover his lifetime. He didn't have to stay at Logan Ranch, but he was a loyal sort.

She and Michael packed up the two babies, two nannies, and their Secret Service detail and flew to the ranch. The babies traveled better this time, thank heaven. Mason was standing out on the runway when they landed. He'd had several of the ranch's truck-bodied SUVs with the Rockin' L logo on them washed and ready to go. He had no idea how many people the mother of twins who is a former president travels with.

The day was mild for November, but every year it seemed to get hotter, and he was in his regular work clothes to meet them: a gray Stetson, which he promptly took off; a professionally laundered white button-down shirt, cuffs rolled up twice; professionally laundered blue jeans with a knife-edge crease; and shiny black boots and matching belt. *If he runs the ranch as well as he dresses himself, we're home free.*

Introductions made, two-month-old Mikey all but launched himself at Mason. Abigail took this as a good sign and handed him over. Emma would stay with her daddy. She liked her parents best. Mikey was soon fishing around in Mason's shirt pocket, had tried to suck one of the buttons off the collar, and was fascinated by the hat. So Mason put it on Mikey, who crowed and gurgled with delight with his head totally obscured.

"I see what you mean about Mikey," Mason said.

Michael put each child's car seat into the back of an SUV with ease. He was now a pro with car seats. Mason and one of the hands got all the baby gear stowed, and they drove to the ranch house. Abby gave up counting wellheads on the ten-minute drive to the main house. She saw virtually no mountain cedar, for which she was grateful. She wheezed and sneezed when it pollinated in December through February.

The huge white house sprawled out along its lawn, two stories, with big stone fireplaces at each end of the front section. Bedroom wings took off down each side of the main house, giving the house a U shape. Huge live oaks shaded the south side of the house.

Mason unlocked the door, and they walked back in time. The rooms had high ceilings and wood plank floors. Laid out to catch the maximum breezes in summer, it was warm in November.

"All the furniture is handmade, much of it here on the property, when the ranch was first built in the 1840s," Mason said. "The first owners brought over a German cabinetmaker who supervised the building of it."

Abigail knew Texas-made antiques like these were priceless these days.

"Later on, when they pulled up all the mesquite, they made some furniture with it. Of course, it's as heavy as lead," Mason said, showing he couldn't budge a low table with a push from this boot.

Mesquite furniture was also precious these days. The kids sure couldn't hurt it; it was as tough as lead, and almost as heavy. Mesquite is a crooked, gnarly wood hated for sucking water from thirsty Texas land. So ranchers dig it up. There's an annual contest to see if anyone can find a three-foot section that is straight. No one ever does. So they cut it up in blocks and build things with it.

"I didn't see any mountain cedar," Abigail said.

"No, ma'am. It's not indigenous, taking thirty plus gallons of water a day away from native vegetation. So we've cleared almost all of it. And everyone breathes better in the winter with it gone," Mason said. "Its only use is as fence posts, and we have darn near a barn full."

The kitchen was huge and straight out of the fifties, but that could be redeemed. Abby counted twelve bedrooms and eight bathrooms. Renovation would take some time, and she was running short of that if everyone was to come at Christmas.

"Yep, this'll do, all right," Abby said to Michael. "What do you think?"

"I don't see why not," Michael said. "Mason, how's the heating? We're thinking of coming for Christmas with all our family."

"It has central air and heat, which are checked out twice a year. It'll be nice to have a family back in here. When I was little, this house was always hopping. An empty house is sad."

"And what are you and your family doing for the holidays?" Abigail asked.

"Oh, it's just me. I usually lay low."

"Well, not this year. We're having a family Christmas here. And your presence is requested. You do know about our family, don't you?" Abigail asked.

"Is there anyone that doesn't? You guys are a rainbow. Is there room at the table for a redneck like me?" he scratched the back of his head.

"Let's see, we've got a *redhead*, Poppy, but no *rednecks*, so sure, you're welcome."

Michael and Abby went around again with Mason, this time pawning the twins off to nannies. Abby took pictures, Michael took notes, and Mason measured things.

The worst problems were the kitchen and baths. The room was huge, but the old fixtures and appliances were completely inadequate to feed twelve. They did some more photos, measurements, and note taking.

Before they pulled away, Abby had Mason shoot a picture of Abby and Michael standing with the twins on the front porch.

"We'll put it on the invitations to Christmas in Texas," Abigail said, hurrying to the car. Besides, Mikey had started beating on his mother's right breast and howling. He wanted to eat. He was starting to look like a bowling ball with eyes, primarily because he always thought he was starving to death.

CHAPTER SEVEN

PUTTING DOWN ROOTS

December
Logan Ranch

O.T. and his men were busy with the restoration of the 1750s house in Virginia, so Regina spent a couple of easy weeks in Texas bossing the upgrade to Logan Ranch. After all, she and Duke did own 49 percent of it. It would be a nice place for all her grandchildren to gather, and the first thing she'd order was a rocking chair for every room. Rocking babies was what made them sweet. Singing hymns made them good. At least, that had worked with Abigail. From what she knew of little Mikey, he'd need a lot of hymns.

Since Abby was essentially a full-time milk machine, Regina knew she'd get no real help from her. Besides, Abigail was always thinking about other things: medicine, then being president of the country, and now, nursing babies. She'd never learned to run a house.

First, she had to have a kitchen and enough laundry capacity.

Regina found a kitchen designer in Dallas who specialized in large home kitchens. The woman arrived at the ranch on time without a frosted hair out of place.

"Honey, you do need me," she said, shaking Regina's hand when Mason showed her into the kitchen. "One refrigerator would be a joke with more than ten adults and four children under two."

"Don't forget we have the Secret Service detail as well," Reege said.

It didn't take the two women long to design the kitchen. Regina insisted on two sinks, one "big enough to bathe a baby in." Everything was enormous and top of the line. Regina even ordered the biggest and best gas range money could buy.

The designer flipped open her phone and called her office from the ranch. "The range is on back order," she said to Regina.

Phrases like that didn't fly with Regina.

"You forget I ran the White House." Regina gave the designer "The Look." The designer called the manufacturer, explained the client was the former President of the United States, and suddenly, the range was to appear on time.

Regina had three dishwashers installed, all with food disposers in them. She'd own a kitchen that flushed if she could. As the house was pier and beam, the designer suggested a drain in the kitchen, "There's room for the U-trap in the crawl space."

"You mean I can just hose this floor down?"

"Indeed I do," the designer said. "Look, I'll get you a pressurized steam and water floor cleaner."

She flipped open one of her books and showed Regina the gadget for commercial kitchens.

"I have died and gone to heaven," Regina said. She hadn't touched a mop in decades and had no desire to start again, but this was a giant leap forward for domestic tranquility—at least in her book.

In fact, everything showed up on time, just the way Regina liked it, including the three washers and dryers, because babies are definitely messy. One was designated for the kids only. If their clothes were stinky now—just wait. There were irons and ironing boards, too. She also put in a commercial-style freezer and refrigerator in the utility room as back up for the very large ones in the kitchen.

Regina was on a roll and decided the bathrooms could be ready for Christmas as well. The kitchen designer learned quickly the best phrase to use with Regina was, "Yes, ma'am." It took an army of plumbers, but all the baths were updated within two days of the arrival of the fixtures. One plumber made the extremely stupid mistake of letting his racist attitude have voice when Regina told him a sink wasn't centered properly.

"I don't take orders from *nigras*," he said with a curled lip, unaware Mason was just down the hall, listening to the whole interchange.

Regina gave him The Look. He didn't back down.

"Get your tools and get out," Regina said as if she was dismissing an errant toddler.

"I want my pay first," he said.

"You didn't finish your job, so you'll get no pay."

"Why you stinkin' black bitch," he got into her face. Regina sniffed the air.

"What stinks around here is your attitude. And as for color, to you, I'm a green witch. I own a large chunk of this ranch. I'm teaching you a lesson you shoulda learned a long time ago. Racism doesn't pay. When you write me an apology, I'll pay you for what you have done.

"I used to make my living working for white folks, some of whom I didn't like. But if I can learn to keep my big mouth shut around people who are putting food on my table, so can you."

The man hurriedly threw his tools together and stormed past Mason.

"Don't set foot on this property again, Jim Bob," Mason seconded Regina. "You'll get half pay with an apology. Someone else will have to finish your job."

Jim Bob Green had always been a bad apple in Mason's book. After he was gone, Mason asked Regina how she was doing.

"I'm sad, Mason, I thought we were past that," she said. "Oh, well, maybe he'll learn to keep his mouth shut."

Regina had a problem with the beds. They were priceless antiques but uncomfortable and too little for anyone except children. So Regina called Abigail.

"Sweet Pea, what do you want me to do with these beds?" Regina explained her problem.

"Well, let's store the ones for adult rooms and buy new ones in a similar style. I might sell them down the line," Abigail said.

"You are not selling these. These are museum quality. You can donate them to some historic home," Regina was continually baffled at Abigail's frugality.

"Yes, ma'am," Abigail said, wondering why Regina bothered to call when she was going to do things her way, anyway.

Pottery Barn coughed up enough beds and mattresses, and Regina ordered a warehouse full of linens from an online company.

The painters finished up four days before everyone arrived, and it was still warm enough to let the house air out while the rooms were readied for their guests. Mason recommended some women from his church in Nickel Slot. They were grateful for the part-time work.

Mason gave Regina as many ranch hands as she needed to complete the "some assembly required" part, and soon the place was looking like a home. The ranch hands put together baby beds for Pris and Sweet Baby James, but just one for Emma and Mikey. Regina was mightily pleased that she was going to have four babies for Christmas.

She felt like crying she was so happy, but she had work to do.

The women Mason hired washed the sheets and towels. Every room was pristine—cleaned according to Regina's written protocol. The kitchen was stocked a full week before everyone was due. There was plenty of wood stacked for the fireplaces.

The last job was to baby-proof the whole house, and a herd of cowboys got down on their hands and knees to put in plug covers, door latches, and the like. No room was spared, and baby gates took up guard positions at the top and bottom of every staircase.

Regina was pretty amazed at what could be done with a computer, a credit card, an army of women from Nickel Slot, and a herd of ranch hands. She was finished with Logan Ranch, including the baths, while O.T. was still in the "deconstruction and catalog phase" in Virginia. *Those fool men planned not only to reuse the nails in the 1750's farmhouse, they took pictures of them. They even found a man to make nails just like the originals, in case they needed more. Men.*

O.T. was allergic to most fresh Christmas trees, so she ordered an enormous pre-lit fake Christmas tree. It needed ornaments, so she called Miss Penny who had a key to the house in Houston. Her grandson, age forty, was dispatched into the attic. Within two days, the tree held the ornaments she had gathered over a lifetime—complete with a beautiful brown-skinned angel for the top of the tree.

A Texas blue norther blew in on December twenty-third, so the air had the tang of Christmas. Legend has it there's nothing between North Texas and the North Pole except a five-strand barbed wire fence, with three strands broken. It sure felt that way.

There was a wreath on the door and mulled cider on simmer. Regina even had personalized stockings for everyone who would be coming. Stocking hangers hung from the fireplace mantel for each one.

People arrived in shifts on the twenty-third, and Regina was happy to see them all.

Uncle Mikey and his man arrived first, and they were pleased with their quarters. Mikey was taking longer naps these days, but he had earned it. Regina thought he arrived first to give himself time to adjust. Harold insisted on serving tea every afternoon, and Regina wouldn't turn that down.

Duke, Kim, and Pris were next. Little Pris saw her Grandma and broke into a run for Regina's outstretched arms. Poppy and Sweet Baby James came later. Chaffee, Chief of Staff to the President, likely wouldn't appear until Christmas Eve—and then only for a day or so. Poppy, too, was glad to be back within Regina's arms. Reege just had a habit of making everything right. Besides, traveling with a busy boy nearing eighteen months would frazzle anyone. Handing him to the crew of mothers and lying down for a nap was delightful.

O.T. appeared and was some kind of happy to see his wife. They'd lived a lifetime apart before they met, and now each hated to be away from the other. He traveled with the Trans who were happy to have some vacation from the shop.

Mr. Tran had finally found someone he trusted to run the place for a few days.

"Don't be fooled, O.T., he'll be snooping around for weeks, making sure everything is still in its right place," Vee said. "I hope this man is acceptable. Tran could use a manager. We want to slow down."

Abby, Michael, Louise, and their brood arrived last as Michael had a public service announcement to shoot on the Infants First program. Abigail refused to let the twins be in it, so look-alike babies appeared. Undoubtedly, their mothers would be proud to know their son or daughter had their first starring role opposite Michael Aston.

Christmas went well, as everyone was happy just being together. At three months, the twins were fascinated with the lights on the Christmas tree. Pris and Sweet Baby James were walking and had to be watched every minute, lest they pull it over. James was a few weeks older, at a year and a half, and Abigail was grateful Regina set the place up to be baby proof. James spent hours rattling the baby gates, trying to get to the stairs.

On Christmas Eve, they had barbecue, which had slow cooked most of the day. The smell of barbecue smoke and a crisp north wind invigorated Abby, who had quickly adapted to the year-round cool and sunny L.A. weather. This felt great.

Abby was eager to hear about Duke's new job. She jumped right in as soon as everyone was seated at the table and after O.T. said the blessing, which was mercifully short.

"So, Duke, I hear you are doing campaign finance compliance at Justice now," Abby said, picking up a rib and biting into it. *Life doesn't get any better than ribs on Christmas Eve.*

"Yes, ma'am, and I'm about as welcome on Capitol Hill as a turd in a punchbowl," he drawled. Regina immediately slapped his arm.

"You know better than to talk like that—especially at the table. How you ever grew up is a mystery to me. It's a wonder you aren't in jail," Reege said, consternated.

"Then let me rephrase, I'm about as welcome as a fart in church," he said, jumping out of Regina's range. Everyone laughed that he would defy Regina again. *Just like Duke.*

"I will send you to your room if you don't shape up," Regina said.

"Yes, ma'am," he smirked and dropped his eyes for a moment. "Actually, we delivered copies of the new regs to the members of Congress before the ink was really dry. Each had to sign that they had received them."

"Do you think they'll find loopholes?" Abby asked.

"Only ones they can hang themselves with. I reminded them I'd indict them for so much as thinking about breaking the laws."

"Good. I hope this will work," Abby said, aware of rib meat stuck between most of her teeth. She grabbed another as the platter went past. She wanted two more ribs but had to leave room for pecan pie.

"We'll see. The regs are straightforward and the penalties severe, so I really don't expect much problem," Duke said. "I could use a little time with Kim and Pris."

The conversation moved on to other topics, and Abby felt certain Duke would be a good "sheriff." Congress surely needed one.

The adults exchanged their gifts once the children were in bed. Putting four under two to bed in a new environment took some effort by nearly all. Papa Mikey, as he was now called, sang lullabies, and Michael's secretary Eileen read to James and Pris, who were sharing a room. Regina rocked all four, and finally Abby fed hers and they went to sleep, though Mikey fought it to the end.

All the grownups tiptoed downstairs, intensely grateful for peace and quiet and some of Regina's spiked eggnog during the gift exchange. Many of the gifts were gag gifts, like Duke's buying Michael athletic shoes on in-line skate wheels, so "you can chase after the twins."

Abigail had drawn Kim's name and got her an antique gold thimble.

"Thank you, Aunt Abby," she said with a dip of her head. "I am thinking of doing a ready-to-wear line this year and was looking for a name. You've given me a name: Thimble." She held up the thimble for everyone to see.

"There goes my quality time with Kim and Pris," Duke groused.

Again, Abigail was amazed at this young woman's gentle spirit and intense drive. She'd started out doing alterations and transitioned to couture without a blink. She made Abigail the gown for her first State Dinner—and her first date with Michael. Now she was nationally known for her bridal line and couture. Adding another business for her was as natural as breathing.

Abigail and Michael did not bring nannies, as all had their own families to go to. Michael did include his secretary, "Irish" Eileen, who fit right in. Papa Mikey loved listening to her stories of Ireland today, and the children loved her gentle ways and serious brogue. Mason drew her name and knew only that she was Irish. He'd never even met her. He spent some time online and bought her a Belleek cream and sugar bowl, as he could think of nothing else.

"Oh, my goodness! How did you know I collected Belleek?" she said, smiling widely at him.

"I didn't." Mason blushed. "It was just a shot in the dark, what with you being Irish and all."

Michael had drawn Abigail's name and when time came he said, "You, Missus, are getting your present in private." Abby blushed, but wondered what it was. Abby hoped it involved sex. If anything, making love with Michael was better than ever, though less frequent, obviously. More than once they'd called a nanny and snuck over to a bungalow at the Bel Air for some afternoon delight. At the end of most days, both were ready for bed about an hour before the babies were.

Tonight, though, Michael had a special gift for Abigail once they were alone. He gave her dangle teardrop-shaped diamond earrings. They took her breath away.

"Michael, these are enormous and gorgeous. You didn't have to do this," she said, reaching up and kissing him. "I'd be happy with a silly gift."

"When I saw you crying with joy at the birth of our babies, I knew then to preserve those tears forever."

"But I didn't get you anything," Abby said.

"I have everything a man could want and more: I have you, the twins, and shoes that double as roller skates."

With the babies asleep in the next room, they loved each other to sleep, Abigail wearing her new earrings and nothing else.

Christmas morning, the big kids were puzzled with the Santa thing but went with it. Michael and Emma were content to watch the lights on the Christmas tree. They weren't even ready to eat the bows and paper yet. Their pretend keys were their favorite present.

Regina did her magic with the turkey, Abigail and Duke bickered over the dark meat. Mrs. Tran set a beautiful table. Papa Mikey sang to the babies in his Irish tenor, and the babies were delighted, even though some of the songs contained some pretty bawdy lyrics. He even sang some Christmas carols as Mrs. Tran set the table.

Mason fit right in, as he got down on all fours and let Pris, then James, ride him. Pris squealed, "Horsey, horsey," at least twenty times that day. Even little Mikey wanted a turn at three months; he hung on like a little monkey, squealing with delight. Emma preferred the safer arms of her father. Sweet Baby James, now rowdy at eighteen months, was the most enthusiastic rider, yelling "More, more."

"Nobody better buy James spurs next year, or I'll be maimed," Mason said good-naturedly as he groaned his way up off the floor.

Abigail was happier than she could imagine, though each time she said little Priscilla's name, she missed her sister. She supposed that would never go away. And there was still an imaginary empty chair at the table.

As usual, Abigail did the dishes. Regina and Michael had long since banned her permanently from anything involved in food preparation. She'd packed rubber gloves and was glad when Eileen and Mason came in to help.

"This is a real treat. Usually I'm Cinderella in here, all by myself."

"Well, I can't cook either," Mason said.

"Oh, I can cook, that's for sure, but Regina said she had a system, and I was to enjoy myself," Eileen said.

"You're a wise woman to do what Regina says," Abigail said, noticing Mason's eyes lit up when Eileen said she could cook. *Michael will need a new secretary before long.*

CHAPTER EIGHT

FIRST STEPS

June

Los Angeles

Mikey was crawling like a maniac anywhere he wanted by nine months. Luckily, the pool was not only fenced, it had an alarm as well. He and Emma adored their time in the water with their parents, but Mikey was a daredevil of the first magnitude. Emma would pat the water from the safety of a parent's arms, while Mikey would hurl himself into the water, instinctively holding his breath.

Emma babbled like crazy, and sometimes Mikey babbled back. Most of the time, he was headed somewhere to get into something. Emma would sit and play, preferably with a doll. Mikey preferred trucks and was quite fond of throwing them. Luckily, Emma was good at ducking.

"Look at him," Abigail said the day before Michael left for his first-ever few nights away. "He has calluses on his knees."

"Fast little devil," Michael said, tossing him into the air. Mikey squealed with glee. The higher the toss, the better he liked it. "You'd better be good for Mama while Daddy's gone."

It was their first separation since the twins were born, and frankly, each was ready to get back into something of their old lives. Michael's transition would be easier, a simple documentary aimed at young inner-city fathers. He could direct that with his eyes closed. For Abigail, the problem was knottier.

She'd been President, but didn't want to hit the lucrative speaking circuit. She didn't need the money, fame, or the travel. The lower a profile she kept, the happier she would be. She missed practicing medicine but couldn't very well go back into the combat zone of emergency medicine. *The Secret Service would have a cow.* She had agreed to write her memoirs, but only because the proceeds went to her three favorite charities: Bookworms, the O.T. Wagner Scholarship Foundation, and the Infants First Endowment. Frankly, the Endowment out-funded the public money allocated, and that was fine with Abigail. At least kids were getting picked up at birth for their developmental screening, and parents had parenting classes.

Michael's work was a documentary for the endowment that he was paying for out of his own pocket. Then he'd pay to distribute the DVD to every Infants First program requesting one.

Abigail had settled into teaching pediatric physical diagnosis at the David Geffen School of Medicine at UCLA one morning a week. She was a natural at it, and her students learned to see babies and children, not as cases, but as someone's best-beloved baby. Often, she took Emma or Mikey with her. So what if ten people looked in their ears? The kids liked it, the students liked it, and Abigail liked it. The Secret Service could live with it. Another morning a week, she did her "admin," answering mail that Michael's assistant handled for her. She had funds for an office but resisted using them.

"Do you realize tomorrow will be the first night we've been apart since we got married?" Michael asked her that night at dinner.

"Yes. It feels weird, but in an okay way," Abigail said.

"I don't know if I'll be able to sleep," Michael said.

Abigail guffawed, almost choking on her food.

"Are you crazy? Of course you'll sleep. No one will awaken you, crying," Abigail laughed.

"Oh, yeah, I hadn't thought of that. Mmm. Four whole nights without crying kids," he smiled.

"Don't rub it in, or I'll check into a spa, leaving you home with the angels," Abigail threatened. *It did sound like bliss.*

"Shall we go away somewhere, just the two of us?" he asked.

"I'd say yes, but, developmentally, this is a bad time for both of us to be away from them. Ask me again in six months?" Abigail said.

"Deal."

"In the meantime, you can book us a weekly afternoon bungalow somewhere nearby, and I'll have a nanny come," Abigail said suggestively.

"You're on," Michael smiled.

By the time Michael came home from his four-day shoot, Mikey had started walking. Or rather, he had started running.

"I go away, and he's all but grown," Michael seemed a bit sad.

"I know, but you'll still get to potty train him," Abigail said with a kiss. "I haven't the vaguest idea what to do about that."

"Yeah, well, I figure..." Michael was interrupted by a crash from the other room.

Both parents dashed into the room. Emma was playing quietly, and Mikey was nowhere to be found. On the floor was a broken souvenir from some trip.

"Where is he?" Michael said, whipping his head from side to side.

Abigail pointed to the top shelf of the bookcase. Mikey was sitting up there, beaming.

"We have a climber. Oh, holy crap," Abigail said. "This is not going to be pretty."

"Cap," Emma piped up and smiled at her own cleverness. Michael and Abigail looked at each other. *Swearing was obviously now officially off-limits.*

"I refuse to acknowledge that Emma's first word was c-r-a-p," Abigail felt the need to spell it out, lest Emma repeat it.

Michael plucked Mikey off the top shelf and put him on the floor. Abigail got into his face.

"Michael Molloy Aston," she said sternly, wagging a finger in his face and then at the bookcase. "Do NOT climb up there again, do you hear me? No. NO."

His smile turned to a frown. He looked at Michael who immediately mimicked Abigail's stern visage.

"You heard what your mother said," he said, pretending to be angry.

Mikey thought for a moment about crying, but decided it would be more fun to run somewhere, and so he ran off. At least he didn't climb the bookcase again…that day.

"I think we handled that well, don't you?" Michael said.

"Gimme a break," Abigail said, hugging her husband. "We were zero for two. Emma's cursing, and Mikey's climbing, and they aren't even one."

"I think it's time we had a nanny around every day," Michael said.

"That or Child Protective Services will have to open a case file on us."

CHAPTER NINE

FIRST BIRTHDAY

In a perfect world, Abigail and Michael's twins would turn one unnoticed by the world at large. Since that wasn't going to happen, Michael arranged a photo shoot a week or so before their birthday. With lots of trial, error, and a super-fast digital SLR camera, the photographer managed to get a shot of both in profile trying to blow out an unlit candle on the cake (he would add a wavering flame digitally). The best part of the shot was Mikey's arm buried elbow deep in the cake.

The photographer also got shots of the family, and Abigail nixed all but one for release: a cute one of them holding the twins but with Mikey and Emma looking at each other, not the camera. The Secret Service had no formal opinion on the former President's children, but Abigail was petrified for their safety. She had made some powerful enemies while in office, and the less people knew about her children, the better.

O.T. and Regina, as well as Mikey and Louise, came for the birthday party itself. Everyone else had to work. Abigail despised overdone children's parties. She thought about baking a cake but realized she didn't know how. Even with instructions, it would be a disaster.

Abby was just punching in the bakery's number when Regina came in and nixed the idea of a store-bought cake.

"I'll make the cake. It's like riding a bicycle," she said with a har-rumph. "Besides, my grandchildren don't eat store-bought birthday cakes."

Abby was tempted to ask how Regina knew such a non-fact but remembered her manners.

For their birthday, Louise showed up with heirloom-quality pink and blue smocked outfits for them to wear "in the pictures." Abby couldn't imagine spending lavishly on baby clothes. She planned to remove them before they got to the cake eating.

On the birthday, Regina whipped up a wonderful devil's food cake. She frosted it with chocolate icing with pink and blue icing balloons, saying, "chocolate makes for better pictures for white babies."

Later that day, everyone assembled in the kitchen. Each child had been enthralled with the pink and blue helium balloons tied to their chairs but soon turned their attention to the cake.

Louise nixed the idea of bibs or having them eat just in a dia-per.

"It's all about the pictures," she said.

The kids were puzzled with the singing and candle thing. But they waved their arms and squealed when Regina plunked a cake down between them. Michael was taping everything and Papa Mikey was snapping away with his camera. Everyone sang "Happy Birthday."

They had help blowing out the candle. Everyone clapped; Abi-gail removed the candle and stepped out of the shot. Emma stuck her finger in the pink balloon and sucked it. She grinned widely and squealed. She deliberately did the same with the chocolate icing with a bigger laugh.

Mikey slapped the blue balloon with an open palm, sending icing flying. Within moments, each had chocolate cake and icing all over their faces and into their hair. Unaware of the camera, or even of each other, each enjoyed "Chocolate Bliss," whether the gooey delights made it to their mouths or not.

After a few minutes of cake freedom, Abigail feared they'd overdose. Chocolate throw-up was not her idea of a celebration. She and Michael each held one child in front of them, as if they were toxic waste, on the way to the bathtub.

Both kids went into the dry tub, from whence their clothes were removed and put in the shower stall. When the babies were naked, Michael began hosing them down with warm water from the handheld faucet. It took two shampooings and two full rinsings to get the chocolate out of their hair. They filled the tub and got the kids clean, but the parents' backs were screaming, not to mention their knees on the tile floor.

"Louise said paybacks were hell," Abby said with a gleam in her eye.

"Would my mom and Regina actually plan this for us?" Michael asked.

"Regina wouldn't. At least I don't think she would," Abby said.

Michael was about to answer when Mikey squirted him with a tub toy.

In moments, both twins were out, dry, and diapered. Abby put ratty clothes on them, because she had no idea what other cruelties the elders might have in mind. She rinsed out their fancy clothes in the shower, but they were probably a total loss.

They loved their presents of new riding toys and a pull along, self-playing xylophone from Papa Mikey. Regina shot him a look, but he ignored it and showed them how to get even louder noise from it.

Their sugar high lasted for hours, fueled in no small part by Papa Mikey and his songs. When they finally crashed for the night, Abigail knew they would sleep through.

The adults slipped out for a quiet dinner, the nannies on guard.

Not even a week later, Mikey weaned himself abruptly from the breast, no doubt desiring chocolate cake instead of breast milk. Soon, Emma wanted to nurse only morning and night. Then one day, she, too, was done with the breast.

Abigail felt horribly, terribly unnecessary. She did not have babies anymore. They were toddlers, or as the English called them, runabout babies. Just when she'd mastered the baby stage, they were out of it.

One day, Fred, the "manny" asked for a moment of Abigail's time.

"Sure. Whassup?" Abigail asked, offering him a glass of iced tea.

"I love my job…"

"I hear a 'but' in there," Abigail said.

"But you and Mr. Aston do almost all the work. I don't get why you have nannies."

"Ah. Good question. Mikey is a daredevil. If I have to go to the bathroom, no telling what all he could do," Abigail said.

"I see," Fred answered. "You need extra eyeballs."

"You got it," then there was a small crash, and Fred took off. He yelled from the other room: "He's fine, nothing's broken."

Abby laughed so hard she nearly cried.

Both twins walked, though Mikey ran. By fourteen months, both had mastered "Mama, Dada, hi, and bye." They practically fed themselves. Abigail's main job shifted from life support to life protection. Mikey seemed hell-bent on destruction, if not of himself, then of his environment.

Abigail and Michael couldn't envision having guests; the rooms held padded furniture and little else. They put tempered, locking glass fronts on the bookcases, only to realize Mikey smeared whatever he could all over the glass. If there was a blank space, Emma watched her reflection and then added her little fingerprints.

When it was Abby's turn to have Bookworms, the group of inner-city girls who loved to read, she had it at a nearby country club to which Michael belonged.

"I thought that since this month's book was about people in a country club, you might enjoy seeing one up close," Abby said. "Actually, we have twins who are fourteen months old, and the house is so child-proof, it's downright ugly."

The girls laughed, and enjoyed being in a private room in a private club. If their hand-me-downs in a sea of designer apparel put them off at all, it didn't show. They learned that good posture, simple ironed clothes, and good grooming would take you most places.

They were the very-welcome guests of a former President. If they were good enough for her, they were good enough for anyone. Abby loved seeing these girls mature just as the Washington group had. The first year's group was graduating from college, and all were doing well.

One night after Michael was happily back at work acting in a buddy movie shot mostly in the L.A. area, he broached the subject of more children with Abigail. If they were going to have more children, it was best not to wait too long.

"Abigail, I am the happiest man in the world," he said.

"And why is that?" Abby said, looking up from an English language international newspaper she'd subscribed to since her days in the White House. This was the first issue she'd had time to read since the twins were born.

"Well, I have you and the twins. The only thing I could ask for is maybe another child," he threw her his best smile.

Abigail put down her paper and went to sit on Michael's lap. She kissed him and nuzzled the spot behind his ear that always aroused him.

"Darling, darling Michael," she said. "If you want another baby, you get yourself pregnant and you deliver it."

He laughed and suggested they practice anyway. Abby was only too happy to comply.

CHAPTER TEN

STEPPING OUT

The first mid-term elections tested the new campaign finance laws. The difference was dramatic. There were many fewer political ads, and as such, voters had to dig a bit to find out about candidates. The candidates noticed voters actually came to see them speak, and they asked a lot of questions. Newspapers and television news delved into issues and candidates' stands.

Candidates running for U.S. House of Representatives seats wooed the wealthy in their district, but donors held onto their checkbooks until they were sure whom they wanted. Many an ad buy was put on a personal credit card by a nervous candidate, praying the funds would come in to cover it.

Voters noticed candidates were listening to them. This was a far cry from years past when a voter couldn't get a word in edgewise. Turnout was higher than expected, and the total amount of money in the races was a fraction of what it had been.

Oddly enough, both the candidates and the voters liked the new system.

"Everything is lower stress. I'm not out begging all over the nation for money," one Congressman said. "I can actually pay attention to the business of my district."

A businessman was more ecstatic, "My Congressman knows he needs me—and all his donors. A campaign donation means something to him. I feel like I'm the important person, and he's the public servant. It used to feel the other way around."

One little old lady, nearing ninety, put it best, "We pay the bills, so they pay attention."

On the other hand, the lobbyists were flopping around like fish on the dock. They could advocate for a position, which was the whole idea in the first place, but without the huge sums coming in and going out of their coffers, their standard of living was plummeting. Federal officials turned down fancy lunches and dinners—it was now income and they had to pay tax on them. They might be up for a burger, dutch, to catch up with their lobbyist friends, but that was about all.

D.C. restaurants either changed their business model or went out of business. What had been a watering hole for the rich and powerful, became a takeout place doing a brisk business for Members of Congress who couldn't cook. They even catered their menu options to fit medical and nutritional requests.

A few Members of Congress actually lost the extra lard all the hard partying had put on them.

Without lobbyists wooing them 24/7, the President stepped up to fill the entertainment void. As a result, much of the vitriolic partisanship of the past was falling away.

Abigail answered the phone just before it went to voicemail. She had to get it out of earshot of the children. The nanny had called in sick today. The kids had given everyone a bug recently. They'd just turned three and were squabbling over nothing but doing so at full volume. *And to think I wanted to stay home with them.*

"Hello," she said. It was Michael saying he was on his way home.

"Madam President, I'm so glad I caught you," Layla Farid said. "I hope this is a good time to talk."

"Oh, Layla, stop with the Madam President bit. I have peanut butter and jelly stains on this shirt," Abigail said with a laugh. "At least, I hope it's peanut butter." The sounds from the playroom continued, contentious but normal.

"They'll be grown before you know it," Layla said.

"I've heard that lie before," Abigail said. "But I'm sure you didn't call to listen to me whine about my three-year-old juvenile delinquents."

"Are they already three? Time flies," Layla said.

"Whether you are having fun or not. How did you raise five?" Abigail asked in wonder.

"I honestly don't remember. It was such a blur, and then one day they were gone."

"I'm waiting," Abigail said. Layla wouldn't feed her any of the "wouldn't miss a moment" crap that other mothers did.

"I have an idea, and you might be just the person to help me with it," Layla said. Layla's ideas helped get the U.S. out of Afghanistan in record time by luring out the wives of the Taliban. She usually had big ideas. Abigail was intrigued. Momentarily.

Abigail heard a crash and wail of pain from the other room.

"Oops. I need to call you back," Abigail said, clicking off and stepping back into the playroom.

Emma's left arm was pinned underneath an overturned table, and Emma was wailing in pain. Mikey stood beside her, crying in sympathy. At least that table didn't hold a lamp he could break, or Mikey would be playing with glass shards.

Abigail lifted the heavy end table off Emma's arm and knew it was broken by the angle of the forearm. Forearms usually are straight-ish. This one was crooked-ish.

"Shhh, shhh, mama's here, it's going to be okay, darlings," Abigail said to soothe the crying children. She'd find out later how this had happened. Right now, she was more concerned with her daughter's injury.

"Can you wiggle your fingers?" she asked. Emma did, but with big, gulping tears. *Good. The hand is pink and warm. Should only need a cast.*

She gently picked up Emma and said, "We are going to go make your arm all better, sweetheart. Mikey, you come too. Mama needs your help."

Even at three, he loved to "help," even though it was sometimes spotty. Once he helped her plant flowers and then accidentally ran through them—breaking half of them—so he could show his arriving dad what he'd accomplished.

She carried Emma gingerly into the bathroom.

"Mikey, can you help mama by going potty?" Abigail had to remind him every hour or so, otherwise, he got busy and "forgot" to go potty.

While he was busy, Abigail gingerly got Emma's top off without disturbing her arm. She pulled an elastic bandage from a drawer and had Emma put her hurt arm against her belly. Then Abigail wrapped the bandage round and round, so the arm wouldn't move. She left the fingers free, so she could keep an eye on them.

Emma was calming down now that mama was taking care of her pain.

"You need to potty, too, sweetheart," Abigail asked Emma also, helping her off with her panties. *I don't want them using hospital rest rooms. I used to wash both before and after using one.*

When both children were finished, she grabbed her purse and headed for the car. Gary Otterman, the Secret Service Agent on duty, helped buckle in Mikey, while she took care to position Emma's seat belt so it didn't touch her arm. Within minutes, they were on the way to the hospital. Gary called ahead.

Abigail knew the drill. One mention of the former President of the United States having a medical emergency would trigger a well-rehearsed drill in the ER. The agent pulled up to the underground entrance that always smelled strongly of car exhaust to Abigail, who was riding in the back between the kids.

Abigail didn't like jumping the line, but she also noticed through the double glass doors that the waiting room was half-empty. She doubted anyone would be seriously inconvenienced. Her fear was having someone die while her lesser emergency was tended to. Still, she understood she couldn't be left in the chaos of an ER waiting room.

A stretcher awaited, and everyone in the waiting area watched as Emma, Abby, and Mikey went straight in. Abigail carried Mikey to an exam room at the back of the ER. The ER doc was at Abigail's side in moments.

"I'm Dr. Peterson," he introduced himself. "What seems to be the problem?"

"I think she has a fractured left radius and ulna, judging by the appearance," Abigail said, unwrapping the elastic bandage. A nurse came in and put an armband on Emma's good arm.

"How'd it happen, Miss Emma?" he asked Emma as he gently touched first her fingers, then her arm.

"We moved the table," Emma said, wincing at the slightest pressure on the fracture site.

"I pushed," Mikey added helpfully.

"I'd say you were a good pusher," Dr. Peterson said. Then he shrugged and turned to Abby. "We have twin boys who're six, and their brother is seven. I keep an emergency kit at home. Last week I sewed up two of them at home. They were whacking each other with plastic baseball bats."

Abigail laughed and shook her head. *He's worse off than I am.* She knew twins conspired to do all manner of mayhem. She just didn't think it would start so soon. And she was grateful the doctor understood. All she needed was Child Protective Services paying her a visit. Within minutes, an x-ray machine appeared, and Emma put her injured arm on the plate. The tech was gentle with Emma, but Emma was not about to let her arm be moved too much. Another fracture sign.

"I need to take a picture of your hurt paw," she said. "You get a sticker if you hold still."

"Do I get one, too?" Mikey asked.

"Well, buddy, you aren't hurt," she said to him, "But I guess I can break the rules. Just this once, though."

Mikey was suitably impressed.

In moments, a digital x-ray appeared on the screen in the room. Emma had small fractures in both the radius and the ulna. Abigail knew the routine: a two-part cast wrapped with elastic bandages to allow for swelling, followed by definitive casting in a couple of days.

As Abigail and the doctor conferred, she had to keep Mikey from going through the equipment drawers.

"That's an ET tube, honey, leave it alone," she said, taking it away from him and putting it back in the drawer. "And leave everything on the red tool cart alone."

If left alone for three minutes, she was certain he'd defibrillate something. *Why me? What did I ever do to deserve curious children?* Then the answer appeared as if by magic. *I had unprotected sex with Michael.*

Emma and Mikey were infinitely curious about everything the doctor did, and he kept up a steady patter of explanations until it was time to go. Emma got some minor pain medicine, and both got a second sticker for being so good. Emma was very proud of her "cast" and sling.

Within an hour and a half, they were home.

Michael rushed out to the car.

"Where have you been? I've been worried sick," he said. "One of the agents said you'd gone to the hospital with Emma and Mikey. Emma hurt her arm?"

"I tried to call, but the cell phones don't work in the hospital," Abigail said, as the kids piled out of the car. Mikey was glad to be able to run and blow off steam, which he did in full "outdoor" voice. A little boy can only be good for so long, and he was well past the sell-by date in that department. He literally ran around in circles, flapping his arms and making noise.

"Look, Daddy, Mikey broke my arm," Emma said, holding her arm in the air. Michael picked her up gingerly from her car seat, and she proudly showed him her bandaged arm.

"And I have to wear a slinky and keep my hand up," Emma garbled "sling."

"Oh, wow. What happened?" Michael asked calmly. He was all but queasy at the thought of his daughter with a broken arm but stayed pleasantly concerned. He had won Oscars for lesser performances.

"The kids were playing in the playroom. I stepped out to answer the phone and heard the commotion. Apparently, they decided to move the table, and it fell onto Emma's arm. Simple fracture of both bones," Abigail said as she kissed him on the cheek.

"How can you be so calm about this?" he asked.

"Pediatric emergencies were my specialty. A hundred years ago, someone would put some useless poultice on it, and wrap it to a board. The kid would favor it for a while, take the board off after a week or so, and that would be the end of it. Now? It'll cost four grand," Abigail only sounded blasé. She knew every complication in the book and decided to keep him calm by not sharing.

Abigail was heartsick over an "unintentional injury" on her watch. *If the table had hit her head, Emma could be on the operating table for a depressed skull fracture. Oh, good grief, get yourself down off the cross. Twins are accidents looking for a place to happen.*

"Daddy, can we have an extra book tonight?" Emma said, playing her hurt arm for all it was worth.

"Sure, darling. Daddy will read you an extra book tonight," Michael said as he carried her inside.

Emma enjoyed her moments in the spotlight of her father's worry. Abigail clucked her genuine sympathy for her hurt daughter, but Michael took his duty as family protector very seriously.

Abigail made grilled cheese sandwiches and tomato soup for dinner. Juanita and Pablo, who lived-in, were vacationing in Mexico with family. This most basic of meals was all the former Leader of the Free World could muster for one of the Sexiest Men Alive and their two hungry children. Anything more would require rifling through the large drawer of takeout menus she hoarded. Even then, the Secret Service would have to call it in to hide Abigail's identity. Michael would have to go pick it up, and frankly, both were drained.

Michael did everything for Emma except chew her food for her, and Emma adored the attention. Mikey did not try to compete, for which Abigail was grateful. They made it through a meal, such as it was, without spills, tears, or fights over real or imagined affronts. The children had just grown out of sippy cups, and this was the first nighttime meal without a spill. *There is hope after all.*

When time came to bathe the children, Abigail wrapped Emma's temporary cast in cling wrap and helped her gently into a separate bath from Mikey. Usually they bathed together, but Abigail knew the bathtub could be a combat zone. Emma had experienced enough combat for one day.

Tomorrow her arm would hurt worse than today, so Abigail gave her a dose of pain medicine before bed. The kids still shared a room by choice. Even when they went to separate "big kid" beds, they wanted to share a room. When they were ready, they'd get separate spaces.

Michael and the twins snuggled on a small sofa in the twins' room. Michael read *Goodnight Moon* and *The Hungry Caterpillar*.

Abigail propped Emma's arm up on two pillows, "If you keep it up on here, it will make it easier to sleep," Abigail caressed her daughter's wild curls and kissed her fingertips. *Still warm and pink. Good.*

Michael and Abigail each kissed both children goodnight.

"Don't forget to kiss each other good night," Emma said. So Michael bent Abby backwards in a theatric dip and kissed her with a loud smooch.

"GROSS," Mikey said.

"Ooooh, yummy," Emma said with a big smile on her face.

Almost immediately, both children fell asleep. But sometime in the middle of the night, Mikey crawled into bed with Emma. When Abigail got up to check on them, Mikey was protecting Emma's arm in the curve of his body. They were so darling; she awakened Michael to see them. He shuffled down the hallway and smiled at his family. He was a very happy man, indeed.

Abby forgot to call Layla for two days. She had to ferry Emma to the orthopedist for casting. Emma dithered for a full minute between neon pink and neon purple. Green was also appealing. Abigail and the doctor waited while Little Madam decided. Pink.

When Abby got back to Layla, she told her of their adventure, "Emma proudly displays her pink cast to anyone she can find."

"Once I was in Casualty in London with one son who'd broken his leg. The nanny brought in another son with a fractured arm. I understand. No one tells you about the dark side of children," she said with a weary chuckle in her voice.

"I wish I didn't worry as much," Abigail said.

"Of course you worry, it's that second X chromosome," Layla said. "Now, let me tell you about my idea...you were very wise to stay away from 'Peace in the Middle East,'" she said.

"I figured when they want it, they'll have it," Abigail said.

"Exactly. And I have an idea to make them want it," Layla replied.

"But why are you talking to me? I'm just a voter now."

"Actually, you are one of the most powerful women in the world, whether you know it or not. Or so says the most widely read newspaper in the world."

"So why don't my kids mind me?" Abigail laughed.

"No matter how horrid they are, you'll still feed them and let them live there. Therefore they win," Layla said. "Anyway, this is my idea…"

Layla called the project "Peace Because." It was a series of cash prizes to be given to essay writers in Israel. Anyone could win money for espousing peace. Only at the end of the article would they self-identify: Hassidic Jew from Jerusalem, Palestinian Muslim from Hebron, whatever. While the reader reads, he or she sees only a human being who wants peace.

"This helps stop the demonization of the other factions," Layla said.

"Can you imagine the problems we'd have in this country if we felt the need to call ourselves a Christian from Iowa or a Buddhist from California, instead of an American?" Abigail asked Layla.

"Yes, well, that is part of the problem, but we need to let everyone speak," Layla replied. "Each week, a winning essay would be chosen on the topic, "I want peace because…" and anticipation for the piece should gain traction."

"Sounds promising. I'm all ears," Abby said.

"I'm so sick of hearing, 'I want peace, but…'" Layla said. "What 'peace, but' means is I don't want peace."

"Okay, so what can I do? I can easily put up some of the prize money," Abigail said. Checks were her primary form of charitable involvement these days. She wanted to spend her time with her children and Michael. His secretary turned down at least fifty invitations a week. If they went out once a month to a function, it was fun for about an hour. Then they were ready to go home.

"Actually, I'm looking not only for funds, for which I thank you, but also for a Jewish woman to head up the Jewish side of things. Marilyn Chernosky, dear thing, is in a very bad way, I hear," Layla said. Abigail's Secretary of State was failing rapidly, her bones turning to dust with rampant osteoporosis. And her husband with Alzheimer's was in a nursing home.

"I spoke to Marilyn just a week ago, and she could barely speak she was in such pain," Abigail said. "I'm thinking some woman of stature, but not political. Do you agree?"

"Yes, and of course, you'll want to run it by President Lafayette," Layla said.

"Oh, I will," Abby said, remembering President Harrington reaming her out about offering an opinion on the Middle East when she was just a Senator. *How many years ago had it been? Five? Six? A lifetime, in any event.*

Over the next week, Abigail chewed on the idea and did a little research online about influential Jewish women. She chose Rachel Gold.

Rachel Gold was a two-time Academy Award© winner whom she and Michael knew socially. She lived down the street—the few weeks a year she was in L.A. She and her husband of ten years had three children under seven, and they roamed the world.

"I want my children to learn, not from books, but from living," she'd told Abby more than once. It was not an appealing lifestyle for Michael and Abby, but the children were well behaved, if infrequent, playmates.

Flamboyantly redheaded, she could "open" any movie, whether acting in a ridiculously overdone epic or as the lead voiceover in an animated movie. And she commanded the film salaries A-list men like Michael earned.

Her husband, Frank Pelham, was no slouch either. Handsome in a rugged, "bad boy" way, he'd never had his broken nose fixed. It added to his marketability. He broke it when his sister tripped him accidentally when he was sixteen, but he lied and said it resulted from a fight in his misspent youth. He was always cast as a villain.

In real life, he was a sweetheart given to ridiculous puns. His giggle would embarrass a teenage girl, and on a full-fledged movie star, it was downright funny. He, too, was in a similar pay bracket to Michael's and realized how ludicrous the money was.

Usually uninterested in the charitable limelight, they made anonymous donations to foundations with good reputations. They did none of the adopting children from every continent and turning them into PR machines. There was no pretending to be an expert in anything as abstruse as sub-Saharan economic debt forgiveness. Nor did they globe trot just to show off watches or espresso machines.

They traveled with their children and tutors, "so they'll grow up to be citizens of the world."

"But what do you do about jet lag?" Abigail asked one night at a party.

"Oh, we have the pilot increase the oxygen to over 50 percent in the cabin of our plane," Rachel said. "So we don't have much jet lag at all."

Abigail smiled and said nothing. She didn't have the vaguest idea whether it worked, but as a physician, she wasn't about to find out. Heaven forbid a spark should blow them all to kingdom come. Until it came out in *JAMA* or the *New England Journal*, she wasn't going to try it or any of the thousand other nutty ideas people peddled to movie stars.

Rachel, while Jewish, was not an overt supporter of Israel, which was important. If she was too Jewish, or Layla was too Muslim, or Abby too American, the plan would backfire. The whole point was to get people, especially women, looking to the future and trying to find a better way forward.

Once she'd mulled over the idea for a while, she called President Lafayette one morning when the kids were at nursery school. She had her notes in front of her, so she wouldn't forget anything. She wiped her clammy palms on her pants. *Why am I intimidated?*

She'd done his job—and done it with distinction. But she'd been up to her ears in babies for nearly three years, and, well, her brain, to say nothing of her belly, had gotten mushy. Sure, she'd gotten her body back in shape, but frankly, her brain was lagging behind. Reading *I Am a*

Bunny two hundred times will make anyone's brain cells dormant. *I just hope mine aren't dead.*

She quickly scanned the online version of *The New York Times* and *WSJ*, and realized she knew what most of the stories were about. *Ergo,* she was allowed to take up the time of the President of the United States…who wouldn't have his job without her having begged him to become her VP.

Lafayette was on the phone in seconds.

"Abigail, how wonderful to hear from you," he sounded sincerely thrilled. "We had Regina and O.T. over the other night for bridge. How are the kids?"

"Away at school this morning, so I can actually finish a thought," Abigail laughed.

"So what can I do for you?" he said.

She detailed the women's plans to move Israelis and Palestinians closer to peace. "If they concentrate on 'I want peace because…' they might, just might, move forward."

"I think it would be a fine idea, especially if the newspapers ran the winning essays on a regular basis."

"Well, we won't know unless we try, now will we?" Abigail asked. "Do you think State would go for it?"

"They will if I tell them to," he said. "If they don't like it, I'll fire their sorry asses. I think you remember doing just that, ten minutes into your term."

"Yes, I did. Boy, was I scared, though," Abigail just shook her head.

"You did good. Keep me posted," Lafayette said, and he was gone.

The President was on board, Layla and Abby were on board, and Rachel accepted also.

"About time someone started to say why they want peace. I'm bloody fed up with this nonsense. Jews building ghettoes is an abomination to someone whose great-grandmother died in the Warsaw ghetto. It's a miracle my grandmother survived the Holocaust."

"Yes, well, don't sugarcoat it, Rachel," Layla said when the three women met at Rachel's house. Abigail didn't know where Rachel had hidden her children, but it was a delight to have a grown-up conversation in a room with no garish plastic in it. Of course, Abigail wore what she called a "paint-by-numbers" outfit from Neiman's sent just for this meeting. *I'm north of forty and still can't dress myself.*

The three women agreed they would form a non-profit, solicit contributions from everyone they'd ever known, and award prizes once a week.

"Money talks," Layla said. "People will lie like a rug to get the winning essay, so we'll have to have someone on the ground vet the stories. I'm sure the newspaper editors can assign someone, even if we have to pay the salary. Sham stories will sink this."

In an hour, they had everything roughed out.

With seed money from all three, Rachel would start things up.

The valet brought in Champagne and Baccarat flutes. The cork sighed when he turned it, and he put some Cristal in each glass.

"To peace," Rachel said.

The clink of their glasses and the tiny, fizzy bubbles bursting in Abby's mouth made her optimistic.

Peace Because was born in the USA and quickly chartered in Israel as well. A website in various languages went up within the week in Israel. Arab and Jewish newspapers signed on to boost readership.

"Almost as good as triple coupons," one editor quipped.

The essays poured in to the various categories, for children, teens, all the way up to the elderly. The most poignant ones were those at either end of the spectrum of life, those with everything to lose or everything already lost to hate and strife.

The in-country administrator handed out the prizes, and Rachel agreed to do an appearance to honor the winners. Layla, too, would appear, but Abigail stayed away.

"Too disruptive," was the line given to the press.

The real reason was Abigail would not engage in Middle East peace initiatives of any sort. Her logic was unassailable: she had feuding twins who vented their anger on her when she intervened. It was no different in the Middle East. The Arabs and Israelis fought, and if anyone tried to be a peacemaker, both sides blamed them for the entire problem.

Slowly, slowly, people on the ground in Israel saw the other side's perspective was the same as theirs. "I want peace because I have lost a child, and I want no one else to feel the way I do," applied to every group.

"I want peace, because I can't work my family's farm with a fence down the middle of it."

"I want peace, because I am a little kid, and I am scared most of the time. It's hard to sleep under the bed at night if people are shooting."

"I want peace because I am old. I cannot see well, but I can't get my eyes fixed because the hospital is full of emergencies from the violence."

The behaviors of the governments hadn't changed, but change would eventually come.

CHAPTER ELEVEN

THE SECOND MIDTERMS

The second mid-term elections went off without a hitch. People were getting into a routine. Parties still existed, but they were one-stop campaign stores where candidates got good deals on placards, balloons, and the like. The party would take a credit card, and candidates prayed they could pay the bills with their donations.

Substance had finally trumped form. The candidates couldn't call each other names and have the public buy into it. The candidates stuck to the issues and were rewarded for it. People felt they had a choice and supported the person they preferred.

The billionaire CEO of a high-tech firm in Silicon Valley tried to funnel money to key employees for them to donate the maximum to a candidate. One employee was wearing his usual nerdy glasses, but this pair had a video camera in the bridge of the nose and audio recorders in the temples. Realizing he was caught, the CEO pled guilty and wanted to get the sentence over with as soon as possible.

On his way into the federal prison in Lompoc, a reporter stuck a microphone in his face.

"What do you think of U.S. Attorney Duke Temple?" one reporter yelled.

"He'd indict his own mother for jaywalking," the man yelled back as the federal marshals hustled him into the building.

At the press conference after the man was imprisoned, Duke said election laws were just like having a daughter.

"If you scare the peewaddle out of the first boy who shows up, the rest behave," he said with a laugh. There were no more election shenanigans.

Another offshoot of the campaign reform was the ease with which a new candidate could run and make himself or herself known. In the past, the party said who ran, and who didn't. Now, if someone wanted to take the risk on their own, they did. As a result, there were more women, Hispanics, Vietnamese, Cambodians, Native Americans, and openly gay people running for Congress. They might or might not win, but the "good old boys" didn't automatically shut them out of the process.

The budget was two-thirds balanced by the second mid-term election, and the law of unintended consequences raised its head. As there was less money to take care of roads, parks, and the like, charities sprung up. Similar to the Infants First Endowment, local charities raised money and did the work on the parks themselves. With greater local participation, more people had a vested interest in keeping the parks clean and safe.

Various cities handled things differently, but it was not at all unusual to see older people in orange vests walking through the park, picking up trash, and chatting away. Community spirit reappeared. After a few months of work, there was less trash. And woe be unto anyone seen littering by the "biddies with pitchforks."

The lack of pork in the budget did offset, to a very small degree, the budget cuts. Still, President Lafayette managed to set priorities and stick to them. Infrastructure repair was critical but very expensive. Inmates in prisons petitioned to work on the projects to shorten their sentences. Non-violent offenders felt they were contributing to their community. Their recidivism rates plummeted as they emerged from prison with job skills and experience.

Inmates in federal prisons petitioned for the ability to grow some of their own vegetables to improve their nutritional status. They also worked out on mechanical training equipment to generate electricity so they could watch television at night. As one inmate put it, "A life without purpose put me here. Purpose now makes it bearable."

Another unintended consequence was the ratcheting down of partisan diatribes. The President went a long way to helping by repeating over and over that he was president of all Americans, not just the ones in his party.

He entertained members of Congress regularly and well, making them all feel welcome in the White House any time.

He even started "Hill Time," two hours a week when any Member of Congress could call on him without an appointment for any reason at all. They could request private or group meetings, or ask to have other officials like a Cabinet Secretary involved, and that, too, would be granted. This was probably the most productive time in decades for everyone in Washington.

But the biggest boondoggle eliminated was Medicare Part D drug prices. Because of lobbying, Medicare Part D had been *prohibited* by federal law from negotiating drug prices, even though the VA medical system negotiated drug costs down to pennies on the dollar. Without lobbyists in the way, the bill was a cakewalk through Congress. The medical tithe also passed. Doctors could deduct donated care to the indigent up to 10 percent of their income. Since Medicaid paid so little in some states, doctors couldn't afford to treat the patients. Now everyone was happy.

The lobbyists who had been behind the Medicare Part D scam were oddly unavailable for comment. Many were, of course, out of their Washington jobs. One network tracked a guy to Grand Cayman where he lived near his offshore money aboard his boat. Another lobbyist had entered the seminary to "atone" for his past sins through continuous prayer and contemplation.

As one comic quipped, "No one would pay him to blather, so he just shut up."

CHAPTER TWELVE

FLYING TIME

July
Logan Ranch

The families had gathered each Christmas and each July at the ranch since the twins were three months old. This year, Emma and Mikey were pushing five, so the year gap between them and the "big" kids had all but disappeared. Poppy's son, James, was a willing partner in crime with Mikey, while Duke's daughter, Pris, and Emma spent endless time with their dollies.

The tradition was comfortable fun for all involved. Regina was the uncrowned queen and ran "The Nickel Slot Hotel" with the precision of Buckingham Palace. She pointed and twirled her finger, and someone did as she commanded, whether it was a ranch hand, some of the ladies from town who appreciated the extra work, or even a certain former President of the United States. Regina, however, cooked most of the dinners, albeit with help from her domestic SWAT team—from which Abigail was permanently banned.

The families looked forward to time for their kids to sprout, even if working fathers and mothers were sometimes in short supply. First and foremost, the ranch was kid territory.

Poppy and Chaffee's son, James, had long since outgrown his nickname "Sweet Baby James." He had not a lick of his mother's red hair or attitude, but was a clone of his dad: sandy-haired and even-tempered. At six, and the oldest, he was marginally more responsible than Mikey, which wasn't saying much.

Pris, Duke and Kim's daughter, would turn six on the Fourth of July. Gentle like her mother, she had her grandmother Regina's innate regal bearing. Her skin was light, like Kim's, and her features a gentle blend of both races. She had Asian eyes, and Abigail predicted men would fall over themselves to get to her when she was grown. She was tall like her dad but with her mother's slim frame and delicate features. She regarded the ranch as her fiefdom.

The twins, eagerly anticipating turning five in September, had spent the last few years following James and Pris around and doing their bidding. This year, Abby predicted they'd feel equal to their older "cousins."

Abby and Michael were a few days late for the July gathering, as she couldn't leave L.A. until she turned in the final proof of her memoirs.

Her editor had been adamant.

"What are you waiting for? Your contract has a drop-dead date of July fourth."

Abby wrote well enough; she just preferred being with her children. The real reason she finished *The Accidental President* was money. All the proceeds would go to Bookworms, the O.T. Wagner Scholarship Fund, the Infants First Endowment, and, as of this year, the Peace Because Endowment.

She turned in her final proof on July third, and they made it to the ranch for Pris's birthday.

The children were immediately a gang of four. Pris, now six, still believed the Fourth of July fireworks were for her birthday. Since she was the oldest, no one could tell her otherwise. James loved being at the ranch, especially since "outside" had been his first word. There was never any question he was every bit Pris's equal.

Emma and Mikey were nearly five, so they had closed the gap between being the little kids. The four "cousins" were tight. They often roamed around together, ranch hands keeping a gentle eye on them. Sometimes they paired off for boy or girl play, but there were remarkably few squabbles.

Regina didn't tolerate squabbling.

"Solve it yourselves," was her standard line for any argument brought to her. If such responses were not sufficient, she'd tell them, "Solve it yourselves. Outside."

If the discord got too loud, the four were banished to their separate bedrooms for an extended cooling off period. All adults took Regina's attitude and within a week, kids stopped airing their gripes to adults.

"If blood isn't flowing, I'm not interested," Regina said one day. "If it is, go see Abby."

As much as Regina taught the children to stand on their own eight feet, she also made sure to slip them a homemade goodie if they happened to wander through the kitchen and were well-behaved. As a result, they were very well-behaved, at least around Regina. And with all their time outdoors during the day, they interacted very little with their parents, which was fine with all concerned. *When had parents started being their children's playmates?*

There was even a new crop of babies coming along. Eileen and Mason had indeed married not long after the first ranch Christmas. It had taken them a while, but Mary Margaret was now six months old. She had red ringlets, a dimply smile, and green eyes. All the adults doted on her. Especially Papa Mikey, whose first love had been a green-eyed, red-haired Colleen.

Kim, too, was expecting. She was due in about six weeks and would need to leave the ranch in a week or so. Her doctor wanted her back in

D.C. after thirty-five weeks. She wanted to stay as long as possible at the ranch, as she, too, loved it there.

There was the occasional skinned knee, and Abigail kept an emergency kit just in case. Surprisingly, she didn't need it very often. With all the things the kids had done as toddlers, neither had been back to the ER in a while. As often as not, ranch hands would show up for sick call, which she had every day at four o'clock. Every once in a while, she'd have to stitch up a ranch hand, and usually all the kids wanted to watch.

July sometimes was short of men. Chaffee didn't always get away from the White House, and occasionally Michael had to work for part of the month. Duke tried to take vacation then, but it was hard. Kim just worked wherever she was.

Thimble, her ready-to-wear line, had not only grown, it had spun off a children's line, Little Thimbles, which took off in part because Mikey and Emma loved wearing the clothes. Now she was launching Baby Thimbles. They were soft, colorful, and, best of all for busy moms, wash and wear. Kim knew the secret was in the textiles, and she was very picky, using only the finest cotton from Texas and Oklahoma. Like her other lines, all the manufacturing was done in the U.S. for a very particular reason.

"Without America, I wouldn't exist," she said. "If a garment costs a dollar more, people can vote with their wallets."

And the votes were overwhelmingly positive. She used a mill in North Carolina to make the stain-releasing fabrics, and the construction was done in a converted computer assembly plant in Texas.

Kim was an unusual employer. She had on-site day care, even a sick bay staffed by a pediatric R.N. A pediatrician was on call for the sick bay, and as a result, absenteeism for sick children was almost zero.

Employees loved working there, and turnover was almost nil. The employee of the month didn't get a stupid parking place; they got a fractional share of the ownership. Similarly, bonuses for a good year resulted in fractional ownership. Kim planned to take the company public in five years. When her company went public, every employee would be a millionaire, down to the janitor.

Mrs. Tran often visited the ranch, in part because she "bossed" the garden. Mr. Tran hated to leave his store for too long. He said it was because business declined when he wasn't there, but everyone knew the store was his social life as well as his business venture.

This year, Mason arranged for professional fireworks. The spring had been a wet one, as had June. Nevertheless, he had a pump beside the pool, just in case.

As always, Pris's birthday cake had sparklers. Everyone oohed and aahed at the fireworks. When the kids finally went to bed after a "bath" in the swimming pool, the grownups gathered in the living room. Michael and Abby held hands. Regina, O.T., Louise, and Papa Mikey were there. Kim was there, very pregnant, but not Duke. Poppy, but not Chaffee. Vee was there, but not Mr. Tran.

Kim was due in six weeks with a boy who would be named for his father. Kim was hot and uncomfortable and spent as much time inside as possible, sketching for the Baby Thimble line and talking on the phone to suppliers, vendors, and whomever else needed her attention.

Those rocking chairs Regina bought were coming in handy as Kim all but lived in one. She had reservations to fly home in a few days per doctor's orders.

Pris could not imagine missing ranch time, so she wouldn't return until it was time for school to start. To a six-year-old, a new baby brother wasn't reason enough to leave the ranch. Duke and Kim could have time alone before the new baby came, and Abigail was delighted to have Pris stay on at the ranch. She could go back to D.C. with Regina, O.T., and Vee, a little closer to the due date.

Abby was glad Vee liked being at the ranch. She came early in the spring to get the garden in, usually with only minimal help from the ranch hands. She also added Vietnamese to the children's mix of languages. Pris's was the best, of course, because Kim only spoke Vietnamese to her daughter at home. Vee's morning walks with Regina had turned into a ritual important to both women. Vee also loved helping with Mary Margaret.

Normally quiet, after the children went to bed on the Fourth of July, Vee finally opened up about her childhood. Abby knew it must contain some awful things and did not pry.

"I am so happy my granddaughter was born on the Fourth of July," Vee said, sipping some iced tea sprigged with fresh mint. "And for us to have such an important family related to us is amazing."

"On the contrary, your life is very American, Vee," Abby said. "Immigrants are our lifeblood." Vee got a faraway look in her eye. No one said a word as Vee told her story.

"I loved my mother and father and all my sisters and brothers. But war is hard on children, and I remember walking over dead people on my way to school. No child should live that way. But I knew nothing else. My sister made most of the money for the family, as she spoke and typed English. She was a secretary at the American Embassy. She knew Saigon would fall and tried to get my family out.

"Finally, my father said that I was to go. I looked older and would blend in with the other secretaries.

"I fled Vietnam when I was only twelve. My sister took me to work with her the last day there. I took nothing with me except my mother's purse. She had filled it with dried fruit as food for us. I put pictures of my family in the side pocket. I was one of those people scrambling up to the helicopter. We held hands so tightly that I thought mine would break. My sister would not let go of me. She pulled until I thought my arm would come off. She would let no one come between us.

"I had never been out of Saigon. I had never flown. Then suddenly, at twelve, I am being yanked into something looking like a giant bug. We went out of the country in a troop transport plane. We sat along the sides of the plane, and a super long seat belt held us all in place. I was so scared; I did not speak for days. We ate the fruit, and I still have only those few pictures of my family. Finally, my sister and I were resettled in a refugee camp, Fort Chaffee in Arkansas, and while I was there, I met Tran.

"America gave me life. I never saw my parents or brothers again. They would not come with us. My father was old and sick, so my mother would not leave him. My brothers were working, so my sister literally snatched me from death. We believe they were all killed because my sister worked for the Americans. It was hard to get information for so many years."

The story gave Abby a chill.

"And Tran, he barely got out. I never knew him in Vietnam. He was fifteen and was one of the boat people. He got onto one of two old ships in Cam Ranh Bay. He said there were five thousand people trying to get on. His boat had one motor working, and they chugged away from the dock at walking speed. The other ship did not work at all. Everyone on that ship died at the hands of the Viet Cong.

"Navy airplanes dropped food and water for them and kept them alive until the boat finally got to the Philippines after three weeks at sea. Many of the old people and some of the babies died. People said words over them and put them in the ocean.

"Once he got to the Philippines, Tran was put in the hospital for a few weeks. He could barely walk as he had given away most of his water to the children or the old people. There he says he got well enough to go to the U.S. We met at the refugee Camp at Fort Chaffee. He was three years older than me, and we became friends while learning English together. When my sister got a job in North Carolina, I moved with her. Tran followed us, and we got married when I was eighteen. My sister Kim died in a car accident not long before my daughter was born, and I named Kim for her. I felt very alone, but I stopped crying every day. Tran was very sweet with me, and soon the three of us became a family. An American family."

Suddenly the Fourth of July took on an even deeper meaning for Abigail. It is a celebration not just for Americans, but also for people who risked everything to become Americans.

Papa Mikey said his parents often spoke of their arrival at Ellis Island. They said the Statue of Liberty was the most beautiful sight they had ever seen.

"They were glad to get away from Ireland. They wanted a place where hard work would fill their bellies. Even if the signs in New York said 'no Irish need apply,' the fact work *existed* encouraged my parents. Then they went to Boston and saw the same signs but started on a real life. They'd approach anyone with red hair and ask about finding work.

"My dad worked his way up to selling vegetables from a cart; my mum ironed her way out of poverty. They scrimped and saved and finally rented rooms in Brookline, where I was born. And my nephew goes and marries the President of the United States. With a little help from me."

Everyone laughed.

That night when she and Michael were getting ready for bed, she mused on how time seemed warped where the kids were concerned.

"I thought the spit up and diapers time lasted at least twenty years," Abigail said. "Now suddenly they can dress themselves. Well, almost. Mikey's tastes are a little weird."

"Shows he's all boy," Michael said.

Emma, on the other hand, was always immaculate in her dressing choices.

Michael wrapped Abigail in his arms.

"I hope you know you've been the making of me, Missus," he said.

"In what way?" Abigail was intrigued. *If anything it was the other way around.*

"I'd had it with the party life. I was looking for a fifty-dollar gold piece of a woman. I knew you were the one the moment I saw you."

Abigail felt one of her blushes spreading from her face down.

"I was shocked, and a little insulted, when you refused all my attempts to see you again," he said of her rejection of his entreaties.

Abigail buried her head in his shoulder. He had his hand in her hair, as he often did, playing with it.

"I had to work, hard, just to see you again. Albright was dead set against it, but Mikey brought him around to letting me come to see you. Then I had to swallow my pride and take a backseat to the country."

"Michael, I really had no choice," Abigail began to protest. He cut her off by putting two fingers to her lips.

"You were right, Abigail. But I'd never been second in a woman's affections."

Abigail didn't tell him she'd never come first in any man's affections until he came along.

"When Lafferty tried to kill you, a part of me died. The old part. The trivial part. I knew I'd spend the rest of my life protecting you and our children."

Abigail burst into tears.

He kissed her tears away and then took her to their bed.

Abigail always loved arriving at the ranch. It had its own smell. In the winter it often smelled of wood smoke coming from a chimney, but in summer, it smelled like dust—dry dirt that's been whittled down as far as it can go.

This summer the kids got ponies. The adults agreed they were ready, and Mason had long since bought them and trained them for their little riders.

Before the ponies, the children played endless games of hide and seek, which was especially fun in the barns, but the girls also loved playing house, while the boys "worked cattle," built forts, climbed trees, and generally stayed out of the house. But ponies were the stuff of dreams to children, especially on a ranch where there are men on big horses.

Mason chose the ponies carefully, and when he "assigned" each pony to a child, none argued. For once. Each got to name his or her pony, and today was the first real riding time.

Mason made sure they knew how to care for their ponies. Priscilla named her pony Petticoat; James named his Spur. Mikey called his Godzilla, and Emma couldn't decide between Barbie and Buttermilk. Abby was secretly pleased when Barbie lost out.

The kids changed so much between visits; Abby made it a point to get videos at least twice a year. On the first day of pony lessons, Abigail captured everything on video.

"Petticoat here is like a person," Mason said patiently to his audience of four sitting on the fence of a small paddock, wearing cowboy hats and real boots. "She not only has to eat and rest, she has feelings too."

"And she poops too. Everybody poops," Mikey announced. "I poop in the potty. Babies poop in their diapers."

"Yes, she does. You guys don't go in your pants, do you?" Mason asked with great gravity.

"No," they all chorused, incensed at the insult. *Grownups could be so stupid.*

"Then you all will get to ride. No babies—just big kids."

Petticoat neighed and stomped a front foot, then horse poop exited beneath her tail. The kids laughed until they almost fell off the fence.

Each got a turn riding while the others watched. Pris got to go first as Petticoat was her pony. She sat straight in the saddle and looked so grown up. Then it was James's turn, and he wanted no help. When it was Mikey's turn, he wanted to make her go faster.

"No," Mason told him. "We're just walking today."

"Yes, sir, Mr. Mason," Mikey answered. The adults taught all the children manners. It was a never-ending lesson. *How could children know all the lines of their favorite books and forget to say please and thank you?*

Even Emma was starting to like riding but insisted Mason hold onto her by her belt, while she held onto the pommel of the saddle as well as the reins.

When the riding lesson was over, they took turns feeding Petticoat pieces of apple from their flattened palms. "That way, Petticoat doesn't think your finger is an apple." They each got to brush her, get her some oats, and lead her over to the water trough. Then they had to go muck out her stable, although none was thrilled with that chore.

"If you can't take care of your pony, you aren't old enough to have one," Mason said. "No one likes to muck out stables, but it goes with having a pony."

They were darling trying to handle pitchforks bigger than they were.

"You guys did great. Tomorrow, everyone learns to saddle his horse, and we'll go out on the trail," Mason said. The kids jumped up and down with glee.

Abby would e-mail the video to everyone in the family who was stuck at work.

The boys were so filthy every night that showers were required. Afterward, the shower floor was muddy. A squirt of baby shampoo and a few more minutes of water made it all gurgle down the drain.

Abigail was glad she had her two. Michael had never again asked for another baby, and that was fine with her. She was acutely aware of the differing needs of twins—at the same moment. Mikey might need a swat on the bottom while Emma needed a hug. There was barely enough of her to go around. While they had nannies if they needed them in L.A. or if they traveled, the ranch was about regular life, chores included. The nannies looked forward to their two months away from their charges: a month at the ranch and usually a month when the family went to Italy without them. Without time off, Abigail knew she'd burn them out and probably scare them away from ever becoming parents themselves.

Every morning, two children went to the hens' enclosure and brought in that day's eggs. The chicken enclosure was almost the size of a small house, and the hens were favorites with the kids. They fed them twice daily and gathered the eggs.

Of course, their enclosure was just made from wood and chicken wire, with a gate and a rudimentary eight-foot tall roof of chicken wire. They had a coop where they could get out of the weather. Even though they were free range, they had to be protected from egg-eating snakes or hawks swooping down to snatch a hen for a meal.

The hens laid their eggs wherever they pleased in the enclosure, so it was like an Easter egg hunt every day. The hens usually preferred a tuft of grass or even the henhouse but not always. The kids watched where they stepped, lest they break an egg. Those eggs were breakfast. Morning glories covered the south side of the enclosure, and they brought joy to Abigail's heart when she saw them and the two children racing toward them every morning. There was a posted rotation schedule; otherwise four kids would end up in there at once. The hens would likely be scarred for life.

All the kids made their beds every morning, put their toys away, washed up before meals, set the table, and took their plates to the kitchen. They said "ma'am" and "sir" as well as "please" and "thank you," though of course it was a constant lesson. Especially for Mikey, who tended to bark orders. Abigail instructed every adult to ignore any child who issued an order. Mikey was the worst at "please" and "thank you." Adults were only to respond to polite requests. She would not have bratty kids.

Abigail had also learned to tune out most of their fights; otherwise she'd have to get a black and white striped shirt and a whistle.

"You settle it yourselves, outside," she would say pleasantly, mimicking Regina. "This is your dispute—not mine."

And as for fighting, there were tussles aplenty, especially between the boys. Michael or Mason stepped in, as Logan Chaffee was seldom at the ranch. He was at the White House, where "vacation" was theory, not practice.

"Boys, you can hit, but you can't hurt each other," Michael said. "Do you understand?"

They nodded.

"And no matter what they do, you don't hit girls. Boys like to play rough, but girls don't. So never, ever hit a girl. Even if she hits you first." Michael was emphatic about this.

Michael, a very smart man, told them that well out of earshot of the girls, who would have beaten them senseless with that information.

Poppy and Abby would occasionally talk politics or current affairs, and since her husband was Chief of Staff for President Lafayette, and Poppy was "on call" for emergencies, Abigail was always pretty much up to speed. As a former President, she got regular briefings, but most of what she knew she learned from Poppy. She was especially pleased to learn polls of both Palestinians and Jews were moving to a more centrist position. Peace Because was doing its job. *What was the saying? Government should get out of the way and let people have peace?*

Lafayette was entering the home stretch of his Presidency, and so the politicking was kicking up.

"Any thought on who'll run?" Abby asked Poppy one afternoon when the kids were outside.

"Right now, it looks like the voters are solidly behind 'none of the above.'"

"What about the Secretary of State?" Abigail asked. Abigail knew she was eyeing the job. The Vice President was barred from running.

"Don't get me started," Poppy said. "Oops. James is crying about something."

She was instantly at the paddock fence, but a look from Mason told her to stay back.

Petticoat had stepped on James's finger, and he really wanted to cry.

"Squeeze your finger real tight and say, 'Man. That hurt like a son of a gun,'" Mason said.

James manfully did both and was soon back to his play.

It isn't often a parent gets to see a child grow, but in that instance, James did grow. And for all of the children, the ranch was a place of magical growth. Whether it was being summoned in the middle of the night to watch a calf being born or catching frog eggs in the creek and waiting for them to turn into tadpoles—it was all real.

The worst part of the day was when it was too hot to play outside. Then Regina insisted they rest.

"I need my rest, so you four have to pretend to rest," she'd say as she headed for her room for a nap. Usually the girls would play dollies and the boys might play at something fairly quiet. They knew if they woke Regina, none of them would get dessert that night. Period.

Kim was at a crossroads. She had to get back to D.C. before she was thirty-five weeks pregnant if she wanted to deliver there, but she also hated to miss a moment at the ranch with Pris and her "cousins." Abby assured her Pris would be fine at the ranch. Kim made her plane reservations for the next day, but Mother Nature intervened when Kim was asleep.

She turned over in the bed to find a large wet spot. She tiptoed into Abby's room.

"Aunt Abby, I hate to wake you, but my water broke," Kim said, a grimace on her face.

"That's fine. Michael and I will drive you to Fort Worth," Abby said, getting up and flipping on the light.

"I'd really prefer to go ahead and fly home," Kim said. "I have it all set up."

"No, dear Kim. You're going to have a baby within twenty-four hours, and by the look on your face, I'm thinking a lot sooner than that," Abby said as she threw on some clothes, and Michael grabbed a key to one of the SUVs. Abby grabbed her emergency kit and alerted her agents.

Abby scribbled a note for Regina, and the three were on the road in less than five minutes.

Abby punched in some search words to her smartphone, and they were soon on their way to the closest hospital set up to handle a preemie in Fort Worth, a forty-five-minute drive—thirty-five in the middle of the night with no traffic. Once they were on the road, Kim began having active contractions. Michael pressed a button above the rearview mirror; an operator came on the speaker.

"I've got a lady who's going to have her second baby any minute. Can you send an ambulance, please?" he said. "I'm pulling off the road."

Michael and Abby quickly got Kim out of her seatbelt.

"Let's get Kim into the back of the SUV, get her some room," Abby said. "Kim, I'll hold your arm while you take off your panties."

Kim had to wait while she had another contraction.

"Michael, see if there's anything halfway clean in the back. I also need a flashlight."

He produced a surgical wattage flashlight from the glove box. There was also a clean blanket and a gallon of distilled water in a zippered bag in the back. *Thank heaven for Mason, Abby thought. He was prepared for injured livestock, but it would work for delivering a baby.* Abby had hand gel, and Michael had a pocketknife, so all should be fine. And she had her emergency kit, though it didn't include a sterile packet of instruments for a sudden delivery. *Oh well, the ambulance will have a precip tray. If it gets here in time.*

Michael quickly flipped down the backseat to give Kim more room and spread out the blanket. The agents stood by, helpless.

Kim was a stoic, but as soon as Abby got her on the blanket and shined a flashlight between her legs, Abby saw curly black hair on the baby's head. The baby was crowning.

"Any minute now, Kim. Just think, your baby's going to be a Texan. Only the best babies are born in the back of a truck."

Abby opened her emergency kit and gelled her hands. She cussed herself for not having sterile gloves. Kim said nothing and just continued to push when she felt like it. Michael offered a hand to hold through the back door, and she darn near broke it with her grip when a pain had her.

The ambulance found them with about two minutes to spare. Abby and an EMT gloved up, opened the sterile delivery tray every ambulance carries, and welcomed Duke Temple Junior into the world at 3:52 a.m.

"I didn't know things could be so easy, or so fast, with a second baby," Kim said, covered with sweat in the hot July night. "I'm just glad I didn't deliver on the airplane."

"They're like greased lightning sometimes," Abigail said. Abby remembered delivering the baby in Gaza. It took so little to do it half-way right.

Everyone, agents included, teared up at Duke's cry.

Duke Jr. was built like an offensive lineman, even though he was five weeks early. He was healthy and had a lusty cry. He sounded positively pissed off at being born in the back of an SUV. Abby dried him off with a sterile towel and sucked out his nose and mouth with a bulb syringe, which he objected to mightily. Then Abby gave him to his mother, and he settled down. Michael snapped a photo of them and called Duke.

"Duke, you're a dad again," Michael said. "Here's Kim. That racket you hear in the background? It's your son."

Abby encouraged Michael to go back to the ranch. "I'll ride to the hospital with Kim and the baby."

Michael kissed Abby good-bye. "I love you more every day, Abigail." Then he drove back toward the ranch; the agents went with Abby.

The ambulance was regulation issue and drove without a siren through the thick darkness of a Texas night.

"Since your baby was delivered in the back of an SUV, the hospital will keep him in the room with you. He's what we call a 'dirty' baby," Abby said.

Kim chuckled and looked at her son with pride. "You're already dirty, little one. You'll fit right in with the big kids."

Duke Jr. scrunched up his eyes and looked at his mother. *I know her voice.*

The doctors pronounced mother and son healthy, and Duke Jr. howled mightily whenever something annoyed him or if a meal wasn't forthcoming within two nanoseconds.

Duke appeared at midday with an enormous bouquet of yellow roses for Kim.

"I'm so sorry I wasn't here," he said.

"But it all turned out fine," Kim said. "It was so quick, there was no time to worry. Besides, his Aunt Abby IS a doctor. It wasn't as if I was alone."

If Duke had been in awe at Priscilla's birth, he was in shock to see a replica of himself in Kim's arms. There was not a trace of Kim in the baby. Duke had big tears streaming down his face. Kim handed him the baby, whom he kissed lovingly on the forehead.

"I just hope I can do as good a job with you as my three aunties did with me," he said, looking into his son's face.

Baby Duke had no problems and went home to the ranch when he was two days old. So now there were six kids under six at the ranch: the gang of four plus the two babies, Baby Duke and Mary Margaret.

It was delightful chaos.

CHAPTER THIRTEEN

NOT NO, BUT HELL NO

August

In the five-and-a-half years they'd been married, Michael and
Abby spent as much time in Italy as possible. After July at the ranch
with everyone, the four of them always went back to Italy. These precious days were coming to an end. Once the kids were in school,
they'd stay in the States during the school year. Neither Abigail nor
Michael was a fan of globetrotting children getting homeschooled
on the fly. They would need the hurly-burly of other school kids—as
well as the discipline of being in school. They were determined to
raise their kids to be responsible, grounded people. And that meant
real school.

Michael and the children delayed their trip to Ravello as Abby had
to do some publicity for her memoirs, *The Accidental President*. The four
stayed at the penthouse at the Franklin Towers.

Abigail started with a makeover by Andre at his salon there. While
she was getting herself organized, Michael would take the kids around
D.C.

"Why don't you take them to the White House? I'm sure Lynne
would love to see them," Abigail said.

"And have Mikey call his sister a poop head or maybe knock over a priceless antique? No thanks," Michael said. "They have to be double-teamed, preferably by Regina and you, to go to the White House."

Just then, they heard a crash and wail. Mikey had tripped over a small table while running through the apartment. The items on the table were shattered, but Mikey was unhurt.

"I rest my case," Michael said, as he took care of the wailing pre-schooler while Abby swept up the mess. "Hey, big guy, inside we walk. Outside is for running. You ready to go to the zoo?"

Once Abigail got to the salon, Andre fussed, fretted, and clucked over her hair and decided her small amount of gray had to go.

"This gray is not the flattering kind. Makes you look washed out."

So Abigail let him color, cut, and condition her hair. *Whatever. She just wanted to look her best for Michael.*

"You're right, it does look better," Abigail said.

"Of course I'm right, baby, I do this for a very, very good living," Andre said, rolling his eyes.

While she had her hands and nails tended to, he worked on her skin care and makeup.

"Twins and traveling have done a number on your skin." He called Bette, his assistant of some nearly nine years, who was no longer a Goth princess dressed all in black. "Bette, darling, can you bring me a prep tray for the President?"

"Hello, Bette," Abigail said fondly to the young woman who was now a platinum blonde with a large fuchsia streak in her hair. Her makeup was overdone, but more like normal than the black lipstick and nails from before. Abigail could even discern the genuine beauty beneath the *maquillage.*

"Good afternoon, Madam President," she replied. Abigail wasn't sure she'd heard Bette speak before. "I'll be making your standard two cases, like we did before. I must say, you did an excellent job of staying camera ready," Bette said. *She had grown up in the years since Abby first met her. Maybe there's hope for my lawless heathens.*

Andre basically did the same makeup but with different skin care products.

"Your skin's starting to dry a bit, so a dab of tinted moisturizer/sunscreen goes on in the morning. Remember, hands, face, and décolletage." He worked quickly.

He held up a tube of roll-on concealer.

"This is new; don't go near a camera unless you are wearing this. No laugh lines, no crow's feet, just glow, glow, glow." He rolled some on Abigail and gave her a magnifying mirror.

"Wow, this is the best concealer I've ever seen." Abby inspected herself.

"It should be," he said. "It's five hundred bucks a pop."

"WHAT?" Abigail all but screamed.

"Pipe down, you'll scare the other customers. Your image is priceless. You're like the Statue of Liberty. You absolutely cannot sag. You owe it to the country," Andre pronounced.

"Besides, you'll sell more books for your charities."

"If you tell a single soul I spent this much money on something so frivolous, I will personally snatch you bald-headed," Abigail said.

"I'm a sphinx where you are concerned," Andre said. Abby knew it was true. He put one in each case. Abigail flinched.

"What have you done to your eyebrows? Have you been mowing them?" Andre asked.

"I've been plucking," Abigail confessed.

"Plucking is for chickens. Your eyebrows are threaded or waxed," he said with a shake of his head. Abby knew his exasperated expression well. She used it often with the twins.

The only thing new to Abigail's routine was a spray tan, just a little bit so she could skip panty hose. She was scared it would turn her orange or make her smell, but oddly enough, it did neither. Of course, Andre lobbied to do her entire body, including her face, but Abigail wasn't buying into that.

"I'll look like I have liver failure," she said, begging off. "Just the legs."

Abigail returned to the penthouse looking like a former head of state—not the harried mother of twins.

Laura brought over an assortment of outfits for Abigail to try. Her needs were simple: a cocktail outfit or two for the launch party and day outfits for the signings.

"Let's start with the launch party outfit," Laura said, producing a sparkling pale-blue beaded cocktail dress. It was very flattering—especially with an hourglass-shaped spandex strapless slip Abby knew to step into. The dress had small straps and a straight-across neckline that showed a little cleavage. There were tailored bows where the straps met the bodice. It even had little hooks for the spandex garment.

"This really shows off your toned arms," Laura said.

"Hauling twins beats pumping iron any day," Abigail said.

Abigail looked at the spandex monster with a combination of hatred and gratitude. *At least I'll have a waistline.*

Laura knew that women's feet often grow in pregnancy, so she had a variety of shoes sent up to her private area. There was a pair that just matched the cocktail dress.

"Oh, Laura, these are wonderful," she said of the strappy sandals that emphasized her long, lean legs.

"You will look spectacular," Laura replied. "And for what people are paying for tickets, you owe them something socko."

She put together the outfits as she had done when Abigail was in office: dress on the hanger, shopping bag with all the accessories.

Abby was good to go—at least for two weeks.

The book launch party doubled the planner's estimated take. As she and Michael did so little in public, people flocked back to New York to attend the party in the Frick Museum. *Boy, am I glad the kids are safely at the hotel with two of their nannies.*

Everyone in the room stood and applauded as they entered. Frankly, she'd heard Hail to the Chief enough that she groaned inwardly. She felt beautiful on Michael's arm, however, and relished just touching his sleeve. His male textures appealed to her: the hair on his chest, the strength of his muscles, a clean dress shirt, even the sleeve of a tux were all off limits to her until he came into her life.

She wore the teardrop diamond earrings, the skinny pale-blue cocktail dress, and carried a clutch with lip gloss, a handkerchief, and a compact in it. She had a wonderful time, even if she didn't eat and drank only sparking water. She was back in the public eye, so she couldn't afford a spilled canapé or a picture of her chowing down.

Regina and O.T. came to the party, mostly because Abby wanted them there, but in part because O.T.'s scholarship was one of the recipients. Most of their D.C. friends had come. Cristo and his wife, Susan Salazar, were there. He was now the superintendent of West Point, an incredible honor for someone who had not been a cadet there.

Peggy Mellon was there and her usual bubbly self; she was escorted by none other than Papa Mikey Molloy. Mikey not only sported a new tuxedo, but his man had polished his silver-topped cane to a gleam.

Abby was thrilled to see Col. Barnett and his wife. She also had fond hugs for Hitch and his wife. Even Thomas Albright, the former head of her Secret Service detail, was there with his wife, Evelyn. She wouldn't let them cough up the thousand dollars a plate minimum to be there, so she sent them "complimentary tickets and rooms at the hotel." It was a flat-out lie, she'd paid for them herself, but she desperately wanted to see her "guys."

Abby understood why Lynne and Jerome didn't come. It was too much trouble to leave the White House. Sure, other presidents had gadded about, but like Abigail, Jerome felt it was simply too expensive and too disruptive.

Marilyn Chernosky sent her regrets, citing poor health. A lifetime of poor nutrition had left her severely osteoporotic. Abby sent her an enormous bouquet and thanked her for her donation.

The Wickers were there. Not only could Laura dress Abby, but she also did a darn good job on herself, wearing a hot pink cocktail dress with a stand up ruffled collar that would flatter most women from seventeen to seventy. Abby couldn't name her fragrance, but she knew it was uniquely Laura, sort of a citrus and floral. They seemed to know everyone who was anyone—far more people than Abby did.

Michael's L.A. friends came to show support. The publisher had generated a guest list of New Yorkers anxious to rub elbows with a former President and her megastar husband.

The party raised two million dollars for the four charities: Bookworms, the O.T. Wagner Scholarship, the Infants First Endowment, and Peace Because. *I guess writing the book was worth it.*

Bookworms had long since gone national, and this extra money would allow a sleep-away camp to teach not only self-reliance but also ratchet up their manners and decorum training. They now had Bookworms for boys too, and this money would really help them. *Even boys need charm school, especially my boy.*

Michael and the twins went on to Ravello the next day, and Abby did all the major interview shows in New York. Then she did signings in New York and D.C. with the Secret Service watching her closely.

She flew to the West Coast and did the talk shows there. She talked to Michael and the twins every night but missed them terribly. This was the longest she'd been away from the twins, and it hurt her soul.

Her book went to number one on the best-seller list, and she was downright exhausted when she arrived in Ravello on the fifteenth of August.

She kissed the twins at least a thousand times and then fell asleep for two solid days. Michael fed and watered her, and the twins tiptoed in to give her kisses and bring her drawings and flowers they'd picked in the garden. She smiled no matter how many times they awakened her. *They and Michael are my joy in life.*

Their first language had been some sort of "twin speak," which they switched to when they didn't want their parents to know what they were saying. Spanish, English, and Italian appeared at the same time. Instinctively, they spoke Italian to Gloriana and Rafael, while they spoke English to their parents. They spoke French to the French-speaking nanny. Abigail envied their ability to switch between English and Italian without a thought. Adults had to work at learning languages; children did it without a thought. They even knew a fair amount of Vietnamese.

Even as a toddler, if Mikey was intent on something, he'd say it in all five languages, hoping the grownups would catch on. Milk, *leche, lait, latte, su'a.*

Both children were naturally very curious, and each parent was constantly giving them answers. If Abby or Michael didn't know something, they looked it up.

"Let's look it up," was spoken dozens of times a day. After finding the answer in English, they found it in Italian, French, and Spanish as well. They looked things up in books and often on the computer, but Abigail didn't let them play kid games or videos. They looked stoned when they were fixated on the screen, and that just couldn't be good for them.

Screen time was minimal, and Abby could have smacked Michael when she came in one day a few days after she got home to Ravello and found the three glued to *Home Alone.*

"Sweetheart, may I have a word?" Abigail asked.

"Just a sec," Michael waved her away, his eyes still glued to the screen. "My favorite part is coming up."

She waited in another room. "Rule One" was they never disagreed about the children in front of them. Michael finally appeared.

"What is it, Missus?" he asked pleasantly.

"Do you know how many injuries that movie caused? That year was the busiest ever at the hospital," Abby hissed at him, so the kids couldn't hear.

"Gee, I hadn't thought of that," he said. "But they love it."

"Just remind them the stunts are pretend, okay?"

"Right," Michael said, scurrying back as the children were squealing with laughter. Still, Abby found the DVDs in the player after she and Michael had been out to dinner or after Michael had "quality" time with them.

Michael usually did one film a year, and Abigail learned films were really piecework. The director shoots scenes together if they used the same sets, even if they were from different parts of the movie. Lead actors might not see each other for weeks unless they had scenes together. Then when shooting was finished, actors disappeared. The director coordinated the editing and getting the music scored and added. While post-production was going on, actors might be working on other films only to return to do the publicity for a film they'd finished nine months earlier, gushing as if it had just wrapped the day before…to sometimes fifty different interviewers in five minute snips, all asking the same questions. *How boring. I'm glad they pay him a lot.*

"I'm surprised you aren't directing again," Abigail said one day. "I will, when the kids are older, but I don't want to be away for long. If I miss a night, it's gone, never to come back. It's not only priceless, it's worth millions to tuck them in at night."

"Even with Emma's endless requests for more books and having to peel Mikey off the ceiling to get him in the bed?"

"All the more reason to stay home. You need the help."

"I can manage them now. They're older and I have Gloriana, Rafael, and Giuseppe," Abigail said. "You can work if you like."

"What?" he had Mikey's wide-eyed look of shock. "Only a crazy man would leave a gorgeous blonde like you unattended in Italy."

Abigail laughed, and then he kissed her—and not at all like a little boy kisses his mother.

August 22

Abigail heard the phone ring but knew Gloriana would pick it up. Besides, the kids were splashing each other in the pool. The day smelled of the cut lemon slices that Gloriana left with the *limonata*. She sipped the lemonade and turned a page in her latest read, an English mystery set just after World War I. Michael had gone into town on an errand. She was enjoying this true vacation time. It would end when the kids started kindergarten after Labor Day in L.A. She heard Gloriana yelling into the phone.

"*PRONTO?*" Gloriana, like many Italians, shouted as often as possible. Abigail had no idea why. *It's amazing they all aren't deaf from daily conversation.*

"*SI, SI, SI. MOMENTO. DOTTORESSA ABBY, LA CASA BIANCA,*" she yelled out to the pool.

While Gloriana brought her a portable phone, Abby asked the children to be quiet while she was on the phone. *I might as well ask them to fly.*

"*Grazie, Gloriana,*" Abigail said as the woman waddled up with the phone.

"This is Abigail Adams," Abby said.

"Madam President, this is Mabel at the White House," the night operator said.

"Oh, Mabel, how are you?" Abby was delighted to talk to her. "Have you changed to days?"

"Yes, I did when President Lafayette came in. I'm right as rain, thanks for asking. You're a better woman than I am to raise twins."

"I didn't have much choice, Mabel. I don't think they have board-ing schools for the preschool set," Abby said with a laugh.

"Oh, he wants to talk to you. Can you hold a moment?"

"Sure."

Abby turned to the children and cocked her left eyebrow. "Quiet while I'm on this call, or you're out of the pool for two days," Abby said, holding up two fingers. But it was "The Look" that convinced them. They knew when Mommy raised her left eyebrow, Mommy meant busi-ness, just like Grandma Regina did.

"Abigail, how are you?" Jerome sounded relaxed and happy.

"I'm terrific. For the record, chasing twins is way harder than being President," she laughed.

"I can only imagine," Jerome said. "There's something I want to talk to you about. What's Poppy told you about the political scene here?"

"Only that 'none of the above' is the front-runner on both sides."

"Well, she's right. And strictly between us, my Secretary of State cannot run. She's losing the battle with the bottle."

"Oh, I'm so sorry to hear that. I thought she was a teetotaler."

"She was. Her father and mother were alcoholics, so she never had a drink until last year. She was in Paris on business last year, and her husband found her passed out at the Embassy, reeking of alcohol."

"How horrible for her, and for her family."

"She is holding on by her fingernails, taking medication to make her throw up if she drinks alcohol, and never being left alone. We're hoping she can stay dry till the end of her term. Then she can go to Betty Ford or Hazelden." Abigail heard him take a sip of his coffee. It was morning in Washington.

"I know you didn't call about your Secretary of State's alcoholism problem…"

"Actually, I'm calling to ask you to run for the Presidency."

Abby hated laughing in the President's ear, so she swallowed it and said, as politely as possible, "I am very honored, sir, but the answer is no.

Been there. Done that. Memoir's selling well. Besides, the primaries are over, and the conventions, or what's left of them, will be in a couple of weeks," she said, hoping that slammed shut all the arguments.

"The polls show you are the only person who could win convincingly. I even asked for an official opinion. Sam Sternberg, the Attorney General, says you can run: no need for petitions as you've held an elective federal office. Also, since you didn't hold a full term, you're eligible. Just file by the day after Labor Day."

"I was a novelty, Mr. President, a one-trick pony, a fluke. Besides, raising twins really is more than a full-time job."

"Well, I had to ask." Jerome sounded dejected.

"I run after kids. That's plenty. By the way, congrats on getting the country back on sound financial footing."

"It hasn't been fun, but the Balanced Budget Amendment helps a lot, as does the Line Item Veto. We need work on the environment but had to clean our financial house first. I figure you're the only person people will sacrifice for. I am begging you. The country needs you. Hell, the planet needs you."

"Oh, please, please don't put that kind of guilt on me. I feel guilty enough just flying by private jet. I must have the carbon footprint of Bigfoot."

"Abigail. We are at, or past, the tipping point for the environment. But people want to gossip, like who's fathered the latest love child. There's even a bill in Congress to ban circumcision for all boys. Meanwhile, the planet is going to hell in a hand basket."

"Jerome. I did my duty. It's . . . someone . . . else's . . . turn." *Not no, but hell no, I won't run.*

"Okay. Whose?" he asked.

"That's not for me to say. I'm way out of the loop."

"Promise me you'll talk to Michael about it."

"He'll tell me to do what I want. And I don't want to do this. I love my life just the way it is," Abigail looked out over the stunning Italian landscape that was just one of her beautiful homes. She could hear the wind rustling in the trees, even a reassuring honk from a truck far below as he was approaching a hairpin turn.

"Just promise me you'll talk to Michael."

"Is this some sort of weird payback? I mean, I thought you liked being President," Abigail lightened up the tone.

"I do like it. Most of the time. Some days, I think a passing street person could do it as well, if not better. You'll get back to me?"

"Yes, sir, I will."

The rest of her day was ruined.

Since the twins had a long swim, she rinsed them off and put them in their pajamas early. Mikey crowed loudly about a loose tooth, while Abby was "checking" his brushing skills. If the tooth was loose, she sure couldn't tell. *He doesn't stop talking even with a toothbrush in his mouth.*

"Yes, but I lost the first tooth," Emma said, displaying a gap in her lower front teeth. "The tooth fairy gave me a dollar."

"Well, I'll get a euro, and that's a lot more."

Sometimes, Abigail wondered if they'd ever stop bickering and just enjoy the lives they had.

Gloriana promised them Italian fairy tales when they were ready for bed. Abigail and Michael walked into the village for a quiet dinner. A few tourists were out, mostly Europeans, but no one disturbed them.

As usual, the *passeggiata* was in progress. Each evening, young men and women stroll around the village, checking out one another. Their grandmothers watch them like hawks and gossip. The men play bocce ball, and mama? She's inside cooking dinner in peace and quiet, probably with a calming glass of wine to help.

When they got to the Villa Margherita, Margherita herself seated them, alone, in a small turret with windows all around to let in the cooler onshore breezes. The scent of lemons wafted up from the groves below. The table with their Secret Service agents partially blocked their door, so they felt relaxed. There was even a bowl of the lemons on their table. She picked up one and sniffed it. It smelled like no lemon in the U.S.

At least Michael was relaxed. He knew Abby had her knickers in a twist about something. Tonight she'd tell him what she was thinking. She never kept things bottled up.

"May I have a very large glass of Prosecco, please?" Abigail said in fluent Italian. She'd worked hard for her Italian. Now she could not only ask a question, she could understand the answer, most of the time. As long as the answer was short, not in a dialect, and didn't involve large numbers, she was fairly good.

"Bring us a bottle, please," Michael said, and then switched to English. "What's up? Were the kids bad this afternoon?"

"No. They're fine." Abby arranged her silverware. Twice.

"Is anyone sick? Reege, Papa Mikey, Baby Duke?" Michael asked with concern.

"No, nothing like that. Baby Duke's doubled his birth weight in less than two months. Most babies do it at five months," Abby said with a big smile. Then it faded. "Jerome called."

The waiter filled small tumblers with cold, sparkling wine. *Leave it to the Italians to keep things simple. The wine tasted wonderful. No flute required.*

"Is something wrong with the President?" Michael felt like he was pulling teeth.

"Yes. He has lost his mind." Abigail chuckled and looked up at Michael. "He wants me to run for President. What passed for primaries are finished, abbreviated conventions are happening the Friday and Saturday after Labor Day, and he thinks I have to run."

"Why?" Michael asked, gently sipping his sparkling white wine. Abigail took a slow sip and let the bubbles play with her nose.

"He says 'none of the above' is the front-runner in each party. Everyone seems to be off on tangents. He thinks the country would get behind me to rescue the environment."

"And how did you leave things?" Michael asked.

"I told him no. Been there, done that, memoir's selling well." Abby laughed at her own joke. "He made me promise to talk to you about it. And so now I have." She smiled a brief smile that turned into a look of pure love. *God, he is gorgeous. I not only get to look at him every day, I know he loves me back.*

"*Dottoressa*, would you like some fresh anchovies? Some just came up from Amalfi," the waiter said in Italian. Italians even had different names for the fresh and salted ones: *alici* and *acciuga*. She loved being called *Dottoressa*, as it was such an honor in Italian. It made her feel like a *Principessa*, a princess. *So much better than being called Madam President. That sounded so starchy and Victorian, almost like Nanny President.*

"Yes, please, with tomatoes and olive oil. Then a broiled fish, please," Abby replied in fluent Italian. *This is the best thing that's happened to me all day.*

"Same for me, but with some *pasta con limone*." Michael was a sucker for anything that included the juice from the softball-sized, sweet Amalfi lemons in front of them. This sauce was a mascarpone cheese with lemon juice over pasta rounds. It was Michael's favorite dish.

After the waiter left, Michael took her hand.

"Abigail, do you remember how you explained to me what heat does to a baby's brain?"

"Vaguely."

"You told me a baby's brain literally starts to cook at a fever of one hundred and seven degrees."

"Yes, it's true. Our thermal window of life is small."

"And do you remember when you were pregnant? You were sweating, and we couldn't get the house much below eighty, because it was a hundred and two degrees outside. There's only so much heat you can lose with high temperatures. And while the air conditioners might make the indoors cooler, they actually add heat to the environment. With global warming, our grandchildren might not be able to keep cool enough. Their precious little brains could bake."

"Oh, Michael, please don't add environmental guilt for our grand-children. I have enough guilt just considering what being President again would do to Mikey and Emma. I'd lose so many moments with them," Abigail said, tears welling up in her eyes. "There's got to be some-one else."

"Well, there *is* Sheila Smart," he said, citing the nitwit of the moment. Any good-looking woman with a mouth could get media attention. She entertained the media with her quips, her five ADHD children, and a knuckle-dragger husband who'd made his fortune off a newly patented hemorrhoid cream.

"She's a moron, and we both know it."

"Well, there's Chuck Schwartz." He was the Senate Majority Leader.

"Michael, he doesn't even believe the earth is round, much less that it's getting too hot."

"So you're really peeved, because Jerome is right, huh? If you don't do it, it won't get done?" Michael asked gently.

She looked Michael squarely in the eye. "Do you really believe that?"

"Yes, I do."

"So you think I should run?" Abby asked.

"Yes, I do."

"Even with what it will do to our family?" Abby asked.

"Especially for what it would do for our family in future genera-tions."

Abigail was quiet for a very long time. Michael let her be. Their food came, and they talked of other things. Over lemon *sorbetto* for des-sert, Abigail returned to Topic One.

"Okay. But on my terms. No one else's," she said, punching the air with her spoon.

"That's my Abigail," Michael said. Then he reached over and kissed her.

CHAPTER FOURTEEN

A CHANGE OF HEART

Abigail and Michael checked on the children, who, for once, were fast asleep. Gloriana bid them both *buona notte* and went to her quarters. Rafael, her husband, was fast asleep in front of a *futbol* match at full volume. She shut off the television. Her husband didn't even notice. She shook him by the shoulder. He harrumphed and followed her to bed.

Abigail got into bed, but couldn't get comfortable. It was a warm night, and they had the huge windows open. They also had a ceiling fan and stone walls two feet thick. The heat usually did not bother her. She got out of bed and took a cool shower. Michael was sitting up in bed reading when she came back to their room. His only concession to the heat was sleeping shirtless. She was pacing in a tissue-weight white cotton gown.

"Michael, I don't know if I can do this," she said.

"Name one thing you've ever failed at," he said.

"I can't dance."

"Okay, so stay off *Dancing with the Stars*, and you'll be fine," he said.

"How can you be so easy about this?" She paced some more.

"Because I know Jerome is right. I should have thought of it myself. Look, without the Electoral College, it's a single election. You campaign nationwide. There's none of this 'we have to get Florida and Ohio' crap."

Abigail remembered campaigning—just for Lawson Gray—and it was all too much. She couldn't live her life on an airplane wooing donors and voters. She'd never see her family.

"Without the electoral voting, you can run one campaign, not fifty," Michael said. *That does help.*

"Besides, we can have an elementary school class in the White House. Mikey and Emma, plus Priscilla and James are basically at the same level. Add six others from the staff, and you've got a great little group. They'd have the rigor of school, and we'd get them a great teacher. And think of the things they'll see and the places we can take them."

"But what about your career?" Abigail asked.

"It's not going anywhere. I probably won't do anything with steamy love scenes, but I can direct. I'm headed toward character parts anyway. I'm a little long in the tooth for leading man roles. Besides, I don't need a paycheck, and neither do you."

"But wouldn't you resent being Mr. Abigail Adams?" Abby asked.

Michael laughed. "Have you ever resented being Mrs. Michael Aston?"

"No. But being First Gentleman might be somewhat, um, demeaning," Abigail said.

Michael patted the bed. Abby sat down. He took her hand and looked into her eyes.

"Abigail, dearest. I will not be serving tea to ladies groups."

Abby had to laugh. "No, Regina enjoys being the Queen Bee."

"Of course, I'll do the protocol stuff, but I could actually help you."

"Help how?" Abby knitted her brow.

"Remember how Eleanor Roosevelt was FDR's legs? She went to see things and do things he couldn't. Once people get past my image, people open up to me—they always have. People will tell me stuff they would be too intimidated to tell you."

"Yeah, the women will give you their phone numbers," Abigail said good-naturedly.

"No, I'm talking about serious things," he said. "It's easier to talk to someone who isn't in charge sometimes."

"I hadn't thought of that," Abigail said. "But you'll also have to take over more of the kid stuff. And I'll really miss those daily moments."

"You know, of course, the real reason I want you to be President again, don't you?" he leered at her.

"No, I'm clueless."

"Air Force One. It's a guy thing. Now that's an airplane."

Abigail remembered their lovemaking in her cabin and blushed.

"Now come here, Missus," he said. "I have something to take your mind off politics for a while."

Abigail called Jerome the next day.

"Okay, you and Michael guilted me into this," Abigail said. "But I'm doing it my way."

"Hallelujah," Jerome said. "What does your way entail?"

"I'll campaign electronically as much as possible. Teleconferenced town halls. Easier on the environment, and I stay home more. But I haven't the vaguest idea of how to run a campaign."

Jerome laughed. "Poppy can run a campaign in her sleep. And with Wicker, your former press secretary, and a webmaster—you're good to start. Oops, gotta run. PDB is starting."

Abigail's stomach lurched. She remembered the daily presentation of what had gone bump in the night. Could she listen to it for six years? Doing it for two was hard enough. She burst into tears. *And the damn panty hose. I won't wear panty hose. I won't, I won't, I won't.*

Michael came in and found her sitting on the bed, pounding it with her fists, crying, and stamping her feet. The resemblance to Emma in full tantrum was amazing. Suddenly he also saw his long-lost little sister as well.

"Missus, what's wrong?" he asked, wrapping her in his big, strong arms.

She blubbered to him about hating the PDB and the panty hose. He gave her a handkerchief.

"Then change things. Put the PDB later in your day, but remember, Iraq and Afghanistan are over, thanks in large part to you. When you win, and win you will, you'll be working to make the world livable for our kids and grandkids. Everything else is just clutter."

Abby cried harder, and Michael just held her. She cried because he was right. *This has to be done, and I have to do it. At least I'll have Michael with me this time. And Andre can spray tan my legs. Screw the panty hose. I won't wear them. I won't.*

CHAPTER FIFTEEN

THE TEAM

Out of instinct, Abigail called Regina first. She needed Reege's comforting voice.

"Reege, I have something to tell you," Abigail said.

"You're running for President," Regina said.

"How did you know?" Abigail rolled her eyes. *I still can't surprise her.*

"Oh, Mabel called me for your phone number in Italy, so I put two and two together. Lord knows, I wouldn't vote for any of the candidates. Not even for dogcatcher, much less President. Where are you putting your headquarters? Houston? L.A.?" Regina asked.

"I haven't gotten that far," Abigail said sheepishly.

"Then do it from the ranch. There's room enough for everyone. I'll come and be the housemother, and Mason can convert the new barn into your office space," Regina was on a roll. "I'll bet Michael can give me the name of one of those catering firms that go on movie locations. We'll use one of them. And I'll get in local help for housecleaning."

She could hear Regina chalking a list on the kitchen blackboard.

"Why, what a smart idea, Regina. The twins will love it," Abby said.

"And have everyone bring their kids. We'll get in a teacher, and they won't miss any school."

"Reege, you are a genius," Abigail said.

"No, I was blessed with the gift of thought. So Poppy will run the campaign; what is Duke going to do?" Regina asked.

"I haven't asked Poppy yet, but I hope she'll help."

"She'll wail and moan, loudly, but she'll do it. Duke will be hurt if you don't ask for his help."

"Well, he's sort of busy with his day job as a U.S. Attorney," Abigail said.

"You'd best call anyway," Regina said, "since his specialty is the new election laws."

"Oh," Abigail said. Once again, Regina outsmarted her. *Maybe Regina should be President. She needed to run the whole planet.*

"O.T. and I will be at the ranch before you get back from Italy. I gotta run, so you can run," Regina said, laughing and hanging up.

Abigail called Poppy.

"You're going to *what?*" Poppy screamed down the line. Abby pulled the receiver away a millisecond too late. Her ear throbbed in pain.

"I'm going to run for President," Abigail said. "Jerome and Michael double-teamed me to save the planet for the grandchildren. I fell for it."

"Well, I can understand Michael talking you straight out of your panties—but running for President? You were the happiest person in the world to get out of that building," Poppy said, and then she paused. "Oh, holy crap. You didn't call to chat. What do you want?"

"I want you to run the campaign. Please?" Abigail moved the phone away again.

"Abby, *no.* I'm having fun as a mommy."

"If I have to do it, you have to do it. Global warming, climate chaos, whatever you call it, will make the world uninhabitable for your grandchildren. You have a moral imperative to help. Just like I do."

"Sometimes I could strangle Pris for dying and leaving me to baby-sit you," Poppy said.

"I'll take that as a yes. Get yourself and James to the ranch ASAP. The campaign will be over in just over two months. We might lose, and then you could say you tried."

"You? Lose the election? Oh, puh-leeze. You're still the most admired woman in the country after six years out of office." Poppy sighed in resignation.

Duke was on the line in seconds when she called.

"Duke, I'm going to run for President," she said. Uncharacteristically, he interrupted her.

"I'll take a leave of absence to help with the campaign. I can keep you up on compliance issues. Plus be your general counsel."

"You don't have to, you know," Abigail asked.

"Oh yes, I do, Aunt Abby. 'Those who need not work, must yet serve.' At least that's what Pris used to say."

"Any ideas for a webmaster?"

"Well, you could see what Charley Garrett is doing. He did a fabulous job on the Five Amendments."

She spent the day on the phone and had her people lined up. Poppy would manage, Duke was treasurer/general counsel, and Charley Garrett was webmaster. Regina was the den mother. She had a few more calls.

Before Abigail called the chairman of "her" party, she spent some time just thinking. This was going to be tricky. The chairman probably hated her, as the campaign finance reform amendment took serious money out of his pocket. For courage, she called Papa Mikey. He knew more about Washington than anyone alive.

"Hello, my darling Abigail. How are you?"

"I'm considering having myself committed to the closest asylum." Abigail laughed.

"Why, my dear? Has Mikey been arrested even before he's started school?" he asked. "After all, I tried a life of crime for a while."

"No, it's just that President Lafayette and your nephew, also known as my husband, have guilted me into running for President. I'm going to do it for one reason," she said.

"And that is?" Mikey asked.

"To save the environment, if it isn't already too late."

"A noble reason, so why are you upset?" Mikey said.

"I have to tell the chairman of the party, and he hates me." Abigail was frankly pouting.

"As well he should. You all but castrated politicos like him and fed them their balls for breakfast. Between campaign finance reform and the abolition of the electoral voting, party hacks are about as useful as spittoons these days. When money goes straight from voter to candidate, political parties have no leverage at all. So what if he is mean to you? He can't eat you."

Abby chuckled.

"Besides, you, my dear, are the one with the sterling reputation. He and his type are pond scum these days."

"I don't think so," Abby snorted.

"My dear, you've been out of the Beltway for six years. Lobbyists are more rare, they wear cheap shoes, and they have very little access to people on the Hill except to advocate for mostly non-profits like AARP and disease societies. Since Senators and Representatives can only raise money from their constituents, they have to keep THEM happy. And the constituents want them to play nice and get their damned work done. My advice? Say your piece, listen for any pearls, and then do as you damned well please. He needs you. You don't need him. You can always run as an independent."

"Excellent advice. I hope you'll come help with the campaign. We're going to run it from the ranch," Abigail said. "I miss you a lot, Mikey."

"Not as much as I miss you, my dearest. I wouldn't miss it for the world. I trust I can bring my 'man' with me?" Mikey wouldn't leave his valet at home.

"Only if Harold is in charge of afternoon tea. I want cranberry scones promptly at four," Abigail said with a bad British accent. She shut her eyes and conjured up the smell of his fresh cranberry scones baking in Regina's enormous stove.

Mikey was right, she *could* run as an independent. That's how she saw herself anyway. Abby put off the call to the party chairman until she'd nailed a Vice President. Her list was short. She hoped he'd say yes.

Cristo Salazar was at his desk at West Point when she called.

She told him about running and said bluntly, "I need a VP. I hope you'll do it. I know you'll need to talk to Susan, but please do consider it."

"I'd be happy to be your wing man, but I have to get the okay from the Boss."

"Great—and tell Susan she looked super in New York. I still want my body to look like hers."

"She'll be happy to hear that," Salazar said. "I'll get back to you."

Abby sat quietly for a few minutes gathering her thoughts about calling Wicker. The phone rang. It was Cristo.

"Susan said not 'yes,' but 'hell, yes,'" he said. Abigail laughed.

"Oh, there is one thing, Cristo. Does West Point have a kindergarten for incorrigibles? Mikey needs one."

"All of ours were incorrigibles, and all of them are upstanding citizens now. They'll grow up about four years after they leave home."

"You promise?"

"I promise."

Abigail laughed again and gave him Regina and Poppy's cell numbers. "Just call them, and they'll get you fixed up." Abby punched in the next number. Thank heaven for smart phones. It still had all her numbers from the White House. She'd even kept "Hail to the Chief" as her ringtone. Somehow, though, "Ruffles and Flourishes" had mysteriously disappeared from her text message tone. After all, it was only for sitting presidents. Former ones could appropriately use "Hail to the Chief."

Wicker, too, was remarkably easy to persuade.

"I think it'd be a kick in the pants to be communications director almost completely electronically," he said, when she told him of her plans. "You'll have to do some live appearances, but no marathon travel. It's not only easier on the environment; it's easier on everyone. I like the idea of all of us at the ranch."

Laura, too, was tickled. "I already have your new measurements. We'll do a slightly different vibe, Abigail, more earth friendly, more organic cottons, but still very Presidential. I'll go to the Dallas Neiman's when we get to the ranch. And if I know Kim, she'll do all the fancy things."

"What?" Abigail said. "You don't think I can wear my old wardrobe after having twins? Laura, I'm shocked, just shocked." Abby laughed and hung up.

The phone rang. It was Kim.

"Duke tells me you are going to run, Aunt Abby. I am so, so happy," she said.

"Well, your husband's life will turn upside down for a few months. I hope you'll be able to cope," Abigail could not imagine running her fashion empire and having Duke at the ranch.

"We're all coming," Kim said.

"Kim, darling, you have two children and a multi-million dollar business to run. Your offer is dear, but, really, not at all necessary," Abby didn't want Kim's business tanking over a stupid election.

"Aunt Abby, I can run the business from anywhere. And when you win, and win you will, I want to do your haute couture."

"Why?" Abigail asked.

"Because it is my creative side. Other women tell me what they want. You leave me alone to design. And you leave Laura alone to choose for you."

"I've always wondered why I'm on the Best Dressed List when I can't buy a blouse and a pair of pants," Abigail said, shaking her head. "Now I know. I don't dress myself."

CHAPTER SIXTEEN

THE CAMPAIGN BEGINS

They flew from Naples, Italy, to Dallas early the next day. Her days of private jets were over; they are too hard on the environment. First class was full, and they ended up almost filling business class, what with the Secret Service flying with them. *At least if I win, I get Air Force One back.*

The children started the flight bickering over the pretzels. *Oh, for crying out loud.* Abby was not about to swat one of them in public. Nor would she allow her hooligans to disturb other people's flight, especially considering what passengers paid for their tickets.

If she had her way, she'd put her kids in locking seatbelts. *At the back of the plane. In a soundproof room. Sedated.*

"Can you deal with this, please, Michael? My way is politically incorrect."

Michael waited until the seatbelt light went off and knelt down beside them in the aisle.

"I am very, very disappointed in your behavior," he said softly and he looked deeply into each child's eyes.

The children pretended to look marginally contrite.

"If you argue over pretzels and disturb people around you, perhaps you two aren't mature enough to have ponies after all. Maybe I'd best give Godzilla and Buttermilk to a petting zoo," Michael said in obvious distress. He even sighed heavily.

They were angels for the rest of the flight. *That's why children need two parents. When one's ready to sell them for a quarter, the other steps in and solves the problem.*

Texas heat billowed into the plane as soon as the jetway door opened. Texas in August is never cool, but they were breaking records this summer.

She was camera ready, down to fresh makeup, artificial tears, and the million-dollar eye goop as she stepped off the plane. In baggage claim, she heard the clicks and whirs of the camera long before she spotted a lone paparazzo at DFW. The shot might sell, as she was traveling with a planetary megastar.

The ride to the ranch seemed interminable. The kids chattered like magpies to the ever-patient Mason. *Why didn't I get in the van with the luggage? Luggage is quiet.*

The kids stampeded for the barn as soon as they'd hugged Regina and O.T., who were already there. It was as if the kids, unable to move around during the flight, could finally let loose their energy. Abby envied them their energy more every year. *Right now, I feel like roadkill. Correction, I feel like baked roadkill.*

Regina hugged Abby until O.T. said, "Excuse me, can I cut in?"

Michael even rated a hug from Regina, a far cry from that first morning when she menaced him with the coffeepot across the breakfast table. Everyone agreed that everyone else looked well, and Abigail headed for the shower, fearing that she not only looked like roadkill, she might smell like it, too.

She took a long, cool shower, shampooed her hair, and felt more human in a tissue weight skirt and sleeveless shirt.

The kids fed the ponies, brushed them, and mucked out Godzilla and Buttermilk's stalls. The pitchforks were still bigger than they were. They were about to drop by the time Regina served an early supper of fried chicken, corn on the cob, and thick-sliced tomatoes. By the time she served the strawberry shortcake, Abigail not only knew she was home, she also knew she was the luckiest woman alive. *Life doesn't get any better than loved ones and Regina's cooking. And to think, I was ready to sell those two a few hours ago. And I probably will be again before the week is out.*

Michael and Abby flipped a coin for bedtime chores. Michael won bath time. Abby would read the bedtime story. Michael always thought the kids smelled like sweaty puppies after a long day of play.

First he gathered Emma's long hair into a ponytail on the top of her head and then drew her bath. He supervised both children's tooth brushing, checking to make sure their teeth were clean. A separate shower and tub made for more mess but less fighting.

He sent Mikey to pee; otherwise, he'd do it in the shower. Emma bathed herself in peace. He put Mikey in the shower, had him drag his nails across the bar of soap, and then handed him a soapy washcloth.

Michael's job was to make sure the soapy washcloth actually contacted most of his son's body. Left alone, Mikey would just play in the water. The soap would remain on the washcloth, and the dirt would stay on the boy. Michael washed his son's dark hair, wrapped him in a towel, and sent him out to his mom. There was dirt all over the shower floor; all of it had come off his son. He shook his head and smiled as he rinsed it down the drain.

Emma's bathwater wasn't crystal clean, but she never matched Mikey in the grime department. Michael lifted Emma out of the tub into a big fluffy towel.

"Daddy, will you do me a sleeping braid?" she asked. She loved it when her Daddy brushed her hair, but not nearly as much as Michael did.

"Sure, sweetheart," he said. She stood on the stool still wrapped in a towel while Michael took out her ponytail, and brushed her hair, starting at the bottom in the back. She needed only a little of the no-tangle spray, and soon he'd put in a single rudimentary braid so her hair wouldn't tangle in the night. He loved the smell of his clean daughter.

"Daddy, why did we come back to the ranch?" she asked.

"Oh, your mom has some work to do," he said nonchalantly.

"Mommy? Work?" Emma asked. "She says her job is taking care of us."

"Yep, it is. We'll tell you all about it in the morning," Michael said, giving her a hug and a kiss on the cheek.

When both kids were in pajamas, Michael kissed them good night. Abigail started on a story for them, but both were asleep within minutes.

Michael and Abby stood in the doorway and watched them sleep.

"They're so defenseless in their sleep," Abby said fondly.

"And such handfuls when they're awake," Michael said.

Abby and Michael fell into bed, only to awaken at four thirty. They put themselves back to sleep the surest way they knew how and awakened again at seven to the smell of Regina's coffee. *Home.*

"Hey, good morning," Abby said to Regina, dropping a kiss on her cheek. "Are the kids up?"

"Up and gone to their ponies. I expect they'll be inside looking for more food any minute," Reege said. "They've grown like kudzu."

After Michael and Abby ate, they called in the kids, who were indeed hungry again.

"Second breakfast?" Regina asked. "Or lunch?"

Abby was the teensiest bit jealous. As a child, she ate what was put in front of her. Choice wasn't an option. But with the twins, Regina was their grandmother and could hand them back. Regina raised Pris, Abby, and Duke with no backup. Not even a husband. *How did she do it?*

"Second breakfast, second breakfast," they said in unison, so O.T. got out the waffle batter and heated up the waffle maker.

While O.T. was fixing their favorite blueberry waffles, Abby and Michael took them into the living room and sat them down.

"Kids, you know Mom was once President of the United States," Michael said.

"Yes," Emma answered, smiling widely. "And then she met you, got married, had us, and lived happily ever after."

"But I didn't quit my job," Abigail said. "I finished it."

"And now she's going to try to have the same job again," Michael said.

"Why?" both kids asked in unison.

"Because the country needs me." Abby tried to keep things simple for five-year-old brains.

"Are you leaving us?" Mikey shrieked in alarm.

"No, no, of course not. We'll all live together in Washington," Abigail said. "Let's look it up."

She pulled up pictures of the White House on her tablet computer and showed them different things. She even showed them the room in which they were conceived, though she didn't tell them that.

"Here was my room," she said, "before I married your daddy. And here's a picture of us the night we met."

"Oooh, there's Daddy," Emma said. "Daddy, you look so handsome."

"He looks like a waiter in a fancy restaurant," Mikey said.

"How would you know? You've never been to a fancy restaurant," Emma countered.

"I saw one on television," he said.

Abby could tell it was time to wrap things up.

"Kids, I have to work to get this job, and everyone who is going to help will be here, living and working with us for the next two months."

"Everyone like who?" Emma asked.

"Like Aunt Poppy, who'll be bringing James, Uncle Duke, probably bringing Priscilla and Kim and Baby Duke, Papa Mikey, and of course, Regina and O.T. will be living here."

"Yeah! No school, no school!" Mikey said. "Just summer."

Michael spoke up.

"'Fraid not, son. We'll have a teacher come here every day, but there will be plenty of time for play."

"Can we help?" Emma asked

"How thoughtful of you," Abby replied. "We'll be getting a lot of mail, so perhaps you could go and meet the mail truck. Of course, you'll probably need a wheelbarrow for all the mail."

After a second breakfast of blueberry waffles, complete with wild Maine blueberry syrup, they were off to their morning's project: finding a wheelbarrow to carry mail. Unfortunately, no one bothered to supervise, and by the time they were finished, mud and muck engulfed what had been the back yard. A rickety wheelbarrow was clean down to its rusted interior. The muck formerly in the wheelbarrow covered Emma and Mikey. As usual, Mikey had the lion's share. Both were prouder than peacocks and dirtier than pigs in a sty.

Regina called Abigail to see the sight.

"It's time for the nannies. Now," Regina commanded and pointed to the filthiest children Abigail had ever seen.

"Yes, ma'am," Abigail replied, swallowing her giggles. She texted the nannies: "Call me. ASAP."

Regina scowled at the children.

"You two are not coming into my clean kitchen dirtier than field hands."

She handed them some soap and a couple of dishtowels. "You certainly know where the water is. Now clean your filthy selves up. Then I'll give you something to eat. On the back steps."

After a half-hearted clean up, they ate peanut butter and jelly sandwiches and washed them down with milk. Then they headed back out to play.

Abby reported two nannies were coming tonight, and the other two would follow tomorrow.

"Good. I can run this house or chase kids. I'm way too old to do both," Regina said with a harrumph. "Besides, I could always take a switch to you or Duke. Switches are way cheaper than nannies."

"My twins do conspire," Abigail said. "At least no one has gone to the hospital in a while."

Duke and Poppy arrived that day. Their families would follow later.

Poppy found Mason and immediately began work on the new steel and concrete barn.

Duke was just there to set up their bank accounts and explained the campaign finance facts of life to Abby. They were remarkably simple. No one could donate to two presidential tickets, unless the first one had dropped out. The Congressional limit was a million dollars per donor, and no ceiling for the candidate. The filing deadline was the day after Labor Day, but she could open her campaign bank account now.

"Gotcha. If we start now, do you think we have a chance?" Abby asked.

"There are lots of candidates, but they've raised diddly. You are the most electable. Other candidates will bow out at your announcement."

Abby didn't agree, but said nothing.

"When do you want to file?" Duke asked.

"Not until everything is more than ready. You're sure I qualify? No petitions or anything?"

"We have an opinion from the Attorney General. You are good to go."

Abigail leafed through it and would read it later.

"Without electoral voting, there really is no need for primaries. A few states had held them, but they were just beauty pageants. Now the bad side. The electronic 'paperwork' is a bitch, but I'm set up to do all of it. Daily donation totals and expenditures are public. Names and addresses of donors are privileged but available for cause."

"I still have trouble believing that with secret ballots, we were posting names and addresses of donors online."

"Dumb," he said, and then continued, "If a declared candidate drops out, the ex-candidate must pay all his outstanding bills, and then return any unused money, pro rata to his donors within sixty days. If they can't be found, it goes to pay down the national debt."

Abigail got a good laugh out of that. With luck the country could get out of debt in about forty to sixty years, but it would take more than chump change.

"Great, but can I get money from their donors right away? What happens to their names on the ballots?"

"The instant they withdraw, their donors are fair game. If the ballots are already printed, votes for the candidate are null and void."

"Thank goodness Labor Day comes late this year. We have just over two weeks to assemble the campaign," Abby said.

Duke and Abby went to the bank and opened the accounts. The bank manager was thrilled. Having a campaign's money flow through the First National Bank of Nickel Slot was the biggest thing ever in his life. He was a part owner of the independent bank, and this would mean a better price when they sold to a bank holding company.

Later in the afternoon, Abby was making one of her mega-lists on her computer. She heard Regina call the kids to come wash up for supper. Emma and Mikey didn't appear.

She checked their rooms; they weren't there. Nor were they in the still muddy backyard. Then she told Abby, who'd just gotten off the computer.

Abby was momentarily panic-stricken, as everyone fanned out in all directions.

"Honey, you stay right here, in case the phone rings," Michael said.

It wasn't five minutes before Mason found them; they were sound asleep in the hay between their ponies. He snapped a picture with his phone.

Still, Abigail felt a chill. Secret Service and nannies were going to be a help, but there were a lot of people in the world who didn't like her one little bit.

CHAPTER SEVENTEEN

A SOCIAL CALL

Abigail knew to stay out of Poppy and Mason's way while they and Charley transformed the barn into Campaign Central. She spent a lot of time boning up on the issues, as soon enough her life would be a blur. The Thursday before Labor Day, she called and made an appointment with the party chairman, Patrick McClure, for the following day in Washington.

She laid out an outfit the night before. Laura was still in the process of producing a new wardrobe for campaigning, and, so far, Abigail did not own a pair of panty hose. *Life's too short for panty hose.* She charged her tablet and smart phone, and she realized it might, just might, be time to buy a new tote. Hers was badly scuffed; after all, it was pushing nine years old. She ordered a new one online. It had almost doubled in price and was now called "The Abigail." *Oh good grief.*

She flew commercial to D.C. early the next morning with one of her agents and went straight to McClure's office. No one seemed to notice the former President as she walked through the terminal at Reagan National in flats and a summery suit. She'd learned to switch on and off the "persona" of President of the United States. Her power heels were in her tote and went on before she entered his building. The persona of the POTUS went on with them. The agent waited outside McClure's office.

"Good morning, Madam President," McClure said frostily. "To what do I owe the honor of this call?"

His office was still grand, but his power was all but gone. The party would be moving into more modest quarters after the election.

"This is a courtesy call to tell you I will be an official candidate for President. I will file shortly."

"Why the fuck are you going to do that?" he all but shouted.

McClure was totally off his game. No one curses at a former President. Abigail stood up to leave, though she could see his point.

"I'm sorry, so sorry." He stood and regrouped. "You caught me completely by surprise. Could we please start over? You're throwing your hat in the ring at the last possible moment. Why?"

Abigail sat back down. McClure annoyingly twiddled his pen back and forth on his desk.

"I'm the only electable candidate with the political capital to reverse global warming. And while I don't want to run, it's my duty," Abigail said in all honesty.

"Well, well, well, the little lady is going to go out and save the world."

Abigail leaned across his desk and got into his face, with a small smile of her own. She could smell his cologne, his toothpaste, and coffee.

He stopped twiddling his pen.

"I've kicked the snot out of people meaner than you'll ever be. You can back me or not. I don't really give a rat's rear," Abigail said sweetly. *Nothing pisses me off more than to be patronized.*

"You see," she said, still in his face, still smiling, "if I get in the race as an independent, fine. I'll win in the runoff. Remember that part of election reform?"

Then Abigail sat back in her chair as if nothing had happened.

"Now, now, let's not be hasty," he said, backpedaling as fast as he could. "We'd be honored to have you head the ticket. I hope you choose one of our hardworking candidates as a running mate."

"Sorry, I already have one," Abigail said, rising from her chair. The party chairman also rose.

"I'll run as an independent. I don't want to deal with you further. You, sir, have the manners of a warthog in a very bad mood."

"But I need your coattails."

"Aw, little man wants to play with the big girls. Too bad." She made small *tsk-tsk* noises. "You slit your own throat."

Abby turned on her power heels and walked out. Once she was out of the office, she allowed herself to limp. She threw her heels in the first trash bin and put on her flats. *I've always hated those shoes. And without panty hose, they're really too small.*

She spoke to each of the declared candidates in her former party before she reached the airport.

Each was crestfallen. They had hoped to succeed Jerome Lafayette, but knew Abigail was the eight-hundred-pound gorilla in the race. Many offered Abigail their support, hoping at least for a Cabinet position.

While waiting to board, she called Poppy for the numbers of the candidates on the other side. She called all of them.

Each was polite but secretly groaning inside. They said they looked forward to a vigorous, clean campaign. Well, most said that. One, Sheila Smart, a one-term governor from Louisiana, who troweled on heavy makeup and fake eyelashes before breakfast, was downright rude.

"You're old news, Adams. I'm hot, and you're not."

Sheila Smart must have taken charm lessons from Senator Cordelia Laurus. Rumor was she was dumber than a box of hair. But Abigail would take her seriously. After all, this campaign was costing money, much of it their own so far.

As far as her résumé went, Smart had a four-year degree from a defunct Bible college. She'd worked in the family business that made a zillion dollars off a new hemorrhoid cream. Her husband did all the work; she did the publicity for the company. That meant she hired an ad agency and little else. They had five children, all with ADHD. She elected to homeschool them, but had to give it up when she became governor. First, she ran for mayor of St. Francisville, then governor. Each child was at least a year behind when he had to enter formal schooling— so Sheila might be Smart, but she was a lousy teacher.

On her watch, the only thing to happen of note was another riot at Angola State Prison, one of the worst in the nation. Twenty prisoners were killed, in part because she authorized the use of automatic weapons from the towers. It was all prisoner-on-prisoner violence in the exercise yard, and all twenty who died were prisoners. No guard or civilian was anywhere near the riot. No one thought to turn the fire hoses onto the rioters. Or to use tear gas. Or pepper spray. Sheila directly ordered the tower guards to use automatic weapon fire, overriding the view of the warden who favored the fire hoses.

"Law and Order means just that," she said afterwards. "They were out of order, and I was within the law."

That incident alone would give any party pause, but she was telegenic and people voted as if the Presidency was a beauty contest, a political version of American Idol. *Abraham Lincoln wouldn't have a chance today.*

Poppy, Abby, and Wicker chose a logo of earth as seen from space. Poppy found a site that sold the image as lapel pins and ordered their entire inventory. She found another vendor for organic cotton tote bags with the same image. Michael and Abigail began autographing the tote bags with green markers as soon as they appeared.

By the Sunday of Labor Day weekend, the barn was Adams Campaign Central, and everyone and their children had arrived. Papa Mikey came for the fun, as he called it, and even brought his "man" with him. The valet/butler steadfastly refused to set foot in the barn, so he pitched in around the house. He even served high tea every afternoon at four. No catering service was going to usurp his chore.

Papa Mikey was in the thick of things, whether political or with the children. He read to them every afternoon from children's classics. They might be devils for their parents, but they were angels for Papa Mikey.

The red steel and concrete barn made remarkably good office space, especially since Poppy called in an environmental engineer who quickly insulated it to within an inch of its life and cooled the place with ultra-fine misting fans and huge attic fans. It was a lot cheaper than air-conditioning. As long as you didn't wear a suit and tie in there, it was fine.

Poppy put her own area in the middle and up a few steps. She could see everyone and everything at once. Office supplies, copiers, and faxes were just below her desk. Everyone else fanned out where she could see them: Abby, Charley, Cristo, Duke.

Wicker had a full television studio, radio studio, and area for still photography in one of the lofts. It was enclosed and had to be air-conditioned for the lighting.

Charley took up the other loft and also air-conditioned it to keep the technology cool. He set up several state of the art teams. One team secured everyone's laptops and phones. Another team did security—doing background checks and turning out badges for everyone. There would be no mole from another campaign on the ranch. A money team handled all the donations and off-site phone banks. The fourth team was involved in polling and data production.

The Secret Service had an area, as usual, as close to the snack table as possible. Their ranks would swell when Abigail announced, but there was room for everyone in an enormous two-story barn.

There was even a conference area. Charley made sure it had all the bells and whistles.

The catering team was on-site and working. They even brought their own tents in which to sleep. They were entirely self-sufficient, and most meals were eaten out under a huge tent.

Regina appointed Eileen assistant manager of the "Hotel Nickel Slot." Eileen used the same four housekeepers who routinely came at Christmas and in July. They worked two shifts a day in housekeeping. They, too, had to go through Charley's background check and wore badges.

Regina and Eileen both counted noses and beds, and it seemed they had enough beds for everyone. Ranch hands helped with luggage, and everyone who arrived knew not to gripe about their accommodations. Most knew arguing with Regina was like arguing with God…while trying to push string…so they took their space and shut up.

Every room had a number on it. It was spotless, and the housekeeping guidelines were posted, so everyone knew what to expect:

> We'll clean your room and change your sheets once a week.

> On your cleaning day, strip your bed and bath linens and leave them in the bathroom.

> Put all your other laundry into your laundry sorter (whites, colors, and black).

> By evening, you'll have a clean room, fresh laundry, and clean sheets.

> Ironing is a waste of energy; so if you want to do it, have at it. Irons, etc. are in the utility room.

> If you need anything more than this, you are on your own.

> Regina Wagner

Sunday, Charley did a last check of what he called a beta test for a "money tsunami," and when the system passed, not once but twice, he informed Abigail she could announce whenever she pleased.

Laura Rowe Wicker took Abby to Neiman's in Dallas and outfitted her only for a campaign wardrobe. While there, Abby got a lot of new shoes. She was shocked that her size had changed.

"Abigail, your feet can grow when you're pregnant," Laura said. "Didn't you know that?"

"No, but I know never to push intravenous phenytoin. Does that count?" Abigail countered, remembering the list she posted of ten things you never wanted to do in an ER. *I'm a slow learner with shoes, but I was busy with other things.*

Susan Salazar set up a full gym in a small barn with misting fans for anyone who wanted to use it. Susan was a petite blonde in her sixties whose body looked thirty years younger. In her forties, she had been in charge of martial arts at West Point and was the one person Abby wanted with her in a street fight.

"What do you want to start on first?" she asked sweetly as she bounced and stretched when Abby showed up in workout clothes the Saturday morning of Labor Day weekend.

"Can you make me look like I didn't have twins?" Abigail asked.

"Sure. Get a tummy tuck," she said, putting her hands flat on the floor and holding the stretch. "But our workouts can make it better."

"But you didn't have a tummy tuck, and you have a flat belly after four boys," Abby started, moving around to warm up. *Are my joints actually making noises?*

"I had mine one at a time," Susan said as if Abigail was a bit dim. Both women broke into giggles and started the workout in earnest.

The four nannies worked out a rotation, so there was some variety for them. All understood they were there for the duration of the campaign. One was in charge of the two little ones, Baby Duke and Mary Margaret. The three others took on the four big kids. Duke's daughter, Priscilla, and Poppy's son, James, were six, while Mikey and Emma were five. Three nannies and four children was not a fair fight if the four split up, but at least that wasn't common.

The two little ones had a playroom all their own. The nannies rotated "baby duty." Whoever was supervising the boys was on "combat duty." Girl duty was "diva time."

Regina let everyone know that she was unavailable between two and three every day while she took her nap. "You may e-mail me, and I'll read it later; if you wake me, you die."

The children weren't up on e-mail, but they knew Reege commanded the sun to come up in the morning and allowed it to go down at night. They were always "shushing" each other if they were inside that time of day. Regina heard it all but made no comment. The adults were actually harder to train, but then again, the children had known about her naptime for a long time.

CHAPTER EIGHTEEN

THE ANNOUNCEMENT

Abigail decided her campaign, as it was so late in starting, had to be overwhelming and overwhelmingly focused. After all, if there was no planet, what other issues mattered?

Duke filed for her in person on Tuesday just before the deadline. The news broke within the hour that she was running and, more importantly, doing so as an independent.

Poppy bought an American flag as big as the side of the big red barn. It took some engineering to get it up on the side of the barn, but Wicker liked the idea.

The candidates in her former party assembled over Labor Day weekend in Jackson Hole and tried to find a way to salvage things. Each had been campaigning vigorously but gaining little, if any, traction. Few had any serious money, so the biggest war chest wasn't a deciding factor.

"Maybe if we fired McClure," one offered. "He's the one who pissed her off."

"Too late," another said. "Besides, he's under contract. His buyout would be enormous at this point."

"I think our best bet is to pick a ticket among ourselves," a third one said.

Their in-house pollster showed them that, in every permutation, they lost to Abigail and Salazar. And in all models involving a three-way race, Abby and Cristo won in the run-off.

It was hopeless.

The sooner they dropped out, the sooner their campaigns stopped bleeding to death. They summoned McClure to Jackson Hole. He flew over the Grand Tetons on a stormy afternoon, and it was the roughest flight of his life. He was white-knuckled and screaming as the thermals of the Rocky Mountains tossed his chartered jet down the east slope of the Tetons like a marble bouncing down tall concrete stairs. By the time he landed, he didn't give a damn about anything other than renting a car for the two-thousand-mile drive home.

The convention was in four days, and no one wanted to run.

They had to decide the best way to commit group suicide. McClure's blood pressure was approaching stroke level trying to get the former candidates to pony up for the money pledged to the convention. He ate antacids by the handful, but the burning in his belly never stopped. He was such a mess; he was smoking and using a nicotine patch. *I should have gotten event cancellation insurance, but we couldn't afford it.*

Only threats of a federal prison sentence by the party legal counsel made former candidates meet their obligations. The rest of the dona-tions they'd return pro rata. Since the convention was expensive, and there were few donors, all the money would go to paying off stood-up vendors. The party avoided bankruptcy by less than five hundred dollars.

Abby had no idea what they were up to, but she was going to let them stew in their own juices. She'd announce formally when she was good and ready. It would be rude to do it on Friday when their conven-tion would have been. Ditto for Saturday when Sheila was having her "coronation." No one ever watched the news on Sunday as the football games always ran over the news.

At the end of the candidate meeting in Abigail's old party, it was a stampede to the exits. On Wednesday, the first candidates in her party dropped out, hoping for a chance at a cabinet position and better luck in six years. The press conferences came swiftly.

"I endorse former President Abigail Adams in her bid for the Presidency. She and Cristo Salazar make a formidable team," each said in one way or another.

"But what about her late entry as an independent, of all things?" The press was pouring alcohol on a cut, hoping for a decent sound bite.

"That is the lady's prerogative," one said. *It's a friggin' knee in the groin.*

"Better late than never," another said. *She cut out my liver and fed it to her dog.*

A few were blunter.

"Our party chairman treated her disrespectfully, a grave error, where the well-mannered President Adams is concerned," Chuck Schwartz said. "Perhaps she would have stayed with us, but frankly, I don't blame her. I've known Abigail and her late sister for many years. You can say many things about them, but they do not suffer fools gladly. They make the fools suffer."

Abigail called the ten savviest people about the environment. Some headed environmental charities, others were academics, some were politicians whose message had been correct but a little too early for the public to get it.

After pleasantries, Abigail got straight to the point.

"I'd like you to join a group of advisers who are tutoring me on reversing climate change. I want you to take a leave of absence until after the presidential election and help me get out the message. Whatever you are being paid, I'll pay you that plus 25 percent for the inconvenience of being away from your family."

Their collective question was, "Why?"

"I didn't want to be President again. But I am electable and can get the country behind me on climate change."

All ten signed on.

Regina had another bunkhouse readied. Charley made sure it was electronically in sync. He'd already noted the cowboys all carried cell phones in little leather holsters, and Mason even kept a minicomputer in his saddlebag if he was on horseback, which was rare. *The world sure was changing.*

The Friday after Labor Day came and went with its usual programming. There was no convention of her former party, as there was no Presidential ticket. Sure, a third of the Senators and all the House seats were up for election, but since each candidate raised and spent his own money, who needed the party trying to tell them what to do?

Abby was content to let Smart's convention go on Saturday night before she showed her face. She wanted to see what they had to offer. She also wanted some momentum to build about why she was waiting. She was waiting to hear what the pundits said during the weekend political shows. Reporters pestered Wicker daily. He said Abigail's announcement was coming "soon."

Smart's convention was a four-hour snoozer on Saturday night. Any duller and it would qualify as general anesthesia. No one watches television on Saturday night in the first place. Since Sheila Boles Smart was the nominee, there was no drama and no reason to watch.

She made a hash of her speech, in part because she only read what was on the teleprompter, and the guy running it mixed up the pages. Not only was she too stupid to have a hard copy of the speech on her lectern—just in case—she was too stupid to notice she'd jumped subjects in midsentence. When she did figure it out, she ignored the first rule of live television: just keep going. She got all confused in front of the nation.

Abigail and Wicker laughed until Abby all but wet her pants.

Then her five hyperactive children and her mouth-breathing, hemorrhoid-ointment-peddling millionaire husband gathered around her and mangled "The Star-Spangled Banner." Even Regina was laughing by this time. She didn't believe in laughing at people who were trying their best, but she couldn't help herself.

Michael called it the "Star-Mangled Banner." Poppy had tears of laughter streaming down her face.

"Well, she just made our job a lot harder," Abigail said.

"How do you figure that?" Poppy asked, still laughing.

"We can't use any of her footage in our ads. It'd be like making fun of the handicapped."

"As bad as she is, you won't need ads," Wicker said. "Think of the money we'll save. You can get elected by doing nothing."

The television ratings were in the toilet for the Smart convention. Even reruns of *The Love Boat* beat out the convention. She was dead last in broadcast and fifteenth if you included basic cable. Sheila was very, very lucky. Few people saw the hash she made of her big night, and most of them were true believers anyway.

Abby announced Monday morning.

The day was hot. Poppy rented outdoor air-conditioning so they wouldn't sweat. They scheduled the announcement just after 7:00 a.m. central time, as the natural lighting would be the best. Abby chose the biggest, oldest live oak on the ranch, and Wicker staged it with some people sitting up on picnic tables, rocking chairs for the elders but with Abigail front and center. In the not-so-distant background were the barn and its flag, set on a nice diagonal.

Everyone had been up since four, and Andre had them all made up to look at least alive. Texas sun, even in the morning, washes out everything. Each grandparent held a child. The ranch dog, Scout, slept through the whole thing. The risk of chaos was high with both animals and children, but Regina had put the fear of God in the children, and Scout was old, tame, and deaf. He hadn't barked at strangers in two years and, besides, Susan held his leash.

The entire family was around Abigail. Michael was on her right, with Emma on his lap. Regina was on her left with Mikey. Everyone in the "family" was there, including Duke, Kim, and the Trans, as well as the Salazars. Polling showed the "tapestry family" was an incredible political plus, as everyone could identify with someone. Those who disliked the mixture still had positive feelings, as Abigail had married Michael Aston, a Hollywood "god."

Major outlets covered the event live in the heavily watched morning shows, and every piece of available office and hotel space between Nickel Slot and Dallas was booked until the election.

While the principals were casually dressed, there was no western garb. The voters remembered Abigail as the perfectly dressed and coiffed President, and today she would be that, but in "business casual." They all wore the little blue ball lapel pins.

That morning Abigail wore espadrilles, a simple red cotton skirt, a belted pale-blue shirt with the collar flipped up, and pearl earrings. Kim engineered her a waistline with industrial strength spandex. Abby looked cool (she was hot and sticky) and calm (her palms were sweaty). The outdoor air-conditioning did help but not a lot.

Michael wore chinos, a dark green polo shirt, and shined loafers. The kids were in school clothes. Everyone wore red, white, and blue or darker shades of green. Moments before the shoot started, Andre flitted around de-shining everyone's noses—with the exception of the children and the dog.

"I am running for President because President Lafayette called me personally and asked me to run. The planet, not just our nation, is in peril. As a mother and a human being, I have a moral and ethical responsibility to pass on a world worth living in. If we don't change our ways in this country—and around the world—the kids will inherit only the wind, and it will be a bitter one indeed.

"Someone explained it this way. If you look at a globe of the earth, the varnish on that globe is about as thick as our atmosphere. Can we afford to do more damage?

"We've all witnessed climate chaos. If you haven't been affected, you will be. Unless we do everything we can to get back on Mother

Nature's good side, it'll only get worse. We must do everything we can, as soon as we can.

"Also, as a doctor, I know our ability to tolerate heat is limited. The human brain begins to literally cook when you have a fever of one hundred seven, just like an egg cooks on a hot car hood. As the earth heats up, there will come a point at which we will die. Of course, it will be the babies who die first, taking our future with them. We could be extinct... gone...in a few generations."

For some reason, Scout chose that moment to look up at Abby, a look of confusion on his old face. Instinctively, Abby reassured him with a pat and went on. The remarks went on for another few minutes, but Abigail wrapped it up simply.

"We're going to campaign smarter and harder than our opponent. We are going to offer you a clear alternative to the other candidate.

"When I was an emergency room doctor, I learned I could only do what Mother Nature would allow me to do. When I helped her, my patients did well. When I thought I knew more than she did, she slapped me down.

"Mother Nature makes the rules, and we've been breaking them. She tells us to clean up after ourselves, and we haven't. She says resources are finite, and we're wasting them. She says the planet has only so much carrying capacity for humans, and our population is exploding past it.

"I am so serious about this campaign, I am willing to give up a perfect life with the man of my dreams and our twins, Emma and Mikey, to make the world a better place for your grandchildren and mine."

"I want to thank the candidates who have stepped aside. They've made a great sacrifice in doing so. Many are diligent and competent leaders. Their endorsements mean the world to me, as does yours.

She explained the abigailadams.com website and how to donate to "get one of the little blue ball lapel pins."

"There are all sorts of things on the website including a place to volunteer. We'll also have a daily best tip about conservation. The best idea of the day will run as a banner, and the winner will get an organic cotton tote bag signed personally not only by me, but also by my husband, Michael Aston."

Abigail paused and looked up at Michael, even yanking a thumb in his direction.

"I figured out a long time ago, I was just a government worker. He's the person everyone wants to see.

"Please, please, get on board. The train has left the station on the environment, and we are running to catch it."

CHAPTER NINETEEN

HOOKING THE VOTERS

The phones and computers lit up, and her campaign raised more than ten million dollars in the first day. The blue ball lapel pins appeared everywhere. They had to rush order another two million. At least the vendor was in New Mexico, so it was fast.

And every day had its own message, its own target demographic, and a report on which tactics yielded the best results. Abigail had suspected it, and the numbers proved her right: Those apocalyptic messages turned people off. Positive messages netted donations. Images that included children did the best, as this was a campaign about their future. Abigail kept her kids in the background, though. Not only for security, but also because Mikey was a wild card. He might start talking about poop or call someone a poopy head on live television.

She and Michael flew to L.A. and hosted a fund-raiser at their own home. Under the new campaign laws, no one else could do it for them. Supporters in Hollywood opened their wallets in honor of Michael. They were already true believers in climate change. The Congressional maximum per donor for the Presidential/Vice Presidential ticket was one million dollars, and Abigail had seventy-eight checks for one million dollars within the first day in California. By three weeks, she had a war chest of over a hundred million dollars. With a short campaign, she had enough money to buy a channel and run her message 24/7.

Duke was starting to squirm.

"Aunt Abby, do you realize you've raised ten times what the others did together?"

"No, but donations are one thing. I have to turn those dollars into votes."

Poppy had a list of cities and towns requesting a teleconferenced town hall meeting. There were two hundred on the list only three days into the campaign.

"Get with Charley and Wicker and see if we can combine any of them without them being too clunky. I can easily do five a day, but it'd be great to combine them so I do a bunch of adjacent areas, as they'll likely have similar concerns."

Poppy got those up and going. The campaign paid for the meetings, but news organizations in the area gave them free coverage. The stations excerpted remarks for the news, but many of their websites crashed when so many people wanted to stream the entire meeting. They gave up and ran them unedited. That meant they had to give equal time to the other side. But Sheila Smart couldn't interact with people for an hour or more. She could sign autographs or wave to the camera. But produce words worth thinking about? No way. She made an hour-long infomercial, and it ran endlessly in the equal time slot.

The first polls showed Abigail with a commanding lead.

"The race is yours to lose, Abby," Wicker said to her. "Do not, I repeat, do not get cocky and don't go off message."

The kids loved all the excitement, and the nannies were earning their money and more just keeping them out of the Campaign Barn, as the press had christened it. Abigail's Secret Service protection was beefed up, and her heart broke the first night she saw what they'd done to protect her. She'd always felt safe covered by a blanket of stars, the Milky Way a wispy "cloud" that never moved. Now the ranch was lighted like a maximum-security prison. The outdoor lights were so bright you could read by them. She felt violated. The Secret Service had taken her private refuge and defaced it. She'd always felt safe in the night at the ranch. Now that safe feeling was gone.

The White House briefed both Abigail and Sheila daily. Abigail wasn't certain whether Sheila understood what she was reading. Abigail wasn't even sure the woman could read.

Michael organized the school for Emma, Mikey, Priscilla, and James. He hired a teacher, and the kids went from eight until eleven thirty, had lunch, then Papa Mikey read them the classics of children's literature for an hour. School resumed from two to four. After a quick snack, they had free play until supper.

Mikey and Emma appointed themselves mail carriers. There was a long discussion with Aunt Poppy about exactly when, how, and why they were entering a workplace, and she put the fear of God into them about doing their job seriously.

"The first time you lose a check, you lose your job," Poppy said. "Got it?"

"Okay, but what's a check?" Mikey asked.

"Silly, that's what the teacher puts on the page when you do okay," Emma said, disgusted with him.

Poppy just shook her head and sighed. *The inmates were running the asylum.*

They had a system. Both came around just after morning school let out. Everyone put outgoing mail into the wheelbarrow. The wheelbarrow was really heavy sometimes, and it took two of them to push it.

Uncle Mason had installed a huge mailbox on the front fence next to the regular Logan Ranch mailbox. Once they were at the box, they took turns. One put the outgoing mail into the box, and the other raised the red flag.

Occasionally Pris and James wanted a turn, but Emma and Mikey were so bossy about Poppy's instructions, that it wasn't much fun.

"You can't run, you can't yell, you can't spill any, you can't stop, you can't talk to the people in the barn"—the list of rules was endless. But Mikey and Emma were up to the job.

The mail came about noon while they were home for lunch. They kept an eye out, and when the red flag was down, they reversed the process. When all the mail was in the wheelbarrow, it took the two of them to push it all the way back to the barn.

Then they'd be really ready for Papa Mikey's reading time. Usually, they were the first ones asleep, and at the end of story hour, the teacher had to wake up everyone. She started with Papa Mikey, so the kids wouldn't realize he slept, too.

Many a day, the Secret Service agent or a nanny picked up stray mail they'd dropped and took it in for them. On the days when Mr. Jim, the regular carrier, was off, Miss Clarisse came with the mail. She was nice also and gave each of them a butterscotch candy.

The catering services kept everyone well fed and watered. Regina had dinner every night for the family and insisted politics not be discussed for those thirty or forty minutes. It was the best part of everyone's day.

The dinner table was crowded with families and generations. From Baby Duke and Mary Margaret all the way up to Papa Mikey, everyone was included. The Trans came for the announcement but went back to D.C. for work. Kim was busy nursing little Duke, whose growth chart looked like the trajectory of a Saturn Five rocket. When Kim wasn't nursing, Regina was filling her with food. In her spare time, she worked at getting her fashion empire onto autopilot, so she could devote herself to design and couture when Abby was elected.

Chaffee, Poppy's husband and Lafayette's Chief of Staff, came every other weekend, if work permitted.

Eileen and Mason had taken to eating at the big house, and Eileen loved having their baby, Mary Margaret, at the table. Mary Margaret and Baby Duke were close enough in age to adore each other. Both existed in awe of the four big kids: James, Pris, Emma, and Mikey.

"When can Baby Duke have a pony?" Emma asked one night.

"When he's bigger," Kim said, wolfing down a third piece of fried chicken. *God bless Regina.*

"But he's already bigger than when he got here," Mikey put in.

"I think he should have to wait until he is five," Priscilla opined. "He still spits up a lot."

"Five it is," his father Duke decreed, and then the talk turned to the end of the baseball season. The women couldn't have cared less, but the men were eager to dissect the chances of another Red Sox pennant.

Abby had a town hall meeting in an hour with the greater L.A. area. She'd spent the better part of the afternoon working with the Emissions Expert and Wicker training the "E.E." how to speak to normal viewers.

Finally, she and Wicker gave up, taught him how to read a teleprompter, and translated his jargon. The "E.E." knew to step from his main mark to his other mark, the day-glow-orange-taped one, when Abby patted him twice on the shoulder. They practiced that as well. He might be brilliant, but he had zero common sense.

Three monitors in the barn studio focused on the three sections of the crowd. There was also a fourth on-air monitor for what was going out to the greater L.A. area. Abby had bought the airtime for that station's market. Even though it was expensive (as was a barn studio), it was a lot easier to do things from home.

Abigail thanked everyone for coming and introduced the Emissions Expert.

The Emissions Expert led off with a scripted talk about how driving less was good. Abby noted that most people sat with crossed arms and a frown on their face. They did not like what they were hearing.

Abby patted him twice on the shoulder only a minute or so into his talk.

He stepped to his other mark, out of the shot. Wicker gave a hand signal to immediately cut the feed from his mike. He sat and watched Abigail.

Abby tactfully stepped in and took a different tack than she'd planned. These people did not want to hear about raising mileage standards and taxing gasoline to build mass transit.

"You're all pretty ticked, aren't you?" she asked.

There was a chorus of "Yes!"

"I hear you. How many of you have kids with breathing trouble, asthma, chronic bronchitis? Just raise your hands, please."

There was a sea of hands.

"A hundred years ago, when cars were just a novelty, maybe one or two of you would have raised your hands. And kids who live where the air is pure have the old-fashioned incidence of asthma."

"How many of you have ever taken your child to the ER when he or she couldn't breathe because of asthma?"

There was another sea of hands, a surprisingly large one, Abigail thought. *I'm going for the jugular.*

"I'll bet you were scared to death. When I was practicing medicine, I actually lost children to asthma."

A hush fell over the audience.

"I miss all of them the most. But I want to tell you about Samantha. She was a darling little three-year-old, her hair in a dozen pigtails, all held with pink barrettes. She even had her toenails painted pink. Her daddy painted them every week.

"Her parents took great care of her, giving her all her medicines, going to every doctor visit. Neither parent was a smoker, nor would they let anyone who was smoking within a hundred yards of their daughter. They got rid of the family pets, as Samantha was allergic. They insisted the landlord rip out the old carpet and put in a floor they could mop, so they could keep the house hospital-clean. Still one night, Samantha woke up gasping for breath at four o'clock in the morning. One gave her a breathing treatment while the other called the ambulance.

"She needed to go onto the heart-lung machine like they use for heart surgery. It takes a few minutes to get it set up and get it primed with warmed blood from the blood bank. We worked like mad while the pump team was setting up as fast as they could. But she was too far gone when she hit the door. Every single person in the room cried when I had to pronounce her dead.

"I thought my heart would break telling those parents," Abigail teared up. "And that was before I had children. I still think of Samantha with her pink barrettes and pink toenails. In a better world, she'd be a teenager now, texting and giggling with her friends—not a bittersweet memory to her family. I heard her parents split up after Samantha died. I'm sure a part of them died with her.

"The sad part is that Samantha is just one of five thousand people who die every year of asthma. That's about a hundred people a week. Fourteen people a day. There's a good chance a Samantha is dying while we are talking.

"In America, with the fanciest medical gizmos on the planet, our air pollution is killing kids and grown-ups alike. Imagine how many little kids are dying in polluted cities in the third world?

"I was going to tell you about my plans to make city air cleaner. But I don't feel much like doing that right now. I just want you to imagine the future with more pollution all over the world. And then I want you to imagine your granddaughter is named Samantha."

She let them all think for a while.

Then she took questions from an entirely different audience than the one that walked into the rooms.

"What do we have to do?"

"When can we start?"

"I'm just one person. How can I make a difference?"

She answered dozens of questions, and for more complex answers, she referred people to the website.

"As to building more freeways, it simply isn't sustainable. Soon we'll just have roads. We'll have to tear down everything just to build them. In Houston, we widened one freeway to twenty-two lanes. What's next? Tearing down the homes near it and making it forty-four lanes?"

As they were winding down, the last question was the most poignant. A middle-aged African-American woman stood up.

"Dr. Abby, I'm Aletha Washington. I moved here to get over losing my little girl, Samantha." The audience gasped. "If I can help prevent anyone else from going through what we did, I want to. What can I do?"

Abigail lost it. She cried. Luckily she had Andre's waterproof mascara and Regina's hanky up her sleeve.

"I'm so sorry I'm not right there, Ms. Washington. One of my staffers will get with you and take things from there. I am very humbled that you stood up. Thank you, thank you for your courage and for confirming that air pollution kills innocent children."

If Abigail hadn't made it real, Samantha's mother did.

The rest of the town hall meetings started by making climate change real to the group involved: people who'd been flooded for the first time ever and farmers whose crops had turned into crap shoots with crazy weather.

She finally realized that the power to persuade was indeed the greatest power of all. And she never forgot Papa Mikey's advice. Find out what the person wants—then sell that to him. People will always vote their own self-interest. And where the environment was concerned, Abigail got to them through their love of family.

The next day Abigail unveiled her MBM plan: microvans, bus, microvans for commuting. People would go online or text the time and place of pick up and final destination. A clean van, powered by alternative fuels, would pick up the commuter who would swipe his credit card through a reader. Once a van was full, it would go directly to the bus terminal. The buses would run in high-speed lanes and deposit passengers downtown at another terminal. A second microvan would deliver them to their destination. Computers would do all the logistics of picking up people the most efficiently.

The commuter would arrive at work in less time than driving, with less pollution, and without parking fees. By using a prepaid card or credit card, the commuter need not carry money, and could reload his or her card at leisure. Best of all, commuting would be a time to read, do the crossword puzzle, or listen to audio media through headphones. With seamless Wi-Fi in the vehicles, you could even do your e-mail or take an online college course.

In one way, we would emulate the Europeans. Their taxis and vans are pristinely clean, as are their drivers. Professional drivers would adhere to a dress code, so everyone would feel safe. No longer would you slog along in traffic and watch as an empty bus drove beside you on the freeway.

CHAPTER TWENTY

UNFAIR FIGHT

Sheila Smart's campaign slogan wasn't bad: Get Smart. Of course, it hearkened back to the 1960s television show about Maxwell Smart, the klutzy spy who was anything but smart. And she was getting sued over her use of copyrighted material. But her believers, and there were many, truly believed. It was her lawyers who persuaded her to find a new slogan. She did.

Sheila Boles Smart's new slogan was "Sheila B. Smart."

Wicker couldn't wait to tell Abby that one. It was an oxymoron, not that Sheila would know what "oxymoron" meant.

Her running mate was Richard Johnson, a two-term Congress-man from Detroit. He was a newlywed; his wife had her own talk show in Detroit.

Abigail questioned the leadership ability of Smart, especially in her handling of the Angola Prison riot. Her running mate, Johnson, had not had time to turn things around in Detroit, which had lost over 25 percent of its population as Americans bought imported autos.

Abigail watched Johnson speak and was underwhelmed by him. He was not a natural public speaker or an articulate one; he often just stood by as Sheila nattered on. Their position on climate change was that it didn't exist.

"Weather changes every day. And if you elect Ms. AA, she'll try to outlaw bad weather," was their general attitude. They believed in the climate equivalent of the Flat Earth Society: Science is bunk.

"Abigail Adams is old news. She probably hasn't changed much since her great-granddaddy John was President. She's everything that is wrong with politics. The people around her were around her six years ago. Doesn't she change with the times?

"Governor Smart and I are running on a campaign of reinvigorating the economy, of creating jobs, of getting the government out of your wallet and your house, and getting you back to work. We'll show the world we're the Smart of the planet, the big kid on the block. We'll send out a message loud and clear that you don't mess with the big dogs."

For Sheila, the message was usually the same hash of mixed metaphors.

"I'm Sheila Smart, and I'll be Smart as President. You can take that to the bank." Then she winked, did a double thumbs up and then a salute. Even the salute was incorrectly done.

Abby and Michael howled. Wicker sat, slack jawed. Cristo snickered, and Laura rolled her eyes. Regina stood up and turned off the television.

"I do not want to see that woman's face ever again."

"Awww, Reege, why not?" Abigail asked.

"I have furniture smarter than she is," Regina said and stomped off. O.T. bid everyone good night and followed her.

October 15

The first face-to-face debate was held in Paducah, Kentucky, which if pressed, Sheila probably could not have found on a map. Many of her professional staff had jumped ship, unable to get through to her. She thought she knew everything and treated professionals as gofers. As a result, if she spoke without a prepared text, she had a severe case of foot-in-mouth disease. Every time she opened her mouth, she not only put her foot in it, she gnawed on it a while. She was so inept; she thought she didn't need help. In politics, that's the worst kind of stupid.

Tonight's debate was on foreign policy, and Sheila's policy could best be summed up as: "Screw 'em, what have they done for us lately?" That might play on talk radio, but it did not bode well in dealing with Abigail Adams, who had spent serious time on foreign policy.

Sheila wore a lime green suit, which meant she was not seen by the Chroma Key cameras they were using. She would be a face, hands, and legs—with nothing in between. The director sent her to change. The only other thing she had to wear was the wrinkled orange linen dress she'd been in all day. It clashed with her super-pink makeup. She clipped on her mike, and the cord dangled down the front of her dress as a disheveled visual distraction.

Abby wore a cornflower-blue, shawl-collar suit with her sister's pin of the Great Seal of the United States. Under it was the hourglass Spandex Monster. She wore her hair more or less as she always did, in a soft chignon. She wore pink baroque pearls, her wedding ring, watch, and pinky ring. She did not wear her engagement ring as she felt its knockout dazzle was a distraction. She also had a backup outfit, something Sheila's media person hadn't taught her.

The two women were instructed to shake hands then wait long enough for still shots of the handshake before retreating to their lecterns. Abigail did as directed, but Sheila forgot, so she was caught turning her back and walking away from a former President before the two had said a word. Plus, she tripped and almost fell over the mike cord. The sound of it hitting the floor was deafening, and the audience waited while she got put back together.

Abby had counted several media mistakes before the poor woman opened her mouth.

The moderator said he would ask a question of a candidate, she would answer, and then the two could discuss the issue.

Sheila got the first question.

"If elected, what will be your policy toward the former Soviet Union, Governor Smart?"

"I think everyone pretty much knows that I've never been a fan of the Commies, and whether they are together or apart, I don't see the need to have much to do with them."

"President Adams?"

"First, Mr. Glasser, I want to thank you for inviting me here for this debate," Abigail said. "When the old Soviet Union disintegrated, their ethnic and political diversity came forward. They are not a block; they are distinct nations. NATO has placed some bases in the former Soviet Union. That's pretty amazing. And our counterterrorism activities are dependent upon the cooperation of Azerbaijan."

"Governor Smart? Do you have a comment?"

"As you buy what?" She was confused.

So Abigail picked up. "We need permission to overfly their air space, and Prime Minister...Oh, my goodness. I'm blanking on the name. That's what chasing twins will do to you."

Abigail turned to Sheila, "I'm sure you know the name of the Prime Minister of Azerbaijan."

Sheila looked like a cross between a deer in the headlights and Edvard Munch's iconic painting "Scream."

Abigail waited no more than a half beat. "Dmitri Alexievitch Shalikashviily, or "Shally," as he is nicknamed, is quite progressive, and we need to be encouraging of his nation—if they are on board with good governance and saving the environment."

"Madam President, what is your policy toward Cuba?" the moderator asked.

"As you know, Castro cannot live forever, although he is doing a good job of faking it. I am taking a wait-and-see attitude. Raul Castro, his brother, is running things, but he, too, is getting on in years. We're not sure exactly what the Cuban people want. The Cuban culture is a vibrant one, and I hope they'll want to become a market economy and a major tourist destination for this hemisphere—but we'll have to see.

"I do think it is important to treat all immigrants equally. And currently under the 'wet foot/dry foot' policy, an illegal immigrant from Cuba can stay if he has one foot on dry land. Not so for a Mexican illegal immigrant. That's not equitable."

"Governor?"

"We ought to take Castro out. Assassinate him. I mean, who needs him and his stupid cigars?" Smart said, and then smiled.

Abigail said politely, "Governor Smart, it is against U.S. law to assassinate heads of state. And for the record, he stopped smoking years ago."

"Oh, really, well, you could have fooled me. We killed Osama, didn't we?"

"He was not a head of state. He was a terrorist."

There were questions about Peace Because.

"Madam President, do you feel it is appropriate for you as a former head of state to insinuate yourself into the internal disputes between Israelis and Palestinians?"

"Absolutely. Whenever three mothers of three faiths come together to promote peace, I think it's appropriate. When the people change their attitudes, government either follows or fails."

"Governor Smart? Do you have a comment?"

"Yes, yes I do," in a gesture of sincerity, she put her hand on top of her dress, thereby partially covering the mike, so the audience endured feedback until she moved her hand.

"I believe in salvation, and the sooner we save those poor heathen Moslems and pagan Jews and Jewesses, the better off they'll be. I'll work for the real peace in the Middle East, the peace that passes all understanding, the peace of universal Christianity."

Abigail had to stop herself from dropping her jaw. *This woman is seriously dangerous. There are enough people who secretly believe what she just said.*

"And now for closing statements," the moderator said.

"I am a Christian and proud of it, and I feel God has called me to lead this nation to head a more Christian world, and to peace based on Jesus's teachings. I'm Sheila B. Smart, and I hope you'll B. Smart and vote for me. I know Jesus would."

"Madam President?"

"Our nation was founded on religious tolerance, and since our Founding Fathers had differing faiths, they chose to leave religion out of government. Indeed, separation of Church and State is in the First Amendment to the Constitution, and it is one of the reasons our government has been so stable. Religion and politics mix about as well as open flames and gasoline vapor.

"Gov. Smart's comments are appropriate for an evangelical minister but are completely out of bounds for anyone aspiring to the Presidency—or any other federal office for that matter.

"If any President tried to spread his or her religious beliefs, whether at home or abroad, I feel certain the House would impeach that President, and the Senate would remove that person from office. It is a violation of the First Amendment to the Constitution. And the President takes an oath to preserve, protect, and defend that Constitution. Governor Smart has just told you she would not preserve, protect, and defend the Constitution. She would ignore it.

"I thank everyone for your kind attention, and I ask for your vote."

Sheila, having recently divined that Jesus would vote for her, declared victory after the debate. She was a lone voice in the wilderness.

Abigail led by fifteen percentage points before the debate but by forty after it. After the domestic debate on the environment, virtually no one could find any Sheila Smart supporters. Abigail had no real feel for whether the people were for her environmental agenda or just had seen Sheila chew on her feet enough.

Oh, Sheila tried, but she thought cap and trade was what guys did with their ball caps. She talked a lot about emissions, until it dawned on Abby: The poor woman was talking about religious missions to other countries.

The Vice Presidential debate was cancelled after the Congressman from Detroit was caught sexting numerous female members of his staff. It was hard to imagine anyone sending that many pictures of his penis with its distinctive birthmark to that many women during a campaign, but it happened. And his unfortunate name, Richard Johnson, lit up the comedy shows in all its permutations. "This guy can't do dick, but his johnson photographs well."

Sheila had the gall to suggest that Abby's people had set him up.

Wicker quickly shot that down.

"President Adams was already well in the lead before Congressman Johnson's scandal broke. Many of the pictures were sent before President Adams even entered the race. The opposing side simply did not vet their candidate appropriately. This is a lack of due diligence by the Smart campaign. President Adams has no comment on what must be a difficult time for Representative Johnson and his family."

Even with the other side's incredible stupidity, Abigail was ticked.

"I wanted a real campaign," she said to Michael one night. "I mean, 'none of the above' could beat Sheila Smart."

"Have you thought that maybe, just maybe, Mother Nature is on your side?"

CHAPTER TWENTY-ONE

GONE

The election was less than three weeks away, and everyone in the Adams campaign was lying low, letting the other side self-destruct. Any efforts on their part would just be seen as piling on. There were lots of card games, as everyone had spare time. Regina, Papa Mikey, and O.T. got their naps, so things couldn't be too busy.

Nickel Slot, Texas, was the closest town to the ranch. Its five thousand souls swelled overnight to twice that many with the press in town. The extra visitors were good for the local economy.

Every village has its idiot, and in Nickel Slot, Darrell and Darwin Rogers were equal contenders. They were dumber than dry dirt and had lived with their mother out in the trailer park until she died. To their credit, they did take good care of her. They waited a few months to tell the Social Security people about her death, so that had given them a cushion. But the cushion was getting pretty thin.

They needed to make some money. There were plenty of jobs to be had, what with the campaign and all, but Darrell and Darwin were allergic to work. They much preferred taking care of Mama, keeping her asleep with her pills except when it was time to watch *Wheel of Fortune*. They spent her money on beer, bean dip, and chips—in that order.

The nation's drop in demand for marijuana had driven their dealer out of business. He was working at Walmart.

"Money's not quite as good, but I get health and dental," he said, then he smiled, showing them his cleaned-up teeth the way a horse would. "And I don't have to worry about no cops."

Darrell, the smarter of the two by a lone IQ point, thought long and hard about how to get some money. He sometimes drilled bowling balls at the bowling lane, but that didn't pay much.

"Hey, let's kidnap those kids whose mama is running for President," Darrell said to Darwin.

"Yeah, she's the one who ran our weed dealer out of business," Darwin agreed.

Darwin had mostly taken care of their mama and considered himself retired. He kept Mama's room clean still, out of respect, but otherwise couldn't figure out what he wanted to do for a job. The pizza place was hiring delivery guys, but that hadn't worked out. One smelled so good, he just had to take a bite out of it.

"We couldn't hurt them. I couldn't hurt a kid," Darrell said. "But we could just get the money and go to Mexico. They still got pot there, right?"

"Yeah, but I think it's hot down there," Darwin replied.

"Nah, remember they got beaches. We might even meet some girls," Darrell said.

He liked girls, but none would give him the time of day. Perhaps it was his massive obesity, perhaps it was the unkempt beard, or that his brother cut his hair twice a year when they cut their toenails. The boys bathed every Saturday night, though why they picked that night was unknown. They didn't go to church. Their body odor cut them a wide swath wherever they went.

They drove past the ranch several times and saw the kids come out to the road one day to get the mail. Sometimes there were men in suits walking around the front of the house, but they didn't impress Darwin. What kind of man wears a suit and tie at a ranch?

"What do they do?" Darwin asked his brother about the men.

"Beats me," Darrell said. "I never seen nobody in a suit, except the guy what runs the funeral parlor."

Darrell drove into Fort Worth and bought a cell phone. They'd never had one, and the salesman said a throwaway phone would be the best. Darrell paid for it and would have called his brother on it, but then he remembered they didn't have a phone in the trailer anymore.

That night, both boys tried to figure out how to use the phone. After two hours, they knew how to make a call and answer one. That was all they needed. They were so tired from the mental effort they polished off a twelve-pack of beer, a big bag of chips, and two cans of bean dip, each, and went to bed.

They even went so far as to hide themselves in the trees across the road one night and sleep until the mail truck came. This time it had a woman driver. The kids excitedly took the candy she offered and helped her put the mail in the wheelbarrow; then they pushed it back toward the house, one taking each handle.

On Thursday night, they parked their car at the bottom of a long hill a mile or so past the ranch gate. They called Leroy to come get them; said they'd had car trouble. *That phone had sure come in handy.*

Most friends would have done some on-scene diagnostics to try to fix the car. Not Leroy. He was not nearly as dumb as Darwin and Darrell, but he was drunk. It was a permanent condition. He picked them up, and then they wound their way back to town.

"Drop us off in town, would you?" Darrell said. The two slept out behind the Pic n-Pac, which was next to the post office.

The next morning, Jim the postal carrier, packed his truck. He must have made a dozen trips from the post office to the van. He was ready to leave about eleven thirty. When they saw him put the key in the ignition, they ran up and whacked him over the head, hard, with a sock they'd filled with buckshot. Jim fell, and the shot went everywhere when the sock busted. Darrell and Darwin could barely stay upright. It was like walking on ball bearings, but they got Jim out of the truck, and Darwin got in to drive.

"The steering's backwards and them gears, too," Darwin said, as grinding noises came from the truck.

So they traded places. That wasn't easy, what with the ball-bearing effect. They looked like fat guys trying to dance with each other.

Darrell tried to drive. His extra IQ point came in handy. He could make the truck at least go. Sort of. They lurched out of town and found a place to hide the truck till just before noon, and then they hiccupped toward the ranch.

"Them gears sound bad," Darwin said.

The Secret Service agent assigned to the front had radioed for backup just before the twins went to meet the mailman.

"Chili, chili," he said. That was code for an emergency bathroom break.

"Roger, copy," his backup said from one of the back barns. "On my way." He headed toward the front of the house. The agent couldn't wait for his relief. He dashed into the main house and barely made it to the bathroom. *That'll teach me to eat ceviche at the local Mexican place.*

The twins were waiting at the gate when the mail truck came.

Mr. Jim was off and so was Miss Clarisse. A new guy was driving today.

He stepped out, but without the sack of mail, grabbed the two children, tossed them to his brother in the back, and drove off in as big a hurry as he could muster. The truck lurched and squeaked down the road a ways; then he put the truck in neutral, and they glided all the way down a long hill.

"Hey," Mikey yelled and kicked at the stinky man. "Put me down."

For her part, Emma bit the guy's hand when he tried to put it over her mouth.

"Ow. That hurt," Darwin said.

"Well, you deserved it," Emma replied, and then she bit him again. He swatted her hand, and she began to wail.

"You shut up, or I'll give you something to cry about," Darwin said. His mama said that when either of them cried. He and his brother usually shut up.

No one except her brother had ever told Emma to shut up. As far as she was concerned that was a grown-up word, like the others she and Mikey were not allowed to use.

Darrell screeched to a stop at the bottom of the long hill and put the truck into the brush by their car.

The men hastily put the twins into a stinky old car. They had to lie on the floor of the big backseat and were loosely covered with quilts. They made lots of turns, and neither Emma nor Mikey had any idea where they were going.

"How are we going to get away from these men?" Emma whispered in Italian to her brother.

"We'll watch, wait till they're asleep, and then get away."

"Hey, cut it out you two. No Mexican talk," the driver said. It came out "Mets-ick-can."

"Did you pick up the food for the kids?" Darrell asked Darwin.

"Aw, shee-ut, I forgot. I'll go to the store when we get home."

"I like peanut butter and jelly," Mikey offered from underneath the quilt.

"Hey, me too," Darwin said.

"With the crusts off," Mikey said.

"Hey, same as me," Darwin agreed.

"Hey, pipe down. You two shut up, or I'll have to hurt you." Darrell slapped at the side of the car for emphasis. The kids jumped but said nothing.

"When we get home, you gotta be quiet. Otherwise, I'll hurt you bad." Darrell did his best to sound mean.

The men wrapped each child in a quilt, whispered to be quiet, and dashed inside the trailer with them. There were a few people home in the middle of the day, but luckily Mama had liked living at the end of the row.

The trailer was a mess, and it smelled of unwashed fat men. Dirty dishes were everywhere, even on the open oven door.

"Sorry it's such a mess, but since Mama died, we've been on our own," the driver said, smacking a fat fly that landed on his arm.

"I'm sorry about your mama. I'd really like to talk to mine," Emma said, fighting back tears.

"You can call her later," the mean one said. "First, I'm going to put you two in Mama's bedroom. It's better'n the one me and Darwin share."

"You better not hurt my sister, or I'll snatch you bald-headed." Mikey didn't know what it meant, but whenever Regina said it, everyone did what she said.

"Darrell, you ought to go get the kids and us some food."

The two brothers took them to the back bedroom, which was as neat as a pin.

"We kept it just like Mama liked it," Darwin said.

"I'll bet she was real proud of you two," Emma said, trying to be nice. Maybe the fat men wouldn't hurt them if she were nice.

"Here's the deal. We won't put duct tape on your mouth if you agree to not scream or anything."

"Deal," Mikey said for both of them.

Then the two men sat the kids on the bed.

"Either of you have to go potty or anything?"

"I need to go," Emma said. "But I want my brother to go with me."

"Okay, you both go, then come right back."

The bathroom was really dirty, and Emma insisted that Mikey wash his hands like she did when they both finished. They saw a tiny, high-up window, but knew they couldn't get out of it.

Inside the back bedroom, the mean one told them to sit on the bed. They did. He duct taped Emma's hands together at the wrists. Then he did the same with her ankles. Mikey was taped the same way.

"I'm going to the store, so you two keep quiet and stay in here. Otherwise, I'll hurt you bad when I get back." Darrell made a mean face.

They nodded. They could see the fatter one in the front room laying back in his recliner. He was drinking a beer and eating bean dip. Emma noticed he watched the same stories that Regina did.

Abigail became catatonic at the disappearance of the twins. One of the most alpha females on earth was in the middle of a living nightmare, and it paralyzed her.

If I hadn't run for office, this would not have happened. My ambition caused my children to be taken from me.

Michael's protestations went ignored and, more frightening to him, unanswered.

"Regina, will you take care of Abby, please, I've got work to do," Michael said and hustled into the room where the Secret Service worked.

The Secret Service explained the momentary lapse in surveillance to Michael. The agent with diarrhea offered his resignation, but no one took him seriously. There was too much work to do. Michael had summoned the sheriff, who was on his way, as were the FBI out of Dallas.

Abby felt dead. She looked blankly into space. Regina put her to bed, where she curled up in the fetal position. Regina kept a warm hand on Abigail.

"They'll find the kids. And remember, those are very smart kids. If there's any way they can help themselves, they will," Regina said, then she rubbed Abby's back and sang hymns real low. Her baby seemed to relax a little. But she spoke not a word.

Regina stepped out to remind Mason about the bad business with the plumber, then she went right back to Abigail.

Mason took the sheriff aside and told him about the words with one of the plumbers, Jim Bob Green.

"I'm his alibi. He's in the jail for being drunk and disorderly. I think it's his hobby," the sheriff said.

The scene yielded little information initially, but the abandoned truck was quickly found and dusted for fingerprints. About then, Mr. Jim, the regular mail carrier, wobbled into the hospital with a big lump on his head.

"Someone hit me over the head," he said. "They must have wanted the mail truck."

The nurse called the post office, and within minutes one of the Secret Service agents appeared and questioned Jim.

"I hear you didn't see the guy, but do you have any impression about him?" he said to the postal carrier.

"Somehow I got the impression of two guys. They sorta seemed familiar, you know?" Jim said.

"Is there anything else you can tell us?" the agent asked. "Did they say anything?"

"Well, neither said anything. I remember going to the truck, then waking up. In between, I felt like it was two guys, but I never saw them, and they didn't say anything. I remember something smelled like dirty socks."

"Not twenty minutes later, the Aston twins were kidnapped," the agent said.

"Oh, no, not those two," Mr. Jim said. "They are the highlight of my day."

Jim had to stay at the hospital; after all, he'd been out cold for an hour or so. His headache nowhere near approached his heartache at the thought of someone snatching those two precious children.

Darrell called the ranch on the way to the store. Little did he know that Charley already had the phones tapped.

When the phone rang, Michael startled. The FBI, just recently arrived via helicopter from Dallas, nodded for Michael to answer the call.

"This is Michael Aston." He hoped he sounded calm. He wasn't.

"I got your kids. You can have them back for two million dollars in cash. Unmarked bills," Darrell said, trying to growl like a bad guy.

"I can do that. Where and when?" Michael asked as calmly as possible.

"I'll let you know."

The line went dead. Darrell accidentally shut the phone off. *Damn. Now I'll have to go home and read the damn book again.*

Luckily for him, it had no GPS. Unluckily for him, Charley could tell which tower the call came from. It was in town.

The cell phone number was a local one. As was his accent. They could safely assume the kidnapper(s) were local. That was reassuring. No jihadist had them. Yet. The FBI was running a fingerprint fragment from the steering wheel of the mail truck.

"He'll call back," Michael said. He was in warrior mode and would likely have strangled the man with his bare hands if he could have.

The vigil continued into the evening. Michael must have paced ten miles in the house. Abigail lay mute in the bed. When she learned the kidnappers were local, she felt a glimmer of hope, but it could not ignite her to action. She knew nothing of what to do. She might have commanded armies, but when it came right down to it, she was a mother whose children were being held against their will. She could not sleep. She would not eat. She had never felt as dead as she did that night. Her body, once filled to overflowing with her two children, was empty, broken. And she could not help at all. Michael worked with the authorities, but Abigail was mute.

Back at the trailer, Darwin and Darrell made the kids PBJs and gave them chocolate milk. Each one fed one child. It didn't dawn on them that with their hands taped in front of them, they could feed themselves. They let them go to the bathroom again, unaware that if they could do that with their hands taped, they could pretty much do anything they wanted to.

The kids asked if they could watch TV, but Darwin said, "We don't have no cable. I don't think there's anything on you should be watching."

The kids pretended to go to sleep, but each would pinch the other every few minutes to keep themselves awake.

Darrell left the house again. The kids had no idea how long he would be gone. They had to work fast.

Darwin was sound asleep in front of the television, snoring loudly.

"Mikey, give me your hands," Emma said in Italian. She began picking at the duct tape with her small fingers and nibbling at it with her teeth. Soon Mikey was free, and within a few seconds, both were untaped.

"Now we need to find a way to get out of here," Emma whispered.

"First, we need to tie up the fat guy." They tippy-toed into the living room. Emma spotted a broken lamp on the kitchen table with an unopened tube of superglue next to it. She pointed to it and Mikey put it in his pocket. They tiptoed back to the bedroom.

"What can we glue him to?" Mikey whispered in Italian.

"Let's glue his hands to the chair he's sitting in," Emma replied.

"Then we'll tie his shoelaces together and put some superglue between his shoes and the floor," Mikey added. "I think we ought to duct tape his mouth too."

"It'll hurt because he's got a beard," Emma said. "I like it."

"Then what do we do? It's dark outside."

"Maybe there's a flashlight somewhere." They began looking around and saw one on the wall, in a holder. They tested it. The bulb was weak, but it worked.

"Okay, who is the quieter one?" Emma asked.

"You are," Mikey said.

"Then I'll do his hands while you tie his shoelaces together."

They went silently toward the snoring hulk in the chair. Emma had the now open tube of superglue in her hand. She hoped he didn't smell it and wake up. If so, she'd squirt it toward his eyes, and they'd just run.

The man was still snoring away when the two children were beside him. She squirted some superglue onto the right arm of the chair and gently, gently pushed his hand down onto the blob.

The man snuffled a bit, and then his head rolled to the other side. He really smelled awful.

While she glued his other hand to the chair, Mikey took the shoelaces. He couldn't really tie his shoes yet, but he could tie a knot. So he did it over and over. The man belched in his sleep, and Emma and Mikey swallowed their fear, lest they scream. There was plenty of glue for his shoes.

He'd probably wake up when they taped his mouth, but what could he do? Emma had checked his hands. They weren't going anywhere.

"Tape the mouth or not?" Emma said.

"Tape it."

They tiptoed back into their room. Unable to rip the tape, they found a pair of scissors and cut two pieces: one for his mouth and the other for his eyes.

He awakened at the feel of the tape, but there was nothing he could do. The last thing they heard from him was mumbles and muffled yells.

The kids took off out of the trailer, flashlight in hand. Their mom had always told them if they were lost to either find a police officer or a lady with kids. A mommy would know what to do.

They realized they were in some sort of place where everyone lived in trailers; at least that's what they thought they were called. Most trailers were dark. The place was pretty quiet.

While they were choosing their safe house, Darrell was on the phone with Michael.

"The bank here has less than ten thousand dollars in cash. My wife, the former President, contacted the head of the Federal Reserve Bank in Dallas, and they can get us two million dollars in unmarked bills. He suggested you take them in hundreds, otherwise they'll weigh a ton," Michael said.

"Fine," Darwin said. "Tomorrow morning."

"Well, it's Friday evening. The Reserve Bank's vault is on a timer and cannot open until Monday at eight a.m. Not even for a former President of the United States."

"Someone can get around that. Tell your wife I want the money tomorrow by five."

"I want to talk to my children."

"No can do." Darwin just shut the phone. He'd gone fifty miles from home for this call and wanted to get some sleep.

As he headed back home, Mikey and Emma listened at the trailers until they heard a lady with a crying baby. They banged on the door with the flashlight.

The youngish woman in jeans and a tee shirt opened the door, her baby on one hip. She expected to see a neighbor griping about the baby noise.

"Hello. Who are you two?" she asked.

"I'm Emma Aston. This is my brother, Mikey. May I please use your phone to call the police?" Emma asked imperiously.

The lady smiled at them. "Sure, help yourself." *Bossy little kid.*

Emma dialed 911.

"Please state your emergency."

"This is Emma Aston. My brother, Mikey, and I were kidnapped earlier today and are now free. We need to go home."

"Oh, thank God. Where are you?" the operator asked.

"Just a minute, I'll give you to the nice lady who let us use the phone."

Within minutes the *whoop-whoop* of police sirens and the strobes of red, white, and blue lights lit up the trailer park. The Secret Service insisted Abby stay home. It took four agents to restrain her.

The police cars screeched to a stop, and Michael was out the door before the car stopped. He swept his children up in his arms, and the woman averted her face. It was too private for her to watch. Besides, she couldn't have seen them through her own tears.

"How did you get away?" Michael asked, squatting down to look them both over.

"When one left, we super-glued the other to his chair," Emma said matter-of-factly.

"And I tied his shoelaces together in knots. Then we super-glued his shoes to the floor," Mikey added excitedly.

"And then we put duct tape over his mouth and eyes."

"Where is he?" Michael was half worried they'd buried him alive.

The twins looked at each other.

"A couple of houses down on this side. His brother should be back in a little while."

The cops hid their cars and turned off their blue lights and shooed everyone back into their trailers and told them to turn off their lights.

Body odor assaulted everyone as they opened the door. Darwin was indeed well trussed into place.

"Is this the man who took you?" a police officer asked the twins. As they ripped the tape off his mouth, Darwin yelped. They were no gentler with his eyes.

"Yes. And you were very, very bad to do such a thing to two little kids," Emma said, while she kicked the crap out of his shin with her pointy-toed cowgirl boot.

"Yes, and you made our mama and daddy worry. Plus Reege and O.T. and Duke and Grandma Louise and everybody," Mikey said, and then he, too, gave Darwin a couple of kicks in the other shin.

"Plus, they said the 's' word," Emma said.

"The 's' word?" Michael asked, confused.

"Shut up." Emma was highly offended.

The police hustled the kids out of the trailer before they did any real damage to their kidnapper. One officer drove them and Michael home while the rest waited for Darrell.

"We should have figured out it was Darrell and Darwin when the mailman said he smelled dirty socks. Those boys stink worse'n anybody in town."

Michael called Abby from the cruiser.

"They're fine, they're both just fine. I'm just glad we got to them before the kids did any real damage to the kidnappers. We'll be home in twenty minutes."

"What are you talking about, Michael?" Abigail was confused, crying in big gulps.

"You remember all those *Home Alone* videos? They came in real handy. The kidnappers definitely got the short end of the stick." Michael laughed and Abigail's tears switched to ones of joy.

The kids ran to greet their mother as soon as the car stopped in front of the house. They all but knocked her down, they were so glad to see her. Each talked nonstop about all the mayhem they'd inflicted on the "bad guy." Abigail looked them over carefully, as did Regina.

"You two did good, you did real good," Regina said. "I think you deserve root beer floats."

They loved telling about how they used their Italian, and how they got out of the duct tape. But each sentence was punctuated with sips of root beer float.

After a bath to get the stink off them, both of the children slept with their parents for what was left of the night. Both kids seemed to sprout more knees and elbows than either parent could remember. Finally, Michael got up, conferred with the Secret Service, and put each child back in his own room. Two agents volunteered to sit up all night, watching over the children.

Michael went back to bed, told Abigail what he'd done, and she snuggled into him and fell fast asleep, a smile on her face.

CHAPTER TWENTY-TWO

ELECTION AND BEYOND

The election was the most lopsided in history. Elections had gone to a two-day weekend in November, and Abigail won 87 percent of the popular vote and was declared the winner within moments of the polls closing the second night on the West Coast.

Sheila did the smartest thing of her entire campaign. She conceded in a three-minute speech and wished "President Adams every success and happiness."

Regina frowned at the television.

"Is that 'our' Sheila? Or did they pay a look-alike?"

Everyone guffawed.

Abigail did her hair and makeup and walked out to the barn with Michael, the children, and Wicker. They had an American flag for a backdrop. She was tired, but as soon as that red light went on, her energy surged toward the camera.

"I am humbled and very happy that so many of you believe I am up to the task at hand. I cannot promise you perfection. I can promise you my best, twenty-four hours a day, seven days a week for the next six years.

"You've elected me to turn the environment around. That is job one. With the love of my family and the guidance of the American people, I feel certain we can get this job done. Thank you and good night."

The children looked up to see Michael give Abby a kiss. Mikey made a pickle face and Emma smiled. No one cared what Abigail said. Everyone was already in love with the imps that were her children.

People demanded a new round of bells and whistles. Kim had already had preliminary designs for new scarves and ties with an environmental theme, but the snow globes were iconic. Abigail gagged, but ordered them in the hundreds in time for the Inauguration.

Then Abigail and her family took a much-needed vacation to Italy, where Abigail felt safer with her children each day. Now the whole family got Secret Service protection. Abigail was still Goldilocks, Michael was Guy, while Mikey was Gallop, and Emma was Glory. Abby wasn't sure if she could ever have them out of her sight again but knew the day would come eventually. At least for the next six years, armed men protected her children.

They stayed at *Bel Vedere* for ten days, and Abigail relaxed by about day five. She and Michael let Gloriana get the kids their breakfasts while they slept in the next few days. Then she got to work on the transition.

Jerome made the transition as seamless as possible, and Abigail found the hardest part was reassembling herself. Her body needed to work out to get her brain in top shape. And with children, it would be harder than ever to compartmentalize things. But she had done this job before, and that helped a lot. Maybe she could work out at six, not five thirty. She had a lot of catching up to do on world affairs.

They visited the White House in early December. The children's eyes were wide. Everything on the first floor was so fancy; neither had ever seen anything like it. When Lynne showed them the Family Quarters, the kids were really excited.

"Mom, Mom, this is big enough to roller skate in," Mikey said. "And great for hide and seek."

"We'll be living on the floor above, darlings. This is just for grown-ups down here." *My children and the Lincoln Bedroom would not fare well together.*

During the transition, Abby, Michael, and the kids lived in the penthouse with Regina and O.T. Lynne helped them set up a school-room in the private quarters, and within days, Emma, Mikey, Pris, James, and six other kids their age from the White House staff started school.

The teacher from the ranch agreed to come live in D.C.

The kids loved having Regina and O.T. with them and were sad when they went to the house in Virginia for some peace and quiet on the weekends. The house restoration was finished, and he and Regina could just relax.

"But we can be quiet, honest," Mikey said.

"Okay, show me," Regina said, looking at her watch. He lasted exactly thirty-seven seconds.

"Mikey, Honey Bear, I love you, but I'm getting old. I need some quiet time," Regina explained.

"You mean like when you tell us if we wake you, we die?" Mikey asked.

"Exactly. You'd best stay home with your mom and dad. Though I'll have y'all out for Sunday lunch."

Mikey felt better. O.T. was teaching him to play checkers. He liked checkers.

Christmas found them all at the ranch, as it should be. If the kids showed any concern over their adventure with Dirt and Dirtier, they never let on. The men had quietly pled guilty, as "dumber than dirt" wasn't one of the choices. Both were safely ensconced at a federal prison for the next forty years. Neither had to work, they got regular meals, but still no cable. No, they didn't share a cell, and they had to get up earlier. Still, it beat any job they could think of.

The biggest, meanest prisoner was deputized to get the boys in shape.

"You stink. If you don't bathe every damn day, I'm going to make hamburger meat out of you, understand?"

"Yes, sir," each tried to be polite to everyone.

But baths alone weren't enough, so men chipped in and bought each of them deodorant.

"Put this on under your arms when you're dry from your shower," the mean guy had to actually show them. "Otherwise, you're hamburger."

The prison barbers shaved each man's head and beard, shocked at what appeared to be a lifelong ignorance of basic hygiene. Heaven only knew what all was in the beard, but the barber did notice old chips and what he hoped was bean dip.

Then the mean guy taught each about shampoo, as the hair would grow back.

Finally Darrell and Darwin were clean, obese men. It would take almost a year of prison food to get them close to anything approaching a normal weight. Their mama would be proud, or at least that's what Darwin wrote in his Big Chief Tablet. He was keeping a journal and hoped to have a bestseller.

Abigail was under no illusions. She and her children had gotten lucky with Darwin and Darrell. She prayed every night there would not be a next time with smarter captors.

The night before the Inauguration, the family moved to Trowbridge House, the part of Blair House reserved for the incoming president. Abigail wasn't the only one with an extra change of clothes. Mikey and Emma had them, too. Regina made them stay in their underwear until it was almost time to leave.

January twentieth was a mild, snowless day, and Abby took the Oath of Office with a clear mind and under the proud view of her children, who had kicked each other only once that she could see. Regina cocked an eyebrow at the offender, and they turned into child-sized statues.

Abigail's speech only ran to ten minutes, and its take-home message was simple.

"The environment is job one. Without a livable planet, everything else is useless. I will look at everything through the prism of saving the environment, much as Roosevelt looked at everything through the prism of winning the war.

"It won't be easy. Some of you will curse me, but your grandchildren will thank me."

As she reentered the Capitol, her new nuclear aide, Capt. Hannaford, gave her only a thumb drive.

"No card, also?"

"No, ma'am. You set your own password," He handed her a keyboard and turned his back. She put in Regina's childhood address, backwards. Twice.

Abigail recalled the moment of terror when Hitch gave her launch codes in her first term. Now she felt only a sense of familiar responsibility. Abby stuck the thumb drive in her bra, and soon she and her family were headed down Constitution Avenue.

The Secret Service nixed walking and provided a bubble top car for them. Of course, the bubble was bulletproof. At five-and-a-half years old, Emma and Mikey got into waving to the crowds. Mikey did not stick his tongue out once. Nor did he pick his nose or put his fingers in his ears and wiggle them. He didn't annoy his sister, either. Abigail wondered how she had been so blessed. Regina had quietly taken him aside just before he entered the car and told him that if he did any of those rude gestures, she would give him a switchin' he'd never forget. He had never had one, but it sounded pretty awful.

"Make me proud, young man," she said. "If you don't, you get a switchin'. If you do, you get a root beer float."

Once back at the White House, each got a root beer float and went to watch the Inaugural Parade. Once their behavior deteriorated to kicking and spitting at each other, Abigail had them taken inside for some quiet time. *I don't care what brain rot they watch, as long as they are quiet.*

Michael and Abigail did the folderol of the Inaugural Parties, which Abigail had spread over three nights as the Inauguration occurred on a Thursday.

By having three nights of festivities, the balls were less crowded. Crammed in like sardines to the various balls, women with sequined gowns had them all but shredded—it was a true waste of a ball gown many would treasure forever. Being conjoined to another woman by the tangled sequins of your dress was not comical at an Inaugural ball.

The evening of the first ball, Michael presented her with another black velvet box with a pink bow.

"Happy Anniversary, Missus. Thought you might use this in your campaign to save the environment," he said. Abigail opened the box to find a large platinum "V" for victory pin with three stones down the fatter side of the "V": an emerald cut ruby, diamond, and sapphire, each about a carat. "Oh, Michael, it's gorgeous."

"It's actually World War One vintage. Apparently the sign started then."

"Odd how it fits the gown perfectly," she said, pinning it onto a blue silk halter-top gown. "I wonder if Kim has seen this?"

"We're running late, Missus," Michael said, hating to start off a new administration with a lie.

They stayed only a short time at each event. Then Abby gave him a night to remember.

The Oval Office was still basically the same. If anything, it seemed calmer. Then she figured out why. The twins weren't in there. It was still a busy hive, and should probably be shut down by the fire marshal, but it was calm compared to any room with her children in it. Try as she might, she couldn't recall a time when at least one of them wasn't talking—except when they were zoned in front of the television. *No wonder parents let their kids fry their brains.*

Abigail found having twins made dealing with Congress easier. Petty bickering had driven her insane when she was in the Senate, but after years of it with her own children, she'd learned to rise above it.

"Solve it yourselves, ladies and gentlemen," she practiced the phrases. "I'm the President, not the referee. Am I wearing black and white stripes and carrying a whistle?"

Regina was again the Official Hostess and had her office in the East Wing. Michael had a small office in the West Wing, which Wicker joked, "protected him from estrogen overload."

Regina and O.T. decided living in was easier, and they spent weekends at their house in Virginia. They were on the lower of the two family floors, and O.T. loved living in the House, not as a servant or a curator, but as a member of the First Family. They chose the Prince of Wales suite that Abigail had during her first term. It had always been O.T.'s favorite.

Regina could do the job of Official Hostess in her sleep, and sleep she did, every afternoon in the Queen's bedroom from two to three. No one awakened her for fear of losing a limb.

The children loved time with O.T., who took them on many a nighttime prowl of the White House. They knew every hidey-hole in the old building.

She also added knockoff "V for Victory" pins and wore hers daily. The "V for Victory" pins went to people who contributed in a meaningful way to save the planet.

As predicted, "The Invitation" in D.C. was for Regina's soul food dinners, which resumed—this time on a Friday night to show they'd come up in the world.

Abby entertained the Members of Congress promptly—and regularly—and Michael charmed all of the female members without even trying. Abby, now sedately married, found the male members harder to charm. Between introducing the women to Michael and feeding the men Regina's food in the Family Quarters, most people came around.

The children stayed out of sight, probably watching *Home Alone* for the millionth time, this time with a Secret Service agent and a nanny also enraptured. As the twins had proven when kidnapped, one adult was at their mercy. They had to be double-teamed, and at least one of those adults had to be armed.

"They need to go," Wicker said, referring to the upcoming State of the Union speech.

"They need to go to jail for the kindergarten set," Abigail said. The twins had been horrid the entire weekend before the State of the Union speech. *No wonder Regina and O.T. left every weekend.*

They'd argued over board games, whined at card games, even turned up their noses at a treasure hunt. Being cooped up on a nasty weekend didn't help. Emma had a full-on tantrum when Mikey told her that her hair looked like rabbit salad (their name for shredded carrots, raisins, and pineapple juice). To retaliate, Emma deliberately tripped him, and he got a bloody nose.

"Look, they are wonderful, darling, precious children, but they are also fully capable of being incorrigible. Mikey has discovered spitting. Because he can't hit his sister, he's taken to spitting on her. They are not docile. They are all but vile sometimes."

Abby had to vent on someone, and Wicker had asked for it.

"How about if we bribe them?" Wicker asked.

"With what?"

"I don't know. A trip to Disney World? Ponies at Camp David?" Wicker said.

"I won't negotiate with terrorists, even if they are my own children," Abby said.

Abby called Regina for help.

"Tell them there will be root beer floats if they are good and a switching if they are bad," Regina said. "And they have to go pick the switch."

Abby hated the idea of corporal punishment, but she'd survived it, and her children were old enough to be good for a half hour at a time. There had been precious few root beer floats for them recently, and they did love those.

On the Monday evening before the State of the Union speech the next night, Abigail and Michael sat the children down and explained what was going to happen.

"Your mom has to give a very important speech, and you can be there to see it, all dressed up, but you have to promise to be good. If you're good, you get a root beer float when we come home. But if you're bad, there will be serious consequences," Michael said sternly.

"So how good do we have to be?" Emma asked. "Exactly."

"You have to be polite, with no shoving, pushing, biting, spitting. Full Regina party manners," Abigail said. Michael nodded.

The kids looked at each other. *Regina's party manners were pretty hard.*

"We'll think about it." Emma spoke for the two of them.

"I would be so proud to have you there watching me speak. It is an event that you will always remember—a part of history for our family and for our country. But because so many people across our country and the world will be watching us on television, you must decide to behave if you are there. You have five minutes," Abigail said. The two huddled in the corner and conferred.

"What exactly is involved in 'consequences'?" Mikey asked after three minutes.

"Well, it won't be fun. When I was little, if I'd been bad, Regina would make me go pick a piece off a bush for a switching. Then she'd flick us across the back of our legs with it. It stung like fire. If you got a piece that was too little, she'd make you go get a bigger one. Children don't get switched any more, but consequences are unpleasant.

"Go, be nice, and get root beer floats. Or stay home. It's all your choice."

The kids came back with a decision a few minutes later.

"We'd like to go, Mommy. But I won't sit next to him," Emma said of her brother.

"Yeah, I want Dad between us," Mikey agreed.

"Very well. I hope you get the root beer floats."

Self-awareness is the first step in growth.

The children were agog when they got to the House chamber. They'd never seen so many people in one room. They wore church clothes that Regina put on them at the very last minute. Michael sat between them, with Regina and O.T. on either side of them. At no point were their four hands unheld.

Abigail decided to wear baby blue for this speech. She wore her "V for Victory" pin on her left shoulder and was, as always, impeccably groomed. Regina kept the kids well away from her, lest Mikey knock over a bottle of perfume or trip and fall onto her with a glass of milk. He was a disaster in motion. Regina even banned him riding with his mother. If all else failed, he could always throw up on her. The children rode with Regina and O.T. Michael rode with Abigail. She was glad for his undivided attention, even if it was just for a few minutes. Abby loved looking at her extended family in the gallery. Having Cristo sit behind her as President of the Senate all but gave her chills. He was a far cry from the first Vice President she had known as a Senator.

Abigail's speech was short, as usual.

After the applause died down, Abigail bowed deeply.

"I am but a servant to three hundred million people. You, the members of Congress, also, are servants. The trust our masters have placed in us is inviolable. It is as sacred as the trust a wife puts in her husband, a child puts in a parent, and a patient puts in a doctor. We may make a mistake, but we must never violate a trust.

"In this last election, the voters told me in no uncertain terms that they wanted us to fix the environment—and fix it, we shall.

"We have what we need to do this: we have the political will, for the first time in history, and we have the scientific resources. All we have to do is ratchet up the second and keep working the problem. Day in and day out.

"Some solutions are simple and cheap. Others are extremely complicated scientifically. We have excellent minds working on the complex problems.

"Luckily there isn't one way; there are many ways. We have air to fix, land to fix, and oceans and rivers to fix. We have to fix it within our budgetary constraints and do so swiftly.

"I will not be the environmental nanny. The best changes come from the people up, not from the government down. I envision government as a good administrator: giving the populace the missing piece that makes their plan work.

"I hope you and your families start the changes that work for you this week. I want your communities to find solutions, and we in Washington will be your advisers and helpers.

"First, we need to 'Buy American,' and if possible, buy local. This not only creates American jobs, it prevents the waste of fuel involved in shipping an article halfway around the world. If it costs a few pennies more, you may choose to buy fewer things. Today's "stuff" is tomorrow's landfill anyway.

"My suit tonight was designed by my niece, Kim Tran, whose business, Thimble, is as all-American as it can be. She could outsource and make more profit, but she is the child of immigrants and believes in giving back to the country that allowed her to exist and prosper.

"No, I won't ask for protective tariffs, but I will ask American companies to bring jobs back to the U.S. Why? An out-of-work American costs us tax dollars. An American with a job generates tax revenue. The Commerce Department estimates the additional cost to consumers for American made products is about 3 percent. That is more than offset by the benefits to our economy as a whole.

"Energy is our stumbling block. I'm from Texas, and our wells won't last forever. Your car doesn't care where its energy comes from. Solar, geothermal, wind, tidal, algae, and nuclear are all there waiting for development and coordination.

"Private enterprise will do the development; government will do the coordination. Just as the government decided on the gauges of railroads so different companies could use the same rail lines, we will perform a similar function in our transition to alternative energy. We might set the rules, but we won't be on any team.

"On the website Earth.gov are literally thousands of suggestions for families in various parts of the country. There are suggestions for communities, cities, counties, states, and other taxing entities. Some changes are easier than others.

"Interestingly enough, the federal government has been the last to come to the environmental party. Believe it or not, many, if not most, of the global oil companies 'got it' decades ago. We are only one of two countries that didn't ratify the Kyoto protocol. Well, that's changing."

The audience erupted into cheers, and Abby looked at the children who were slack jawed. *People were clapping for Mommy.*

"Every decision that crosses every federal desk will have to pass the environmental sniff test. If it hurts, we won't do it. If it helps, we can go for it. I hope states and local governments will adopt preserving the environment as "Job One" also.

"In our dealings with foreign governments, they get points for good governance and for environmental friendliness. If they have neither, they can forget U.S. support.

"I don't like corporate tax incentives. They get gamed. But I do like them for individuals. We'll help homeowners and apartment owners make homes more energy efficient via tax deductions. We'll sponsor environmental science fairs and invite venture capitalists to them to marry new technology with private money—not taxpayer money.

"We'll give local communities planning money to decide which building code changes make sense for them. For example, air lock doors, like those used in shopping malls, should be routine in every house that either uses heat or air conditioning. The Dutch have been doing it for generations.

"We will offer competitive scholarships to students in environmental engineering. Just as we had a national priority to put a man on the moon within a decade in 1960, I challenge you to help me reduce global warming before I leave office in six years. Period."

The applause was thunderous.

"I'm from Texas, where oil's in our blood. But we must use it for its optimum use: in petrochemicals, in plastics, solvents, paints, and for products that make our world a better place. Hospitals cannot go back to glass syringes or rubber intravenous tubing. Gasoline and electrical energy generation is the most wasteful use of oil.

"And I have a special word for you out there, the NIMBYs of the nation—Not in My BackYarders. Your backyard is no more special than anyone else's. I'm sorry if you don't want to look at offshore wind farms. Deal with it. Their carbon footprint is minimal.

"I will be sending a number of bills to Congress to implement a variety of environmental solutions. I will also be exercising the line item veto on anything that is bad for the environment. I will also veto anything that smacks of pork. The voters sent us here to get the job done, not to dither, bicker, blather, and backstab as we have in the past.

"Change is coming. Get on board. Get ready. Some of it will be wrenching. Jobs will be lost in one industry and created in another. You might have to move or learn a new skill.

"Mother Nature's law is simple: adapt or die. We will not just adapt, we will thrive while doing so. We have no choice but to change if we want to stay on this planet.

"Thank you and good night."

The applause was deafening, and both children got their root beer floats.

Abigail fell into a workable schedule easily: workout at six, breakfast with her family at seven, in the office by eight thirty. Then she endured the PDB. As usual, she put the protocol things early in the day and substantive work in the afternoon with a break for after-school snacks with the kids for thirty minutes. That time was sacred. She sat and listened to them babble about school. She was trying to get them to talk one at a time and figured she had six years in which to accomplish this. Changing her children was as hard as changing the environment.

School started at eight thirty. They had a morning recess and an afternoon recess. They had a quiet time as well. School was out at three thirty, and one day a week, Abigail or Michael took the rest of that afternoon off. She might do nothing with them except play outside. Other times, the class had field trips around Washington. She would not keep her children imprisoned in the White House. It wasn't fair to them. Whether it was Michael or Reege or a nanny with the kids, it was still less hassle for people in Washington than if Abby went. So the President never got a guided tour of the Air and Space Museum or a dozen other places she wanted to see.

Michael and she switched off supervising homework time if they were at home. It was no trouble for Abigail to set an example. She had a pile of documents to deal with every night.

On nights when they had functions to attend, they didn't have the luxury of supervising bath and bedtime. Regina and O.T. pitched in. But she and Michael always kissed the children good night, before and after their function.

The first spring, there was a state dinner for the Queen of the Netherlands, a beloved figure in her homeland. The arrival ceremony was on a Saturday, and the kids could watch from the Truman Balcony. Somehow Mikey had found a squirt gun in the cache of toys they'd brought with them. There was something of a breeze and it put his aim off, but he was diligently trying to hit the feathers on the Queen's hat.

He felt a tap on his shoulder and turned around, fearing Regina had caught him. It wasn't Regina. It was one of the snipers from the roof. With his real gun.

He held out his hand, and Mikey surrendered his weapon.

"Are you going to tell?" Mikey wanted to know.

"What do you think?" the sniper said with some menace in his voice.

"I don't know," Mikey was terrified of the man all in black.

"Next time, account for the wind," he said with a curt nod of the head.

Then he turned and left.

Mikey lived in fear for a week, but apparently the man said nothing. No more water pistols threatened State visits.

The changes came fast and furious in the legislation to clean up the environment. Deliberate corporate water pollution became a federal offense and after two CEOs went to jail, it slowed dramatically. In a third very high profile case, the CEO of a Fortune 100 company was hauled off to the federal pen accompanied by the COO and the Chief Environmental Officer. It stopped for good then.

"You will be caught. You will go to jail. You will not get out, as this is federal prison," Abigail said in a weekly press conference. "We have limited resources, and they cannot be fouled."

In March, Abigail hosted a Presidential Commission on Reversing Climate Change. Unlike most Presidential commissions, she was committed to implementing their suggestions, whether through legislation or administrative changes.

She gave a great deal of thought as to where to put the hundred or so people who were writing the blueprint for the future. Camp David was too small; besides, they needed a place where nature inspired them. She stuck them at a resort near Austin that was lovely, but warm, in March. It had its own naturalist, and when they weren't working on the environment, they were learning about the ecosystem around them. They even had a field trip to the Lady Bird Johnson Wildflower Center in Austin, where they also learned a lot.

The University of Texas, about fifty miles away from the resort, was happy to provide all their technical support, giving graduate students in environmental science credit for being gofers and number crunchers for the group.

And Dell Computers graciously donated all their technology. Michael Dell himself hosted them at his home in Austin, as did the Chancellor of the University of Texas.

At the resort, they would also be able to play golf, go horseback riding, play tennis, even have a massage.

Abby could have flown in for the first session, but decided to teleconference her remarks and invited them, and their spouses, to a dinner at the White House when they presented their findings.

She also asked them to serve as a vetting committee for the Presidential Globe of Progress, an award she was creating and funding pri-

vately to award to companies that made the most environmental progress. All were willing.

"I'm going to announce it as soon as the trophy is designed and
will award it before Thanksgiving."

The family schedule was, de facto, that of the White House. The
Easter Egg Roll went off without a hitch, thanks to the volunteers. Abigail and Michael explained that some children with disabilities would
be there and that as good hosts, Mikey and Emma should make sure
everyone had a good time.

Mikey helped a child in a wheelchair, and Emma found a visually
impaired child to help. Abigail forbade pictures of them doing good
deeds.

"They can't be rewarded for doing what they should do anyway,"
she said to Ken Clutter who was still the White House Photographer.

The Commission Report came in after Easter, and Abigail spent
a long time going over it. All of it was sensible; most of it wasn't too
expensive. It was highly technical and way above the average citizen's
head. She might have trouble selling what looked like gobbledygook.
Even if she could, it wouldn't fit into the Balanced Budget.

*Money was the easier sell. Gobbledygook was harder. Solve the easier
problem first.* She and Cristo and the relevant Cabinet members squab-
bled and fought over how to pay for it. They were all at the point where
no one believed they could find the money to pay for it.

One night, as Abby was kissing the children good night, she
noticed their piggy banks. The next morning, she called the Treasurer of
the United States.

"I need to know how much change is hanging around the country,"
Abby said.

"I'm not sure I follow you," Treasurer Takazaki said.

"You know, how much is in piggy banks, or in jars where guys put
their pocket change."

"Off hand, I cannot say, but I will look into it."

Treasurer Takazaki called all his kids and had them count their change. Then he had his personal secretary to do the same thing. That should be a good enough sample.

"Madam President, I estimate the average household has at least ten dollars in change lying around," he said.

"What was your methodology? Or did someone at Treasury just know?" Abigail said. She, too, had gone through her family's change.

"I asked my kids and my secretary and her kids," he admitted with a chuckle.

"Me, too," Abigail laughed.

With just over a hundred million households, that was a billion dollars. *Bingo.*

Abigail did a brief speech to the nation, asking for their spare change to fund environmental changes made by the Commission. Banks put up bins for change, counted it and sent in money to the Special Fund for the Environment.

The country was so tickled with the program, they didn't even want much explanation of the gobbledygook on the website. Nevertheless, Abigail cornered a couple of science geek interns and had them translate as best they could for Charley Garrett.

Within a month, the legislation was on its way, securely funded without having to override the Balanced Budget amendment.

The bill provided a myriad of pilot programs, so we could know what would and would not work. Cap and trade was pitted against the European model. There were science prizes for best solar energy design, best energy retrofitting of homes in various climates, best tidal energy design in low tide areas and high tide areas, best kinetic energy design, best people moving solutions, best solutions for moving of goods. To be considered, a system had to reduce energy use by at least 20 percent.

Many a college offered summer courses to work on these prizes, as well as hundreds of people tinkering in their basements, garages, and warehouses.

After the Fourth of the July party at the White House, they went to the ranch for a month, where the kids could be as free as any children watched by the Secret Service could be. Priscilla figured out the fireworks weren't just for her birthday, but at least she got to do it at the White House. Petite and gracious like her mother, she still felt a special glow whenever she saw fireworks.

In September, Abigail succeeded in heading off the White House Decorations Committee before they got really geared up. She met with the volunteers in September, just as they were ready to begin behind-the-scenes preparation at a warehouse in Virginia.

At a tea on the lower floor of the Private Quarters, Abigail praised their Executive Committee to the hilt, realizing full well Regina knew she was lying through her teeth. Regina didn't even bother with The Look. She was savvy enough about politics to know that a good lie can be better than a bad truth.

"You've made the White House a Christmas showpiece for many years, but we have to dial things way back in the spirit of conserva..."

The chairman of the organization interrupted.

"But we reuse our decorations from year to year," the well-upholstered matron said with condescension in her voice.

"But the public doesn't know that," Abigail said. "We need to model that less is more for the American people." *Rude witch.* "And model that, we shall."

Abigail fixed her with The Look and the matron sniffed but didn't back down. *I do wish assassination was legal for overbearing volunteer matrons.*

"Well, we've never had an interfering President," the woman's face was turning purple.

"I'm not interfering, I'm commanding. Argue further, I'll have you banned from entering the building," Abigail said pleasantly.

"When you redo your plans, show them to Regina please, for her approval," Abigail said. She stood, turned on her heel, and left. All the women creaked to their feet. The meeting was over.

Earlier in the year, with cooperation from the VFW, she set up Operation Homecoming, a nonprofit to get WWII vets to visit Washington on Veteran's Day. Peggy Mellon, her friend from the Senate, was the chairman. The sticking point was airfare, which could be prohibitive. Abigail had Poppy get every CEO of every airline on the line for her. There was nothing to do but be presidential about it. She lied like a rug. Regina might give her a switching for lying, but she loved every minute of it.

"Every other airline CEO has signed on for a special one-hundred-dollar round-trip fare for the veteran and a companion. You don't want to look cheap, do you?" Abigail asked. Each caved in. Had she not kept all the others waiting on the line, they might have had a chance to talk among themselves.

The first autumn, Cristo and Peggy Mellon put on a helluva Homecoming on Veteran's Day. The Mall was a sea of tents, one for each branch of the service. Each tent was not only heated, it was wheelchair accessible. Every entrance had a computer for a vet to log in and find out where his old unit was. They could even find buddies from other units.

The Pentagon had unearthed enough paraphernalia to decorate the tents with authentic memorabilia. A fleet of Jeeps driven by young service members dressed in WWII uniforms was a favorite spot for photos.

Peggy and Cristo assumed none of the vets would be mobile, so they commandeered all the golf carts the military had at golf courses and trucked those in. On Homecoming weekend, everyone either walked the courses or stayed home. It was a small inconvenience.

Entertainers donated their services, and the mall was hopping with WWII music—to Michael's mind, some of the best ever written.

Since WWII had run on coffee and doughnuts, Dunkin' Donuts and Starbucks both ponied up for the refreshments for free. The war also ran on cigarettes, but Abby drew the line there. The ones who'd never given up cigarettes were long gone anyway.

Abby and Michael showed up in uniforms and posed for endless pictures at each tent. The White House photography department did this sort of mass photo mailing for a living, and within days each vet would have a picture in his or her mailbox. Abby regretted she couldn't listen to each story, but she insisted each vet take time to contribute to the video history project in the works by the Smithsonian. Their stories were dying with them, and that was a tragedy.

The events took up all of a three-day weekend, and on Monday night, Abigail and Michael put their feet in cold-water baths.

Many of the vets stuck around to see not only the WWII Memorial, but also to spend time with old buddies and maybe to admire what they'd fought to protect.

On Wednesday evening, Wicker disturbed her at the residence.

"Whassup?" she asked pleasantly.

"A GI and his former flame found each other," he said.

"Oh, how sweet," Abigail said.

"They want to get married, and I thought you should perform the service."

"Can I?"

"Yes, you can."

"Then find them a time and place in the schedule, and I'll be there."

John Eagleton and Marie Schneider were pushing ninety, but their eyes held a love Abigail recognized as true. She married them in the Oval Office in front of family Abigail had flown in. She held a reception for them in the Roosevelt Room and cried when the happy couple left, each holding a cane in one hand and their spouse's hand in the other. Michael gave the wedding party a weekend at the Four Seasons.

"I hope they don't die trying to have sex," Abby said when she crawled into bed with Michael later that night. They were both exhausted from a long day.

"At least they'll die happy," he said. "I've already optioned their story for a movie, by the way. Know anyone to play POTUS?"

CHAPTER TWENTY-THREE

FIRST CHRISTMAS IN THE WHITE HOUSE

Abigail made a big deal out of the Globe of Progress Awards ceremony just before Thanksgiving. Yes, she'd pardon the stupid turkey, but this was more important.

Hundreds of companies entered, and the winners were invited to dine and sleep over at the White House the weekend before Thanksgiving. The committee vetted over a thousand entrants and awarded five prizes, based on a company's size.

The event was as fancy as Abigail could make it, without being over the top.

Wicker described it as "approaching a State Dinner to demonstrate the President's commitment to environmental progress." He went on to detail that after dinner and before presentation of the awards, the President had invited Ashley Duncan, a child opera prodigy to perform.

"Her voice cannot exist in a polluted world," he said.

Of course, to Abigail, this was just another function. Michael said he was going to snore loudly if the opera singer sang too loud. Abigail went to slap him on the forearm, then, remembering that was Regina's way of showing displeasure, she kissed him on the cheek.

"No sex for snorers," she smiled sweetly. She made a mental note to have Ashley perform just one aria.

Everything went well, from the organic food through *O Mio Babbino Caro.*

Abigail panicked momentarily, afraid that her high notes would shatter the crystal trophies. *And I thought the snow globes were expensive.* But all went well, and the crowd loved the little girl who was only eleven. The children came into the back of the room for the performance, and afterwards, Ashley thundered up the stairs with her hooligans.

Abigail handed out awards.

"Our first Environmental Progress Award goes to White Manufacturing, a small tool company that has reduced their carbon footprint by 75 percent," Abigail said.

When she handed Mr. White the crystal globe, etched with all the continents, he held it aloft. He was nervous and it slipped from his grip, shattering into a million pieces on the floor of the East Room. He was horror-stricken.

Abigail did not miss a beat. She put an arm around his shoulder.

"If ever there was an appropriate analogy for the power we hold over our world, this is it. We cannot drop the ball, although of course, Mr. White, I had a spare made just because they are so delicate," Abigail said, reaching to the back of the line of globes.

She gave him another, and he cradled it as he would a newborn.

"Thank you, Madam President. This really goes to Cora, our housekeeping lady. She nagged me until I gave in and did everything she had researched. Until my dying day, I will hear her saying, 'Do you think there is a Cora to clean up the world? No. We all have to clean up. And here is the list.'"

The crowd applauded him, and in a few minutes all the trophies were gone. No one dropped another.

Abigail and Michael took their leave and found Ashley and the kids upstairs. All three were singing opera, but only one could carry a tune.

The White House announced earlier in the fall that it would have a live Christmas tree and encouraged other Americans to follow suit.

"Then, you can plant your tree in your yard," Wicker said at the Daily Press Briefing. "Or your city will take the tree and plant it in a needed area."

The National Christmas Tree was not large, but to drum up interest, there was a daily video on digging the hole, digging up the tree, etc. Kids all over the country learned about trees from this feed.

In honor of Regina, Abigail insisted the tree be topped with a black angel. Regina was not about to let her prized one sit out in the open air, so O.T. crafted one in perfect scale from an antique bisque masque like those used at *Carnevale* in Venice. He painted the face and created the angel's hair and body. A solar-powered battery powered the spotlight to illuminate it at night.

There was only one tree on the State Floor of the White House, and it, too, was live, its root ball disguised under a *papier-mâché* mountain with a little train chugging to the top.

As usual, there were gingerbread houses in various places, but the numbers were down dramatically. Abigail was glad the decorations were maybe 10 percent of normal.

One day, a week or so before Christmas proper, Abigail noticed one of the gingerbread houses was missing. She headed upstairs and found much of it in the trash in Mikey's room. She called Chef Dahm to make sure it had nothing toxic in it.

"No. No. Only natural ingredients. Of course, I bake it for looks not taste."

"Michael Molloy Aston, I need to speak with you," Abigail said, summoning him out of the classroom.

She took him to his room and pointed at the trashcan.

"Please explain yourself," Abigail said simply.

"Well, I, um, thought it would taste good, so I thought I could put a little one up here and snack on it," Mikey said. *At least he wasn't lying—yet.*

"And so you took it without permission," his mother said.

"Well, it was just sitting there. And this is our house," Mikey waffled.

"No, this is not our house. This house belongs to the American people. We just get to live here because of my job."

"Oh."

"And the gingerbread house was for everyone to enjoy, not just you," Abigail said.

"I'm sorry," he said, pulling a sad face and cutting his eyes to the left—a sign he was sorry he'd been caught, not sorry for what he'd done.

"So if you wanted to eat it, why did you put it in the trash can?"

"It tasted yucky."

"Okay. You will go down and apologize to Chef Dahm for destroying something he spent hours making. And there will be no screen time and no dessert for a week."

"A week? At Christmas?" Mikey protested.

"Argue and it will be two. Mikey, how would you feel if someone destroyed something you'd spent hours building?" Abigail was trying to teach some empathy.

"I would be pretty mad."

Abigail marched him down to the kitchen and found the chef. She took them to a private corner and put her hand on Mikey's back.

"I'm sorry I took your ginger house, sir. I know you worked hard on it." Mikey really was sorry, and it came through in his voice. He was especially sorry about a week of no screen time and no dessert.

"I accept your apology, Mikey," Chef Dahm boomed. He always boomed. "Perhaps next year, you and your sister would like to help make one."

"Yes, sir, that'd be great," Mikey said. Then he spontaneously hugged the chef. Chef Dahm slipped a gingersnap into Mikey's hand. Abigail pretended not to see.

The week without dessert at Christmastime was awful. Especially since everyone else seemed to be enjoying extra servings, and he had not been excused from the table.

Santa would come to the White House, and then they would go to the ranch for a few days.

One night as they were getting ready for bed, Abigail asked Michael about Santa.

"Do you think the kids still believe?"

"Oh, I don't know. I'd say they are in the 'maybe' camp right about now."

Abigail thought about it and came up with a plan.

Mikey certainly was still big on all things having to do with poop. So Abigail met with the chef and concocted a plan. Chef Dahm baked up a large batch of reindeer 'poop,' a mixture of raisins and egg whites, dusted with cinnamon. He baked it to make sure it would hold together.

The kids hedged their bets. They made elaborate lists just in case Santa was real. They talked a lot about which chimney Santa would choose—there were so many. This was just to play along if it was Mom and Dad. They didn't want to hurt their feelings.

On Christmas morning, they looked around the chimneys on their floor, and there was no sign of Santa. There was no sign of him on the floor where Regina and O.T. lived, though of course, their looking awakened them. Finally, on the State Floor in front of the fireplace in the East Room, there were their gifts.

The kids raced to their stash and were thrilled Santa had found them.

"Of course, he did. After all, if he knows whether you've been good or bad, then he easily knows where you are," Abby said, still in her robe and slippers.

"And I'll bet he chose this fireplace as its chimney goes all the way to the ground," Michael added.

Mikey nodded in grave assent. *Pris and James were wrong.*

Regina, however, was not pleased. There were also muddy footprints along the hearth, and at least one tangerine had been dropped in the soot.

"I can't believe Santa would be so messy, and in the White House of all places," she said with consternation. The children ignored her and ripped into their toys. Each got a "forever" ornament, this one a handpainted miniature White House with their name and date on it. Abigail swiftly removed them to safety.

Mikey got a real toy train (O.T.'s idea), and he and O.T. got to work on putting it together. Papa Mikey made sure one station said "County Cork" for Ireland.

Emma got American Girl Dolls. She couldn't make up her mind which one she wanted more, so Santa brought two.

There were smaller gifts as well in their stockings. Michael insisted on Pez dispensers and extra Pez packages, a tradition in his family. Regina added tangerines, as she had done for Abby, Duke, and the late Pris. The ever-practical Abigail added buzzy toothbrushes, as they needed new ones anyway. Papa Mikey added caramels, and Louise put in jacks for Emma and a yo-yo for Mikey.

After playing for a while, Mikey asked, "Hey, I saw Santa ate the cookies and milk, but I wonder if the reindeer ate their carrots."

"I have no idea," Abby said.

They bundled up against the chill, and Mikey skittered to a stop on the South Lawn. There were large piles of reindeer poop about eight feet behind the gnawed carrots.

Regina was apoplectic.

"O.T. can you believe those reindeer did that?" she pointed at the poop piles. "And on the nice clean sidewalks of the White House?"

"Yes, Miss Regina. I heard they did that during the Roosevelt Administration regularly. But I'll have the Chief Usher look into why this wasn't already cleaned up."

Mikey had seen proof with his own eyes. *Pris and James were just teasing them about Santa being your parents.*

By the Second State of the Union address, Abigail was able to report real progress.

"We have ratified the Kyoto Protocol, albeit a decade late, but it is done."

Water usage was down across the nation by 20 percent as people became more aware of their water usage.

"No one is skipping brushing their teeth, they've just stopped leaving the water on while they do it," she quipped. "And Navy showers aren't such a bad idea."

Congress had passed a law overturning restrictive covenants prohibiting line drying of laundry. In the South and West, much laundry dried either in garages or carports.

"No sense paying for heat that is free outside," was Abigail's take on it. "Even the White House hangs out laundry a lot of the time." This, too, had decreased energy consumption by another 4 percent. In the winter, people went back to drying laundry in their basements, if they had one.

Cities and towns were experimenting with ways to decrease petroleum use. One town did a trial where only half the cars could be on the road on any one day depending on whether their license plate had an odd or even number at the end. Exceptions were made for emergencies, obviously, but after initial grousing, people adapted to the situation. Many people went to hybrids and electric cars exempt from the system.

"The real test will be down the road. Will people feel deprived or just fine?"

Another town offered to be the testing site for cars that ran on alternative fuels. The gas stations sold biodiesel, compressed natural gas, or let you charge your electric car. People were happy with their cars and the easy availability of fuels; the "power station" owners felt economically neutral compared with previous gasoline and diesel sales.

Houston, a flat city that regarded air-conditioning as Freon-based life support, did a massive bike lane improvement on conduits to the major thoroughfares and retrofitted various buildings with locker rooms, so people could cycle to work, then shower and dress there. Those participating in the program had a weight loss of about twenty pounds over the first year.

Another city, Denver, adopted the Singaporean approach. Every car had an EZ tag, and there were readers all over the city. You were debited for where you went and when you went there. Go downtown on Monday morning and it might cost you five bucks. Go on Saturday afternoon, and it was free.

The science prizes would contribute, and the winners of the fairs had all found venture capitalists to back them. "Hopefully, energy-efficiency moguls will be our next crop of billionaires," Abby commented in her weekly environmental update briefings.

"I'm also happy to report the Department of Education has offered age-appropriate curricula on financial literacy and energy conservation. Early habits are the hardest to break. Schools can pick and choose which seem to work for them, but we must educate our children to make good choices."

"Each building has an energy conservation officer, and, by shelling out up front for motion sensor lights, buildings are paying for these devices within a year. That's a good investment. Everyone fit enough is taking the stairs for one floor up and two down. Next year, we'll aim for two up and four down."

"During my medical training, our heart surgeons had no time for exercise, so they never used the elevators. They thundered up and down their ten-story building all the time. Not one of them was overweight. Some ended up with bum knees at sixty, but hey, they weren't fat." That quip got a good laugh.

"Whatever all three hundred million of us want, we can have. Just keep coming up with the ideas."

National polls were overwhelmingly positive. The country felt optimistic for the first time in a long time. The money-sucking wars were over, and the wounded and maimed were healing. Without lobbyist interference, Lafayette had passed sound fiscal laws. It would be harder to be a Bernie Madoff, but it would also be harder to get a mortgage for a house you couldn't afford. Credit cards did not flow like cheap beer at a college party.

Now Abigail was telling them they were making progress, albeit slowly, on the environment. She knew she had to keep it fun and positive. Deprivation did not work in weight loss diets, and it would not work in changing the environment. People had to see a purpose and to feel like they were involved in something greater than themselves for environmental changes to work.

CHAPTER TWENTY-FOUR

A WORLD OF TREES

The first midterm elections into Abigail's term were remarkably calm. Campaign reform had tamed the vitriol out of the candidates, and people were coming to Washington to solve problems—not create them by throwing political temper tantrums.

Abigail, as an independent, had no problem working with either party and kept up with her entertaining, even though it cut into time with the children. She still did the goldfish bowl thing, getting everyone in Washington into the White House, as well as their wild cards. The latest newsmaker was always on the list.

She also continued Hill Time but increased it to three hours. Anyone in Congress could request up to an hour of her time, bring who they pleased, and work the problem right then and there. It was incredibly efficient. Good government required goodwill between the Congress and the White House, and nothing generated it more than Hill Time.

One night at dinner, Emma, now seven, brought up the subject of trees.

"Our teacher says that trees are the other half of children," she said. "They take what we breathe out and give it back as clean oxygen." The last word came out "ox-da-gen."

"Yeah, we breathe out carbon 'dinoxide,'" Mikey added, as if it was something evil.

"Our teacher says we need more trees," Emma pronounced as if her father and mother had never heard of such a thing.

"Really?" Michael said, momentarily pausing over his favorite food, Regina's meatloaf. No sushi-grade tuna for this guy, he grew up on meatloaf and loved it.

"So Mikey and I were thinking we could have a lemonade stand or something like that to raise money for trees."

"Yeah, a whole world of trees," Mikey said, his gesture overturning his milk glass. A Navy steward handed him a towel, and Mikey cleaned up his own mess. He did a lot of that, and yet cause and effect still eluded him.

"That would take a lot of lemonade," Michael said. Abby tapped his shin under the table and shot him a look. *They need encouragement.*

"Every tree helps," Michael said. "Lemonade's a good idea. You could put up a stand in the West Wing."

"And another in the East Wing," Abigail added.

"Yeah! Yeah!" the twins began screaming in unison.

Michael figured it would take at least a thousand dollar's worth of staff time to clean up after them.

"I'll match whatever money you raise," Michael said.

"And I will too. Your daddy and I are very proud of you."

The rest of the meal was all about their plans.

Heading for bed that night, Abigail was rubbing some sort of lotion into her hands and arms. Michael adored watching her ritual, knowing she would offer him the hairbrush. He often brushed her hair at night, and it was a bond as surely as their lovemaking was. After seven years of marriage, he loved her even more than the day they wed.

He was pleased to take some of the burden for her. Visitors were sometimes happy to have him as a stand-in at photo shoots. And Uncle Mikey's vision was failing a bit, so Michael took up his job handing Abigail a daily file with oddments from the various newspapers and magazines.

Mikey and Emma told their teacher about their plans. Soon lemonade stands to buy trees was a class project. The class worked on signs and recipes and learned the basics of budgeting and marketing. They even learned about hygiene when handling food.

Mikey asked everyone who left the bathroom, "Did you wash your hands? We can't have poop in the lemonade."

Abby hoped that at seven, he'd get off the poop kick. She dared not introduce him to a visiting dignitary, lest Mikey ask about his bowel habits.

They put up two stands: one in the Roosevelt Room and one in the East Wing break room. The kids stayed after school for an hour to work each stand.

They charged fifty cents per glass with one free refill.

When the class hit up Wicker to buy a glass of lemonade in the Roosevelt Room, he had a great idea.

He pitched it to Abby, and she agreed.

"A World of Trees" was created.

Michael called Nickelodeon and the Disney Channel to find someone to run with the idea as an independent foundation. They took the lead and other child-oriented businesses pitched in to match funds.

Schoolchildren in the U.S. held bake sales, hosted pancake breakfasts, washed cars, and put on watermelon suppers to raise money for A World of Trees. Nickelodeon and the Disney Channel appreciated their partners. Going it alone would have been financial suicide.

Just to punk Michael and Abigail, staffers began giving the kids more than their asking price.

"Sorry, all I've got is a five," they said. "Keep the rest for your tree fund."

When the kids presented their "bill" to be matched, Michael and Abby nearly fainted. Abby did some quick calculations and realized the staff had gotten them good. Both parents wrote their checks, but told the children they could only accept the fifty cents a glass.

"You need to learn how to make change," Michael told them.

At least when school was out for the Christmas holidays, the stand would disappear for a while.

With a new Congress sworn in, Abigail was getting to work on paying down the national debt. Forty years was probably too optimistic, sixty was probably doable, and Abigail held a number of meetings with the pertinent players about how to accomplish this.

The plan they came up with was a simple one. There would be a surtax on payroll deductions. Ten percent above the payroll tax would go straight to principal reduction. If the taxpayer got a refund, fine, but he or she could not get back the surtax.

Amazingly, people did not balk. They knew it had to be done. They were spending less money on energy because of voluntary conservation, and this would be a wash in their home budgets. Abigail was flabbergasted when it passed both Houses intact and signed the bill as soon as it hit her desk.

Wicker said, "The President is so thrilled, she's thrown in an extra 10 percent of her payroll deduction."

No sooner did he say that, than most of the wealthy individuals in the country began writing checks to the National Debt Fund. Maybe forty years wasn't impossible after all.

Abigail had the actuaries run very sophisticated numbers on death taxes. She felt the money had been taxed once, during the person's lifetime, and should not be taxed again upon his or her death. She did not want to appear self-dealing in repealing the Inheritance Taxes. She realized she had not earned her money, but inherited it—after estate taxes were paid. So she sent a bill to Congress that had a two-tier approach.

If someone earned the money and paid income taxes on it, at death it passed untaxed.

For the next generations, if the inheritance money appreciated, it was taxed at death at 15 percent, the capital gains tax.

"This way people will feel they can excel, can build wealth, without having the Grim Tax Reaper come in and snatch it away. Family farms can stay intact; family businesses can stay intact. But people who haven't worked for the money will have to share a little of their good fortune with the rest of us."

The bill passed unanimously.

Its unintended consequence was a huge outflow into charities, including the one that would help their great-grandchildren the most. "I'd rather give it to the National Debt Fund than to the IRS."

By the end of the school year, A World of Trees reported there was enough money in the fund to reforest burned areas in the U.S. While wild fires do have an ecological purpose, some areas near populated areas needed replanting to prevent devastating mudslides that would damage intact homes and expensive infrastructure. A World of Trees also began reforestation of Haiti, with a lot left over to start on the Amazon.

The charity went global. When Emma and Mikey announced they wanted donations instead of birthday presents, mothers everywhere rejoiced.

A World of Trees began offering nature-themed unisex hand-crafted items, all made in third world countries from fallen wood. Busy moms went online, bought the birthday child credits, printed off a cute card to give at the party, and were finished.

The children spent their credits as they pleased. The charms were the "in" thing for school-age children, and Abigail was thrilled to know the following generation was on board to save the planet. The variety of charms was endless, from beads for bracelets, necklaces and hair ornaments, there were sets of animal charms the kids could collect and trade. As demand grew, wooden jewelry and handcrafted maps of various countries appeared.

She was even more thrilled to get kids away from the culture of acquiring crap toys that would be debris in two days. Getting money directly to people in need of work made for a three-way win.

For the Fourth of July fireworks, Abigail remembered her first Fourth of July at the White House. She had goose bumps that she was able to give her children a front-row seat to the best of America.

She could swear she saw her sister in the crowd on the roof of the White House. But she blinked, and Pris was gone. But there was her voice as clear as ever, not reassuring her, but teasing her.

"Now do you see why I wanted all of this for you?"

CHAPTER TWENTY-FIVE

HOMECOMING

Abby went to the ranch after the Fourth of July, but she worked most of the time she was there. What was important was family tradition. The kids were big enough to work roundup, tag calves, worm them, and the like. Emma had taken a shine to ranch work, which surprised her parents. She was up at dawn and often the last one to hit the showers. To make hair care easier, she asked Regina to do cornrows of her long curly blonde hair, and Abigail delighted seeing her daughter's bouncing braids as she worked around the ranch. Abby disciplined herself to stop work at dinner, so she and Michael could have some downtime with the family. They played cards or did puzzles, but the kids could bathe themselves without supervision. There were no electronic gadgets for the kids to focus on at the ranch. Ranch time was all about life.

The White House had displayed only balled, living Christmas trees on their first Christmas there. Afterward, the trees were planted on the property. Abigail still had to fend off the SWAT team in panty hose. The head of the Executive Committee actually stopped Abigail on her way to the West Wing and demanded some of her time.

"Madam President, last year's decorations looked positively shabby," the old biddy said.

"They were elegantly simple," Abigail said.

The woman tried to press her point again, this time putting a restraining arm onto Abigail's. That was a true breach of protocol, and the woman knew it: no one touches the President unless she reaches out first. Abigail picked up the woman's hand with two of her manicured fingers and removed it as if it were an offensive insect.

"Do you have any idea how destructive my children can be? They all but maimed their kidnappers. If I were you, I'd keep things very simple until they are long gone. Now if you will excuse me. You are making me late," Abigail said. "I will not be countermanded by a volunteer. Do I make myself clear?"

The woman did not like this six-year term idea at all. It would be years before she could implement her grandest design of all: Christmas Around the World. She'd wanted so much to do a Hawaiian Christmas in the Blue Room.

By year three, the sales of cut trees dropped enormously, and balled trees were the new norm. Soon people were decorating not just evergreens, but whatever kind of tree they wanted for their yards, even if the limbs were bare. If they didn't have a yard, their city would plant it in a park in their name.

There was a vacancy on the Supreme Court, and Samuel Sternberg finally got what he'd always wanted. Abby wanted to appoint Duke to the federal bench, but decided that would be nepotism. Maybe the next President could do that. Duke was a splendid U.S. Attorney and had made a name for himself in overseeing the federal elections. He was batting a thousand where violators were concerned.

Papa Mikey got older and slower physically but mentally stayed just as sharp. He came in daily until there was a small fire at his house. Then Abigail asked him and his man to stay at the White House. The valet made small protesting noises about moving in with his niece, but he was thrilled to go from Windsor to a private home to the White House. At least they were civilized enough to live on the same floor with Regina and O.T. Abigail could keep a closer eye on them, anyway.

Poppy ran Abigail's presidency with the same iron fist in the chain mail glove as she had done before. Actually, it was easier this time, as Logan decided to "stay home" with James, who, of course, was schooled at the White House.

"That means you got some time to help out around here, bud," Poppy said to him and assigned him a desk not far from hers. Abigail gave up and put him on the payroll half time. He could work until James was out of school. Abby sincerely tried to get Poppy home for supper at least four nights out of five.

CHAPTER TWENTY-SIX

HITTING THE GLIDE PATH

By the fifth State of the Union speech, Abigail felt she had some solid progress in motion. When she walked into the now-familiar House chamber, she could look around and see a nation of consensus for the first time in a long time. She still felt mauled by the aisle hogs that all but pummeled her on her way down. She looked up and saw her family. The kids were safely separated by Michael and bookended by Regina and O.T.

When the applause died down, Abigail felt the need to give them the good news first.

"Saving the planet seems to be growing our economic pie. The GDP is up 3.5 percent. We're doing something right. Just as the personal computer changed forever how we do business and allowed for the growth of new industries, saving the planet is growing new businesses at a good clip. It's always better to grow the pie than to bicker over who gets which piece.

"Early on, we sponsored a few 'science fairs' with socko prizes. The venture capitalists came to them, and ideas are now in the marketplace.

"Solar panels now come as roof shingles and are now installed on high-end houses. Soon they'll be affordable for regular houses. While the homeowner is at work, the house will sell its power to the grid.

When the homeowner comes home, he'll essentially use his appliances for free.

"Soon schools, libraries, and municipal buildings will be partially self-powered on sunny days. On rainy days, they buy power from the grid, and on sunny weekends, they sell power to it.

"Schools are not only leading the charge in the environment, they are teaching age-appropriate financial literacy skills. When a kid graduates from high school, they'll know the difference on the interest on a certificate of deposit versus the interest on a credit card. They will not go into the financial marketplace as fresh meat. We have also stopped many of the predatory lending processes. Without lobbyists shelling out money by the boatload, common sense has returned inside the Beltway.

"One skyscraper is going up with a solar-generating film as its 'skin' and if it works, the innovator with that patent will be a zillionaire.

"Another guy has patented a programmable breaker box, complete with a remote. This thing is selling like cold beer on a hot day. You tell it when to turn off which breakers. At bedtime, everything shuts down except air-conditioning, refrigerators, house alarms, and nightlights. Before you wake up in the morning, it turns everything back on. If you go away, your house's energy consumption can drop to near zero. As will your utility bills. I can't figure out how he resets the clocks and gets the coffee brewed in the morning, but man, it's a great idea.

"Zip vehicles of all sizes have made huge inroads in densely populated areas. People have figured out car "user-ship" is more economical than car ownership. If you need an SUV to bring stuff home, you rent one for a couple of hours—you don't have to buy it.

"More cities are using the microvans, buses, and microvans concept with a consequent reduction in gasoline usage in those cities by nearly 50 percent. With Wi-Fi on them, enrollment in online classes has doubled, giving workers more job flexibility.

"The federal government was asked by no fewer than 1,125 municipal entities to standardize recycling categories. So we've not only standardized what is recycled, we've designed a recycling tower for the home that includes all the standard recycle categories in a two foot square footprint. There's even a space for hearing aid batteries. They'll be available at nominal cost from your city or town starting next week.

"One of the more exciting concepts, at least if you have an animal, is urban composting. Animal waste is natural fertilizer, but has parasites in it. One company has successfully piloted a program in Charlotte, North Carolina, where you just dump animal waste, bag and all, into a receptacle not unlike a mailbox. Bacteria in the box eat the bag, and enzymes destroy the parasites. Then the company packages it and uses it as fertilizer. A portion is given to the city to use in parks, the rest is sold to consumers. The trick is there is no odor around the receptacle.

"Knowing some people's propensity for vandalism, especially where poop is concerned, the containers are federal property and tampering with one is a federal offense, just like messing with a mailbox."

She got a big laugh at this line. To her credit, she did not look at Mikey.

"Tidal power, wind power, algae power, and solar power all are growing and producing energy for the grid. One gym even made its machines into dynamos that generated electric power to offset their power bills.

"One of my favorites is a kiosk in malls that lets kids bounce on trampolines to recharge their battery-powered toys. The parents love having their kids in a mesh cage, blowing off steam while they shop. And by federal law, all toy batteries must be rechargeable. The toys might break, but the batteries won't.

"Ultralight push mowers have replaced most home lawnmowers, and gasoline-powered leaf blowers have given way to silent solar-powered ones. No one needs to give up his chainsaw, though. I think those are covered by the Second Amendment."

That got a hearty laugh.

"As far as home lawns are concerned, they pose a unique environmental challenge. Texas A&M has patented SuperGrass that thrives in a wide range of horticultural zones and requires no mowing. It's only good for about 70 percent of lawns, but that's better than nothing.

"In the West, where drought has led to vicious cycles of fires, we have started a pilot program that takes rising sea water, desalinates it through reverse osmosis, and pumps it into aquifer recharge zones. While this is an expensive program, we have to start somewhere.

"One man has a patent on water-absorbing concrete for road surfaces, driveways, sidewalks, and patios. This will help prevent flooding, as streets won't fill up with water as fast. If you live in a low-lying area, this is crucial to preventing property damage.

"We have also changed the insane law that made the federal government the reinsurer for properties built on barrier islands. Your flood insurance will pay you once. After that, you are on your own. And by federal law, all beaches beyond the vegetation line, if they do not belong to the state, now belong to the nation. If the vegetation line changes, you can lose your home or business. This is our way of saying 'stop building on barrier islands.' They have an important ecological purpose—and your beach house isn't it.

"We've learned a lot. First, we are all in this together. Second, there isn't one solution—there are thousands. Third, developing technology to save the planet grows the economy.

"We are getting closer to fixing the environment, but we are not there yet. We don't feel a sense of deprivation about our efforts; we feel a sense of anticipation about what comes next. This is a victory in and of itself. A few years ago, no one even had hope.

"We have more to do. Each of us independently and all of us collectively must act. I hope you will stay on board. Keep coming up with new ideas, and keep sending them into the website.

"We are part of a global village, and I am happy to report that our fellow villagers have the same sense of urgency that we do. Finally, everyone on the planet knows the little blue ball is in peril. We have taken the first steps on the journey, but we still have a lot to do.

"We have to fall out of love with the internal combustion engine, once and for all, without impairing our ability to move people and things. That's still a huge stumbling block, but we will overcome it.

"Thank you and good night."

Abby had more in her speech, but decided to wrap it up there. Why? If her kids were fidgeting, which they were, so were most of the adults watching at home.

The other part of the speech was the downer part anyway: raising gasoline taxes and some techno speak about the need for negative population growth. The Chinese had a one-child law. They didn't need persuasion.

India was trying mightily to control population growth, and indeed birth rates had plummeted in the last several decades. However, with such a huge population base, they were trying to do even more, especially as the poverty of their people was so severe.

Europe's population was rising, due in part to immigrant groups with high birthrates. France would be a Muslim country by 2050 unless they could persuade immigrants to have fewer babies. They'd given up and imposed a stiff fine for anyone having a third child. The fine for a fourth child was even higher. France's population changed not at all from 1900 to 1950 because men of reproductive age were wiped out by two wars. In the decades since, the population had exploded with immigrant children. They, too, had adopted infant education classes, in part to integrate Muslims into mainline French culture.

Holland had immigrants, but to become a Dutch citizen you had to pass rigorous Dutch culture and language classes. This was too much effort for many would-be immigrants with a marginal interest in the

Netherlands, but the classes assisted assimilation by committed individuals into their new community. If you can't be Dutch, you can't live in Holland. It might seem harsh, but after the murder of Theo van Gogh, descendant of Vincent van Gogh, that country became less tolerant.

The Arab world was changing rapidly in many ways. They realized extremism would get them nowhere in the global village, even if the terrorists threatened the stability of royal families. Al Jazeera, by giving both sides of the story, was creating a demand for facts, not propaganda. The Internet, too, was opening their eyes. A real education, not one memorizing the Qur'an, would be required if they wanted to manage their resources well. The Qur'an is a great religious text but a lousy engineering text.

North America was energy independent and had no need for the Middle East. The Great Satan was no longer the Great Sugar Daddy of the Middle East.

They'd have to do it the old-fashioned way. The sheikhs insisted their children get properly educated and then work for the money previously squandered on them. They paid top salaries to teachers—whether kindergarten or PhD advisors—and within a generation they could solve their own problems. Gone were the days when Arabs outsourced work to Westerners if it involved brainpower—and to third world immigrants if it didn't.

The Arab street also figured out two children would be adequate. They, too, were getting the message about global warming. Petroleum might be their lifeline, but it could be their death knell also. Their governments were looking beyond petrodollars. Strategic planning for a changing economy was spreading everywhere.

Abigail's nemesis on population was the Pope. He had huge influence on population growth in South America. *Now, there was a tough nut to crack.*

In environmental terms, his intransigence was environmental suicide. If he would get on board with zero population growth, it would be a huge coup for Abby.

She brainstormed with Catholic leaders in the U.S., where parishioners, or what was left of them, felt free to ignore the Church's stand on anything they liked. After all, the church had betrayed their trust with tolerating pedophile priests, and before that, it had encouraged women to stay with battering husbands.

"Ma'am, with all due respect, we've been trying to get His Holiness to change his mind for twenty years," one Cardinal told her in the Oval Office.

"Have you told him he might kill us all?"

"Not in so many words, no."

"Okay, then, Cardinal, you're deputized to speak for me. Get the message to him. If he ignores me, tell him he does so at his peril. I appreciate the solar panels at the Vatican, but population is a problem he should address."

The man blanched.

"I'm not sure he'll take my call," he said.

"He should if you tell him you are calling at my request. That is only simple courtesy. You are carrying an urgent message from the President of the United States for His Holiness."

Abigail waited two weeks before she called the Cardinal.

"What did His Holiness say?"

"He did not take my call. I called three times using your name."

"Thank you so much."

That night as they were getting ready for bed, she told Michael about the situation with the Pope.

"I don't know what to do," she said, as she creamed her face and slathered lotion on her arms.

"You'd best think fast. We're supposed to meet with him when we go to Europe next month."

"Can you help distract me from problems with the Pope?" she asked, slipping a nightgown strap off her shoulder.

"Maybe," he said, kissing that shoulder.

Abby decided she had nothing to lose. She wasn't running for any office. She walked into the Press Room the next day at the one-thirty briefing, as she'd done a lot of times. As usual, she was in her highest heels. At least these didn't hurt, because they weren't too small.

All popped to their feet.

"Have a seat. As you know, I am going to Europe next month and have decided not to make my planned visit to His Holiness, the Pope. Saving the planet is a moral issue, and if he wants to be a moral leader, he cannot escort us to the brink of extinction by opposing population planning. As far as I'm concerned, whoever encourages people to grow the planet's population is exhorting us toward planetary suicide and committing a crime against humanity."

Then she turned on her heel and left.

Wicker was in the Oval Office instantly.

"What in the *hell* was *that?*" he said putting his head in his hands and then raising his face toward the heavens.

"I just thought I'd put the ball in play and see what people do with it. I'm outta here after my term is over."

"But you accused the Pope, of all people, of a crime against humanity," Wicker wailed. "I'm too old for this."

"So? I dare him—I double-dog dare him—to defend planetary suicide. And you can quote me on that."

Wicker knew better than to do so. He had his hands full with what she did say.

As usual, Abigail lobbed her grenade then stepped back to watch the fireworks. The world press lit up at this one. Wicker, as usual, was instructed to show her only the editorials that disagreed with her. All were from Catholic newspapers and all sidestepped the issue of population control, concentrating only on Abigail's "disrespect" for His Holiness. Nowhere did they say she was wrong. A couple got huffy about her lack of support for organized religion, but Abigail was no fool. She knew the evangelicals of all stripes were strongly in favor of saving the environment.

The Pope had no public comment. Abigail thought that highly unusual. She must have really ticked him off.

Michael just shook his head. She still could surprise even him.

HEAVY IS THE HEAD

She and Michael had a lovely, busy trip to Europe. The Queen welcomed them again to England, this time to Buckingham Palace. Abigail was charmed by the contradictions it posed.

The windows opened—but lacked screens. Not a speck of dust was anywhere in the vast building, even in the midst of downtown London. It was stuffed with priceless art, but the beds were lumpy and old. The light bulb on their bedside table was forty watts, not even enough to read by. The "backyard," thirty acres of downtown London, was remarkably quiet.

The children's whole class accompanied the President, but they stayed at the American Embassy. The Queen did invite the class for a small garden party with the royal children that were their ages.

"I do know to keep children outdoors," Her Majesty said. "Mine were downright hellions. They once took straws and dried peas into some ceremony or other and damned near blinded half the peerage."

"Oh, please, don't tell our kids that story," Abigail begged. "They need no help at all."

Emma came running up and waited for a pause in the conversation.

"Mrs. Queen, is it true you wear a crown sometimes?" Emma asked.

"You address the Queen as 'Your Majesty,' Emma," Abigail said.

"Mrs. Your Majesty, do you really have crowns?" Emma asked. The Queen chuckled.

"Yes, I do. In fact, I am wearing one tomorrow. Would you and your friends like to see it?"

"Yes, ma'am." Emma ran off and summoned the children.

"Follow me and hold hands. This is a look-but-don't-touch house," the Queen said. Abigail was quaking in her shoes. She gave the American kids The Look, and they were suddenly sedate.

They went into the Palace and were soon in the Queen's private quarters. Abigail noticed an old clock radio, vintage 1950 on her bedside table. The plastic had yellowed it was so old. The table, however, was probably worth a fortune. Abigail prayed Mikey wouldn't fake needing a trip to the bathroom. He was still very interested in anything related to human waste and was fascinated by toilets in different countries.

"The Crowns stay in the Tower, but tomorrow I have to wear this one when I open Parliament." The Queen produced the Imperial State Crown from its red leather case. The children were openmouthed. The sides of the box flipped down, like a magician's box.

"When my great-great-grandfather wore it, this cross fell off in the street," she said. The children laughed. "Luckily someone picked it up and returned it. Would anyone like to try it on? I'll hold it, as it is very heavy."

Her Majesty then put the crown on all the American children, holding the weight off their little necks. Abigail, with Her Majesty's permission, snapped pictures of all the kids.

"Now, would you like to try it?" she asked Abigail.

Abby couldn't help herself. *Protocol be damned.* The Queen put it on Abigail, and Abby could barely hold it up. Her Majesty snapped a picture of Abby.

"Heavy is the head…" Her Majesty said.

"In more ways than one," Abigail said.

Then Her Majesty offered it to her own great-grandchildren, who had all tried it on before.

"Thanks, but we'd love to go back outside for more lemon creams," they said without even whining. How remarkable.

That night, they attended a State Dinner, again at Windsor. Abigail met Mohammed al Ozedin, a Peace Prize winner and a British subject. Egyptian by birth, he was a nuclear physicist. He'd won the Peace Prize for his work on the IAEA, the arm of the UN that deals with nuclear regulation. In the nuclear world, he was known simply as The Wizard of Oz.

Soon the two were chatting away about Abigail's idea for cookie-cutter nuclear plants in third-world countries.

"That's easy enough to do," he said, with a shrug.

"But…?" Abigail knew there had to be a "but." "When the Chinese raised it, it went nowhere in my first administration."

"The problem is engineering. We must make them stand up to double the worst that Mother Nature is inflicting, and here's the expensive part, replace them with new technology every thirty years."

"Why's that?"

"They're like hospitals. After thirty years, you need to tear them down. A hospital is full of germs, and a nuclear reactor is out of date."

"Do you think we could get the world to sign on, especially after Fukishima?" Abigail said.

"What choice do we have? Oil will kill us, coal will kill us faster, and the sun only shines half the day."

"What about nuclear waste?"

"Ah, that's where the French are smart. You know they are all nuclear, right?"

"Yes."

"They 'restock it' and use it 'later' when technology permits. The amount of waste is minuscule. Their PR is fantastic."

"So if we did the cookie-cutter thing in third world countries, where would you 'restock' it for later use?"

"Oh, probably on some remote uninhabited island where it would be safeguarded."

"Like Diego Garcia?"

"You read my mind."

"How do we get around the expense of putting in a grid in the country?" Abby asked.

"Offer them the engineering. Have them provide the labor. That's the most expensive part."

When Abigail got home, she called in the U.S. Ambassador to the UN and asked him what he thought.

"The biggest problem the UN is dealing with right now is parking tickets," he said. "The members hide behind diplomatic immunity and tie up Manhattan traffic by parking wherever they like. The only way it could be worse was if they rode donkeys and parked them wherever they wanted—claiming the donkey poop had diplomatic immunity." *Mikey may not give up on poop. This guy hadn't.*

"Okay. If I work on that, will you work on the nuclear thing?"

"If you can fix that, you're the Wizard, not Oz."

"I've got it. Tell the member nations that the U.S. will veto putting any nuclear plant in any country that breaks New York City's parking laws."

"I'd kiss you, but you're married," he said. For the first time in a long time, the man smiled.

Abigail could see the light at the end of her Presidency's tunnel, and it did not appear to be an oncoming train. The debt was getting paid down, the budget was balanced, and there was excellent progress on the environment. The biggest stumbling block was still population, but Abigail secretly knew that Mother Nature was going to take out chunks of people every time she could. If the Pope would get on board, it would be an enormous help.

There was even progress in the Middle East. The Peace Because initiative was handing out money right and left and people began to talk in terms of "when peace comes," not "if peace comes."

Abby stayed well away from it, though, dropping out as soon as she announced her candidacy for President. She felt that when the time was right, governments would get out of the way and let people have the peace they wanted.

Layla sent her articles that tore at her heart.

"I want peace because I am Jewish, and my best friend is Palestinian. We are like brothers. I beat him at chess half the time; he beats me the other half. At least until yesterday when he was killed by a stray bullet fired by an Israeli army member. The soldier said he was trying to break up a gang of kids throwing rocks. He said he fired into the air. I don't care what he says, because my friend is gone, and I will never have another as good as he was."

"I want peace, because I have lost my last child. I had two miscarriages, which I still mourn. Then I had three healthy children. A suicide bomber killed one when she was three. The next died when he was five—another suicide bomber. The third and last died yesterday of a ruptured appendix. There was no one to operate on him in Gaza. I am fifty and too old to have more. I just want peace so I can grieve without worrying my nieces or nephews will die also. Isn't it enough to have taken all of my children? Can't we please stop killing children? We have no future without them."

Abby read these and wept.

But she had to stand her ground. When the Israeli and Palestinian people demand their leaders make peace, it will happen. And until they both want peace at the same time, it could never come.

ROMEO AND JULIET

The girl threw the Frisbee with the wobbly skill of an overachieving novice. It flew high and wide then plummeted toward the ground. She covered her mouth and laughed at her erratic attempt. The boy would not lose face by missing the catch. He leapt sideways and snagged it but fell into the muddy grass, holding his trophy aloft.

The girl wanted to make sure he had not hurt himself—but held back. He was up in a second, his shirt was covered with mud, and his face sported a muddy half-sided grin. He couldn't be hurt. Besides, her father would not approve of her touching any male, much less a Jewish one. Where she lived in the H1 zone of Hebron, Jews were rare. Here, every other person was one. At least the other half was Palestinian/Muslim like she was.

The journey to Peace Camp had been an adventure in itself.

Everything was new to all the teenagers at the camp in the Maine woods. Even cool forests were new to them. Hana, at sixteen, was used to the hot hubbub of her city, and the replacement of that with calls of the loons on the lake was eerie. But she'd only been there two days, not even time to get over the jet lag, really. She had another nineteen days before she went home, and she was in no rush to leave.

The boy with the muddy shirt was an Israeli named Ari. They were just two of the thirty campers enjoying three weeks of peace—that rarest of things between their cultures.

The Institute for World Peace sponsored this camp every year, and the counselors were all graduates who had returned while in college. To participate, an applicant had to display leadership skills (not a problem for Hana who made top marks in school), speak the rudiments of a common language (either Hebrew or English), and have parental permission. The Institute paid for all expenses.

Hana, the younger of two daughters, was the smartest in her family and wanted to become a doctor. Her mother understood Hana's gift and her need to step beyond the boundaries her mother had endured. Abra had miscarried three times, all boys, and was surprised her husband had not taken a second wife. He might have, but their house was very small.

Her father, well, he was her father, and he expected her to be a good Muslim girl and marry a man of his choosing. A career was not normal in his mind. Perhaps he'd been better when he was a young man, but life had hardened him into a fundamentalist. Hana's role was to submit to Allah's will, her father's will, and then to her husband's will.

Luckily, between his religious activities and owning a string of struggling repair shops for anything with a small engine, he was often out of the house. And when he was home, he preferred the company of his friends, all male. Hana, her sister Farah, or her mother, Abra, waited on the men, usually leaving the other two females virtually invisible to the men. Always covered in the presence of the men, they never really knew who was waiting on them if the women were quiet.

Right now, he thought Hana was visiting her maternal aunt who had just had twins. If he found out about the conspiracy of lies, only Allah knew what he would do. Thanks be to Allah, her aunt lived in an area where cell coverage was poor. Hana's mother took a terrible risk in sending her to this camp, but she believed Hana needed to flower—something neither she nor any of the women before her enjoyed.

She routinely used what anonymity was available to her to protect her daughters against the brutalities of Islam. She believed more in her own experience than she did in what any man in power told her. She would not allow her daughters to be mutilated as she had been. In memory of her younger sister who had died after she'd been cut on with a dirty knife, she would never allow anyone to touch her daughters.

When time came for ritual female circumcision, Abra took them to her sister's farm where the two women told the girls what it was that they were being spared. The girls were horrified and grateful. The women gave the girls laxatives for several days so they would look sick when they got home.

"Better to have diarrhea, my beauties, much better," her mother said when they protested at yet another dose of laxative. "One day, you will thank your aunt and me for doing this."

Hana would not disappoint her mother, who risked everything to make a better life for Hana and her older sister, Farah. Farah wanted to be a hairdresser, and as a result, last night was the first night she could ever remember when her sister did not brush her thick, wavy, dark hair before bed.

There were eighteen girls in her cabin, including the three counselors. Half were Jewish, and half were Palestinian. No one cared if she wore the headscarf, so she chose not to—just to see what it felt like. Some of the girls did, some didn't. Modesty was not a problem, as it was still chilly, though hot weather was expected. She didn't know how much of her body she felt comfortable exposing to boys, but she did like having a choice. At home, even when it was sweltering, she had to be fully covered including her face. Now *that* was hot.

She'd sat next to Esther on the flight over, a blonde, blue-eyed Jewish girl from Tel Aviv who also wanted to study medicine, but she wanted to be a vet.

"I want to work on large animals, and to do so, I have to live in the country," she said with a twinkle in her eye. "That means I can move out of Tel Aviv where my father is a rabbi. Trust me, you do not want to be a rabbi's daughter."

"Why is that?" Hana asked, taking a swig from her water bottle.

"Everyone watches you and tells your mother if you are not being devout enough," Esther said. "I swear I'd be better behaved if he were a shoemaker. I started smoking just to annoy him."

"Did you really?" Hana could not imagine smoking. She hated the smell of her father's cigarettes.

"Yes, but I don't like it. I only do it around women from the temple," Esther said. The girls dissolved into laughter.

They decided to be bunkmates, and the only bad thing Hana had noticed about Esther was that she snored very, very softly.

Ari noticed the pretty girl who threw the Frisbee and, at dinner that night, made it a point to introduce himself. He was pretty sure of himself where girls were concerned—especially considering he had three sisters and no brothers—but he'd never dated a Palestinian. *Oh, well, there's a first time for everything.*

"I'm Ari," he said, offering his hand to shake. He could do that, as he was not Orthodox. "And you are the girl who made me eat dirt this afternoon. Do you have a name? Or shall I call you Miss Frisbee?"

Hana did not know what to do. She had never touched a boy who was not her brother or cousin. But this was about peace, so she shook his hand. Both of them had clammy palms.

"I'm Hana. Hana El-Hibri."

"I'm Ari Mandelbaum. So where are you from, Miss El-Hibri?" he said with his all-but-patented half smile he reserved for girls. It highlighted the dimple in that cheek.

"Hebron. And you, where are you from, Ari?" Hana asked with a small smile.

"Me too," he replied. "H2, of course, and you?"

"H1."

Already the battle lines were drawn. Hebron has two sections. H1 is all Palestinians; H2, overwhelmingly Palestinian, has a few Jews living in relative luxury there. But they were here to find a way get along, not to prolong the divisiveness in their own city.

There was an awkward pause.

"But I doubt there is Frisbee in either section," Hana said. "My toss was terrible. I was afraid you had hurt yourself."

"Only my pride. My bunk mates called me 'The Dirt Eater' all afternoon."

Hana's laugh was musical. She blushed, then shyly covered her face. At that moment, Ari was instantly smitten. He knew so few girls who were at all shy or reserved. And when she blushed, he would have thrown himself at her feet, but there were people around.

They could have passed for siblings with their dark, wavy hair and black-brown eyes. She was petite, coming only to about the middle of his chest, while he was a strapping young man pushing two meters tall. Each was at a loss for more words.

"It is nice to meet you, Ari," Hana said. "I have to go now."

She turned and walked away. She did not want to be with him more, because she was afraid of her feelings. She hoped no one noticed that he made her blush. She could feel him looking at her as she moved toward her cabin.

He came running after her just as she was headed toward the yellow light on the porch of her cabin.

"Hana. Wait," he said. He had to think of something else to say. He couldn't say what was in his heart.

"Tomorrow morning, we all have to have a partner for our leadership exercises. Will you be mine?" he asked, slightly out of breath.

"Me? I am so small. Wouldn't you like a stronger partner?"

"You'll do just fine. I'm certain I want you," he said.

"Very well, I suppose I can use someone bigger and stronger," she teased him. "Just don't expect me to carry you anywhere."

"I won't," he said. Then he turned and jogged back to the main clubhouse. *Yes, she likes me.*

It rapidly became apparent to everyone in the camp that they were a pair. At the teamwork exercises the next morning, she easily fell backwards into his arms. He hesitated, lest he knock them both down, but she planted her feet and took his full weight with a stagger and grunt. In the obstacle climb, they worked in tandem—she doing the things that required fine motor skills and precision, he working on things that required strength. Within a day, they were virtually inseparable.

The camp counselors were used to the puppy love they saw every year, but usually after a week or so, each one of the couple moved on to someone else. Not Ari and Hana. Nor did they stray out of sight, one of the camp prohibitions. Heaven forbid someone should go home pregnant. That would be the end of Peace Camp. If caught out of bounds, they'd be sent home, but each was content simply to be together, whether it was while mastering knots (Hana learned to tie the fastest bowline in history) or charting a hiking trail (Ari's height was a big advantage there), they calmly excelled as a team. As the teams of two coalesced into larger teams, they remained the default co-leaders of their group, the self-named Maniacs. The other team called themselves the Wickeds. In Maine, something very good is deemed, "wicked."

They talked about their families, their friends, their dreams for the future. Hana was shocked that Ari supported her desire to be a doctor.

"Why shouldn't girls do as they please?" he asked, fumbling with a half hitch. "It is your life after all."

"But my father wants me to marry a man of his choosing and make a home," Hana said, studying the next knot in the booklet. Knot tying would be important if she were a doctor.

"Fine, then let your father marry him," he retorted. He would do almost anything to make her laugh. Once he stood on his head. Another time he threatened to eat a worm if she didn't laugh. He dangled the earthworm over his mouth, until she could stand it no longer and erupted into giggles.

"Ah," he said, putting the worm down. "Hana has saved you from being eaten by a giant."

If Ari was at all frustrated by the lack of physical contact, he did not show it. As a Muslim girl, Hana was probably not only a virgin but had likely never even been kissed. In his group of friends in Israel, almost everyone had ditched their virginity long ago, but he understood that this was not an option for Hana. He would not push her, even though he could tell that she desired him.

For her part, Hana was aware of feelings she had never felt before. Sometimes she had a dampness in her underwear that wasn't her monthly. It only appeared when she was around Ari. She swore Esther to secrecy and whispered her question one night after lights out.

"What is happening, Esther? No one has told me," Hana said, picking her way painfully through the question.

"Hana, dear Hana, it is your body's way of saying you want sex," Esther said.

"Oh, but I don't," Hana hissed. "I'm Muslim. I shall be a virgin on the day I marry."

"Your brain might not want sex, but your body is wanting it. It is very normal. Now go to sleep, I want to dream that I'm the one wanting sex," Esther said.

Hana still did not know what her mother had spared her by not cutting her, but when she thought of Ari, at least she knew what desire was. And she liked the feeling very much indeed.

As camp neared its end, everyone was amazed at how they'd grown—not only in the feats they could accomplish but also in their ability to operate as a team. To take everyone's input into making a decision and implementing it, and almost seamlessly, was something new to these teens.

One of the most instructive sessions was one where each team designed and built something from scavenged twigs and bits found out in nature. Ari and Hana's team built an Eiffel Tower about three feet high. The other team made a model of a Native American hut, about the same scale as the Eiffel Tower. It was shaped roughly like an Airstream trailer. Built from twigs and interlaced with pieces of found bark, their structure had a hole in the top to let out the smoke from a fire as well as the benches around the sides where people slept.

When each presented their pieces, the pride showed on all their faces. Someone from each team presented a brief talk on the project. After all, each team had spent the better part of a week designing and making their creations. As the counselors handed out the envelopes, each side hoped for a first prize.

Instead, inside was an instruction to destroy the other side's creation, then using pictures of the object—rebuild it.

"Wait," Hana said. "Why should we destroy something our friends built?"

"You are going back to the Middle East where destruction is a daily occurrence," the counselor said. "You must learn to keep rebuilding."

"No," Ari said, looking around at his team. All were shaking their heads "no."

"Anyone can destroy something," the leader of the other side said. "Destruction is easy, building is hard. We will not do it, either."

"But this is just a game to show you how easy it is to destroy, and how hard it is to rebuild," the counselors said, knowing full well these kids weren't about to destroy anything. "If you do not do it, you cannot win the award as best team."

"I want no part of best team, if that is the price," Hana said.

All agreed. So the counselors shrugged and opened the next envelope, reading from it.

"As both teams have refused to engage in destruction, we declare both teams co-winners of the Peace Prize."

The chef rolled out an enormous chocolate cake, decorated with the names of each of the campers.

"I have no qualms about destroying this," one kid said, and soon all were laughing and enjoying not only the cake and ice cream but also admiring the designs of the other team.

Only one last project remained, and this was a cooperative one. Tradition held each group should leave behind something for the next group.

They'd decided what to leave behind for next year's campers and worked hard on it.

They foraged for a freshly fallen tree, and then managed to saw a piece of wood large enough for a plaque. They planed and sanded it in the woodshop, then a team inked in the letters, just so. The kids best with wood carving tools carved out the letters, and another team sanded and sealed the front. Everyone signed the back, and it too was sealed with two coats of polyurethane. They added hooks and hung it over the massive fireplace in the center of the clubhouse. It was the gathering place on many a chilly night. And many summer nights in Maine were chilly.

In English, Arabic, and Hebrew, they carved "When your heart is ready, peace will come looking for you. Ajahn Chah."

"It's only right that a Buddhist should show Israelis and Palestinians how to get along. We certainly don't do a very good job ourselves," Ari said. Everyone applauded.

The last night was silly skits, including a song about "Ari, the Dirt Eater" and "Hebron Hana, queen of the wild frontier." Esther signed up to come back as a counselor, and as much as Hana would love to, she knew it was impossible. Her task was to go home and find a way out of her father's house and into a world where women have value. At least she had a passport, so if worse came to worst, she could leave the country, though she did not want to leave her mother and sister.

The thirty kids took the same flight back to Tel Aviv. Hana and Ari sat together, at last touching one another. It was impossible not to touch your seatmate in coach. He turned the armrest up, and she rested her head on his shoulder most of the way home—her headscarf in her bag. She slept fitfully, and Ari would occasionally kiss the top of her head and whisper, "Shhh… into her clean, sweet hair. Ever so softly, he said to her, "I love you, Hana."

"And I love you," she whispered back. "I always will."

As they began their descent into Tel Aviv, the atmosphere of the campers changed. They would be assuming their old roles, but they could never be the same.

"How are we going to see each other?" Ari asked.

"I don't know. We both have cell phones, I assume we can make arrangements?" Hana asked. They put all their info into each other's cell phone and knew there was at least that link available to them. They lived less than a mile apart but might as well have been in different galaxies. Different languages, customs, religious beliefs, and more importantly, a wish for the destruction of the other separated them, at least in the hearts of the adults.

"We will see each other, somehow," Ari said.

"But people will see us together. Your family and mine will find out," Hana said.

"We'll find a way to meet someplace far away," Ari said. "When your heart is ready, peace will come to you. The same is true of love."

Hana said goodbye to Ari in immigration, and they went into different lines. Her aunt was there to meet her and take her to the farm before she went back to Hebron. Hana knew the address to which Ari went but could only imagine the lies he would tell his parents. Or the truths he could never tell them.

Once Hana was back home, Farah wanted all the details of the camp. Hana talked a lot about everything except Ari. She mentioned Esther and her smoking, even about how one night it would be cold, another hot, even the black flies that could bite. Farah could be loose with her comments. Hana knew the only way to keep something secret was to tell no one, especially her blabbermouth sister whom she adored anyway.

"Who is Ari?" Farah asked one morning as she was practicing yet another beauty school coiffure on Hana. Hana blushed.

"Ari?" Hana asked.

"You talk in your sleep, sister."

"He's Jewish, but NOTHING happened," Hana said. "We are friends, nothing more."

"That's not what it sounded like in your dreams," Farah said, pinning a stray lock into place.

Hana's hair didn't look like the picture, so she pulled everything out and started over.

"And since when do dreams count?" Hana retorted.

"When papa has picked a husband for you," Farah said.

"No. That's not true. Mama would have told me," Hana said, panic rising in her voice. For once, she was as still as statuary, and Farah could work faster on her sister's hair.

"I heard them talking last night. He is one of Papa's suppliers, and Papa owes him money. The man's wife died while you were away, and he needs someone to take care of the children," Farah said, matter-of-factly. "He will forgive the debt; you will be married and live nearby. Only the man's father is still alive, so you will not have a horrible mother-in-law to boss you around."

Hana paid no attention to what Farah was doing with her hair, even though Farah was wreathing her head in a toxic cloud of hairspray.

"How many children does he have?" Hana felt her hopes sinking. She could never become a doctor. She could never see Ari again. Peace

Camp was a fraud, just a dream to get her hopes up. She could not imagine feeling desire for anyone other than Ari. She could not imagine another man even touching her.

"Four. The oldest is six," Farah said gently.

Hana began to cry. Farah could not take a picture of the hairstyle to e-mail to her teacher, not with her sister in tears. Soon, Hana had ripped it apart in fury, and her tears flowed for hours.

The next morning, Hana had made up her mind. She would meet this Mahmoud and see if she might be able to stand him. If not, she would beg her father not to marry her off to him. If he persisted, she would stall for time. Maybe she and Ari could run away somewhere. She could no more choose to enslave herself to this man almost old enough to be her father than she could choose to breathe. She had never even seen a man naked, and the idea of a man she didn't love sticking something like a turkey neck into her was repugnant.

If she had not met Ari, had not known the intensity of first love, perhaps this marriage would have been tolerable. But she knew what it was like to be content to be in the presence of him, to want to touch him, to feel the sweet pleasure of her head against his shoulder. She wanted to determine her future; she was smart enough, and, at least for now, Ari was part of her future. Maybe after she became a doctor, she would not want him. But for now she wanted a boyfriend, not a husband. Holding hands with Ari was worth the world to her.

"When may I meet Mahmoud?" Hana asked her father the next day.

"Why do you ask such a question?" he said mildly.

"Father, this is the rest of my life we are talking about. Would you not indulge me just a little by letting me at least meet him?" Hana was offering him sweets, knowing how much he liked them.

"I suppose it would not hurt. But the marriage contract is arranged," he said. "I cannot go back on my word."

Hana sought her mother's advice but received little solace from her mother.

"I had nothing to do with this, Hana, and there is little I can do to help you now." Abra looked weary and defeated. "I prevented you from being cut, and I allowed you a glimpse into a different world. Perhaps I was wrong. Now you do not want the world you have. You want one you cannot have."

"Oh, mama, I love you. You have tried," Hana said, hugging her mother. "Perhaps we will figure out something. Maybe Mahmoud will fall into a very large hole on the way to meet me and never be seen again."

Even as she said it, she knew it was a girlish dream. Mahmoud loomed as her future husband and jailer.

Ari and Hana texted each other but could not make plans to see each other. It was one thing to be together in America, but they would have to meet somewhere outside Hebron, and that was a problem for Hana. As a Jew, he could travel anywhere, but as a Palestinian, Hana's movements were restricted. Even their texts were formal, as discovery would have unleashed the dogs of hell upon them both. She dare not tell him about Mahmoud lest he do something stupid, like try to spirit her away in the night.

On the day she was to meet Mahmoud, Hana slept late and made no attempt to groom herself as befits a bride-to-be. Perhaps if she were ugly or surly enough, he would back out. Her mother and Farah watched from the far end of the living room as she walked toward Mahmoud.

Her heart sunk when she saw him. He was a small man, wiry and graying, older even than her father. His skin was leathery, and he stank of cigarettes and garlic. He smelled as if he had not bathed in some time, and his breath smelled of rotten teeth. Indeed, his mouth caved in from lack of many teeth. His nails were ragged and dirty, and his clothes were none too clean. Before he even spoke, she was repulsed.

Her father and Mahmoud sat in the living room taking coffee and eating sweets. Mahmoud showed her father the pictures of his children. Her father passed them to Hana, who briefly glanced at the children and handed the pictures back wordlessly. She knew she was being rude, but she did not care. She sat in defiant silence until she could stand it no longer.

She stood up abruptly and said to the two men who were staring at her, "Father, Mr. Mahmoud, I am honored you would consider me as the mother for your children, but I will not become your wife. Not now, not ever."

Hana turned and left the room. She waited in the room she shared with Farah. She knew her father was capable of enormous wrath when confronted, and she had not only confronted him, she had defied him in front of another man. She expected to be beaten.

Her father was at the door in seconds, and he grabbed her by her arm, dragging her into the living area, now absent Mr. Mahmoud.

"What on earth has possessed you to act like a whore? No decent woman speaks like that to her father and her future husband." he was not yelling, but hissing his disapproval. She knew that when he was like this, to reason with him was useless.

"Mahmoud has gone," her father said.

"I am sorry if I dishonored you in front of your Mr. Mahmoud," Hana said. That was almost true. "Surely he cannot want anyone as bad as me for a wife."

"On the contrary, he looks forward to taming you to his ways," her father said.

"So you will not let me out of the contract?" Hana looked up into her father's face and saw only stone.

"No. You will marry Mahmoud."

"You should think very carefully, father. I will never speak to you again as long as I shall live. You cannot love me and ask me to submit to that stinking man," Hana all but spit her words in her father's face.

She was not surprised when he slapped her full across the face. She grabbed a chair to keep herself from falling.

"Careful, father, you do not want to make the bride ugly," she said, putting her hand to her face's puffy lip and spitting out a chip off of a tooth. She refused to cry.

"You are little better than a whore, speaking back to me in this way. If I were not a good father, I would abandon you to the streets," he said.

"It would be better than marrying a man who stinks worse than a male goat," she spat back at him. She wanted him to throw her out. Ari would help her, somehow.

Her father locked her in her room for the next three days. He allowed her mother to bring her food and water and to take away her waste. But he forbade his wife from speaking to Hana, who lay on her bed paralyzed at the prospect of a life without Ari and with the Goat Man, as she had come to think of him. She ate nothing and took only sips of the water. Many times she thought of reaching out to Ari, but what could he do? She was locked in her room, and her father held the only key.

On the fourth day, her father unlocked the door. Hana had not washed or changed her clothes. When she was commanded to stand, she could barely do so.

"Will you defy me again?" he asked.

"Yes."

The father again locked her in the room.

Farah had snuck in with the mother to take food and water. The food remained untouched, and Hana's urine was stinking from the decay within Hana's body. Farah slid her hand under Hana's mattress and found her phone, slipping it into her pocket.

Once she was alone, she read the texts. *So this was why Hana was adamant about Mahmoud.* Farah did not know what to do. Her mother felt there was nothing she could do for Hana. Perhaps Mahmoud would be kind, or maybe Hana could somehow tame him, rather than the other way around. After all, Hana was a very bright girl, and Mahmoud seemed quite dull.

On the sixth day, Hana again was brought out of the room, still weak and dizzy but unbowed in her defiance of the marriage to Mahmoud.

"Very well. You leave me no option," her father said.

He sat her in a kitchen chair in the front room and bound her hands behind the chair and her feet in front. Farah, knowing only this was unlike anything she had ever seen, texted Ari: "COME NOW" followed by their address. He would have to immediately pick up and come more swiftly than a bird could fly to prevent what Farah feared.

The clock in the room ticked, its pacing driving the father who took his time walking into the kitchen and sharpening the largest knife in the drawer. Farah wanted to scream and flail at her father, as did her mother, but each hoped Hana would see the knife and know she had to submit. There was no use calling the police, as her father was doing nothing illegal.

Neither Farah nor her mother knew Hana was ready to die. Her life was already over. She had known love, even though her only kiss had been on the top of her head. She had dreams of a simple life with Ari, becoming a doctor, of doing good deeds. She had opened her heart, and peace had come into it. If she could not have a real life, she would rather die. Dying would only take a few moments. Living with Mahmoud would be an eternity.

The father returned to the front room with the knife. Hana's head was bowed.

"Do you see this?" he father said.

Hana said nothing.

"You will dishonor me by not marrying Mahmoud?" he asked. Farah could tell he was stalling for time. He did not want to kill Hana, but he would if he had to.

"Yes. But it is you who dishonors me," Hana said.

The father grabbed Hana's hair and yanked her head back, just as Ari ran through the door. He saw Hana and screamed, "NOOOOOOOOOOOOOO." The father glanced at him and then made a deep, clean slice across her throat, as if he was butchering an animal, not his daughter. Bright red blood pumped into the room.

Ari's voice was the last sound that Hana heard. Her almost severed head lolled back over the chair; blood was everywhere. The mother was holding tight to her remaining daughter, trying to hide her face from the slaughterhouse their home had become. Both screamed endlessly in horror.

Ari instantly grappled with Hana's father, wrenching the older man's arm so hard, the knife fell from it. They both slipped in the ocean of blood, fell to the floor, and Ari found himself face to face with Hana's murderer. Enraged beyond all human limits, he banged the elder man's head onto the tile floor. Ari's world was blood red and reverberated with screams—his own and the women's. He could no more stop than he could undo what the father had just done.

At first the man protested, then he went quiet, and as Ari continued to bang him against the floor, he became dead weight. The monster had destroyed the first person outside his own family that Ari had ever loved. Now Hana was gone.

Ari knew that the screams had changed somehow, and he stopped banging the father's head when his rage ebbed. When the world stopped being red screams and the father moved no more, he looked around the room, befuddled and very, very tired.

There was his beloved, dead, tied to a chair. The father, too, was obviously dead. Two women who resembled Hana still screamed at him in Arabic.

Ari shook his head, as if to clear his mind. He knew he had killed Hana's father, but oddly that did not bother him. Dazed, he stood and backed away, slipping in Hana's blood and nearly falling to the floor. He regained his footing and made himself look at Hana's beautiful face hanging backward over the chair.

He had killed. He felt no remorse for it, only incredible remorse that he could not stop Hana's death. His life was over, now that Hana, and her father were dead. Only horrid, crazy things would follow.

He saw stairs and took them two at a time to the top of the three-story house. Once on the roof, the plan appeared. He knew Hana was nearby. He had only to join her. He would fall into Hana's arms, as he had done that first morning of the teamwork exercise. He walked to the edge of the flat-topped house. Standing with his back to the street, he gave her time to position her feet to take his weight without faltering.

"Are you ready, Hana?" he asked.

He could hear her musical laugh, even over the roar of blood pumping in his head.

"Sure, Ari, I will catch you. I won't let you fall," he heard the lilt of her voice.

He leaned back and fell into her arms for eternity.

CHAPTER TWENTY-EIGHT

GIVE PEACE A CHANCE

Just as the PDB was breaking up, Poppy announced the American Ambassador to Israel was on the phone.

"He says it's urgent," Poppy said.

Abigail motioned for everyone to stay seated.

"Good morning, Ambassador Paulsen. I have you on speakerphone with everyone from the PDB," Abigail said. "What's up?"

"I've just received word of three deaths in Hebron. It seems a young Jewish boy and a Palestinian girl were in love. We've picked it up on the police scanner just now. Details are sketchy, but the father killed her in an honor killing."

Abby felt a knot forming in the pit of her stomach. *The idea a father could kill a daughter for disobedience made Abigail all but irrational.*

The ambassador continued, "Somehow, the boy walked in on the killing and beat the father to death, then committed suicide."

"Oh, what a tragedy," Abigail said. She had tears in her eyes, but then again, so did some of the others, all veterans of the violence in the Middle East.

"I'm trying to get more facts, but I think this is potentially explosive," Paulsen said.

"Yes. If anyone asks you for a comment, just say our hearts go out to both the families who must be devastated. And when you get more information, let me know ASAP."

"Yes, ma'am." Abigail broke the connection.

"Ideas anyone?" said to the group gathered for the PDB.

"Well, both cultures demand burials within twenty-four hours, so we have to work quickly to get in front of the story," Wicker said.

"Good point. Where can we get quick information?" Abby asked.

"Al Jazeera should be running with it," Wicker said. "Let's see what they are saying."

"Poppy, would you ask Michael to do the after-school snack today?"

"No prob."

Everyone trooped down to the Situation Room. Within moments an Arab translator from the Pentagon was relaying English translation over the Al Jazeera video feed.

"A young Jew named Ari Mandelbaum is dead in the street in the Palestinian sector of Hebron. He lived in the H2 sector. The dead girl is Hana El-Hibri. Her sister, Farah, texted the boy to come immediately, hoping he could stop the father. Hana had been refusing for a week to marry her father's choice of husband: a much older widower with four young children.

"According to the mother and sister, Mandelbaum burst through the door to see El-Hibri slit his daughter's throat," the translator paused, shaken. Everyone in the room gasped. "Apparently the enraged Mandelbaum, who was a large and fit young man, took the knife from El-Hibri's hand and threw it away. Then he wrestled the weaker man to the ground and pounded his head repeatedly against the concrete floor. The mother and sister watched in horror and shock. Finally Mandelbaum stopped, looked around, then went to the roof of the three-story house, turned his back to the street, and fell backward to his own death."

The video up to now had been generic of the neighborhood outside of the house and the police presence. But there was a brief interior shot. It looked as if someone had taken gallons of red paint and sloshed it into the room.

The mother and sister had blood spatters on their faces but were sitting, dazed, and huddled in blankets on a warm day.

"Wait, wait," the translator said, "Here comes someone now, a middle-aged couple. He's wearing a yarmulke, and both are screaming and wailing. It must be the boy's parents. We can't get close enough to them because of the police."

The herky-jerky shot of the parents ceased without comment, and the screen went black. Everyone in the room sat in stunned horror. Finally Abigail spoke.

"I want Layla Farid and Rachel Gold on the line. Now."

Everyone stayed silent until they were patched in and brought up to speed in a conference call.

"Layla, what do you think?" Abigail asked.

"I hate to sound like a vulture, but this could be our tipping point. Our polling shows more and more interest in peace among all groups in Israel."

"Rachel?"

"I agree with Layla."

"Thanks. Not a word to the press, please? From either of you. Let me do the talking," Abigail said. "Sometimes I hate this job. Today is one of those times."

Abby instructed both women to quietly go to the American Embassy in Tel Aviv immediately, and both agreed. "I want you both in country, in case I need to show you there."

Then, as she had done many times in her first term, she went into the bathroom and threw up her breakfast. *Maybe this proves I'm human, not scared.*

As if things weren't bad enough, not fifteen minutes after the first live feed, Al Jazeera reported that both the teens had attended Peace Camp in the U.S. Abby learned of it at the same time as everyone else.

As the day wore on, Abigail learned more from her various sources. When it came out the mother of the girl had hidden her participation in Peace Camp from the father, Abby saw her opening.

Layla would attend the girl's funeral, as she was welcome anywhere in the Arab world. Indeed, she was a hero of Arab women who secretly applauded her handling of Al Qaeda wives.

Hopefully, the girl and her father would have separate funerals, but it would be tricky for Layla to pull off.

Rachel would attend the boy's funeral.

Little did Abigail know, things would get worse before they got better. They were bad enough already.

CHAPTER TWENTY-NINE

EXTRACTION

Layla's chartered jet left Nice, France, in less than two hours after Abigail's call. En route, it took her four phone calls to locate the widow and her remaining daughter who were staying on Abra's sister's farm. With the permission of both Abigail and the Palestinian authorities, an intermediary ascertained Abra would receive her early the following morning.

The farm appeared no more or less successful than the ones around it. Abra's sister's family grew centuries-old olive trees. Goats and chickens roamed around a very old and very simple stone house. It looked like it had grown up from the land to shelter its inhabitants. The most colorful part of the house was the door. It had once been bright blue, but the harsh Mediterranean sun had faded and flaked it to a soft turquoise.

It was a place of refuge for Abra and her remaining daughter.

Layla's driver waited outside in the heat, as she went to the door and knocked. The door opened, and Layla took off her shoes and entered. The brother-in-law, who was stone deaf and elderly, did not participate in the visit. This was an incredible stroke of luck. Layla had wondered what difficulties the men of the family would pose.

Twin baby boys about four months old were a pleasant diversion, while Abra's sister served tea and dates. Layla found it distasteful that the gnarled old man was still having sex with a wife in her thirties. Layla would not wish a sex life like this wife's on anyone.

Layla offered her condolences, "As a woman, as a Muslim, and as the representative of the President of the United States—I want you to know that we are both saddened and shocked at the events of the last day. May we alleviate your suffering in any way at all? I speak for President Adams who says she will move heaven and earth to help you. She has two children and cannot imagine how horrible this must be for you."

It was word for word what Abigail had drafted.

"I thank you, as does my daughter," Abra said. "Thanks to you, I have a little money put by. I won one of the Peace Because prizes."

The sister was summoned and produced the copy she had hidden from her husband.

Layla read over it and could not help but weep.

"I want peace because I have two daughters, and I want them to determine their own futures. Allah gave us all a mind. If he did not want women to think, why did he give us a mind? Surely, men are jealous, not only of our power to produce the next generation, but also of our power to shape it. That is why they must keep us down. We must all submit to Allah's will, and men must realize that Allah's will includes that women should think."

"You are a fine writer," Layla said.

"Thank you, but I only spoke it. Hana wrote it. My father forbade my learning to read and write."

"What a loss for all. How may I help you?"

"I have never been in this situation, so I don't yet know what I need. But I do know I want to leave my husband's body to be eaten by the jackals."

"I can understand, but I'm afraid I can't help with that." Layla said with a rueful smile.

"Then I shall have to bury him shortly. As for my daughter, I do not want her near her father."

"Both of those wishes can be arranged," Layla said.

Farah had clung silently to her mother's arm. When she spoke, it was barely a whisper.

"If you really want to help us, get us out of this place. My uncle says my sister disgraced the family. My future and my mother's are to be a servant in this house for the rest of our lives."

Layla looked at the mother. Abra appeared shocked at her daughter's insolent request.

"I must apologize for my daughter's outspokenness. Perhaps I have been too gentle with them."

"Do you wish to leave also, Abra?" Layla said. "For if you do, I will take both of you with me right this moment."

"But what of the funerals?"

"We will leave immediately afterwards."

The two women looked at her, and both burst into tears.

"Do you want to bring your sister and her twins?"

"She was born on this farm, and she loves it very much. She looks forward to the day her husband dies, as she has twin sons. She need never leave here. I know her heart. I also know I cannot trust her to ask her this."

"I understand," Layla said. Taking the sister and babies would have made the job a lot harder, anyway.

The funerals had to occur within twenty-four hours of the deaths by Muslim custom. With a few phone calls from her car, Layla arranged to move the bodies to the farm to avoid the crazy crowds that would accompany such a spectacle in Hebron. One call was to Abigail.

"I want to bring the widow and daughter to my house in France. Can you arrange for them to have an appropriate passport?"

"Sure, when?" Abigail asked. *The Israelis would love to get them out of the country.*

"In about four hours?" Layla asked, her voice a bit timid.

Abigail had to laugh.

"What are you going to do? Take their passport pictures with your phone?"

"What a great idea. That's exactly what I'll do."

In the Jewish section of Hebron, Rachel Gold was sitting with the family of Ari Mandelbaum. His mother was showing her pictures of him as a baby, then as a toddler.

"He never crawled. He went straight to running," she said.

"I have one like that," Rachel said.

"My mother-in-law said he would. That's what my husband did," Mrs. Mandelbaum said. Then she burst into tears anew. "I am sorry. I weep all the time."

"Don't be. Crying is natural at this time," Rachel held her hand and looked into Mr. Mandelbaum's face.

"Rachel is right, my dear. Let the sadness flow out of you," he said, giving her yet another fresh handkerchief. Thanks be to God, he had a drawer full of them.

"I entered the contest you sponsored," the mother said. "I didn't win much, but it felt good to see my words for peace in print. Jacob, will you go get the piece?"

In a few moments, Rachel held a yellowing piece of newsprint.

"I want peace today. Until seventy years ago, my family's history had been a relatively peaceful one in western Poland. First Hitler killed so many of my family, but my orphaned grandparents were spirited out as children and ended up in Israel. There was the War for Independence that killed older cousins, then always another war. Each war took someone I knew or loved. If we don't stop, there will only be one person left in this country, and he will have to shoot himself out of loneliness."

Rachel bit her lower lip hard. She could not enter the mourning as fully as her heart would have her do. She had work to begin.

"Mr. and Mrs. Mandelbaum, you know I am here at the request of President Adams. She would come herself, but her presence would be too disruptive."

"She's right to stay out of this mess," Jacob Mandelbaum said. "We won't have peace until we all want it. Every American President tries, even goes so far as to claim victory, but we go on killing each other."

Abigail got the phone photos of Farah and Abra and sent them to the Israeli Prime Minister who was only too happy to issue passports for the two women. They were messengered to Layla's driver at the farm and arrived just after the end of the funeral.

Hana and a casket full of rocks were buried in the family plot, in full view of the television cameras. When they loaded up and left, the women waited for darkness. Then Layla, Abra, Farah, and the driver dug a shallow grave in a meadow and buried the father. Abra dug the fastest to spend her anger. She barely flinched when she hit a rock that jolted her all the way to her shoulders.

"Let the goats crap on him," she said, when all was done.

"May all your troubles be behind you," Layla said. It was a standard condolence in Arabic. And for once, it was half right. Abra would have no sadness that her husband was gone; she was free to mourn only her daughter now.

Abra and Farah took a loving leave of the twins and their mother the next morning.

"We are grateful that Layla will drive us back to Hebron," Abra lied to her sister.

"Allah willing, I will see you soon."

"*Insh'Allah.*"

CHAPTER THIRTY

PEACE PEEKS OUT

The press would not let the Romeo and Juliet story die. The local papers and international press endlessly interviewed anyone who knew Ari and Hana and the other members of their class at Peace Camp. All the major news magazines gobbled up information. *People Magazine* put them on the cover. The tabloids paid handsomely for insider stories, but no one had an unkind or salacious word to utter. Snapshots went for the price of fine art to the tabs.

"I've never seen anyone my age find their soul mate," one girl said. "They even looked alike."

A Jewish boy at camp had another take on Ari and Hana.

"He knew about the taboos of her culture and respected them. They are bound for eternity, but there was no physical romance between them. I never saw him even hold her hand."

Esther, Hana's friend, said, "I saw her fall asleep on his shoulder on the plane home. That's the closest I ever saw to boyfriend/girlfriend touching. Sure, they worked together as teammates, but romantic touching? Didn't happen."

Then Esther blushed.

"In a way, it made their love all the sweeter."

The Mandelbaums called Rachel and asked for sanctuary away from the press.

"The press will not leave us alone. Anywhere we hide in Israel, they find us. We have moved three times in a week, and my wife is about to lose her mind."

"Give me a few minutes, and I'll get back to you."

She conferenced with Abigail and Layla.

It was Abby who broached the idea of putting them with the mother and sister at Layla's.

"Perhaps they would unite as their children did and advance the peace initiative further," Abigail said. "Of course, they could just as easily hate each other..."

Both families agreed to meet one another that evening after the Mandelbaums arrived with Layla.

The next morning, the Mandelbaums left Israel for the short flight to the French Riviera on a jet Layla sent for them.

Layla called the French President, a personal friend of many years, who sent someone to take care of customs and immigration. As the jet taxied into the hangar and cut its engines, the man boarded the plane and stamped their passports.

"The French President sends you his condolences," he said and took his leave.

The hangar doors shut behind him, and the two passengers came down to meet Layla.

"I trust you had an uneventful flight," she said to the couple.

Mr. Mandelbaum was a big man, probably in his late forties, his black hair shot through with gray. He did not wear a yarmulke, beard, or any other mark of a particularly observant Jew. He also shook Layla's hand, so he could not be Orthodox. The wife hung back a bit but did manage a weak "hello."

"I am pleased that I can offer you seclusion in your bereavement," Layla said as she walked them to her waiting vehicle.

Layla's limo had blacked out windows. They left the hangar through a back garage-sized door. She offered them refreshments from a small cooler under an empty seat next to hers. Each accepted a bottle of water.

Their trip to the villa was largely quiet. Layla noticed the wife was pinched and pale, her hands continuously twisting a handkerchief.

"I'm Layla, but I don't know your first names," she said.

"I'm Jacob, and this is Ruth," the man said. "Forgive my poor manners."

"Your manners are fine, Jacob, if you don't mind my calling you by your first names."

Jacob and Ruth managed a weak smile of assent.

"We should be at my home in under an hour. You will have a completely private bungalow, and I suggest you rest as long as you wish... hours, days, weeks...until you feel up to meeting Abra and her daughter, Farah. Many people have found this area a balm to the soul."

"That is a wise idea," Jacob said, patting his wife's hand. "I think my wife is about to collapse in every way possible."

"Just pick up the phone for anything you may need or want. You are welcome as long as you wish to stay. Oh, and do you keep kosher?" Layla asked. She'd found a local woman who had a kosher kitchen and was prepared to have her cater everything for the Mandelbaums.

"No. But we do not eat pork or shellfish," Mrs. Mandelbaum said.

"Of course," Layla answered. "I don't eat pork, but I am grateful I can eat lobster."

This provoked a small smile from Jacob, but nothing from his wife.

After three days of sleep and meals brought in on trays, the two began to venture into the private courtyard of their quarters. They spent another few days soaking up sunshine, reading, and walking to the beach and back.

On the seventh day, they rang Layla directly.

"We would like to meet Hana's family," Jacob said. "That is, if they want to meet us."

"How about this afternoon over tea? I will come for you at four," Layla said.

Ruth's color was better, but she still was stunned with grief as she and Jacob walked with Layla up to the main house. Anyone else would have noticed the gorgeous views of the Mediterranean down below, but Ruth was blinded by grief.

Layla arranged for a "high tea" with both sweet and savory items in a room that overlooked the setting sun. There was enough food for at least ten hungry footballers. The families could visit into the wee hours with the spread she put on for them.

Layla knocked once and entered the room. Abra and Farah stood. Layla introduced the Mandelbaums as "Ruth and Jacob."

An older woman entered the room. She was lumpish but pleasant in her appearance.

"This is my personal assistant, Naomi, who speaks both Arabic and Hebrew," Layla said. "She is the soul of discretion and has heard many secrets. She will keep your thoughts in her heart—not even to share them with me."

All five shook hands, and Layla took her leave.

"Please, share something to eat and drink. If you wish something stronger than tea, just ring the bell, and my man will attend to your needs. Stay as long a time, or as short, as you wish. There is no protocol for this. Just follow your hearts," Layla said.

When she had heard nothing from the room in two hours, she assumed the four were getting along. At hour three, they invited Layla into the room.

"What may I do for you?" she asked.

"We four have decided that it is time for the killing to end," Jacob said. The three women nodded their heads. Naomi's face was neutral.

"And how can that happen?" Layla asked.

"We want the Israeli and Palestinian leaders to answer to us, and to all grieving people in our nation, how they can guarantee this will never happen again. No family should go through what we have gone through," Abra said, her voice clear and crisp.

"Let me make a few phone calls, so I can give you some options."

CHAPTER THIRTY-ONE

NEGOTIATIONS

Abigail insisted that the Israeli Prime Minister and the Palestinian equivalent deal with the families as full partners: "I won't have these families tortured by having to deal with useless placeholders."

"Each family member gets the same vote as a head of state. They are the ones with the most skin in the game, so they are the ones whose opinion counts the most," Rachel chimed in.

"What about the U.S.?" Layla asked.

"We've been called in to referee too many times. They want us as a scapegoat for when they screw up. I'm stupid, but I'm not that stupid," Abigail was hot. "I don't have a dog in this fight."

"But you are a part of Peace Because," Rachel said.

"And that was an essay contest, not Middle East peace negotiations," Abby said. "I have bickering twins, and that's exactly what the Middle East players are. I don't wear a black and white striped shirt and carry a whistle at home, and I will not do it for the Middle East."

"I understand," Layla said.

"Me, too," Rachel said.

"So you want me to host the conference?" Layla said. "I'm a Muslim."

"And I'm a Jew," Rachel said.

"And I'm an idiot if this goes down the tubes," Abigail said. "Okay, here's what I'll do. I'll issue the invitations. I'll show up for the first night and the last night. Otherwise, they are free to screw it up any way they like."

In the five days it took to get the officials in place, along with their inevitable bickering entourages, and enough security for a small nation, the families of the two teens discovered they liked each other a great deal. They could see their children happy in each other's company. In a more perfect world, they would have been in-laws, so that is how they began to think of themselves.

Sadness, of course, overshadowed everything, but each day, some little light of laughter permeated the gloom. Each day, one learned something new about one of the others, or of themselves for that matter. At the end of the week, they knew they were bonded, even if Naomi had to translate for everyone.

"My tongue is getting tired," she said one night to Layla.

"Not much longer, Naomi. Besides, you could go into the history books," Layla said.

"Yes, as the first woman who died of tongue failure."

When everyone had arrived at Layla's on a Monday, Abigail and Michael appeared briefly to start the conference. First, they met in private with each family. Then after a light dinner, they spoke to the heads of state and the families as a group.

Abigail's remarks were blunt and written on the plane over.

"How many of you have had a first love?"

Most people raised their hands. Farah did not raise hers.

"There is no greater way to honor the memory of two lost teenagers who had found their first love than to lead their people to peace. Make peace for Ari and Hana, and for yourselves, and your children.

"You've never done it before. I'm not sure you've got what it takes. I fear you like the drama of a grudge more than you like peace.

"If you can make peace, you'll be heroes. If not, you'll be like murdering thieves in the night, stealing the only thing these families have left: hope that other families never endure what they are going through.

"Their grief will never end. It never ends for a lost child. You, the leaders, can lessen it by manning up and creating a just and lasting peace.

"I am not here as a referee or as a participant. I am here to tell you the civilized world is watching to see if you want to enter it. It is very simple.

"Palestinians, you must agree that Israel has a right to exist and stop the endless call for its destruction. That's all you have to do. Say the words once, 'Israel has a right to exist,' and be done with it.

"Then live it.

"Israelis, you must agree that Palestinians have a right to exist peaceably on their lands. You must agree they have as much right to be in Israel as Jews do. We're not talking rocket science here.

"Thirdly, if you leaders are really smart, and I doubt that seriously, you will make Jerusalem a religious 'Switzerland,' a font from which three of the world's great religions arose. And you will make sure that, just as each religion values peace, Jerusalem is the most peaceful place on the face of the earth.

"I am the mother of bickering twins. Your behavior is worse, and that is saying a lot.

"Frankly? I think you will fail, just as Hana and Ari were doomed by their cultures. Over and over, Arabs and Israelis slit their own throats rather than have peace.

"It is right and proper that each family member have one vote, just as each faction has one vote. Why? Their loss was far greater than your investment could ever be. You are jaded; you have seen all the atrocities. You may have engineered some of them.

"But these parents and this sister have seen hell on earth. You must answer to them, as they are 'righteous' in their anger and 'strong' in their beliefs. If you leaders had been faster, these two families would have their children. You are too late for Ari and Hana. Please move quickly, lest other children be lost."

Abigail gave each minister The Look, and then she and Michael took their leave.

Marine One took them back to Air Force One in Nice, and they headed home. Michael held her as she cried.

"The Mandelbaums have lost their Mikey. And Abra and Farah have lost their Emma. What on earth is the matter with these leaders?" she wailed and sobbed. "I felt like taking a bullwhip to the Israeli Prime Minister and the head of the Palestinians. Don't they care they are killing children?"

"Shh, shh…it'll be okay, Missus," Michael whispered over and over as they crossed the Atlantic.

As soon as Abigail left the room, Layla rose to speak.

"Well, I guess we can tell that President Adams is not optimistic. I hope we can prove her wrong. Let's do a little housekeeping business tonight and get started in the morning."

Everyone agreed that Layla and Rachel would trade off facilitating the sessions. Naomi would remain as translator. They also agreed that the Israelis would have one vote, the Palestinians one vote, the Mandelbaums two votes, and Abra and Farah two votes. While a professional mediator might be better, it would take weeks to find one the two sides would agree on, so Layla and Rachel it was.

The Palestinians had to be persuaded that an illiterate woman and her teenaged daughter deserved a full vote.

"No one would let my smart, beautiful mother learn to read, so she had me taught in private. She cannot read, but she is smarter than several of you put together. As for me, while we are speaking freely, I saw my sister get her throat slit. How many of you have seen that?"

No one raised a hand.

"Give us our votes or we leave. As Palestinian men, you would not have stopped my father from butchering my sister."

Abra and Farah got their votes.

"I think we've done enough work for one night. Shall we reassemble in the morning at ten o'clock?" Layla asked. *That is if you don't murder each other in the night.*

In the morning, Rachel appeared and called the group to order.

"I have here all of the winning Peace Because essays. I suggest we read one at the opening and at the closing of each day. I suggest we start with those written by the participants.

"Oh, and no matter how well things are going, we will stop every day at five. There will be time for recreation, dining, and socializing among ourselves."

On day one, after the opening essay, Jacob reminded everyone of a central truth. His son and Abra's daughter were watching them. They expected politicos to get out of the way and let people have peace.

"When your heart is ready, peace will come looking for you," Jacob reminded them of the saying Hana and Ari's group had left for following Peace Camp members.

"Please, please be ready, because peace is looking for us all."

He could see the political types gulp. He had hit the right nerve.

It took a few days for the group to gel. The first night, Abra beat the Israeli Prime Minister at chess four times out of five, even though she could neither read nor write. When he complimented her on her skill, she said simply, "I am illiterate. I am not stupid. Your second move in the last game was incredibly dumb, Eli."

He erupted into a deep belly laugh. *That move had been dumb.*

Farah immediately took to tennis to blow off steam. Once Layla had taught her the basics, she began cramming anger-fueled serves down the Palestinian Prime Minister's throat. After she wiped the court with his fat ass a few times, he started to respect her.

Each day the talks went nowhere, but the games let them compartmentalize their animosity.

Jacob was a whiz at table tennis, of all things. He and the Palestinian Prime Minister played endless ping-pong games going back and forth, point to point. Finally, they decided they were better as tennis partners and took on the Israeli Prime Minister and Rachel Gold, who had a killer backhand. The games lightened up, and the meetings did also.

Ruth won a small fortune from Layla at backgammon—well, a few euros anyway, but both took their business seriously.

When talks stalled over a minor negotiating point, Farah exploded as only a teenaged girl can.

"I haven't heard this much goatshit in a long time," she said, slamming her palms on the table, rattling glasses and making the adults jump. "You *old* people don't get it. *Your* stupid sense of pride incites *my* generation to kill," she said, slapping her chest with her hand. "Not just physically, like my sister who got her throat cut, but you . . . you . . . you dogs are killing our *hope*. Forget the stupid past. It is *over*. Give us *hope*. Hope is to our souls what water is to our bodies. Are we to have peace or not?"

She left the room, slamming the door behind her.

"I apologize for my daughter's rudeness, but I cannot apologize for truth," Abra said.

"Ari said the same to us not long before he went to Peace Camp. Our youngsters do want peace. We are standing in the way," Ruth Mandelbaum replied.

"But it is not that simple," the Israeli Prime Minister said.

"Yes, it is," Ruth Mandelbaum said, looking into his eyes. "The children are right. We are the problem. We have had a lifetime of war and hatred, so we think it is normal."

By the end of the week, Abra had gained the undying gratitude from the Israeli Prime Minister for "letting" him win two chess games in a row. More importantly, they agreed. Israel had a right to exist in peace, as did Palestine. They roughed out the borders, agreed on them, and each was ready to take it to the group for a vote.

"Abra and I have a plan. I think we should vote it up or down. If you vote against it, you and a member of the other side must come up with another plan," the Israeli Prime Minister said.

Everyone at the table read the plan.

There were polite questions.

"What will we do about the wall?" Jacob asked.

"We will tear it down. It is incredibly ugly," the Israeli Prime Minister said.

"What about checkpoints into and out of Arab/Jewish territory?" Ruth asked.

"They take up too much time. Let's just go on about our business," Abra said.

"How will people know where they are, whether they are in Jewish or Muslim territory?" Farah wanted to know.

"The street signs will be different color background. Also, in Palestinian areas, the Arabic sign will be on top, while in Israeli territory the Hebrew sign will be on top."

"And disputes?"

"They are matters for the police where the dispute occurs," the Palestinian Prime Minister said. "Not for armies or terrorists."

"And what can we do about the horrible poverty in the Arab areas?" Ruth asked. "I don't want to live like they do in India, just letting poor people rot." Ruth wanted to know.

"We are hopeful that in peace, the Arab economy can grow. We are also thinking of full education for females. It is silly to run a country on half its talent," the Palestinian leader cast a sideways glance at Farah and Abra.

"Finally," Abra said.

"What will we do with Muslim extremists?" Farah asked. "With men like my father who would rather slaughter their own child than see her hold hands with a Jew?"

"We will enforce the laws on the books for the treatment of females. They are adequate. It is enforcement that is needed," the Palestinian leader said.

"We'll loan you the money for that," the Israeli Prime Minister said.

"In addition, we see no reason that Arabs cannot work for Israelis and vice versa. The more we are together, the better we will like each other," the Israeli Prime Minister said with a glance at Abra.

Everyone mulled over whether either side could sell the peace plan to their countrymen.

"What of the people who want violence?" Farah asked.

Ruth offered an unusual perspective.

"I think that since Jerusalem will be a World Heritage Site overseen by the United Nations, it should be a place of peace. No weapons allowed in. It will become a place of asylum for people tired of violence."

"Can everyone get in?" Abra asked with a laugh.

"When we de-politicize violence and make it a police matter, I think discord will die down," the Palestinian Minister said. "We will not tolerate violence for any reason."

"Nor will we."

"And what about weapons? The Jews have them, but the Arabs are not supposed to," Farah was not going to let these crazy grownups off the hook.

The older generation looked around and thought for a while.

"Each household can have a long gun and a box of ammunition. After all, many people live on farms and need to kill a predator," the Israeli Prime Minister said.

"We will go house to house and confiscate everything else," the Palestinian said. "Who in his right mind needs a grenade in his home— much less in a crowded city? This applies to Jews and Arabs alike."

"We will agree to that. Our military weapons will stay in an armory. I've never liked the idea of armed soldiers walking down a street," the Israeli Prime Minister said.

"And what shall we do with institutions? Will we have two hospitals, two jails, two courts?" the Israeli Minister asked.

"I really don't see the need. Perhaps we could share some essential services like hospitals?" the Palestinian leader needed hospitals desperately.

"I think we can do something about it," the Israeli Prime Minister said.

"And what will you do for language?" Naomi asked.

Everyone laughed.

"Can I suggest you teach the kids to be bilingual? The first hurdle to peace is to speak to your neighbor," she said.

When Abigail got word that the two sides were ready to present their plan, she thought that Hell had surely frozen over. When she arrived at Layla's villa and saw a budding flirtation between the widowed Israeli Prime Minister and Hana's illiterate mother, she knew the River Styx was ready for ice-skating; Hell had indeed frozen over.

The plan was solid. The UN would go for it. If the Israeli and the Palestinian people didn't, they were bigger fools than she thought they were. The two sides even asked for UN Peacekeepers.

The UN would administer Jerusalem. It would be Abby's dream: a religious Switzerland. Abby hoped she could sell the UN on a plan to have an institute of religious history there. Maybe then people would figure out that killing others to save them was a stupid idea.

CHAPTER THIRTY-TWO

THE POPE SPEAKS

Months after the hoopla with the Pope was forgotten, His Holiness announced a change in his interpretation of God's law.

"By the grace of God, we have been given a beautiful home. It is my profound wish that it remain habitable for the miracle of miracles, the birth of new children. They cannot come into a world without clean air and water, without food to feed them, or parents to love them. I am encouraging every woman to keep her body sacred for the birth of one child, conceived in marriage, and loved by two parents and four grand-parents. If the resources of her country can support a second child, I think that should be the family's choice."

Abigail whooped with joy. Birth control stocks went through the roof. The Pope endorsed a one-child policy. Sort of. More importantly, he had endorsed a woman's right to her own body. The Roman Catholic Church was responsible for billions of births the planet could not support, but, finally, this Pope made it to the party.

By her fifth year in office, the UN had built, owned, and operated cookie-cutter nuclear plants in twenty-three countries. This generated thousands of mining and engineering jobs in the U.S. as well as construction jobs of the grids by the nationals. In addition, another forty-three plants were in development. And New York had solved its UN parking problem.

She departed from the environmental focus to introduce a bill requiring mandatory public service for all American kids upon leaving high school. Yes, it was expensive, but the rewards were priceless.

She finagled an invitation to speak at her own high school's graduation where she announced the plan.

Even though the ceremony was indoors, and she insisted on handing out the diplomas, it was still sticky under the robes. She was thrilled she had not worn panty hose in the last five years. Today would certainly have done her in.

"We've done a lot for kids recently. The Infants First program came along after you guys were born, but your parents have had ongoing parenting classes at school, and you've all been screened for all sorts of things at the appropriate time. Our public and private schools have improved, and you are all now as well educated as any kid on the planet.

"You didn't think I'd let you have something for nothing, did you? So it's time to give back. I'm proposing a year of national service to follow high school graduation. But this graduating class can relax—it can't start before next year."

That got a big laugh. And a large round of applause.

The legislation passed. Congress was tired of seeing ill-prepared twits turn down jobs they saw as "beneath" them. This would be a leveling experience, much as the military was.

Every child attended a three-month boot camp designed by an elite team of educators. Chief among them was Cristo Salazar and his wife, Susan. Kids were away from home with people from other parts of the country, living in barracks, getting up early, making their beds, learning to respect authority, and working as a team to solve problems.

Before a hearty breakfast, they did an hour of rigorous exercise. They ate well, developed their muscles, and were allowed only one hour of free time a day. There was a communal computer in each barracks, and most kids got to check their e-mail twice a week. During free time, they had to do things like polish their shoes and sew on buttons.

At the end of the day, they wanted their beds. Badly.

After boot camp, they chose how to give back for the following nine months.

Many worked in early-childhood programs. Others worked with the elderly, especially the ones who wanted to stay in their own homes. Some worked with Habitat for Humanity, building houses. Some chose to work in the outdoors, cleaning parks and getting rid of graffiti. Many were all-purpose FEMA "boots on the ground," ready to go on a moment's notice to do what needed to be done. Some went into the military. But whatever they did, they got back more than they gave. They were paid a modest wage, lived in designated housing, and learned the basics of budgeting time and money. There was a curriculum for the year. Those who entered as high school dropouts, worked on a GED while serving their country.

When their year of service was over, if college was in their plans, they went as young adults. They were ready for the rigors of an education, not for a four-year session of beer swilling and hooking up.

If they went into the workforce, they had good work habits. All could fill out a job application and have it look literate. Apprentice programs reappeared, shoving out some of the commercial "schools" that didn't do a very good job of training someone to be a computer technologist—but charged the student a fortune to do so.

Of course, the twins were not looking forward to what their mother had cooked up for them when they graduated from school, but they were still good kids. They still bickered, but Abby wouldn't believe they were her own children if they stopped arguing for more than declared holidays or command performances.

The school at the White House was fun, and they had the best field trips in the world. Whenever Abby went someplace interesting, all the kids at the school came too on Abigail's nickel. They saw the Great Pyramids, the Great Wall of China, Machu Picchu—even Paris, but with a lesson plan involved.

"Remember how we said we didn't want globe-trotting kids," Michael asked one night on a trip to Paris.

"Well, we've got them," Abigail said. "But they are learning."

She and Michael were happy in the White House. As promised, he did a lot of fact-finding for her. He also took over Bookworms and the O.T. Wagner scholarships. Bookworms had been hugely successful, and Abigail was proud that all the members of Bookworms not only attended college—but also graduated. Every child of a White House employee who was accepted to college had the funds to go.

A World of Trees still had annual lemonade stands, as well as a wealth of other activities to entice children into saving the environment.

Wicker decided to retire when Abigail left office, as there was truly nothing left for him to do in his career. Wicker Washington would continue in its media training, but he and Laura wanted to retire to Camden, Maine. Both loved the area and had bought waterfront land when it was cheap. They looked forward to building a dream house that would "see them out."

Abby wanted a major change to the national health care system and got it. Everyone had to carry insurance, but mutual insurance companies and co-ops reappeared, where policyholders were also the stockholders. Each could decide how much to pay their CEO, and most managed fine with the head honcho making a million a year or less. The companies had no incentive for high overhead and ran on 5 percent for administrative costs, the same as Medicare. In short, everyone was covered but with no added dollars to the system.

Medicaid became a vetting place for charitable care. Doctors would care for Medicaid patients, just like any other patient, but would not send anyone a bill. Instead, the doctor could deduct up to 10% of his patient revenues as a charitable donation. Medicaid spent its precious dollars on inpatient care, not on doctors.

Commercial insurance behemoths had to adapt or die. They died. Consumers stampeded to the lower-cost mutual companies or co-ops. No one mourned the behemoths. And without a lobby on Capitol Hill, no one tried to resurrect them.

Premiums were based on your health habits. Those who flunked the blood test for smoking or drug use were rated up. Those who documented regular exercise by logging into a gym's computer system were rated down. Cigarettes were taxed to cover what they cost society and went to nearly twenty dollars a pack over the next five years. Few took up the habit, and smokers quit in droves. Abigail estimated that within five years, no one in the U.S. would smoke.

People could choose what kind of policy they wanted, and policies were standardized. First dollar coverage was the most expensive, higher deductibles less expensive. Policy A from company X was the same as from any other insurer. The system was transparent.

For seniors on Medicare, there were options. Indigent patients had first dollar care. The wealthier you were, the higher your deductible. People in the top 5 percent had only catastrophic coverage as an option: a $10,000 deductible.

Doctors found they enjoyed practicing medicine again as their electronic health record of a patient visit generated a claim that was paid usually overnight. Hospitals, too, received timely reimbursement. Happy doctors made for happy patients.

Fraud was tougher with the electronic health record and was severely punished. Since the federal government was involved, the perps went to federal prisons—without parole.

By year six, North America was energy self-sufficient. Alternative fuels were up to 40 percent of total energy use in the U.S. and higher in Canada. The nice part of that was that the region really didn't care what happened in the Middle East on any given day. Petroleum was increasingly being used not as fuel but as feedstock for petrochemicals—its best use anyway.

Mexico, freed of the scourge of U.S. drug demand, could turn to growing its economy. The U.S. bought their oil and loaned them a fleet of heavy equipment to stop the burning of the sugarcane fields in the spring. The annual haze that had drifted over Texas each May, sending thousands to the doctor with breathing problems, finally stopped. Clean air was a treat, and soon it became an expectation.

Sure, we still weren't completely weaned off the internal combustion engine, but at least we weren't at the mercy of the Middle East.

There was peace in the Middle East, but no one knew how long it would last. Six months was a world record, and the Israelis were tearing down the wall that made the Berlin Wall look like a white picket fence. People all over Palestine and Israel celebrated, and miracle of miracles, suicide bombing had gone out of fashion. It was no longer an objective of Arab countries to destroy Israel. They had local problems that needed fixing, like making sure everyone could read and write.

In the first half of the term, Abigail tried to institute things that didn't hurt too much. Then she got down to the hard part, which she'd hoped to save for the end of her term. Gasoline taxes had to be raised to cut consumption. Voluntary changes had prompted a decrease of 20 percent in emissions. But that would not cut it.

Abigail told people early and often that if they needed to replace a car, they should choose one that ran on alternative fuels.

"Gasoline as fuel will be phased out, and the first step will be increased gasoline taxes. Using oil to generate power or run a car is folly. It's like running your car on perfume, when plain water will do."

Congress bitched, but Congress raised taxes on gasoline to European levels in year six, with the taxes going to clean air projects. With other travel options now readily available, consumption plummeted.

"We have to fall out of love with the internal combustion engine," was Abigail's mantra the last two years of her term.

Airlines diversified, buying other—more profitable—segments of transportation. There were fewer planes flying short hauls, as rail was cheaper and easier. Old track was replaced with electromagnetic track that allowed express trains to achieve incredible speeds.

People still flew, but many were long-haul flights, which were higher profit anyway. The big engine makers developed more efficient engines, and Boeing and McDonnell-Douglas designed lighter, more fuel-efficient aircraft by designing planes to fly at high cruising altitudes where there was less drag.

Abigail ordered the post office to send mail by the most environmentally friendly route.

Congress basically banned junk mail. Why? Not only because people hated it, but also because it was a waste of resources to create, a waste of resources to move, and a waste of resources to recycle it. The 1 percent of the consumers who bought something from junk mail could not justify the cost to the nation of the other 99 percent.

The country loved that. The bulk mail industry hated it, but they were the only ones. If lobbyists still existed, so would junk mail. As it was, each had to get jobs in other industries. No one felt sorry for them, except maybe the people on *Extreme Coupon* shows.

Abigail had wanted to drive a stake through the IRS and simplify taxes, but there was only so much she could do in six years.

As her term neared its end, Abigail could not say whether the planet had turned the corner. She thought perhaps it had. There were fewer weather disasters, but that could be a fluke. In Mother Nature's time line, six years was the blink of an eye.

She gave the commencement address at West Point her last year in office. Certainly, she had a life of service, first as a physician, then as President, but she felt somehow inadequate compared to the young men and women who worked diligently to get an appointment to a service academy. Harvard and Yale seemed like wussy schools to her when compared with West Point.

Certainly, she was well educated in the University of Texas system. After all, they owned enough oil royalties to join OPEC, and she valued her quality education. But she never felt quite good enough when she saw a cadet at West Point.

Abigail worked hard on her graduation speech for an institution she revered. She wanted to hit just the right note. Michael and the kids came with her. The twins were pushing eleven, and this was their first foray without nannies or Regina. Maybe, just maybe, armed Secret Service agents alone could contain Mikey.

She began her speech by taking out a digital camera and taking pictures of the corps of cadets. They all laughed.

"Hey, you're taking pictures of me; I thought I'd get some of you," she said with a smile. Then she settled into her text. She needed no notes, only one sad list.

"When I look at you, my heart is full. As an outgoing President, I am full of pride in you. As a citizen, I am full of respect for you. And as a mother, I am full of fear for you.

"Having sent many of your predecessors into harm's way, I know the risks you will be taking. I pray nightly for your safety. I cannot stand here without honoring those West Point graduates who gave what Lincoln called "the last full measure of devotion" for their country when I was Commander in Chief."

She took out the list and read it.

"Captain Joseph Abrams. His mom told me he'd always wanted to be a soldier. When he was little, he insisted on being called G.I. Joe.

"Lieutenant Gardner Adams. He wanted to be career military and become a doctor in the Army."

"Lieutenant Deborah Furness. Her mom said all she ever wanted to be was a pilot. From the time she was two, she was pointing to things in the sky. Her mother reassured me that her daughter had died doing what she loved."

The list was not terribly long, but it was terribly poignant.

"That even one person is on this list breaks my heart. I pray that no one else joins the list before I leave office. I know that warriors are essential to peace. And that peace is only understood by those willing to die to keep it.

"Politicians do not keep the peace; the men and women in uniform keep us at peace.

"I became a Senator by accident, and then I became President the same way. In my first few days in office, I was scared beyond belief. I threw up every morning, and I cried myself to sleep at night. But I had no choice. I had to do it. You know the three words that guided me."

The corps of cadets shouted in unison, "Duty. Honor. Country."

Abigail fought back tears.

"It's good to know the black and white of life, because much of the world is lived in shades of gray. But whatever else you have learned, I know you have learned the difference between right and wrong while you were here.

"Cadets, do the right thing, whether on the battlefield or off. It is often the hardest choice, the steepest path, and the one least likely to bring you public honor. But it will let you look yourself in the eye in the morning. And it will keep you and our country strong.

"I cannot approach the rhetoric of MacArthur in his farewell address to West Point. But I pray that you memorize it and take it with you as an article of faith.

"Leadership only starts with 'follow me.' It then goes on to never asking someone to do something you wouldn't do yourself. If the people under your leadership fail, you take the responsibility. Then you show them the right way, quietly and privately. If they succeed, the credit is all theirs. Leadership also means that you are thinking as far ahead as possible and being willing and able to adapt to changing situations.

"As a leader, fear is not your enemy. Fear sharpens your senses and makes your training kick in; it puts you in your zone. Your real enemy is hubris. No one is invincible, and a sense of invincibility is a fatal flaw, not only for you, but also for the men and women who will be under your command. Hubris has many partners: sloth, ignorance, fatigue, and assumptions. These deadly sins have vanquished many.

"Knowledge is expanding faster than we can acquire it, so be humble in what you think you know and never, never, never stop learning.

"Because of men and women like you, I do not fear the future. I am excited at what it brings. I know that you are there, part of the long, gray line, to keep not only my family and me safe, but also our country. For that service, I thank you, and I salute you. Good luck and God speed."

Abigail shared the Nobel Peace Prize with Layla Farid and Rachel Gold in the last days of her term. The three founders of Peace Because shared a ceremony on December tenth in Oslo, Norway. The Peace Prize is awarded separately from the other prizes, which are presented in Stockholm. Upon the announcement, Abigail started what she called the Peace Prize Diet: half rations, double workouts.

Kim insisted on making Abigail a gown for the white tie Peace Prize ceremony. She wanted the gown to be white in honor of peace. Abby nixed that.

"I'll look like a whale," she said.

"Abby, you have gained two inches in your waist since you had twins. Your weight is the same."

"But my girth has rearranged itself in an exceedingly unflattering way."

The gown had a portrait neckline of white satin and ended up being a sheath of navy silk crepe with long sleeves for winter. Michael had already secretly bought her a new piece of jewelry, and Kim designed the dress around it.

Michael asked Marion Glober in Houston to do a cipher of the "V for Victory" and an "A" for their last initials. She did it in rubies and sapphires and diamonds, and Kim put it at the vee of the neckline. As usual, Abigail was too busy to notice much about the dress design. She trusted that Kim would make her look good.

Laura packed for Abigail and would travel with her. She was in charge of the cipher pin. Her husband, Wicker, was also going, so that made things more fun. Layla and Rachel were going separately, but all would stay at the American Embassy as Abigail's guests. Poppy backed out when James came down with mono.

"Sometimes being a mom sucks," she said with Poppy-ish precision.

Michael and Abby were both tired by the time they got to a brand new Air Force One for the late night flight to Oslo. They tucked the kids into their pod flat beds and retreated to their bedroom. They'd likely fly on it two, maybe three times more before the new President got it.

"So, what do you think, Mister?" Abigail said alluringly.

"Think about what?" Michael asked innocently.

"Don't you think we ought to christen the new Air Force One?" Abby began peeling off her clothes.

"Oh, I don't know," Michael said. "Maybe we should let the next President pop its cherry."

"Like hell," Abigail said, tugging at his shirt and all but popping the buttons off of it.

As Abigail dressed for the occasion at the American Embassy, she slipped the gown out of its garment bag. She planned to wear her teardrop diamonds that Michael had given her right after the twins were born. She forgot to ask if they put a medallion around her neck or handed it to her in a box. *Oh well, I'll skip a necklace.*

Kim zipped her into the gown, and Abby stuck the launch codes into her bra. As always, she was grateful for the hourglass-shaped span-dex undergarment. She could pretend she had a waist. She loved her children, but they'd done a job on her body, as had time. She'd thickened up a bit, and Andre kept her hair its "own" color. "You can gray on your own time, but the country needs your youth, so pipe down."

Kim made her twirl slowly to make sure there wasn't a snippet of thread out of place.

"Aunt Abby, can you imagine that we are here?" Kim said.

"Honestly? No. I can remember you and Laura getting me through my sister's funeral, but never, ever, in my wildest imagination, could I envision this," Abby said, her eyes welling with tears.

"And I could never have imagined the happiness we've all had these last fourteen years," Kim gave way to tears, and Abigail went to comfort her.

"No, no. My makeup will ruin your dress," Kim said, backing away, laughing and crying at the same time.

Just then, Michael chose to make his appearance.

"Is this a bad time?" he asked.

"No, not at all. My goodness, you look so handsome in white tie," Abigail said.

"Considering someone kept me up half the night, I'd say I look damned good," Michael said, kissing his wife on the cheek.

The children appeared dressed and ready. Regina had Mikey by the hand, lest he do any of a thousand things to get dirty. He was almost out of elementary school and still was a dirt magnet. He was in a little suit and tie. O.T. was escorting Emma, who was wearing the fanciest dress she'd ever owned. It was a high-waisted white taffeta dress with a skirt that flared out a bit to mid-calf. She wore white tights and white Mary Janes with it. Her Aunt Kim had made it just for her.

"I have a present for you, my darling Emma," Michael said. He produced a black box with a pink bow. Abigail was about to burst with love for her husband. She knew nothing about this.

Emma opened it. Inside was a single strand of pearls, perfect for a growing girl.

"Oh, thank you, Daddy, they are beautiful," she said, hugging her dad.

Michael put them on her, and then she pranced off to find a mirror. Mikey looked a little crestfallen.

Michael produced another black velvet box, this one with a white bow.

Inside was a money clip with Mikey's initials. In the money clip was an assortment of small Euro notes.

"A gentleman always has walk-around money, just as he always has a clean handkerchief."

Placated, Mikey went to show his sister that he, too, had gotten a present.

"They'll just bicker over who got more," Abigail said. Michael chuckled.

Then he produced another box for Abigail.

"Michael?" she asked. "I have everything a woman could need."

"Okay, I'll give it to my mom. She appreciates nice jewelry."

"Oh, please don't. I'll love it, I promise," she said.

She opened the box from Marion. Nestled inside was an elaborate round pin of an intertwining *V* and *A* in rubies and sapphires and diamonds.

"It's a cipher of sorts. The V is for victory in your endeavors, the A is for our initials," Michael said.

Abigail blinked rapidly and leaned her head back to fend off tears.

"I designed the dress around it. May I put it on you?" Kim asked.

"Of course. You were in on this?" Abigail asked.

"Oh, yes. I made Marion make it bigger," Kim giggled.

Kim had put tiny stitches where the pin should enter and exit the dress to be perfectly centered. The thing was as big around as a circle made by Abby's thumb and middle finger and was the focal point of the gown. *Very serious bling. The Queen would love to have this.*

Abigail donned a full-length navy cashmere coat Kim had made to go with the gown. Her red clutch accented the rubies in the pin.

Emma's coat was an exact copy of her mother's but shorter and in white. She wore white kid gloves for warmth. Michael and Mikey had matching charcoal topcoats and gray mufflers. O.T. wore his regular topcoat. Regina wore her full-length mink.

"I dare anyone to say anything about my wearing fur," she harrumphed. "Especially if they have on leather shoes."

Once honored, it was Abigail's duty to make short remarks. Neither Rachel nor Layla wished to do the major job, so the task fell to Abby. The audience included the Israeli Prime Minister seated next to the Palestinian leader. Both families were there.

"It is everyone's duty to leave the world a better place than they found it. When Layla Farid approached me about an essay contest to encourage peace in the Middle East, I thought I'd write a check, and that would be the end of it. We roped Rachel Gold into helping us, so that we could have representatives of Muslim, Christian, and Jewish faiths on the committee.

"The essay contest nudged the rock up the hill with its nose every day, and it rolled back down every night. But over time, polls showed that people were starting to see "the other" had the same emotions about peace. For that brilliant thought, Layla gets all the credit.

"History has a way of choosing a moment. When Ari Mandelbaum and Hana El-Hibri died, God...Allah...wept. Layla reached out, Rachel reached out, and everyone pulled together. Perhaps the most important voice in the group was Farah El-Hibri's. She spoke, force-fully, for the youth of the area who were tired of their elders keeping peace from them.

"At Peace Camp, Ari and Hana and their other campers made a plaque that quoted the Buddhist Ajahn Chah: 'When your heart is ready, peace will come looking for you.'

"Peace came looking for the Middle East after Hana and Ari died, because the essays had opened hearts, and because this classic story of lost first love due to the enmity of others is truly a tragic one.

"I spoke with the group of parents and leaders, and I spoke with anger in my heart that something as pure as 'first love' had been destroyed. I never thought the two sides could do it. I am humbled, and very grateful, that they made their hearts ready and proved me wrong."

Abigail received a standing ovation, bowed, and took her seat on the stage.

Layla spoke next. "I, too, never thought I would see peace in the Middle East in my lifetime. I wish we had succeeded before the deaths of Hana and Ari. But they are the ones who found peace first, and their memory made peace possible."

Rachel had little to say, a first for an actress with a room full of awards.

"Nothing can top this," she said, and then too overcome to speak, she waited a few moments. "Thank you and may you walk in peace all the days of your lives."

By the time the three left the stage, their faces were flooded in tears. For once, Abigail didn't care if her mascara ran. They all got another standing ovation.

That night there was a state banquet followed by a concert. Michael wanted to stay with the kids and watch videos, but Abigail nixed his plans.

"Whoever sleeps with the President has certain boring obligations. Besides, I want to skip it, too."

They sat through the concert doing erotic things to the other's hands, totally unnoticed by the people around them. Abigail would stroke Michael's palm with her middle finger, ever so lightly. Then she'd remove her hand and put it in her lap. He'd gently take it back, and do the same to her palm, all the while whispering remembrances of trysts past. She had goose bumps just from his whispers—just as she had the first night she met him.

Once back from Oslo, it was time to hit the glide path out of office. President-Elect Brown, an experienced centrist, was on board to continue Abigail's vision of climate change, peace, and economic sanity.

There were holiday functions every night, it seemed, and Abigail allowed her eleven-year-olds into the parties for a few minutes if they wished. Then they disappeared upstairs no later than eight.

Both she and Michael were determined the kids would go to the ranch the day after Christmas, even if she was too busy, which she was. She had a million things to do to leave office. She still had no desire to have a Presidential Library. Her ego was big; it just wasn't that big. Texas A&M asked for her artifacts to add to the George H.W. Bush Library, and she figured that was honor aplenty: to put the things of the least qualified President with those of the most.

Michael had a directing gig lined up in March.

"I want to do something the kids will like. It's animated," he said. Little did he realize that the twins were outgrowing animated films.

CHAPTER THIRTY-THREE

LEAVING HISTORY, AGAIN

They had their last Christmas in the White House, and Abigail and Michael felt blessed that all made it to this landmark: Mikey Molloy walked more slowly and never without his silver-topped cane tapping on the old hollow floors. But he was still full of political mischief.

Regina and O.T. looked ageless.

Poppy and Logan Chaffee were still happily married, and puberty was hitting James. Overnight, his voice was changing, and there was fuzz on his upper lip. He was sprouting into a handsome young man. He did not have his mother's red hair, but he did inherit her need for glasses. He opted instead for contacts.

Laura and Wicker were there, as usual, both casually elegant.

Kim and Duke were fine—Kim as successful as ever, even though it seemed effortless. Priscilla was also blossoming into a tall, thin, and exotic beauty. Little Duke was six and anything but little, and Abigail was glad Duke had come into his money. He probably couldn't feed that boy on just a U.S. Attorney's salary.

Mason and Eileen brought Mary Margaret, nearly seven, with her mass of red ringlets to the White House. She was very impressed to see it, but once she and the others ran up to the kids' domain, all were their normal selves.

It snowed enough to track a cat on Christmas Eve, and Abigail took this as a sign that Mother Nature was pleased with Abigail's obeisance to her.

On Christmas morning, after they'd opened their presents, Mikey took the "little" ones outside to see if the reindeer had eaten their carrots. Duke and Mary Margaret were iffy about Santa so the big kids made sure they pretended to believe. Not only had the reindeer eaten the carrots, Mikey showed them the reindeer poop. Mary Margaret was disgusted at the "fact," but little Duke's eyes were big as saucers.

As always, they cooked their own Christmas meal. They sent non-essential staffers home. Everyone brought the usual "signature" items. Over the years, any deviation from the menu brought howls of disapproval, so people had long since stopped looking for new recipes. Abigail cleaned up, but this year all four of the big kids volunteered to help. Abigail was at first suspicious, then it dawned on her that Regina might finally have civilized them.

Abigail and Michael were planning furiously for leaving the White House. The children were already registered in schools in L.A. and would waste no time in starting after the Inauguration. The teacher was making sure they were in sync with the school in L.A. The kids wanted to go to the ranch after Christmas, as they had always done, but Abigail didn't have the time to go with them.

Michael took them all for a week, and Abigail thought she'd never been as lonesome in her life. Then she remembered they'd be back shortly, and she'd long for peace and quiet.

Scout, the ranch dog, had died, and the cousins were in love with Patches, the three-month-old mutt who had taken his place. Patches tagged along after any of the children and was usually found in a different bed every morning. Mary Margaret didn't mind sharing him, as she lived at the ranch full time. Patches would end up hers in the long run.

The kids returned on New Year's Day, and Abigail was glad to see them. They'd yet to master talking one at a time, but that was this year's project.

"Uncle Mason says Patches is at the needle-teeth stage," Mikey held out his arm as a badge of honor. It was covered with scratches. *Only Mikey would allow himself to be a chew toy for a puppy.*

"And the little kids got their ponies," Emma said. "Duke named his Judge. Mary Margaret chose First Lady. Oh, and Regina taught me how to fry chicken," Emma said.

"She says you can't even find the stove, Mom."

"I can, too. I just don't know how to work it," Abigail said.

Abigail absorbed all the stories that spilled out in a hodge podge, and by nightfall she was exhausted and glad to fall into bed with Michael.

"How did you cope with the non-stop talk of six kids?" she asked, as she snuggled into their spooning position.

"Pretty soon, our kids will stop talking, if I remember puberty correctly. I knew this was the calm before the storm," he said.

She knew that, come January twentieth, she would miss Duke and his family tremendously. And leaving Regina and O.T. would hurt more than she could imagine.

July and Christmas at the ranch were still going to be on everyone's agenda for the foreseeable future. It was central—not only geographically—but also to them as a family.

Michael and Abby could always stay at the penthouse at Franklin Towers in D.C. if they wanted to see Regina and Duke. And they'd always keep *Bel Vedere*.

Suddenly it was their anniversary again, and a new President was taking office.

Tradition dictated that Abby leave a hand-written letter for him on the desk in the Oval Office. Abigail's was brief.

"Dear President Brown,

Welcome to the second hardest job on earth. Being the mother of multiple children is the hardest. At least I had a lot of help with that. As President, you have no real partner, no moral back-up. It's just you.

I will never second guess you publicly, and I am always available to you if you need me. It's hard to get the truth in this office, so don't hesitate to ask. If you are unsure of what to do, look at the guy hanging over the fireplace or the busts of the two men who flank it. Between Washington, Franklin, and Jefferson, you can't go wrong.

I wished I'd had time to drive a stake through the heart of the IRS and simplify taxes, but there's only so much one person can do in six years.

Fondly, Abigail Adams

P.S. You got my vote."

Abigail looked around the Oval Office for one last time and felt an intense sense of gratitude and relief that she had not screwed up this job. From her first night in the little study until this morning, she'd never had to use those launch codes.

That alone was success.

But the country was in better shape now than it was when she started in this room, and that is every citizen's job—not just every President's.

The jury was still out on her kids, though.

She headed back to the Residence and grabbed Michael a few moments before the President-Elect and his wife came for coffee. He was finishing dressing.

"Do you think you could clear your schedule for a couple of weeks?"

"I don't see why not. What's up?" Michael asked, fiddling with his cufflinks. Abigail took over the job.

"I'm taking you on a trip," she said, straightening his tie.

"Where?" he asked, checking his appearance a last time in the mirror. Abigail knew her appearance was perfect. She'd long since mastered it. *I can't cook or pick out clothes, but I can do hair and makeup. And I do have a Nobel Peace Prize.*

"It's a secret," she smiled.

"Who will keep the kids?" he asked.

"What kids? Oh, you mean our kids? I thought we'd leave them home alone."

"Very funny," Michael said, turning around and encircling her in his arms.

"Well, O.T., Regina, Papa Mikey, and Louise have agreed to go to L.A. with them."

"I thought that's where we were going. It's kind of late to repack a bag," he said, nuzzling her neck and sending goose bumps down that side of her body.

"You can get essentials where we're going. Besides, you're going to be naked most of the time."

The End

ACKNOWLEDGEMENTS

Writing is a solitary pursuit. You put your manuscript to bed each night, and in the morning it has typos in it. Then you find out how many people you really depend on. Editors like Laura Burns and Ellen Burns, copy editors like Jan Marino, readers like Carol Witham and Lora Nita Parsons who track down those typos, then smack 'em down.

Then there are the people at EMSI that help me get the word out about my work. They are all treasures. Joe and Raquel Thomas of Left Brain Digital are masters of cyberspace, cover design, and free psychotherapy.

Of course, nothing would get written without the patience and love of my family, Deke and Debbie, who read until they get cross-eyed, all the while telling me every sentence, even "The End" is brilliant. *Yeah, sure.*

There are also women of grace, authors who encouraged me when they didn't have to, lovely people like Karleen Koen and Jacquelyn Mitchard. I thank them both. A lot.

How do I classify the unique support of Jane Moser and Rose Graham? Or the people at River Oaks Bookstore or Past Era? They are all rock-solid, good people who went out of their way to help a fledgling storyteller.

People ask me where I get my inspiration. I tell them I get it at 3 Dogs Café from Steve Watts or from Matt Doucette. My inspiration is a grande non-fat mocha latte, with an extra shot of espresso.

So, I guess writing isn't so solitary after all...

Dixie Swanson
Rockport ME
September 2012
dixie@dixieswanson.com
www.dixieswanson.com

www.ingramcontent.com/pod-product-compliance
Lightning Source LLC
Chambersburg PA
CBHW051234260626
47162CB00002B/422